ReEvolution

ReEvolution

a crispr novel

~ Alex M. Grant ~

PUBLISHER'S NOTE:
ReEvolution is a work of fiction. Names, characters, places, and incidents are the product of the author's imagination or are used fictitiously. Any resemblance to actual persons, living or dead, businesses, companies, actual events, or locales is coincidental.

ISBN: 978-0-578-45858-8 (paperback)

To my lovely wife Kim, whose support, grace and editing made this novel possible.

With gratitude to Jeffrey Levin,
for his insights and support.

1

Liu Wei, Chairman of Xian Corporation was about to go into a meeting of the Politburo. He had just met with his top scientific advisor, and thought this was a great time to be alive, especially if you held a position controlling 1.4 billion people. The reason for his good mood was he'd just been told that humanity was on the cusp of something huge.

Although most people in his country were blocked from searches using Google, he Googled it and found that it was actually real. It was called CRISPR, and as best as he could understand it, it changed a body's DNA. It could edit or remove genes that cause diseases. In theory, it had the potential to change a person's height, hair color, strength, intelligence, and perhaps even lifespan.

Liu could still hear his science advisor's explanation that, "This new technology, CRISPR, will change the way evolution occurs; no longer a gradual occurring process of natural selection, but now immediate and man-made. Within the next ten to fifteen years," his expert stated with certainty, "evolution will be completely under human control."

According to Google, the advisor could be right. In the United States, there were some patent fights in progress over the technology, but in the US, China and other places around the world, it was already in use to improve plants and had been tested and proven to cure ailments in animals, and even humans.

Liu knew there was excitement in the Politburo over the new technology. Even though they had not publicized it, CRISPR was already successfully employed to change dogs and other animals. He had been briefed on successful research involving beagles with double the muscle mass of a normal beagle caused by deleting a gene. Those dogs were stronger, faster, and good for hunting or policing.

He wondered if they would find such genes in humans. He knew a lot of athletes, and pretty much everyone else, who would not mind a little more muscle on their bones. And the best part of all was that the dogs could naturally pass on the mutation to their puppies.

He had also been briefed on the disastrous first attempts to modify human embryos using CRISPR, which resulted in unexpected gene mutations. This was a black eye for the research and was well-publicized, resulting in condemnation by different world organizations and researchers. This had to be avoided, at all costs, if there were problems with future research efforts.

Even though it was very controversial to use CRISPR research to change the characteristics of human beings, it didn't matter to Liu. Hell, when one Chinese scientist recently claimed to have success with twins born with HIV resistance, it still met with world-wide condemnation. Such thinking was short-sighted, in Liu's opinion.

Most of the individuals in the top echelons of Chinese society, however, including Chairman Liu himself, were extremely interested in moving forward. As such, they permitted the creation of a Chinese company, called Xian Corporation, to do the research that needed to be done – without the glare of the international press or other countries' scientists being focused on those efforts.

Chairman Liu knew that in a command economy, the right officials could ensure that the proper funding was in place, and would look the other way to ensure the mission was completed. If the right people wanted the research and development to happen, it would happen. The arrangement also gave the officials involved plausible deniability if the crap hit the fan.

And there would be two types of research for the CRISPR technology in China. One was white-ops, done by university professors and experts in large, well-known research facilities. The other involved affecting a gene's expressions in organisms, including humans, to mimic evolution. That was what some select members of the Party elite were most interested in, and that required black-ops. And for this enterprise, the term black ops meant through use of all means necessary – no holds barred.

Liu also had an ulterior motive for being gung-ho about the program. His only son, Ping, was born with a congenital heart defect which limited his physical activity, his attention span and mental stamina. On top of that, Ping also had Asperger's Syndrome. Maybe these two things could be corrected, and his beautiful Ping could become a prominent member of the party, and lead the life he was meant to live.

It may have been wishful thinking, but from what Liu saw, it had the potential to work; relieving his son's suffering and maybe the suffering of millions of others, too.

He knew that, off the record, many of the people who counted in government and business wanted to go full steam ahead with the project. The theoretical possibilities were endless: creating people with exceptionally high IQs, incredible speed, strength, and stamina and who would be disease-free and capable of passing the traits on to their progeny.

Many officials briefed on CRISPR convinced themselves it was their solemn duty to manipulate the genetic code for the good of their children's futures, their country and mankind. To them, failure to move forward at this time in history would be societal negligence. Who knows what 'enhanced' people could do for society, and if those people were their children, so much the better.

These officials considered the work on CRISPR a sort of 'Manhattan Project' for genes, instead of nuclear power. Moreover, this new genetic revolution was more vital to humanity than nuclear power ever would be. This made time of the essence.

Advancing CRISPR research was also in harmony with the mandate from heads of government who wanted China to lead in high-tech, biotech, infrastructure, and space technology, and indeed to raise their game to 'commanding heights.' CRISPR fit the bill as a technology at the highest of heights.

2

It was a cold, windy autumn day. The kind of day you felt like staying in bed, but John Ordell bounded out of bed with an abundance of energy.

He had a lot of things on his mind, including what he was going to do now that he was done with school. He reflected back on his academic career, and the fast friends he'd made. He was going to miss the professors, beer and pizza with his buddies, and talking shop about genetic engineering.

To him, math and science always came easily – with formulas dancing in his head as they whispered their secrets in his ear. John always loved science, and when he was young he had microscopes, telescopes, and all kinds of science paraphernalia that his parents would get him – even when money was tight.

But now, it almost seemed like a dream – the accolades in high school, and his top grades in science and math when he was a pimply faced college kid studying at Columbia. He always seemed to be ahead of the curve, at least when it came to science. He also liked beating out other kids, who had the benefit of attending private schools but not his innate abilities.

Unfortunately, when he took the GRE test he didn't do as well as he thought he would. It might have been the pesky English and social studies, which he didn't especially care for, that held him back. While the math formulas spoke to him, the same couldn't be said for reading and writing.

Because of his score, and tuition assistance and stipends offered to him at Washington University in St. Louis, he decided to do his PhD there. Although it wasn't an Ivy League school, it was still prestigious and boasted the third best medical school in the country. It was a good fit for a science nerd like him.

He thought back to the long nights spent studying molecular biology, organic and physical chemistry at Columbia, and competing with some of the best students in the country – and besting many of them. He remembered numerous occasions, in the dead of night waking and unwinding the solution to some obscure science or math problem which evaded him during the day – like some divine inspiration. He loved those late-night insights, when his mind would race through the problem and the answer became clear. But now that he graduated, he had the challenging task of going forth in the world and earning a living.

John was weighing a number of options. The problem as he saw it, was choosing which would make him happiest, and which would put him in the best position to repay his student loans.

Before college, his father, who had been a Green Beret, suggested enlisting in the military so the government would pay for school. While that appealed to John, he knew that Desert Storm had forever changed his father, and not for the better. Moreover, his mother before she died, would tell him over and over how much she hated wars, even though she fell in love with his father, a soldier. Go figure.

As he thought about his Mom, he instinctively tilted his head down at almost a forty-five degree angle to his body. His mother always encouraged him and tried to bring out the best in him; his father always made fun of him because of his bookish ways, and called him college boy. His mother called him her little Einstein; his father goaded him for not being a good athlete or having the best eye-hand coordination. His mother had always raised him up; while his father, with the supposed goal of making him tough, always tore him down.

Then, when he was 13 years old, his world fell apart when his Mom got the big C – cancer. It was apparently a family trait that his grandmother and some of his aunts also inherited. How he and his entire family hated that word. It was a word that was uncontrollable and deadly. It was a decree that seemed to touch everyone. But you especially didn't want to hear about it at 13 years old.

He recalled the doctors telling them there was almost no chance of a cure for his Mom's particular type of cancer. Her body was wasting away and there was no way to combat it except with poisonous chemotherapy and radiation. One doctor said that it was a problem in her genes – a mutation – that made cells start growing very quickly. The fast-growing cells turned into tumors. The chemo and radiation worked best on the fast-growing cells, but they also did damage to the rest of the body. John just couldn't stop thinking about doing something to affect the genes, change them, fix them, do anything to stop his mother's pain and save her life.

He could never forget his mother's pain – being lucid one minute, and then not remembering anyone around her the next. He would always remember the look in her eyes and the anguish, and fear, which he would have given anything to be able to relieve. But he was 13, and even if he was 63, there was nothing that could be done, no means to help. All he could do was hold his head in his hands and cry.

His father chalked it up to fate, or the human condition, and just shrugged his shoulders. Unlike John, his father was not a crier. He had seen a lot of bad stuff in his lifetime, and knew there was nothing that could be done. He could only look away when he saw his son overcome by anguish, frustration and grief.

His father thought it best that John learn this lesson now. Life is what it is, and is not necessarily fair. You can't change it, make it better, or stop the inevitable. His wife's fate was in God's hands, and from what he'd seen, it's not always merciful or pretty. Anyway, his son with all his books, microscopes, and science, didn't have the power to change anything.

3

What to do, what to do, what to do?

There was a lot going on in gene therapy research and the very recent breakthrough called CRISPR was changing the rules. It was clear to anybody who knew anything about DNA research that the world was going to change in profound ways, in the near future. For very little money, one could even buy a CRISPR kit and perform serious research in the comfort of a small laboratory.

The world was his oyster, John thought. He could be part of the next big thing, and CRISPR technology was just that. So that was the direction he wanted to take.

He decided it was more to his liking to find the right city where he'd try working in private industry or for the government, and then see where that would lead him. After a few years maybe he'd start his own lab in his basement. That thought appealed to him. He knew of friends who had built new websites, or developed new games, or apps, and sold them for millions, but for most people making enough money was problematic.

His father, on the other hand, was old school. His profession had been the military, but what he had to show for his years of service was a lost limb from an IED and a small pension. His father believed that John should become part of something bigger than himself, like the Army, or a blue-chip company, because that was the only way to go.

When John shared his far-flung plans about the future with his father, and that he might like to become an entrepreneur, his father would remind him of some dumb thing he did as a kid as proof that it wouldn't work out.

It had been very different with his Mom. She used to reassure him and tell him that he could do anything. Now, it was time to move on, and only time would tell.

Although he was no business major, he knew he needed to get a job. This would allow him to get some real-world experience on his resume, and hopefully some money in his pocket to begin paying off his student loans.

He dreamed of making his mark early at NIH or in big pharma and developing breakthroughs in gene therapy research, and maybe finding a cure for cancer, heart disease, mental illness, or Parkinson's. When he told his Dad about these goals, he laughed at John and said, "I'll believe it when I see it."

But it was also very appealing to be the next Bill Gates, but in biotech. John read a book about Gates, and he also started from scratch. These days, everyone wanted to be like him, a multibillionaire at an early age. Hell, Gates even went to Harvard but dropped out. John figured if Gates could do it without a diploma, then why couldn't he, armed with his degrees?

John had sent out a few resumes and received some interest from NIH, the National Institutes of Health, in Bethesda, Maryland, a close suburb of Washington, DC. He had spent a summer in DC when he was in college and loved the town.

He remembered his first day there. He'd driven down to meet his friend Jeff Leonard so they could find a place to live, while they both did Federal government internships. They met at Chad's, on Wisconsin Avenue, where they ate chicken wings and drank Harp beer. Afterwards, they drove around DC for hours trying to find a cheap place to crash.

When they were unsuccessful, they slept in the car overnight, even though the humidity was 100%. John was rudely awakened the next morning by the sight of a man walking his dog in what seemed like a sketchy neighborhood. Just at the moment he awoke, the dog was lifting his leg on the left rear tire.

What he remembered most about that summer was how he and Jeff were continually impressed with the bars in Washington. Although John was shy like many science guys, he held a certain appeal with the opposite sex. He was also 6 feet tall and in pretty good shape, even though he had almost no athletic ability.

His parents always said he got his physique from his father, and his brains and disposition from his mother, who despite a 158 IQ, was a high school teacher. John's father used to joke with him that he inherited the best two out of three genes from them: he got the book smarts and the brawn, but he missed the manly character traits of decisiveness and athletic prowess that were instrumental in getting his father into the Green Berets. His Dad used to say, "Two out of three ain't bad," although he didn't really mean it.

John also considered going to the West Coast, but decided that it wasn't his cup of tea. Silicon Valley was very expensive and a better spot for tech people, though it did have a large biotech sector. Further south, in LA, it seemed like everyone was far too busy trying to be Hollywood cool, bleach blonde, and phony. He thought that he might be giving California a bad rap, especially since he had only been there once in his life, but the other coast was definitely not for him.

Thus, he came to the fateful conclusion that DC, with its myriad of biotech companies just to the north in Maryland, wins by default.

4

Artie Cohen had just moved into the three bedroom apartment on Connecticut Avenue, directly across from the National Zoo. The apartment was small and stuffy, with a tiny kitchen and an old, original bathroom. Nonetheless the price was right, and if he could find suitable roommates to defray his costs, he would be able to live off the inheritance from his grandmother for at least three years.

He just moved his things from Long Island to DC and found the trip exhausting. The Southern State Parkway wasn't too bad, but when he got to the Belt, he found traffic at a near standstill. He hated driving through Brooklyn; it was overcrowded and filled with what he considered to be many Neanderthals.

Not that he was Albert Einstein or anything, but he did graduate from SUNY Stoneybrook, with a business degree, then followed that up with an MBA from Hofstra University. He had saved a lot of money by living at home, but it was now time to leave New York. He was hoping to get hooked up with a management position at an IT company, or a biotech company, that could support the meteoric rise that he so desired. He just had to figure out where he would find the right fit.

Artie's grad school friends all talked about working for one of the Fortune 500 companies, but most of those jobs, and even internships, were very hard to get. Being from Hofstra didn't help, since it didn't have a top-tier MBA program. Also, he didn't graduate anywhere near the top of his class. Since he wasn't inheriting a family business, he bought into the mantra of other similarly situated classmates, that being an entrepreneur was the way to go.

Since his second semester in the MBA program, he imagined being involved with a startup. He hoped to carve out a niche for himself in a company where there were talented people who would develop a new product. The company would then get a patent and license the technology to a multinational corporation that would do all the marketing and production work. It was the way of the world now, where big players would buy upstarts to remove competition or to capitalize on their ideas. He figured that this was a pipe dream, but it was his dream.

On the other hand, maybe he would line up the financing himself, go into production with his idea, start making a profit, then do an IPO and retire a multimillionaire. It was funny how his daydreams always ended with him retiring before the age of thirty-five with a fat bank account.

He knew he didn't want to stay in New York, where he'd be a tiny fish in an enormous pond, and where he'd have to live in a tiny rat hole of an apartment, or commute for an eternity. He decided it would be cheaper to move out of New York, to try and set up some type of consulting company and get on his feet, while he still had his nest egg.

Artie decided to seek his fortune in Washington, DC, because the close-in suburbs of Maryland and Virginia offered strong biotech corridors, as well as IT companies galore. DC was becoming hip, and housing costs were going up, but it was not yet as expensive as New York.

There were also a number of think tanks and universities to tap into as resources, and the US Patent Office was located there. Artie knew a lot of neighborhoods were being re-gentrified and there was a decent nightlife, including a great male to female ratio favoring men, which was a compelling reason to hang his hat there. He also had a number of friends in DC.

He figured that if worst came to worst, he could get a nine-to-five job at an association, or with the government. So he packed up his stuff and moved to DC.

5

Glen Brennan was in a state of high anxiety. He had been accepted to four law schools, none of which he wanted to attend. Fordham was a good school, but going to school in Manhattan would be cost prohibitive, a fancy phrase for next to impossible. Rutgers had a decent reputation and, being a state school, was fairly reasonable. Unfortunately, it was located in New Jersey. The other two schools he'd heard from didn't meet the standards of a snob who graduated from Cornell. Unfortunately, he'd had a bad day when the LSAT was given and his score reflected it.

He was mortified when he opened the envelope and found that he had been ranked at the 81st percentile on the test. He remembered sitting on the top step of his group house in Ithaca, New York, stunned – thinking his world had just come to an end. Goodbye Harvard, sayonara Yale, so long Stanford. But he felt he could still salvage something if he could just get into Georgetown, or even George Washington Law School. He'd heard that going to school in DC was a great experience and, after all, it was the Nation's capital, where laws were made.

The only problem, was that he was wait-listed at both Georgetown and GW. He'd spoken to people in the admissions offices of both schools. He thought he had almost no chance of getting into Georgetown, even though it boasted a larger student body than any other law school in the country, because he was so far down the list.

That left GW, located in Foggy Bottom. It seemed like it could be a nice place to live and study. Well, maybe he'd be better off at GW anyway.

His parents always said, "Things always happen for a reason," or "Things always turnout for the best," although sometimes it was hard to believe.

In any event, he still hadn't heard from GW. The registrar told Glen that he was close to the top of the list, and because many GW applicants get accepted to higher ranked schools, they could fall off the waiting list and he might get lucky. He could be notified any day. It was only four weeks until classes were scheduled to begin, and consequently he was sweating bullets.

Finally, one rainy, dreary Monday, Glen went to his mailbox, looked inside and pulled out the letter which told him he'd be living in Washington, DC for the next 3 years.

6

Artie placed an ad on Craigslist for 2 roommates. His first choice would be a tall blonde with a killer body, who would be really into him, with great looking friends. For the other he hoped, just someone who's not a total loser, who could afford to pay the rent each month. Like the title of the movie he watched the previous night on Netflix, 'Reality Bites,' and he'd have to see what the cat dragged in. Anyway, who knew how long he'd have to stay in this dive of an apartment building.

He woke up at 9:30 AM, put on his favorite vintage T-shirt from the Grand Canyon and went downstairs to get a coffee and read the news on his cell phone. He walked to the Starbucks coffee shop around the corner and checked his phone. He loved going there. It was cozy, and the aroma of heavy, rich coffee beans was always inviting. You could watch people's faces, as their eyes began to show signs of life, when the caffeine kicked in.

He also liked watching the people on weekdays, as they scurried about, their lives so important that they would scowl if it took more than a minute to get waited on. They'd then run out to their offices, so as not to be late for their dismal, dead-end jobs. It was much more fun to sit on the overstuffed chairs, smile at the pretty girls and pretend you didn't have a care in the world. It was even better when the girls smiled back.

This was Sunday so most of the Washingtonians were mellow and relaxed. Artie walked over to the counter and waited in line. There was one thin young woman and an older gentleman in front of him, with a

New York Times under his arm. Artie almost struck up a conversation with the guy, but decided against it.

He looked over at the shelf where the *New York Times, Washington Times, Washington Post* and *USA Today* newspapers were stacked and wondered why anybody would buy a newspaper if they had a cell phone. Although, he liked to read the *New York Post* occasionally, because it had gritty stories and a great sports section.

He heard the woman in front of him order a decaf latte wet, and thought to himself, whoever thought of the idea to sell $4.00 cups of coffee to overpaid hipsters was a genius. Creating a whole new language to describe the coffee was also an inventive move; if it sounds expensive people will probably spend a lot of money for it. He also pondered what they meant by, "Wet."

Artie finally got to the register and saw the familiar face behind the counter. She worked at the shop six mornings a week and he thought she was real cute. He found it funny, though, that she had brown hair, brown eyes, and rich creamy skin – very much like the coffee she sold. Coincidence, he thought not. He said, "Hi," to the girl and she smiled back with her big white teeth, which looked disturbingly like sugar cubes, and gave Artie his change.

He wondered about the girl behind the counter. Was she a college graduate? Did she have some grand plan for her life? Was she happy waiting on politicos, hipsters, weirdos, and uptight working stiffs, or did she just live for the moment? Artie felt sorry for her because he believed it was really easy to roll along with a mundane, hum-drum job and suddenly find that you've become an old person.

Artie looked over and found an overstuffed chair that called out to him. He burrowed in and opened his cell phone to the Craigslist site. He scanned down the ads for apartments, and then he saw it. He couldn't believe his eyes, his ad read as follows:

> "Seeking two roommates, M or F to share Cleveland Park three bedroom apartment. Spacious, light, no pets, no smokers, $7100 per month."

Artie's face started getting red. He couldn't believe his mistake. How stupid he had been. What a freakin' idiot; dumbass, stupid, shit-head. How could I do this, Artie thought. It's a simple clerical function. It doesn't take a genius to input the proper rent – which was, by the way, $710 per month. Why didn't he proofread before he emailed the posting to them? He just screwed up any chance of renting the other two rooms this weekend. Artie began muttering under his breath, "Why does this crap always happen to me? Is it too much to ask that I get roommates so I don't have to use up my meager inheritance, and then have to get a dead-end job just to stay afloat? Son of a bitch!"

As fate would have it, sitting in an adjacent overstuffed chair, sipping a large coffee was John Ordell.

7

John looked over at the guy sitting next to him and thought, what's wrong with that joker? The guy didn't look too bright, was muttering like a mental patient who just got out of a halfway house, and just kept staring at his cell phone. What a dope.

John decided that it might be funny to find out what was bothering the cretin, so he asked Artie, "Is everything OK?"

Artie looked over at John and thought, why is this guy bothering me? He looks like a total loser.

Artie said, "I put an ad on Craigslist for roommates, and it's f'd up. Instead of listing the price as $710 per month, I put down an extra zero."

John said, "That's a bad break, because it sounds like a good price and I bet with the right amount, your phone would be ringing off the hook. Anyway, it shouldn't be too hard to fix."

Artie responded, "Wow, you must be a rocket scientist to figure that one out."

John gave Artie a dirty look that conveyed, 'Are you for real?' Then he said, "No, actually I'm a PhD Biochemist who's new in town and looking for a place to live. But your $7,100 Taj Mahal sounds too rich for my blood." John and Artie were both surprised when they saw each other laugh.

John said, "When you're done with your coffee, why don't we go and have a look at the place?"

The two walked out of the coffee shop and around the corner to Artie's apartment. It looked like it was going to be a beautiful day, it was sunny, 80 degrees, and the plants on Connecticut Avenue were blooming.

John thought that the outside of the building looked large and imposing, but it was clearly an old building that was not well-maintained. There were a number of storefronts directly in front of the courtyard to the building. One of them was a bar.

He had been in many buildings in DC; a good number had beautiful granite lobbies which were ornate. But not this building. Instead, it looked more like a cut-rate, no-frills affair, complete with a sixty-year old guard at the front door, who looked like he could be blown over by a strong wind.

John recognized a smell of mildew in the lobby, which reminded him of the old apartment building his grandmother lived in up in the Bronx. He hoped the smell wouldn't make him sneeze and knock down the old security guard. He looked like he needed the job and the paycheck.

As they walked to the elevator Artie said, "The old guy is Frank. He's pretty good at taking packages and other messages for you and he'll call the police if someone takes your parking spot out back."

John responded, "I bet you sleep great in a high security building like this one. But, tell me more about the parking." Artie told John that they had parking in the rear and that he could get his own numbered spot. It was convenient because zoo visitors would often try to park anywhere close, and if you didn't have your own spot, it was hard to park near the building.

John asked, "What do you do if someone takes your spot, even though it has your number?"

Artie told him about the time three weeks before when someone took his spot and he was coming back from grocery shopping, "I returned home and saw a stupid Dodge Minivan in my spot. I got so pissed because all the spots were taken and I had some groceries that needed to get to the fridge. I told Frank and he called the cops. It took them a good hour to get there, and then they made me fill out a complaint and an affidavit that I rented the space. By the time they finished, the moron and his family were already in their van getting ready to leave. I started screaming at the cop and he ran over and gave them a ticket."

Artie continued, "It broke my heart that this jerk and his family didn't come back just a little later, to discover that their precious van was towed. Then they would have spent a few hundred bucks and the rest of the day getting the van out of a police impoundment lot. If they screwed with my day, why can't I ruin theirs? Unfortunately, he only got a $250 ticket. I guess, better luck next time."

John looked at Artie and thought, what a twisted guy, in an amusing and obnoxious New York kind of way. He reminded him of a number of friends back in the City, and wondered what his deal was.

8

When they entered the apartment, John was a little surprised. It was nicer and more spacious than he expected. It had a nice view of the courtyard from one window, and you could even see the National Zoo if you looked out of one of the bathroom windows. The configuration of the rooms was also interesting. All of the bedrooms were off the living room area and the kitchen and dining room were off to the side. It was a very good use of space which made the common areas comfortable and the bedrooms private.

He also noticed that there were a lot of birds in the trees in the courtyard and it looked like someone, probably a master gardener, was tending a magnificent garden. John saw roses, forsythia, azaleas, and other more exotic plants that he couldn't identify.

But then he came back to reality when he feasted his eyes on Artie's pride and joy – a mammoth 80-inch high definition TV. "Holy Shit," John said, "Sold! Where do I sign? Get me a lease immediately!"

Artie thought, this guy seems all right, smiled and said, "I guess you saw the TV, because I don't think my furniture could close the deal."

Artie pulled two Sam Adams from the refrigerator and they opened them, then clinked the bottles to celebrate their new status as roommates. Artie thought that this could either be good or bad – a day he signed up to room with a putz for a year and never sees him again, or a day where he meets a guy who lives with him a while, becomes good friends and ten years later sends you cards once a year at Christmas with pictures of his kids.

Artie usually didn't like science nerds because they were too serious, or were often like Sheldon Cooper on 'The Big Bang Theory,' socially inept people who prattled on about things that normal people hated – like formulas and equations. But this guy seemed a little different, and might not be too bad to hang out with.

Just then Artie's cell phone rang and he noticed that he had four messages. He answered, "Hello," and heard the person on the other end of the phone blurt out, "Hi, I'm Glen Brennan, are you still looking for roommates? And is the rent that's listed on Craigslist a mistake or is it some upscale modern building?"

Artie responded, "I still have one room available, and the rent was a mistake. It's $710 a month. I'm here right now if you want to come over." He then gave the address of the apartment and said, "I'll see you in about 45 minutes."

Artie then listened to his other messages on speaker while John read over the form lease. The first message was a wrong number from a guy trying to reach Barbara. Artie said, "Aren't we all?" Then John piped in, "They probably met in some bar and she made up a number, and now he'll keep calling until he realizes that she's not the next love of his life. So sad."

Artie said, "Amen, brother," and they both laughed again.

The next call was from another guy inquiring about the apartment. It was a rambling, twangy message, and the guy was interested, but wouldn't be moving to DC from Texas for a least a month, since his new job started in eight weeks. Artie turned to John and said, "Doesn't sound like we have a winner." John shook his head in agreement. Artie added, "He's probably either too old, too boring, or too much of a redneck. Either way, if I can get someone in sooner, then Mr. Texas is out of the running."

The next message was in Spanish and Artie made a face like he couldn't understand. John said, "Hey, call that guy back. He sounds like the perfect roommate. You can't understand a thing he says, so he can't ask to borrow anything, and he can't complain about anything, either." Artie responded that he took Spanish in high school and the caller didn't leave a number. At least he didn't think so.

The last call was another inquiry for the apartment, but it was a couple who were looking for an ultra-luxury apartment, and it was clear they were not interested in his place.

9

As they sat watching TV, they heard a knock on the door. Artie opened it to reveal a short, thin, disheveled looking guy. The guy dressed in khakis and a button-down shirt stood about 5'5" with thinning hair and horn-rimmed glasses. This guy was the caricature of a DC lawyer, sans briefcase.

Artie invited him in stating, "You must be Glen, the guy who called about the apartment, come on in and join the party." Glen replied, "Thanks," as he entered the living room. Artie proceeded to give Glen the grand tour, complete with an introduction to John. Glen didn't seem to care much about the surroundings and was only mildly impressed by the big screen TV.

Artie asked Glen about his moving plans. Glen said that he needed a place right away, since he had orientation at GW Law School in a couple of days. Artie probed, "So you're starting law school soon?" Glen responded, "Yes, and I've heard first year is a killer, so I'm looking for a quiet place to crash after long nights of studying. Unfortunately, because I was wait-listed I couldn't get campus housing, and I'm scrambling for a place to live."

Curious, John asked Glen, "What kind of law do you want to practice?" Glen answered, "I'm not sure, but in all likelihood corporate law because that's where the money is. Besides, I was a business major at Cornell."

Artie and John had both sized up the situation quickly. This guy might be a workaholic, pompous putz, but he'd never be around to bother anyone, and might even have some cute coed friends. Artie looked over at John and could see he was on the same wavelength.

Grinning, Artie offered, "Well, it looks like you came to the right place. John over there just finished his PhD in Biochemistry and I got my MBA from Hofstra in May. If you can afford the rent, and you're interested, we'd love to have you." Artie added, "There are lots of restaurants nearby, and there are Metro stops North and South of here on Connecticut Avenue. I might even throw in some help with your corporate law classes."

Glen smiled as he thought to himself, with an MBA from Hofstra, he must be crazy if he thinks he's going to help me in law school. But who cares? These two look pretty mellow, and the rent is $200 less than the last dump I saw – and this place doesn't look half bad. Also, if I don't take this, I'll have to ride around in this sauna of a city, with its crazy humidity, for an eternity to find another place. Also, I can walk to the Red Line Metro. Forget it, done deal.

Glen said, "I'll take it," as he stuck out his hand to shake on it. He said, "It's a deal, let's sign the lease. Any chance I can move in today?" Artie agreed, and Glen proceeded to unload the used VW beetle that his parents gave him as a graduation present. John had already staked out the second largest room as his own.

10

Glen and John carried their things into the apartment and set up their rooms. Later, they celebrated their newfound apartment at an Indian restaurant about four blocks down the street near the bridge over Rock Creek Park. Artie didn't join them, since he already had plans to meet one of his friends.

As the two walked down Connecticut Avenue, John asked Glen why he decided to go to law school. Glen explained, "Most of my life I did well in English classes, and I've also got some skills with computers. After law school, I hope to get a job with a dotcom company. My plan is to grow with it, get stock options, and retire on some beach when I'm 45, preferably with a margarita in one hand and a beautiful companion on the other."

Glen, more serious, offered, "I took a lot of pre-law classes at Cornell, and I thought it would be interesting to practice law. Even if you don't work in a law firm, it's good training for anything else you might want to do."

John asked, "Come on, why would you go to law school if you don't want to be a lawyer?" He smiled and in a good-natured way jabbed, "I bet you want to be like one of those guys on the show "Suits," or on "The Good Wife", or, better yet, one of those guys defending multinational corporations against little old ladies."

Glen retorted, "Well, I really don't know what I'll be doing in a few years. It's kind of nerve-wracking, because if you don't graduate from a top tier school, you have to be at the top of your class or your job prospects are bleak. I have friends who either went to law school, or are in law school now, and it's nothing like TV."

He continued, "The job market is scary. It's an expensive undertaking to attend law school. I can't believe I won't do great, with my Ivy League background, but I know smart guys who didn't do well and are now living in their parents' basements beating the bushes for temp jobs. Before I made the decision, I looked at a lot of websites and saw a lot of negative posts, but I still was determined law school would be right for me. Hopefully, after I graduate first in my class, I'll be fine," he chuckled, although he truthfully expected this outcome.

John considered what his new friend had to say, preferring to believe the TV version, which was that lawyers, all lawyers, made millions and never had money problems.

As they turned the corner to enter Bindaas, John thought that even pre-lawyers are full of themselves and talk too much. He just hoped that this one wasn't too much of a whiner.

11

When they entered the restaurant, John said, "Two, and can we have a booth please?" After they sat down Glen asked John, "Now that you've landed in the Nation's Capital, what are your plans?"

John reflected for a second and said," I have an interview at a company called Geneteka, which does recombinant DNA research, catalogues the human genome and works on something called CRISPR. It could be a good opportunity for me."

Glen remembered reading an article about CRISPR on his cell phone. In an effort to be funny, he asked, "What is that, like trying to play God with genes to create a Frankenstein monster, only without the bolts?"

John said, "I don't know about Mary Shelley or Frankenstein, but CRISPR's potential can blow your mind. CRISPR actually stands for clustered regularly interspaced short palindromic repeats. The name comes from how they first saw the phenomenon, in bacterial immune systems."

Glen, genuinely curious asked, "Well, can you explain how it works?"

John confidently responded, "It's really not that complicated. Each person has 23 chromosomes in the nucleus of their cells which are made of strands of DNA. Each chromosome contains hundreds to thousands of genes. Different genes determine the different characteristics, or traits, of an organism.

To oversimplify, one gene might determine the color of a bird's feathers, while another gene would determine the shape of its beak.

CRISPR targets a particular gene on a chromosome, whether it is diseased or just unwanted, and then it can change the gene or just remove it. This edits the targeted gene in every cell in the body. The genes taken together on chromosomes constitute who you are and what you are – how you look."

John continued, "CRISPR can deactivate a gene by removing it. RNA finds the gene to be removed and Cas9 cuts it. When you remove a gene, the two cut ends of the remaining DNA can join back together without the gene being present. Sometimes the body may try and recreate the missing gene, but it often gets it wrong. In that case, a gene is deactivated."

Excited, John took a deep breath and continued, "Another way to do CRISPR is by adding another gene between the 2 cuts. This introduces a new gene, with a new expression, into the animal or plant.

The beauty of the system is that it's very easy to do, and you can actually buy kits for very little money.

CRISPR also can be modified to turn existing genes on or off to activate gene expression. The portion that turns on or off is called a transcription factor and it activates or silences genes. During an animal's life genes actually turn on and off to make sure they are expressed in the right cell, at the right time and in the right amount. It functions to coordinate and direct cell division, growth and death.

Theoretically, scientists could repress genes that manifest changes in humans, like stopping a person's hair from turning gray, stopping osteoporosis, and maybe stopping cancer. Who knows, maybe we will find a cure for old age."

John, a little cocky, said, "The possibilities of CRISPR must make you feel like studying law is rather inconsequential."

Glen considered the brash statement and without missing a beat replied, "Yes, until you get sued for bringing a plague on the earth, then you'll be begging for me, the best lawyer money can buy, to get you off."

"Touché" John said, but thought this a virtual impossibility, with all the safeguards used in DNA research.

He chuckled, "Who knows, if we gave you the new genes, it could make you a starting forward for the Knicks or even smart enough to get a 4.0 in law school."

After the waiter appeared and took their orders, it was Glen's turn. Not letting it go, he asked, "Let me get this straight, you're planning to do DNA research, so that you can engineer super humans. I'll put in an order to be 6' 2', blue eyes, 210 pounds with a two hundred IQ."

John shook his head while saying, "No, you have it all wrong. I shouldn't have said it that way. It may be able to do that in the future, but not now. Biotech is one of the hottest fields around today. The CRISPR revolution is a real thing. And you may appreciate the fact that there's a patent war going on to determine who's entitled to patent the technology. Once that's decided, all hell's going to break loose."

John continued, "The technology isn't meant to be used to create designer people, but to revolutionize healthcare worldwide. It could lead to a whole new era in treating different diseases, like cancer, and it has already cured muscular dystrophy in mice and created disease resistant wheat crops. In the future it may be able to change people's genetic codes, so they won't contract or be susceptible to various diseases, like heart disease or cancer. It's true CRISPR could be used to create human enhancement, but that's not the goal."

John continued, "No one is sure exactly how genes interact and which genes can give rise to certain traits. There are about 21,000 genes in the human genome, and less than 3600 have been linked to a trait so far. Also, the international science community opposes using the technology for enhancements and vanity purposes. Although, you could probably do well with a couple of enhancements."

Glen thought to himself, this is pure science fiction. This guy's not a scientist, but a CRISPR salesman. He's overselling this CRISPR thing and is quite possibly delusional. Hoping to change the subject Glen joked, "You must subscribe to the SciFi channel, because this sounds like pure fantasy."

Unabated, John continued, "You can't imagine what strides will be made in the next 40 years in biotechnology. Do you know how many Nobel prizes are waiting to be won, how many lives can be changed for the better, and how many billions are waiting to be made? Large banks have already invested millions of dollars in technology that has yet to be developed."

John went on, "This revolutionary research will drastically change the world. Can you envision a scenario where science has unlocked the key to your genetic code; where they not only map it, like we did recently, but they also isolate the genes inside of you that cause diseases, like muscular dystrophy, cancer or heart disease?

Can you imagine a world where a simple DNA test can identify what diseases you are at risk of developing and you receive an injection which prevents their onset? CRISPR can actually cut out those bad genes or replace them with good genes. And even more incredible, your kids will inherit the new genes that CRISPR installs into your body. That's true."

Glen frowned and said, "I wouldn't necessarily trust the science community to do the right thing – not to create a Frankenstein monster, or a super virus that could destroy mankind, while playing God in the lab, especially if there's a profit to be made. That's the more likely outcome, at least in the movies I've seen."

"Well, I wouldn't lose sleep over it," John said, "because it's too soon to use on humans to change their traits. The Chinese actually tried it on embryonic cells, and to make them HIV resistant, but they had some pretty bad outcomes and stopped. Although now that you mention it, recently one of their scientists publicized that he did it in twins and that they were born healthy."

Not permitting his concerns to be so easily dismissed, Glen then said, “Friend, it still sounds suspiciously like the eugenics movement. Whether it’s seven-foot giants with blonde hair and blue eyes taking over the world, or geniuses telling everyone else what to do and I think it’s an ethical minefield.”

Glen continued sardonically, “What could possibly go wrong? In a world of international terrorism, rogue nations, and totalitarian countries like China, Russia, and North Korea – I cannot imagine how this technology could become problematic.”

Digging his heels in, John said, “Well, I happen to believe CRISPR is a really good thing. Researchers have located the genes that cause anemia, cleft palate, hemophilia B and colorblindness and other diseases. Once the gene is found a lucky pharmaceutical company, in all likelihood, may find cures for these common maladies by cutting or altering the genes. The more common the disease, the more money can be made in the cure. The stuff that you call sci-fi will be heavily regulated and will come later, if at all.”

As he reflected back on his parochial school days, Glen said, “That’s pretty far out there, and even if it’s possible I’m not so sure I like it. I think there are a lot of religious people, including my priest, and even ethics professors who would believe this was improper. Human beings are more than just the sum of their genetics. There’s a spiritual component, in addition to a chemical component, to life. What you’re talking about, controlling the genetic make-up of human beings, could probably fill 10 medical ethics books on what not to do, and screw-up mankind forever. No offense, but I don’t want a guy like you screwing with my DNA.”

John concluded with, “I think that if God didn’t want humans to understand how to do this, we wouldn’t have the intelligence to understand it. And for my purposes, there may be a vault full of money in them there genes.”

As the soup arrived, Glen countered, "If people are smart enough to do this, then they should be smart enough to know not to do it." Glen was trying to figure out what to make of this guy. People like John were a little too enthusiastic and self-assured. Glen thought that he was bound to learn the hard way that things don't always turn out the way you want.

12

That evening, John and Artie sat on the couch watching the Redskins game on the huge TV. John thought this is how life is supposed to be – sitting in a comfortable chair with a beer watching your favorite sporting event.

He turned to Artie and asked, "Do you have a heavy schedule this week?"

"I have a couple of meetings, but nothing too tough," Artie replied.

"Who are you meeting with?" John asked.

Artie looked at John, who apparently was just trying to make conversation, and said, "Who wants to know?"

John, a little taken aback said, "Inquiring minds want to know."

"Well, if you promise it's off the record, Mr. Inquirer, I'll tell you. I have a few friends from Long Island in the DC area who are trying to open start-up companies in the tech field, and they require my expertise in drafting a prospectus to enable their companies to get financing from banks or venture capitalists," Artie said with a grin.

"What kinds of companies are these?" asked John, with genuine curiosity.

Artie answered, "The ones I have lined up are Internet companies; my friends are computer wizards who set up websites. Some of them are in incubators. Two of them have what appear to be good ideas for selling specialty items over the Internet. One has an existing porno site and he knows girls who pose, and occasionally go online live.

Believe it or not, he's the one most likely to make money. He's looking for financing so he can sell video downloads and other porn paraphernalia online. The toughest parts are figuring how payments can be made and getting financing. Isn't technology great?"

"That sounds morally uplifting, do these guys actually pay money for this advice?" John asked inquisitively.

"Hell, yeah. Not only do I help them prepare a prospectus, but I also help them with presentations to get funding. I accompany them when they meet bankers and potential investors. I also help with their online promotion and sources of funding. It's not as easy as it looks, and a lot of these guys don't exactly have stellar personalities or my flair to impress corporate types." Artie exclaimed.

"Yeah, Artie, you're an impressive guy," John agreed.

Well, I'm not Thomas Edison or George Foreman," Artie conceded, "but I'm still a heck of a good pitch man, and I bet good old Tom wasn't too great at that."

John wondered what this young guy had successfully pitched in his short career as he asked, "How much do these guys pay for your services?"

"Well, it depends on the business and the amount of work required. At this point I usually get a small retainer to cover expenses and then I get a percentage of equity in the company, in the event I assist in securing funding," Artie explained.

John shook his head and admitted, "I'll tell you the truth, I never really understood the business end of those types of things. I used to try and read the business section of the *Times*, but I never really grasped the terminology. For instance, what's the difference between a stock, an equity stake, or a bond? What's the difference between a president and a member of the board of directors? And I never really understood what a hostile takeover is."

Artie said, "Those answers are for paying customers, and if you become a paying customer, you get the benefit of my insight."

John said, "Don't count on it."

Artie thought it's nice he tried to be honest about not knowing. He then turned to John and asked, "What's on your agenda for next week?"

John said, "I have two interviews scheduled. One with a company that is working on the human genome and doing research on genetic engineering in Rockville, MD. The other with a chemical company that makes plastics and adhesives. I'd kill to get the job in Rockville." John added, "I also have resumes out to other smaller biotech companies doing DNA research."

Artie didn't look too impressed and commented, "Oh, I guess you're just trying to get a job. Well, good luck working for someone else. Let them get fat and rich off your brains and hard work."

John responded, "Do you realize how important the genome research is to curing disease, finding new drugs and, dare I say, understanding the nature of life?"

Artie said, "Yeah, yeah, but in this country, a guy like you should set up his own company, with yours truly helping out. Otherwise, you'll be working to unravel the DNA code for most of your life and then hope to retire with a gold watch, if you're lucky, and a happy horseshit handshake. Meanwhile the CEO of the company you slaved for, incapable of spelling DNA, has houses on the east coast, west coast, Aspen and exits with a golden parachute worth 150 million bucks. That's why I like working with entrepreneurs. Their heads are in the right place."

"Speaking of rewards, my porn client provided me with a sample download of his merchandise," Artie said with a glint in his eye. "Any interest in watching on the big screen? The TV makes the participants look life-sized and the action may help you with your scientific research."

John laughed and said, "To quote my father's favorite sportscaster, Warner Wolfe, let's go to the videotape."

13

John Ordell drove up Rockville Pike, past the Big Screen TV store, a couple of Metro stops, Pike & Rose, and then he finally exited the Pike into a large corporate park that bore a logo for Geneteka. The logo almost looked like a religious symbol. It consisted of a large circle criss-crossed by double helixes, within the circle was the da Vinci sketch of the man in a circle with his arms and legs in two positions; one with his legs and arms out to the side and the other up over his head. Both positions touched the circle made up of the sides of the double helix.

As he drove into the parking lot, he saw an available visitor's spot in the first row. He hoped, please let this be a sign that I'll get this job.

John looked at his watch, realizing he was about 30 minutes early for his appointment. He decided to search for the coffee shop. Most corporate parks had at least one building with a coffee shop, and looking at the directory, he saw this one was no exception.

He walked down the stairs, into a small room, and saw a stout Hispanic woman behind a counter that held newspapers, pre-packaged doughnuts, candy and other sundry items.

John noticed a guy buying a newspaper who asked him, "Are you here for the Raytheon conference?" When John responded, "No," the guy continued, "They're a good group and have free doughnuts and coffee upstairs, and I bet they wouldn't mind if you took some." John thanked the guy but declined the offer.

At the counter John ordered a large coffee. He sat down at one of the three small tables, looked at his phone to check his Facebook page, but was too nervous to read. Even though he sometimes felt old using Facebook, he still kind of liked it.

He pulled out the letter setting up the interview with Dr. Alan Duretts. He had looked up Dr. Duretts immediately after he received the letter from Geneteka, and was not surprised by what he read.

Dr. Duretts received his B.S. in chemical engineering from Columbia, then went on to study at Harvard, where he received his MD and a PhD in organic chemistry, with a concentration in biochemistry. John thought how amazing it was that this guy was both a medical doctor and a scientist, with a strong engineering background. He wondered if there was anything this guy couldn't do if he put his mind to it. John couldn't wait to meet this scientist who was on the forefront of biotech research.

John looked down at his shoes and thought, I should have had these polished before the interview. This guy will think I'm one of those scatterbrained scientists with his head in the clouds and his unpolished shoes under the desk – damn. He should have taken care of that.

John sat drinking his coffee, pretending to read what he'd downloaded, thinking that he couldn't believe how nervous he was. It just showed how much he wanted the job. He wondered how many others were being interviewed, and whether any of them were from MIT, Cal Tech, Harvard or Yale. He recalled meeting a guy named Bruce Katz during an academic convention when he was in his PhD program. The guy was a brilliant math student who had done an incredible thesis on biochemistry and mapping genes for CRISPR. If Katz was in the running, he'd be stiff competition. God knows who else was out there to prevent him from getting this job.

At ten minutes before 10 o'clock, John stood up, took his last slug of coffee, and walked up to the reception area for Geneteka.

He approached the receptionist who looked to be in her twenties. She was slim with blonde hair, and a pretty smile. John thought how pleasant it would be to see her every morning before work. He introduced himself and told her he had a 10:00 AM interview scheduled with Dr. Duretts. She directed him to take a seat and buzzed the doctor.

After five minutes, Dr. Duretts appeared, shook John's hand and offered him coffee. John accepted the offer and Dr. Duretts asked the receptionist to get some for both of them. Dr. Duretts walked with John to the nearby conference room.

Dr. Duretts was a large man, who appeared amiable rather than imposing. He stood about 6'3" tall and probably weighed about 250 pounds. His eyes revealed an intense intellect and thoughtfulness, and he did not come off as arrogant or overbearing. He had the eyes of someone who took everything in. He radiated the aura of a brilliant mind, one who didn't have to flaunt it. John wondered for a moment if maybe he was reading too much into his first impression of the doctor.

They sat down in luxurious Italian leather chairs surrounding a large mahogany table in a paneled conference room that whispered, rather than screamed, I'm expensive. Dr. Duretts directed John, "Tell me about yourself and what I should know that would convince me that you're the best candidate for the job."

John hated these standard, meatball questions but responded, "I've done some work with Dr. Johnson at Washington St. Louis regarding the detection, operation and function of control regions in DNA and specifically in moths. This is the area where I concentrated on my thesis. We first mapped out a portion of the gypsy moths genes, specifically concentrating on one chromosome which changed when the caterpillar became a moth. We then determined where the control regions – which regulated and turned on the transformation from caterpillar to moth- were located. We did it by comparing the gene sequence for moths, before and after they underwent metamorphosis, and located at least two sites which had changed. We were preparing it to inject the larvae with CRISPR material to turn 'on' the control region and make the change occur early in the organisms or even to turn 'off' the control region and make the moth turn back to a larvae. I think they are still in the process of doing the injections."

Dr. Duretts asked, "Did your findings get published in any journals?"

John said, "Yes, they did. The Journal of Molecular Biology published an article written about the calculations we did about where and how the changes occurred and how they likely changed the appearance of the moth. I co-authored it with Dr. Johnson."

"I see," said Dr. Duretts.

John added, "Dr. Johnson was very excited about the project and on a number of occasions said he believed that this area of study could bring home a Nobel prize. He's still doing CRISPR research attempting to locate and switch different moth genes on and off, particularly the ones where the larva changes to a moth."

Dr. Duretts gave John a funny look and thought, how presumptuous this youngster is to come here and talk about Nobel prizes. It's like a toddler saying he'll become the world's fastest man before he can even walk. Duretts laughed inwardly, but there was something he liked about this candidate. His naiveté was almost charming, and he was certainly smart enough to do the legwork on the project. What a shame that there were so many other candidates with more stellar credentials than this fellow.

Dr. Duretts said, "So it's a Nobel prize you're after, eh?"

John continued, "Well, not really. I'd prefer to get involved with a quality lab, work with a collegial team, be challenged. I want to look forward to waking up every day to go to work on something I believe in, and where I feel my career is advancing. I've looked up some of the scientists here and I think I could grow as a scientist with this company because it's a world class institution."

Dr. Duretts liked what he heard, because it reminded him of himself many years ago, before the reality of huge egos, cynical scientists and shareholders' profit margins began to surpass the importance of the work. He also recalled his own promising future, where he'd had so much potential, always first in his class, always the rising star, but later years' disappointment and failure to achieve that potential.

He also remembered some of his less talented colleagues who went the 'easy route,' into management. Some were lucky enough to get in on the ground floors of pharmaceutical companies, where they hit it big financially. Those friends pursued MBAs and no longer did the actual work in labs, but instead attended board meetings, watched the bottom line and eventually struck it rich.

Many times, when he was working late at the lab missing his family, he'd reflect on what his father, a tailor, used to say: "You might not think I'm rich, but I feel rich," sadly that wisdom didn't seem to ring true when heard through his ears as a 59-year-old Director of Research at a prestigious lab in a high cost of living area, where his salary was competitive but not overly generous.

Dr. Duretts continued, "Before we go any further, let me describe the position that we are seeking to fill. It's a junior level position where you would be monitoring and re-checking data from chemical mixing bins and using computer models to determine specific locations of genes and how they express themselves. We're actually looking for somebody with superior computer skills. And, to be quite honest, the work is not very glamorous. After all, you have to crawl before you walk, you know." Dr. Duretts thought it an apt metaphor for this conversation.

John began to feel a certain comradery with Dr. Duretts, so he too became forthcoming. John responded: "I know the work of junior scientists is rarely very exciting on a day to day basis, but to work in a place like this, being exposed to cutting edge techniques and top-flight scientists. It sounds too good to pass up."

Dr. Duretts replied, "That's a nice sentiment, and I agree with it in principle, but the actual business of ground-breaking research can be every bit as unfair as other types of endeavors. For instance, have you ever read *Double Helix* – that's what research is really like – a rush to the solution, trying to beat the other guy before he beats you and publishes his findings. The guy who publishes first gets huge grants for his work, speaking engagements, praise from his colleagues, and possibly a shot at the Nobel you mentioned. The other guy gets to stay in his lab for another twenty years, with the smell of acetone, and retires at 65, with a small pension, a pat on the back and a fare-thee-well."

Dr. Duretts looked at John thoughtfully and said, "I'm sorry, I think that was somewhat inappropriate for an interview, so let's get back on track, tell me more about yourself."

John offered, "I grew up in New York City, in Brooklyn. I went to public schools and graduated from the Bronx High School of Science. My father was a Green Beret, and we lived in a blue-collar neighborhood. I attended Columbia and Washington University in St. Louis on a scholarship."

As he looked at John's resume, Duretts noticed the DC address, and commented, "I see a DC address on your resume, is that correct?"

John explained, "Yes, I moved down here because I liked DC and felt like there were a lot of opportunities here. I'm renting from a guy from Long Island, who has an MBA and works as a consultant advising start-up companies."

Dr. Duretts paused and thought that was interesting. He'd have to keep that in mind. He then asked John, "Do you have any questions about the job or the selection process?"

John asked, "Does the company do any work with CRISPR?"

Dr. Duretts had a sparkle in his eye as he continued, "Everybody doing this type of work has been working on CRISPR. We have been doing a lot of work on plants and even animals. The big boys are actually fighting it out regarding who has the rights to the patents. Hundreds of millions of dollars have been raised by investors based on the simple hope – probably still years away – that CRISPR drugs and treatments will pay off handsomely."

He continued, "We do have a division working with the technology.

We also had people who were involved with its predecessor, zinc finger nuclease technology and TAL effector nuclease technology, which was terribly slow, and like most things nowadays is already obsolete. I'm also acquainted with people outside of the company who are very seriously pursuing CRISPR. I even know one of the individuals at Editas Medicine where they're doing a $100 million initial public offering to begin clinical trials for a rare genetic disease for blindness. If you have a special interest in that area, that's not the particular job we're offering now."

John then said, "I understand, and that's fine. You have to start somewhere." then followed with, "What's the timetable for your selection and is there more than one interview?"

Dr. Duretts replied, "The process should take about three weeks, and we have a number of other candidates to interview, but you should hear from us in writing before the end of the month. If you're selected for the first cut, there will be a second interview with a panel of three scientists who will go into your background and knowledge of molecular biology in much greater depth than I did."

"In any event, John," Dr. Duretts stated in a sincere manner, "It really was a pleasure meeting you and I wish you good luck. You seem like a top quality young scientist. I hope we can keep in touch, and I truly mean that. I have a hunch your career may be one to watch, and if you don't mind, I may reach out to you from time to time, if that is all right?"

"Sure," said John.

As they shook hands and John started to leave, Dr. Duretts again thought that it was a shame that there were so many other candidates with Ivy league credentials and experience vastly superior to John's, and that it was most unlikely that John would merit a second interview, even with his imprimatur. He had another fleeting thought that John might be the perfect candidate for his 'outside the box' plans. He would have to give it a lot of thought, but he just may have found the right fit.

14

John returned to the apartment early in the afternoon and saw Glen sitting in the living room with a big bag of books in front of him, and a look of consternation on his face. John asked, "How you doing, Glen?"

Glen looked up and jibed, "So what, you're Wendy Williams now? I went over to GW Law School to pick up my course materials and get my schedule. I can't believe it, I'm already behind. I've got massive reading assignments and classes aren't scheduled to begin until next week. This isn't going to be as easy as I thought."

John went to the refrigerator, got himself a beer, and told Glen, "Don't worry, when I lived in St. Louis some of my friends were in law school, and they all said the first year was a killer and the second and third years were a piece of cake. So you only have one tough year to look forward to, then it's all good."

Glen said, "Yeah, I know I heard something similar, but my friends' version was, the first year they work you to death, and the second and third years they bore you to death. Anyway, I'm pretty sure that I'll do fine, and I've been told that a little hard work never hurt anyone."

Glen then added, "So, where are you coming from?"

John appeared a little nervous when broaching the subject and responded, "I just came from a job interview, and I'd kill to get this job. Now I'm going to do some more research on the guy who interviewed me. Maybe, I'll get some good material for my thank you letter."

Glen said, "I might as well start reading these overpriced textbooks to begin my dazzling legal career. Good luck finding the dish on your new colleague."

John proceeded to his room, picked up his antiquated iPhone 7, and entered his password 'CRISPR.' He Googled the website set up by the people at the publication, *Who's Who in Science.*

He then heard Artie's footfalls as he came toward John's door. Artie knocked but then barreled into John's room and asked, "What are you up to, searching sluts.com?"

John ignoring him said, "I just interviewed with a guy named Dr. Duretts and I'm checking him out."

John typed in the site name and was prompted with a request that he enter the scientist's name. He typed, then selected, Duretts, scientist, Maryland. A moment later, he was looking at Duretts' complete biography. It highlighted that he won a Westinghouse competition when he was in high school. While John already knew a little about Duretts' academic accomplishments, he learned that the doctor spoke three languages: German, Russian, and Mandarin Chinese. The bio also noted that Dr. Duretts graduated Phi Beta Kappa, and was listed as a Kulner scholar at Columbia, which meant he was in the top 5% of the school academically and that his last year he presented an honors thesis. After Columbia, he entered the joint MD/PhD program at Harvard.

Boy, John exclaimed to himself, this guy must have aced the MCAT and GRE examinations to gain entry to Harvard. John turned to Artie, who was reading over his shoulder, and uttered, "See why I want to work with this guy?"

Artie teased, "Read on, because I'm interested in the part where Mr. Perfect is put in a mental institution or axe murders his whole family."

"Not this guy," John responded, and they read on, "After receiving his PhD at Harvard Dr. Duretts became a research fellow at Harvard and performed research in genetic engineering and gene mapping, but abruptly left after approximately one and a half years, before the fellowship was completed and before the research had been published. Dr. Duretts then went into research in the private sector, where he was responsible for a string of minor advances in technology that could read genetic material used for forensic purposes and for advances in gene sequencing technology used to map the genes of fruit flies, worms and other creatures. It was a precursor to the type used in the human genome project. He also co-authored a number of papers in the area of genetics and wrote two books, one a scientific work which was well-received by his peers, but went out of publication shortly thereafter. The other, was a book targeting the popular market as a scientific non-fiction work for laymen. The second book met with negative reviews and was unsuccessful. The doctor subsequently became active in the human genome project and was appointed as a director at Geneteka, the company where he is currently employed."

John thought, "How odd. Why would he leave Harvard so soon, especially before he finished his fellowship?" It just didn't add up.

Artie said, looking over John's shoulder, "I guess I was wrong, he's just another boring nerd after all." Artie then walked out, leaving John still curious about why Dr. Duretts left Harvard.

John decided to continue his search on Bing and went to the website set up by a group against the continuation of genetic research, for such things as genetically altered foods, cloning technology, and genetically altered animal research. He hoped their site would reveal any dirt on Geneteka or Dr. Duretts, if it existed.

He logged on to www.saynotodna.org and got an eyeful. Boy, he thought, these zealots are vehemently opposed to recombinant DNA research. What kind of a screwed-up world view would make them think that it made sense to halt DNA research with all its infinite possibilities – from curing diseases, to making new food sources resistant to pests, to creating new organisms that could do all sorts of things, including breaking up oil spills.

It's just crazy to believe it's an apocalyptic event every time DNA research breakthroughs occur, and that anyone who wants to develop the technology is evil. What a bunch of kooks. If they, or someone they loved, had a genetic disorder, like a predisposition to breast cancer, you know they'd be the first ones yelling for unlimited genetic research. Just like the old fart Senators who opposed stem cell research, until they realized that it might cure them if they developed Alzheimer's.

Anyway, the site had what he was looking for.

On its list of top ten 'criminals,' i.e., those who were misguided enough to play God with DNA molecules, the name Dr. Alan Duretts was prominently featured.

The site downplayed Dr. Duretts' impressive schooling and claimed he was a fallen Catholic, and now a secular humanist critical of religion. It even suggested that Dr. Duretts was a megalomaniac, with no need for a belief in God because of his intellectual gifts. That didn't mean, however, that he was entitled to affect human life – and mess with people's souls. They predicted Armageddon, where a rogue bacteria or virus would wipeout humans on the planet, or that engineered animals would take over the earth. And finally John's favorite, the creation of an Antichrist via genetic engineering.

John thought the site was unbalanced and unfair in its viewpoint, that it omitted the incredible benefits of the new technology, its modest cost, and its potential to improve life on the planet. They left out the litany of CRISPR discoveries, including breakthroughs such as the mouse that was cured of muscular dystrophy. John figured the people who set up the website still probably believed the earth was flat.

He couldn't take anymore. He clicked off his phone and thought that certain politicians and fanatics just didn't get it. They were the kids in school who would get a C or D in science class, and then hated science for the rest of their lives, even though they benefited from the fruits of science every day. Such is the way of the world.

15

John woke up the next morning at 10:15 AM, and when he walked into the kitchen he bumped into Glen who was gulping down some juice. John said, "What's going on, you look a little messed up."

Glen said, "It's my first day of classes. I read the assignment, but it's all gibberish. It's like they made up a whole new language, with words I don't understand." He winced, "I think the professors actually ask questions the first day. I keep thinking of an old movie 'The Paper Chase,' where Professor Kingsfield tells his student 'Here's a dime, go call your mother and tell her you're not going to be a law-w-w-yer.' I've got to go."

Glen left John shaking his head, thinking: Lawyers. They probably just use incomprehensible language so regular people can't follow what's going on, so they can justify making money doing their thing.

John got dressed in a pair of sweatpants, Nike running shoes and a t-shirt. He went downstairs and saw the sunlight streaming into the windows at the front of the building. He was happily thinking about the great day ahead.

The birds were singing outside and traffic was streaming by on Connecticut Avenue, as he went to the apartment's mailbox. Opening it, he found a few bills, two solicitations for credit cards – he may already qualify for $10,000 of credit – and at the bottom of the pile, a letter from Geneteka. It almost took his breath away.

This was it, the karma was right. It seemed like perfect timing. He could start working, finally get on with his life and maybe get his own big screen TV. He ripped open the letter and the smile evaporated from his face. It was a short letter, three sentences long. It said:

"Thank you for your interest in employment opportunities at Geneteka. We regret to inform you, however, that you have not been selected for a second interview.

Good luck with your future endeavors."

He was stunned, and his eyes began to well up. His throat began to close and a nauseous feeling came over him. He then noticed some handwriting on the bottom of the letter. It was from Dr. Duretts. John wondered, what could he possibly want to add?

The handwriting was legible, and Dr. Duretts wrote: "I'm sorry you won't get the job, but you have a lot of potential. Would you like to meet with me, maybe get a beer and discuss your future?"

Why, thought John, would he want to do that? Maybe he's a decent guy who wants to help another person he connected with, even though the interview didn't work out.

Duretts included the number for his private line in the letter. John said to himself, in a barely audible voice, "That and $2.75 will get me a ride on the New York City subway."

16

Demoralized, John went back to the apartment. He walked to the elevator and listened as the elevator clunked down to where he waited on the first floor. He didn't remember hearing that sound before. The elevator doors opened, he walked inside, pressed the button and the doors closed with a loud thud. He started thinking that maybe it was a mistake to move to DC, and that things wouldn't all just work out.

His Dad might have been right, that he should set his sights lower. Maybe he could get a job with the Feds, possibly at the National Institutes of Health, because he wouldn't have to work too hard. If he got the right gig, it could even be interesting. Those jobs, however, were still tough to get and usually you had to know somebody who could pull a few strings.

John got off the elevator, walked down the hallway, which smelled of mildew, and opened his door which creaked more than before. He felt hot in the apartment.

Artie was already there talking to someone on his cell phone. John entered the living room, sat on the sofa, and began flipping through the channels. Artie walked over looked at John's face and asked, "Why so glum?" John answered, "I just got a letter from Geneteka and I got shot down; but the guy who interviewed me wrote that he wanted to talk with me and meet me for a beer."

Artie optimistically offered, "That's strange, but I think it's great. You need contacts, maybe hook in with whatever social media accounts he has. He could be someone who can help you meet top people in the industry, that's how DC and corporate America works. It's not what you know, it's who you know."

John asked, "So, you think it's a good idea to call him?"

"It can't hurt to go see him, unless you think he may be into you other than as a mentor. And you're not interested... definitely not interested," advised Artie. As he prepared to leave, Artie added, "it probably won't lead to a job with his company, but he must have some awesome connections."

John agreed that meeting Duretts would be a good idea, but he really hoped it wouldn't be for a 'hook up,' because he already felt like he'd gotten royally screwed.

17

Artie was on his way to DuPont Circle so he could meet his friend, Frank Nathie. They were working on a prospectus to secure financing for a new business venture. The deal wasn't a lock, since the gaming program wasn't finished and few investors would provide money to start-up companies that didn't have product. If you didn't have money, and you didn't have the goods, then you didn't have much at all.

Still, Frank had been a good buddy from school. It would only take an afternoon to meet, then another few days to put together a reasonable prospectus. Artie had nothing else going on, and it would be good practice, since he'd only written three before, if you counted the one he'd gotten an A for at Hofstra. It was an easy decision.

He rode the escalator into the Metro which struck him as spotless, mostly because it didn't smell anything like the New York City subway, with which he was intimately familiar. The Metro even had lights on the platform floor that flashed on and off when the trains approached. The New York City subway definitely didn't have that.

He rode one quick stop, exited the train and took the escalator up to Connecticut Avenue. He walked over to Starbucks, bought two venti coffees and then went up to Frank's apartment. It was a nice building off Connecticut Avenue in what was known as Kalorama, an affluent, well-heeled neighborhood. Frank's parents must have been doing pretty well to put him up in this luxe neighborhood. There's no way an unemployed programmer two years out of college was paying for this pad.

Artie turned left off of Connecticut Avenue and walked three blocks in the warm sunshine. He thought of the scant documents he reviewed; still, if the idea worked it could be big. It was supposed to be a super-fast program which could permit games to interface with the cloud more quickly and over various platforms.

As he understood it, it was supposed to work by shrinking the program files to a form that could be transferred over the Internet more quickly. It also had the capability of translating through different types of gaming programs. Frank claimed that it would be 35% faster than what was currently available, meaning that gaming instructions could be transferred much faster. However, there were still glitches to overcome to get the program to run seamlessly.

Artie went into the condominium building and noticed the lobby's beautiful green granite floor. It made the expansive room cool and soothing. There was a valet behind the desk to hold deliveries and help people who lived in the building. Artie thought, 'this is the way to live,' and just then one of the elevator doors opened. He entered and pressed 7.

The elevator door opened into a hallway which had a regal looking carpet with a subtle star pattern. He rang the doorbell to Frank's condo and Frank invited him in.

Artie said, "I love this apartment, man. The furniture all matches, and it's color coordinated. Did your mom, or sister help out?" Frank responded, "Dude, I had an interior decorator in and we did it together. She showed me some ideas, but I picked out everything. She was pretty hot for an older woman."

They moved to the dining room table to discuss the prospectus that Artie had worked on. He said, "I have a few questions about the business. First, how did you figure out how to write the program, and do you own the rights to the program?"

Frank grinned at Artie, and said, "Do you think that I'd call you if I didn't own it? Anyway, one of my friends from my programming classes at American University wrote it, and I purchased it from him. I got a few of my parent's friends to invest in getting the rights to the program and I bought the idea, but he still has to work out the bugs if he wants to get any money. If he does, I'd like to license the program to one of the major gaming companies."

Frank, suddenly more serious said, "Look Artie, I like you a lot, but my parents and their friends want their lawyers and business advisors to go over this and get a deal done, including establishing the corporation, preparing licensing agreements, and obtaining patents. We also have an independent engineer lined up to certify that the technology works, once we get the bugs worked out."

Frank stepped back and said, "Don't look so surprised. In a few years you'll be the one doing all that, and in the meantime, my parents insist. Anyway, there are some great bars in the neighborhood. I'm buying. Let's go."

Artie, disappointed in the turn of events, marveled how great it must be to go through life as a trust fund baby, as he said, "Well, that's got to be the best offer I've had all day."

18

John's father called from New York to tell him, "Your Aunt Sylvia is sick and in the hospital. She had a mild heart attack, but she'll probably be OK. Did you get a job yet, or what?"

John replied, "I'm sorry to hear about Aunt Sylvia. It makes me sad to think of her being sick." His father sensed that there was something more, but John didn't feel like getting into it with his father today. He simply said, "One job that I was especially interested in, fell through, but I have some other job leads. The other places are also biotech companies."

John just shook his head at the phone, which was on speaker, and mumbled, "Great talk. Anyway, tell Aunt Sylvia I said I was sorry to hear about her, I might be back in New York in the next couple of weeks. Take it easy."

John began thinking, maybe his father was right, that he was just chasing pipe dreams, and his mother had been wrong. Maybe her beautiful, genius boy wasn't so great after all, and grew up to be just another ordinary guy. Maybe he was just a loser.

But no, he was determined to make his father eat his words – to drive up to his father's modest house in an expensive car, and show him once and for all that he was wrong.

Only now, John was unsure of how to make that happen, or even if it would ever be possible.

19

After John called Dr. Duretts, he thought the choice of meeting place a bit odd. Duretts asked John to meet him at 7 o'clock at Miller's Ale House, on Rockville Pike. John speculated about what kind of casual conversation he might have with an old guy who'd just crushed his dreams.

John was desperate to find the right job, and not just any job. He was already getting responses from resumes he'd sent out, but the bites he got were for what he considered to be dead-end jobs – say hello to developing the next generation of plastic food wrap.

The only job that held any interest for him was with a pharmaceutical company that made cold medicine. It was for a job doing research on the effects of drugs, and the pay was pretty good. Still, he held out hope that Dr. Duretts might be able to provide him with leads for jobs with top people, and maybe even be willing to make a call or two. Although, probably not. After all, he had been rejected by Duretts' own company.

20

John drove into the parking lot and saw a number of SUVs. The bar looked like a little box, with the usual Budweiser, Michelob and Coors neon lights in the windows. It wasn't the kind of place he usually frequented, but it had a sports bar feel to it, was clearly into the NFL, and was only a few short miles north of the Beltway. Since they were meeting in Rockville, he was surprised that Dr. Duretts hadn't chosen one of the newer, swankier bars in Town Center. Anyway, here he was.

When he walked through the door, he noticed that the lighting was dark, and was struck by the smell of cheap beer. Three men sat at the bar, drinking whatever was on tap, and another was eating a sandwich with his beer. They were all watching sports on the televisions behind the bar. To the left was a row of booths made of wood.

John glanced at his watch and saw it was about 6:50 PM, so he was 10 minutes early. He didn't see Dr. Duretts anywhere. As he moved toward the booths, he saw that the last two at the end were empty. He slid into the last booth in the row, looking toward the entrance. It was dark in the corner, with posts that obscured the view.

The waitress came over as John, once again, wondered why Dr. Duretts had picked this particular bar to meet. Was he thinking he had a new frat buddie or what? The waitress, a middle-aged blond with her hair up, asked, "What will it be, honey?" John smiled and asked, "What do you have on tap?" She answered, "We have Budweiser, Miller, and Coors Light, and that card lists the bottled beer selections," she smiled as she pointed to the card stuck in a Lucite holder. He said, "I'll have a Sam

Adams and I'm waiting for someone. We'll probably order dinner." She left to get his beer.

Just then, Dr. Duretts walked into the bar. He was wearing jeans, a T-shirt and boots. Very different from what he looked like when John had seen him at work. Now he looked like an ordinary Joe, like an electrician or plumber just getting off work, having a pop before going home to the wife and kids. Dr. Duretts waved when he saw John in the end booth, and walked over.

John greeted him, "Hey, Dr. Duretts."

Duretts reached over the table to shake hands and said, "Hello, John. You don't have to call me that, in fact I'd prefer that you just call me Alan." He slid into the booth, smiled in an obsequious manner, looked over at the bar and ordered a Coors Light when the waitress returned.

He asked John how the job search was going. John answered, "I have some leads but they're not so great. I would have liked to get an offer at Geneteka, but you already know how that panned out." John frowned, but wished he hadn't.

Duretts earnestly sympathetic said, "I gave you a strong recommendation in my memorandum, but I didn't think you'd get the nod from our HR department. They are not very flexible. It may not seem like it now, but you're probably better off because many young scientists become experts in sub-sub-specialties and become mired in doing the legwork. Besides, you strike me as an entrepreneurial young man; someone who isn't afraid to take risks if the reward is great enough."

John responded, "I like to think I am, but I don't have money or experience, so I'm not sure. Some friends who got MBAs went into the business side of science, but I think I want to do the research, especially with all that CRISPR can do, it's revolutionary."

Duretts interrupted, "Well you know that all the work, the research, the 'increasing of knowledge' is really ultimately fueled by money. The basic research is paid for by taxpayers and people like you perform the research in universities or at NIH. If the basic research is fruitful, then the idea is co-opted by private companies. It's ultimately licensed to them so that they can capitalize on it, to make higher profits. Universities do make some money, however, in reality it's socialism for big pharma and others who reap the greatest rewards without taking the commensurate risks; although, they do have to pay to have the drugs approved and products marketed."

"Don't get me wrong," Duretts continued, "the system seems to work OK; but people like us, who figure out the answers and get the results, sometimes have to look out for ourselves."

He looked straight at John and said, "It's a rough and tumble world with people trying to take from you every step of the way. That's why guys like you and me, scientists – the guys who make it happen – need to stick together."

John thought it an unusual statement, but clearly Alan had a point he wanted to make. John looked back at Alan, who still looked at him with intensity, as he asked, "How do we stick together?"

John hoped this drama was leading up to Alan saying he knew someone who could hire John. He anxiously awaited Alan's next words.

Alan continued, "I have a lot of colleagues who spent 20 or 30 years working in labs at Geneteka with little to show for it. They were lower level employees, did not get stock options, dividends or have golden parachutes. Their pension benefits were decreased, even though the company's profits went through the roof."

Alan looking at his hands, went on, "Unfortunately, this happened to me and all my colleagues in my department. I guess we were good at the science, we just weren't very good at corporate politics. The CEO, now after he does his stint, he walks away quite comfortable – fat and happy – but not my friends, and not me. It begins to strain your loyalty."

Alan then took a deep breath and continued, "You come to the realization that it's necessary to start thinking about yourself, like all those

MBAs and bankers. And maybe derive greater financial benefit from what you or your team discovered, for yourself, and more importantly, for your family."

Alan continued, "Consider Bill Gates. He started his business by selling an operating system to IBM that didn't even exist. It had yet to be developed. He ended up buying the idea from a talented programmer for something in the neighborhood of fifty-grand. Gates' real stroke of genius was to convince the brain trust at IBM to lease the idea, rather than purchase it. Since IBM was fearful of being accused of antitrust violations, it did just that. The irony is that Microsoft, itself, was convicted of antitrust violations a few short years later."

Alan proceeded, "But at the end of the day, Bill Gates is still one of the richest men in the world. His children will never know want, nor will his grandchildren nor their grandchildren's grandchildren. Sadly, that is not the case for me or for my friends, at least not yet."

John smiled nervously, not really following where Alan was going with this.

Alan asked, "Have you ever see the movie, *The Big Short,* where they exposed all the fraud going on with the banks, rating agencies, and mortgage brokers, where all of these folks made tons of money? Well, it was rampant and I daresay the same players are still doing the same thing. So, my lab friends and I decided that if it's good enough for them, it should be good enough for us."

John looked on, intrigued, but still not following.

"Can I trust you, John? What I want to tell you is very sensitive and confidential. We're looking for somebody with just the right amount of smarts, and who'll be able to pull off a startup company without too many people questioning what actually happened. We want someone to help us capitalize on something me and my team discovered."

It was unbelievable to John that this accomplished scientist felt this way, and even more unbelievable that he was telling John about it. But then he remembered his father's words, that 'people get angriest and motivated to action when they feel they're getting ripped off.'

John didn't mind playing this game, no matter how hypothetical he thought it might be. Jokingly he replied, "I'd rather just win the lottery and be done with it." As soon as the words left his mouth, he wished he hadn't uttered them.

Duretts, intently focused on John, was not smiling.

Instinctively, John immediately responded, "All joking aside, I never really thought it was an option before, but who wouldn't want to be the next Bill Gates?"

Duretts, considering John's words, looked directly at him, and stated, "That could be closer to reality than you think."

John froze, and the hairs on the back of his neck actually stood up.

Just then, a different waitress approached their table and said, "Sorry, I didn't see you come in." She then took their food order and went to get the beer, which had never made it to their table.

Dr. Duretts, suddenly at ease, asked, "What would you say if I told you we could give you a methodology to create a CRISPR based compound which you, as a front for us, could sell for a great deal of money?"

This was a question that John couldn't have anticipated.

He wondered, did he still have a shot at getting the job at Geneteka? Was this some innovative interview technique? If he says the right thing, he's offered the job on the spot? Unlikely, he thought. It was probably just a powerful old guy messing with his head. John thought, two can play that game, and figured he'd lay it on thick.

John said, "I'd say, we have a deal. You bet I would. If it worked for Microsoft, why couldn't it work for us? I'd rather work at a new enterprise, where I could make a mark, as well as a lot of money, too."

Duretts, satisfied that he had found the right guy, felt very hungry all of a sudden. Just then, the waitress arrived with their order. She brought the food and beer at the same time.

Dr. Duretts attacked his sandwich with gusto. They lapsed into small talk, and shared accounts of mishaps and pranks in labs they'd worked in. John regaled Alan with his experiences working in the lab as a graduate student, where one of his crazier classmates took to throwing phosphorus out the windows at passing pedestrians during snowstorms, because it exploded when it hit the snow.

As they prepared to leave, Dr. Duretts said, "I'd like to do this again very soon. I also have a couple of friends I'd like you to meet. One is a programmer and the other is a scientist at Geneteka. Next time we'll meet someplace else, maybe in Gaithersburg."

John responded to the invitation saying, "Sure I'll call you at Geneteka to get our plans straight."

Duretts, disconcerted, said, "Please don't call me. I'll call you." He dropped some bills on the table before they headed out the door.

21

The next morning, when John saw Artie he couldn't wait to talk. Artie was in a hurry to get out the door because he was on his way out for a run. Before he could leave, John said, "Did I tell you that I had dinner with Dr. Duretts last night, up in Rockville? Man, it was strange."

Artie considered John, who stood before him with a perplexed look on his face, and said, "I'd rather talk about it later, but it looks like this can't wait. I'll give you my two cents, short and sweet. Isn't this the guy who rejected you for your dream job? Why do you care if he's a little eccentric, or even nuts? It's not like he can fire you, or do anything to screw up your future. If I were you, I'd just roll with it. You have nothing to lose."

John said, "Thanks, that's actually pretty good advice. Run a mile for me, would ya?"

Three days later when John's cell phone rang, the caller ID displayed a number he didn't recognize. Since it hadn't come up 'unavailable,' he picked up.

He was greeted by Dr. Duretts' voice on the line. Duretts said, "Hello John. I hope things are well with you." John replied, "Yeah, how's it going with you? And why is my phone showing a weird number?"

Dr. Duretts responded, "I'm well, thank you. I'm using a disposable cell phone, I think your generation calls it a 'burner.' How is the job search going?"

John replied, "I'm going to another interview in about two weeks. This one's with AgriTechnologies, Inc., to work on genetically altered foods and agricultural products. The pay seems a little low, and although they use CRISPR technology, I wouldn't be working in that department. I'm just not sure it's the right thing for me. Do you know anything about them?"

Duretts thought he'd better move fast if he was to get John committed to what he had in mind.

Duretts said, "I heard Dr. Green is over there. He's a good man, and they do some interesting things with fruits and vegetables. Let me know how it goes. On another note, I'd like to meet with you at the end of the week. Would Friday's on Rockville Pike be convenient for you?" It was the right kind of place; always crowded, dark, noisy, anonymous – not a place anyone would notice four scientists sitting in a booth.

John said, "I can do that." Dr. Duretts asked, "How's Thursday at 8:00 PM?" John in a weak attempt at unemployment humor said, "Let me check my schedule," then added, "it looks like I'm free." Duretts didn't laugh, but said, "I look forward to seeing you then, and I will be bringing two friends."

John said, "OK, see you Thursday. Bye," and hung up.

22

It was Thursday, and John found himself ensnarled in traffic as he drove up Connecticut Avenue at 7:15 PM. He could not believe the traffic. It was crazy. There were so few roads connecting the suburbs and the District that it was simply ridiculous. He felt sorry for the poor slobs who had to do this commute every single day of their lives. Torturously long commutes are just a way of life for the hoi polloi, he thought.

He cut across Jones Bridge Road, to Wisconsin Avenue, which he was pretty sure turned into Rockville Pike. Why do the names of roads change like this around DC, he wondered. As you drive down a street, suddenly its name changes. He noticed this more than once while driving around DC and its suburbs. It just added to the confusion.

Anyway, he guessed it didn't matter as long as the GPS worked.

As he drove up the Pike, he saw a number of strip malls, bars and restaurants. He took mental notes on the different places he might try in the future, hopefully with a date, if he ever got a job.

John pulled into the parking lot for the TGIFridays, beside a Pier One store, across the street from a Silver Diner. He thought this nondescript strip mall could be found in any city, in any state in the country.

23

John homed in on a spot in the parking lot right in front of the TGIFridays, and felt it had to be a good sign.

He walked into the restaurant and recognized Dr. Duretts at a booth in the back corner. He was sitting with two other guys. The one he could see was sitting beside Duretts. He looked short by comparison, was partially bald and wore thick glasses. He had a sour look on his face, appearing annoyed or bitter about something, or maybe that was just the way he always looked. As John walked over to the table, Dr. Duretts said, "Hello, John. Meet Dr. Bob Daniels." Bob looked up and shook John's hand.

The person across the table looked like a stick figure, he was skinny and almost sickly looking. Dr. Duretts introduced him to John, "And this is my friend, David Goldblum. He's what can best be described as a prodigy programmer."

John sat down and Duretts began, "John, I'm going to be direct with you, and not beat around the bush. I've known Bob for more than 30 years and we've both worked for corporations over those many years. After talking to you, I thought you might be the right person to discuss something that we've come up with."

As Duretts shifted his eyes from his beer to John's face, he continued, "Can you keep a secret? Can we trust you, even if you're not interested in pursuing what we have to say?"

Dr. Duretts looked at John, believing in his gut that his assessment had been right. If he had miscalculated, however, it could present a huge problem.

John looked sincere when he said, "I'm not the kind of guy who violates a confidence. Also, as you know, I hold fellow scientists in high regard, and would not ever do anything like that. I thought about what you said when we last talked, and I agree."

Dr. Duretts was pleased by what John said. Bob, considering what they were about to embark on, had to consciously stop himself from rolling his eyes or showing disdain at the thought of having to cut this unproven youngster in on the plan.

Dr. Duretts then said, "Like most things, there is more to the story. When we were employed by various companies, including Geneteka, we had to sign anti-competition agreements so that we could not use or apply for patents relating to any of our work as employees of the companies. The laws are such that the companies own the rights to anything we create while working in their labs. The corporate CEO and the shareholders keep all rights to every idea and are not shy about going to court to protect those rights."

John said, "OK."

Dr. Duretts looked over at Bob and continued, "Bob is a highly trained scientist who went to public College at SUNY Binghamton, and then got a scholarship to Purdue University for his PhD. He's a bright guy, and a decent guy too, I might add, but not much of a politician. He doesn't know how to kiss up, so he's stuck on a lower rung at Geneteka. He's not a director or VP, but he is great at the science.

He has two kids, both fairly gifted, who are about to attend college. They should have the opportunity to go to the best schools they can get into, and money shouldn't be an issue, but of course, it is."

John looked serious as he said, "I know exactly what you mean, I've accumulated a significant amount of debt as I've pursued my education, and I wish I hadn't. It was all to understand the science of genes, which I love. I also hate diseases, although it sounds stupid when I say it out loud."

Dr. Duretts thought, true, it may sound stupid, but this was useful information.

Dr. Duretts continued, "Bob and some of our colleagues were working long hours doing research on the human genome project, and decided to do some overtime off the books work. We also used our man David, here, as an independent consultant to create an algorithm with AI to analyze and extrapolate from the findings."

Dr. Duretts said, "Bob and his assistants worked on their own time, weekends and evenings, looking at specific areas on genes with their effect on different traits. David figured out ways to predict certain genes, and what their function is, in different animals and it even had some limited application in people."

Dr. Duretts continued, "As luck would have it, Bob, and 3 bald techs, along with David, stumbled on the genes that deal with the growth of hair on people's heads. He compared the genes of the janitor, Lou, and many others who had full heads of hair at 57 years-old, with the bald-headed techs and other bald friends, then ran it through a computer. They were pretty sure they identified two genes that control when hair falls out causing baldness."

Dr. Duretts said, "The process took about two years, and we tested and compared the genes of numerous bald and non-bald people, and we were able to locate the genes which regulated at what specific age hair falls out. In Bob's case the age was 27, in Lou's case he never lost his hair. Bob and David also located and isolated the 2 genes and the control region on the balding gene. He thought that if you change the two genes then voila! The patient re-grows his original full head of hair – it's Minoxidil that works for everyone and right away. It also carries over to your future children and prevents baldness in them, too."

Dr. Duretts continued, "We were able to test it by applying it topically on the bald head of one of the techs. It actually worked and the tech agreed, off the record of course, to try a CRISPR injection. He now has a full head of brown hair."

Bob was studying John, wondering if this was such a good idea. John had a skeptical look on his face and asked, "If that's the case, why are you telling me? That's the breakthrough I should be reading about in a scientific journal."

Dr. Duretts continued to explain, "You will not see it in any journal – because no one knows about the discovery."

Duretts paused before continuing, "You see, Bob here has two sets of books at the lab. One for them; one for us. I've also been working on this little project, and between the two of us we have enough data for someone to successfully reverse engineer the process. It would look especially convincing if the group doing the research copied notebooks or a zip drive with our results, providing the rationale for starting and moving the research into the particular area – something that we've also thought a lot about. Writing the notebook, in your own handwriting, or typing it into a tablet would be a nice touch. Also, you can hire David to assist."

Dr. Duretts hoped he wasn't making a grave error in laying out the plan in such detail, and so soon. John's demeanor was off, like his muscles were tightening up and his eyes were contracting into a squint. Dr. Duretts said, "You must tell us what you're thinking. I need to be forthright here, and equally, we need you to be upfront with us. Again, my impression when I met you was that you were a stand-up type of young man who could handle something like this."

John responded "Isn't this really just like stealing from the company that hired you? And, isn't it illegal and unethical to test on humans?"

Bob then weighed in and said, "Well John, I'd like to answer these if Alan doesn't object. Alan and I have both worked at labs for well over 30 years. Do you have any idea how much money this cure is worth – considering that Minoxidil sales are in the multimillions? Our treatment is far superior and should work on everyone. Also, no one was hurt in the trials. We were able to test it topically first, then David's program provided us a backstop that analyzed the differences in the genes of bald men and men with full heads of hair, at least for this limited application. The tech, a friend of mine, volunteered to be our human guinea pig. So, again, what's the harm?"

Bob continued, "Alan and I were also instrumental in figuring out some clever ways to crack the human genome in a quarter of the time that the original method would have yielded. We even had to use the zinc finger nuclease method for the initial research, which was backbreaking."

He went on, "And you know that when it comes time for the payoff – which will probably be billions of dollars to pharmaceutical companies – no one would have given us appropriate compensation for the blood and sweat that got the job done."

Bob said, "With both of my kids in college next year, I expect to use a substantial portion of my 401K to pay their tuition. Who knows when, or if, I'll ever be able to retire."

Dr. Duretts interjected, "Look, had we found a site involved in curing cancer, then we would feel obligated to publish the findings and ultimately give our research up to Geneteka, so that humanity would benefit and they could make a fortune off of our discovery. But we didn't cure cancer. At least not yet, but it does have tremendous commercial appeal, just like Viagra. And here we are."

John looked torn, and Bob could tell they had more work to do if they were to convince him. So Bob jumped in and said, "Both Alan and I have contracts with our company. The contracts have strict anti-competition clauses, which they vigorously enforce. This means any findings or techniques uncovered by us at work, or even on our own time, are considered to be the property of Geneteka."

Bob continued, "If we left and then started a company, it would look very suspicious. Geneteka has cadres of lawyers just waiting to sue us, which would tie our sorry asses up in court for years, and is something neither of us would look forward to. But you, a neophyte, a virtual unknown, credentialed enough to be believable, would be untraceable to us. Also, with Alan's connections, we could probably get you financing to set up the operation for our, I mean 'your,' idea."

Bob said, "To lay it all out for you – we can provide you with everything you need to make yourself a player in the biotech community and to make you rich enough so you can do anything your heart desires, all within a couple of years. Grow a pair of balls, be a man and do something good for yourself. It's a no-brainer. Say yes and we all win. Your future wife and kids will thank you every day."

John still appeared stunned by what had been revealed to him, but was uncertain about what to do. Bob made a lot of sense, even if it was not really 100% right. But who does what is right anymore? It was confusing. And he didn't appreciate being admonished to 'grow a pair and be a man,' when it could land him in jail. Despite his inner conflict, with no other decent employment options, it was easy for him to make up his mind.

Bob and Dr. Duretts were looking directly at John when he meekly said, "I'll do it; I'll work with you guys. If this CRISPR thing looks viable, I'm your guy."

Just then their meals arrived. They instantly switched topics and began discussing the Redskin's chances for a Super Bowl ring this season, and then made other small talk, but the air was thick with the energy and excitement of their conspiracy. They clinked their beer mugs together in unspoken glee as partners in crime, intent on stealing back what was stolen from them.

24

For the rest of the evening, none of them even mentioned the plan again. Dr. Duretts merely said, "My young friend, my crystal ball tells me you are looking at a magnificent future."

Duretts continued, "Please, take this burner phone that I purchased for you. When we need to talk, only call me from this phone. Don't call me from any other phone and don't call me at any other number. I've already pre-programmed it with my contact number."

Then they paid the bill in cash, and as they prepared to leave, Bob winked, smiled for the first time all night and said, "Don't call me at all." David, on the other hand, said nothing and was expressionless.

Before he stood up to walk out of the restaurant, Dr. Duretts told John, "Next time you hear from me, I'll give you a list of equipment you must purchase to do the research and to set up the business. It includes a specific brand of supercomputer David will require. In order to help us get data to put into the computer, you will also need to set up a department for DNA testing for the public."

John drove back to the apartment still feeling conflicted. The angst of not getting a decent job offer still bothered him, but he felt a calling to be part of the CRISPR biotech revolution. He couldn't do it himself, but wanted to feel like he could make a difference, even if it was actually Bob, or someone else, who was on the frontlines making the discovery.

What would his mother think? She probably wouldn't have approved, and would have wanted him to choose differently. But she was gone, and he didn't seem to have the prospect of securing a great job, or any job at all. His Dad would just laugh if he got a dead-end job, going nowhere fast and burdened as he was with student loan debt.

He remembered his favorite professor in college who said if you had a good idea, the difference between making it big or not, simply had to do with timing. Being at the right place at the right time. He hadn't really gotten into whether or not you should bend the rules when the timing was right.

John drove into his parking spot behind the building, walked down the dingy hallway and took the elevator to his apartment. Artie was watching the Wizards game on the mammoth TV.

John asked, "How's it going?" Artie shook his head and replied, "Not so great, the Wizards are down by 9, with a minute and thirty-five seconds to go. It looks like the fat lady's about to sing."

John then asked, "So what are your prospects with the friend you met? Did anything pan out?"

Artie said, "It doesn't look good. These guys are all putzes, except for the dude with the porn site. I have a special place in my heart for him, and especially his employees."

"I'll bet," John smiled, then asked, "Have you ever done any work in biotech?"

Artie said, "No, but with what I do, it's all the same. I just ask the client to explain what the company can do and help formulate the business plan. You need to have a well thought out plan to get financing. You need to convince the bankers or money people that you have a commodity – you hold a valuable license or something else of value that can be used as collateral.

Intellectual capital – your people – and institutional knowledge is also important, but not as important. The bankers are in it for the money, if they think you can make them money, it's all good. If not, it's no go. Like in the case of Internet companies, they've become very skeptical.

Biotech, probably less so. But in those areas, a track record – or showing that you really have something in the works – really helps."

John asked, "How do you get paid for the work you do?"

Artie asked, "What do you mean?"

John looked quizzically and said, "What I mean is, uh, do you only get paid if you're successful in getting money for your clients, or do you get paid per hour, or something else?"

Artie replied, "Oh, I see. To be honest, it really depends on the company and what I'm doing. I really haven't been doing this very long, and I'm usually doing it with friends and I'm flexible. Sometimes I get paid a percentage of the money I get. Usually about 2%, or I might get a piece of the action, especially if they're cash-strapped and I think it's a good deal." Without letting on, Artie was merely parroting what he heard from others in the field.

John said, "Not to show my lack of business acumen, but what do you mean 'a piece of the action?'"

Artie suddenly screamed at the TV, "What the hell is John Wall doing, throwing the ball away like that?" Not missing a beat, he turned toward John and said, "A piece of the action means that I get an ownership stake in the company."

John waited for more, and finally Artie continued, "I get some shares in the company if it's a corporation, or a small percent of ownership if it's a partnership. So, if the company does well after the financing is in place, I get a piece of the pie; if it doesn't work out, then the guy who hired me doesn't have to pay me. It's a crap shoot, but think of the payoff if I had brokered financing for Microsoft. It's better odds than the lotto."

"So, if it doesn't work out, you don't get any fee?" John probed, and Artie said, "I hate to admit it, but yes, if that's the agreement, I get nothing."

John then raised his eyebrows and said, "I was thinking about trying to set up a company to do biotech research in gene therapy, is that something you'd feel comfortable working on?" Artie looked at John's face and saw he was actually serious.

Artie trying to be kind said, "Dude, you need a serious track record of profits to show you know what you're doing, or you need capital or some kind of collateral. You have to be able to convince some old codger to agree to fork over a ton of money, and he needs to feel comfortable that you not only know what you're doing, but that you will earn him a tidy profit in short order. It's a tough thing to do. Not to burst your bubble, but I don't think that you can do it, especially not at your age."

John retorted, "Why not? I have topnotch training, I did research in the same area for my PhD and actually got some good published results. I don't see why they wouldn't go for it." John continued, "Also, this new technology called CRISPR is as revolutionary as any idea that's come along in the last 20 years, maybe longer. I bet you could sell that."

Artie responded, "Well, a lot of bankers don't understand bio-tech, and some of those that do got burned by tech companies in the last down-turn. You might not get it, but bankers either require a proven track record – and I don't think you've have that going for you – or that you have property or other collateral for the loan. No offense, but because you're living here, in this apartment, I don't think that's the case."

Artie continued, "And if you think the people who do this for a living are nice guys, who want to help you out, they're not. But you can't really blame them, particularly after the bubble burst in the late 1990s and then in 2008 when the great recession hit."

Artie asked, "So, do you have any hidden assets I don't know about?"

John dejectedly answered with a simple, "No."

Artie, feeling a little guilty about kicking John when he was already down, offered, "Look, dude, I'd be willing to give it a try, but only for you roomie. I just want you to know that I'm not promising any miracles." He nodded at John, thinking to himself, what do I have to lose? After all, he's my roommate and one never knows. Although in this case, he was pretty sure of exactly what the outcome would be – nada.

Artie, in an effort to dampen John's expectations, said, "If you have a concrete business idea, and you want to give it a shot, I'd be happy to help you draft a business plan and prospectus. Yeah, why not?"

Artie thought it might even be fun working with John, totally dismissing the notion that there was any chance of finding a pot of gold at the end of this particular rainbow.

25

The next morning, after a sleepless night spent tossing and turning, John awoke without needing an alarm. He took a quick shower, dressed and downed a cup of coffee, then called Dr. Duretts on the burner phone.

John speculated, this must be what it's like to be a spy. I'm actually taking the first step in this cockamamie scheme. It almost felt dirty, but was also invigorating. He again thought of spy thrillers and the adrenaline rush that people engaged in espionage must experience. But this wasn't a novel, this was real.

John hit the automatic dial button for Duretts' burner phone and hoped it would be Alan who answered. If he didn't answer, John wouldn't leave a message but he wanted to get the ball rolling. On the second ring he heard Dr. Duretts' voice ask, "May I help you?"

"It's me, your pseudo protégé," John answered, in an attempt to be clever, like the Mafia guys who never use names on the phone. He thought of using the name Johnny Double Helix, but thought better of it since it sounded more like a porn alias, and probably wouldn't be appreciated by Duretts, anyway.

Dr. Duretts whispered into the phone, "I think it is important that you be my very discreet protégé. Anyway, we need to meet. I was thinking of the Brass Monkey in Georgetown. Do you know it?"

John said, "No, but I'll find it.

"How about 9:30 Friday evening?" Dr. Duretts asked.

"I'll be there," John replied. Though he didn't know the place, the location alone made it a strange choice, especially since Dr. Duretts, an older, distinguished-looking gentleman, might stand out like a gray thumb.

"Until then," Duretts responded, then hung up as he walked down the hall to his office. Once there, he closed the door and picked up his other burner phone to call Lisa, the daughter of his second cousin.

26

Lisa was a tall brunette, with big eyes and an ethnic Mediterranean look. Her hair flowed long and wavy, and most guys thought she was exotic looking, if not exactly beautiful. She was the type whose beauty actually came from her imperfections; not like a Barbie doll, she had a sultry look with an air of cool intelligence.

As Duretts dialed her number, he thought how much he liked Lisa. He hadn't seen her often, even after she moved to Washington from Harrisburg.

Hers was a sad story. She was an only child. Her father and mother were killed in an automobile accident when she was just a junior at Bucknell University. Though she graduated with a major in art history, she seemed unmoored since her terrible loss.

Duretts felt like he'd let her down and was sorry that he hadn't made greater efforts to stay in touch. He recalled a brief conversation he'd had with her about her future plans shortly after the accident. She'd confided that the life insurance money was not as much as you would think. Her father had been a salesman for a small business and money had always been tight. He had a $350,000 policy that she planned to use to cover the cost of her last year at college, and to pay off her student loans. She really had no idea of what she wanted to do once she graduated. To him it seemed she'd lost her compass.

Though he couldn't blame her, to Duretts, Lisa seemed to be floating through life. She had always been very outgoing and ambitious, but the accident changed all that. She drifted from one dead-end job to another;

at first selling perfume at a department store, then working at a veterinarian's office cleaning kennels and helping with the animals, then working as a receptionist at a law firm.

In the early years of their marriage, before Lisa was born, her parents had lived a few houses down from Duretts in Harrisburg. He had been friends with her father, Richard, in their youth.

After they moved to Washington, Duretts' wife, Judith, used to be in contact with the family a few times a year. Over time it dropped off. For all intents and purposes, they had lost touch and there was no direct link between Duretts and Lisa. He was counting on that lack of traceability.

Lisa quickly answered the phone and Duretts said, "Hello, Lisa. It's Alan, Alan Duretts. A little bird told me you were in town and I would like to see you. How is Washington treating you?"

Lisa replied, "What a nice surprise. I like it here. It's so much more exciting than Harrisburg, a little more fast-paced, but I'm adjusting."

"Well, that's wonderful" offered Dr. Duretts, and Lisa added, "How are Judith and the kids doing?"

Duretts replied that all were fine. He then asked, "How does your schedule look for dinner this week, it's my treat?" She said, "That sounds nice. I usually go out with friends on Thursday, so would Wednesday work for you?"

Pleased, Duretts said, "Excellent. I'll pick you up at seven. If something comes up, let me know and we can change plans. I look forward to seeing you."

27

Duretts drove his Passat wagon down Rt. 270, exited onto Wisconsin Avenue and drove into Georgetown. He followed some winding side streets to Lisa's apartment building. The traffic was fairly light because rush hour was ending and the bulk of the traffic went the other direction. He pulled up in front of the building, parked, and thought it looked pretty nice for someone so young.

Duretts entered the vestibule and was impressed by the lobby's appearance. It had a desk with a doorman and honed marble floors. Something didn't sit right with him. He knew she had some money left from her parent's estate, but he didn't think she was the type to blow it all on something like this. Well, depending how things went, he might sit down with her and have a talk.

Judith had wanted to come along, but this was to be a private meeting. Duretts had serious things to discuss with Lisa. Despite their limited contact, he felt he had a stronger bond with Lisa, than most of her other relatives. They seemed to be on the same wavelength and he loved her intelligence. Also, there was nothing like engaging with a young person, who had her whole life in front of her. Despite their limited contact over the years, he knew that he liked her.

Duretts rode the elevator to the fifth floor. As he exited into a hallway, he noticed the wine-colored carpeting accented with a taupe and navy border. He knocked on the door and a very attractive, twenty-something blonde girl answered. Duretts, believing it was the wrong apartment, flushed with embarrassment.

The girl stated, "You must be here for Lisa." Relieved that there had been no mistake, Dr. Duretts inquired, "Yes, and who might you be?" She answered "I'm Lori, her roommate. We also have another roommate, Gina, who's not home. Please make yourself at home, I'll get Lisa."

Duretts stood in the foyer of the apartment. It contained some inexpensive furniture, probably from Ikea, and it smelled good. Like the scent of nubile young women. His chemistry training made him think it was probably the scent of estrogen or some female pheromone. It put a smile on his face, even at his age.

Lisa entered the room, looking a lot like the last time he'd seen her. She smiled and greeted him, "Hi, there." Duretts returned the smile and with sincerity said, "It's been way too long, but it's good to see you again." They left the apartment and walked to J. Paul's in Georgetown for dinner.

As they walked to the restaurant, Duretts gently questioned her about her living situation and how she was supporting herself. He asked, "So how are you finding it to be living in our fair city?"

Lisa responded, "So far, so good. I'm enjoying the city, I like where I live, and I like the girls I live with. We go out and have a good time, and we also take advantage of a lot of the free things the city has to offer, like the museums, concerts and stuff. I don't know my way around outside the city, but I like DC, though living here is pretty expensive."

Duretts agreed, "Yes, it's certainly become less affordable to live here than it used to be. By the way, how are you doing financially? Do you have enough to get by?"

"Yes, Alan, don't worry about me," Lisa said, as she looked down at the sidewalk. "I have two roommates, so we split the rent, and I still have some money left over from the insurance." Duretts thought Lisa looked pained, so he didn't say much during the rest of the short walk to the restaurant.

When they were seated, Dr. Duretts said, "Judith and I are very concerned about you. We want to make sure you're settling in and that things are going well for you. In fact, this conversation is probably long overdue."

Lisa quietly said, "It's been hard. As you can imagine, I think about my parents a lot. I just needed to get away from Harrisburg, because everyone I knew treated me differently. Here the people I meet are interesting and fun, and they don't know all about my tragic life story. There are cultural things to do here, but there are also a lot of bars and stuff to do at night."

Dr. Duretts was happy to hear her say that. She did seem to be healing, and was starting to focus on boys and fun. Life was moving on.

He said, "You're right, but I've heard more than one woman complain that the guys here are wimpy, and the ratio isn't in your favor. But I have no doubt you'll have no trouble meeting suitable young men. Have you seen any of your uncles recently, or for that matter, any of your friends from back home?"

Lisa told him that she returned to Harrisburg every couple of months or so. "I still keep in touch with my best friend Sharon, and Uncle Paul and I still talk regularly – he's keeping an eye on me, you know," she said with a little smile.

Duretts, glad to hear that she was maintaining those close contacts, probed a little further, "Have you seen any therapists since you moved here?" She confided that she participated in a support group once a week.

Duretts relieved, remarked, "That's certainly good to hear. You mentioned that you're OK financially, but I must admit, I did have an ulterior motive for meeting with you tonight. What are you doing for work now?"

She told him, "I work part-time at a coffee shop, and they give me health coverage. I like my co-workers and, for the most part, the customers are nice."

He proceeded with his plan, since he wouldn't be tearing her away from a promising career, or one she had a passion for. "I have a proposition for you, but I want you to promise me that if I let you in on a little secret, that you will keep it confidential." She agreed with a mystified look on her face.

With a serious countenance emphasized by the ladder of his furrowed brow, he began, "I know a young man who I feel has real potential. I once interviewed him, but his goals were pretty ambitious. I've heard he's trying to start a new biotech company, and I think it could be a wonderful ground floor opportunity for someone like you."

Alan continued, "I have remained in contact with him and would like to have someone I can trust on the inside, so to speak, to keep an eye on things. But you'd have to be very discreet about it. I don't want anyone to know about our connection."

He went on, "It would probably seem unfair to others if they thought you were given such an opportunity because you know me. And on the off chance that the company is successful, you could make out very well financially. You could get stock options, like the secretaries who worked at Microsoft in the beginning. Those who got in early received shares in the company. The ones who held onto those shares eventually became millionaires."

"It could be a great opportunity for all of us, you, me, and him." He looked at her for any telltale signs of reluctance. When none were apparent, he continued, "Because this is such a monumental opportunity, I think we can both help each other. Before we get into specifics, I'd like to know what you think about all of this. For that matter, whether or not you're even interested?"

Her brown eyes sparked with interest and her smile brightened when she looked at Dr. Duretts and said, "I'm definitely interested. I can be discreet, and it's not like I'm leaving a fantastic job. What kind of job and salary are we talking about?"

Duretts thought that she was a good pick for this. She had the right combination of intelligence, and maturity to recognize this gift horse.

And he was pretty certain that life's hard knocks meant that she wouldn't blow it.

Duretts responded, "While it's difficult to predict the future, what I can tell you is that it has potential to really take off. Anyway, I'm sure that they would pay you a generous starting salary, probably as an executive assistant, so you're not really taking any risk. Worst case, you can just walk away, but the upside is very high."

Lisa intrigued by what she heard said, "If you don't mind my asking, tell me more about this guy and what makes you think it will work out?"

Duretts wanted to tell her the whole story, the fact that the fix was in, that they'd already developed the product that would propel the enterprise, but thought better of it. He thought it best for all concerned that she not know the full story – plausible deniability – at least not yet.

Duretts went on, "I know some finance guys, who can help us get the proper funding to get the company up and running. I interviewed the lead scientist, John, the guy I've been telling you about, who appears to have a strong work ethic, an entrepreneurial bent, and some great ideas. With you in the picture, I would be around, discreetly, to help out in any way I can. Through you, I'll maintain a stake in the company. With some luck, and my stealthy assistance, it could be very lucrative for all of us."

Lisa said, "Why don't you just start your own company? Then you don't need me, or him, for that matter."

Duretts then wanted to take back his prior thought that her intelligence was a plus – sometimes ignorance is bliss.

He paused, then responded, "Because I'm employed by a large company that does DNA research, and if I left and started my own company, they would watch me like a hawk. If they thought that I was using patents or trade secrets developed while working for them, I would be in court for years. It would be me against a well-heeled corporation, with cadres of lawyers and large amounts of money to stop me – regardless of whether they were right or wrong. Any scientific advances could be waylaid for decades."

Lisa, with full trust in her third cousin, said, "Sounds reasonable to me. OK, count me in."

Enthusiastic from her response, Alan said, "Great! I would like you to start right away. I'm scheduled to meet John at 9:30 on Friday night at the Brass Monkey in Georgetown. I'd like you to go in my place."

Duretts described John as, "6' tall, with brown hair, probably what you'd call classically handsome. And remember he must be the only person who knows of the connection between us – that is something you must remember. Promise me."

She regarded Duretts, a face that she knew well from her childhood, but it had a seriousness which she did not recognize. She returned his gaze with an equal measure of seriousness and pledged, "I promise."

28

As Lisa walked to the Brass Monkey, she was pleased that Alan had thoughtfully arranged the meeting convenient to where she lived in Georgetown. Funny, how things sometimes worked out.

Anxiety crept in as she prepared to meet John for the first time. Even though it was technically a business meeting, it still felt like a blind date. Except that this would be with a nerd, whom she reminded herself could be her future boss. She wondered if he wore horn-rimmed glasses? She then reminded herself that this was simply a business deal, an interview arranged by Alan, and he was in her corner.

Lisa walked into the Brass Monkey and immediately saw two boys, who looked like Georgetown University students standing by the bar. They were clearly checking her out in a drunken and obvious way. Their stares just annoyed Lisa as she proceeded toward the bar. An overwhelming stench of beer and deep-fried food met her nostrils. Strange place for a business meeting, she thought.

She looked around but didn't see anyone who resembled the 'John' character described by Alan. As she sat down on an open stool, his tardiness began to irritate her. It wasn't a good sign, especially for someone who had been portrayed as a 'real go getter,' she thought.

Suddenly, off to her right, she noticed a guy sitting at a high top table by himself, subtly scanning the bar. Can't be him, she thought. He didn't look that nerdy, not like a scientist. That was not her guy, but with no other candidates that fit the description, Lisa walked over to where he sat, smiled and, after a slightly awkward pause asked, "Are you John?"

John surveying her with a certain amount of anxiety of his own replied, "Do I know you? You look familiar."

She decided to have some fun with him, before letting the cat out of the bag. Lisa said, "I can't believe that you don't remember me. I met you at a bar in Adams Morgan and you said you'd call, but never did." As she said it, Lisa attempted to appear angry.

John continued, "You know, I never forget a face, especially one like yours, but I think you've mistaken me for someone else. I'm expecting someone."

Lisa thought, while this may be fun, I'd better nip this in the bud. "Actually, I was sent here by Alan Duretts," she blurted out, "I think it's him you're expecting. He sent me instead to talk to you about your new company. He said that you might be interested in hiring me."

John quite shocked, automatically responded, "Excuse me?"

As she looked directly into his eyes, Lisa raised her eyebrows and said, "That's right. Alan told me about your new venture and he wanted me to be involved in it, in some way. Anyway, he thinks that I could help and be a sort of go between, between you and him. He was also emphatic that no one but you, him and I know of my connection to him. I don't know why, but he even made me promise him."

John was starting to get the picture, and said, "I think that your cousin, Alan, is a very smart guy. I also think he's probably right to do it this way. But, if you don't mind my asking, what exactly is your connection to Dr. Duretts?"

"Well, if you're the only other person to know about it, do you really need to understand our connection?" Lisa asked.

John offered, "You got me there, I guess I don't." As he smiled at Lisa, he thought she's not drop dead gorgeous, but she does have a certain sex appeal. Although she wasn't really his type, he almost wished that she'd just approached him at the bar and begun talking to him, instead of being sent by Dr. Duretts. He disliked Alan's manipulating their meeting, and not being upfront with him.

John continued, "I was wondering just what he had in mind for you; almost a liaison, between me and my partner in crime." John immediately thought it was a bad choice of words. Lisa, dismayed by his attitude, was about to turn on her heel and leave.

Instead, she matter-of-factly said, "I think he wants me to work with you as you start the company and to offer me some kind of stock option when, or if, the company takes off. I'm a college grad, have a good head on my shoulders and could be an administrative assistant or office manager. I can start as soon as you need me, and I'll do temp work or continue to work at the coffee shop until you're ready. I think this is very important to Alan."

John wondered what Alan was thinking, what this was all about and whether this girl was serious, but he just said, "OK, give me your name, address and phone number. Send me your resume, it doesn't have to be anything fancy, email it to me and I'll call you when we're ready to hire."

John pulled out his phone and said, "Give me your number, let me send you an email, then you can send it to me when it's ready." She said, "I have a draft already. I'll finalize it, then send it to you."

She finally sat down expecting John to offer her a drink, but it never happened. They sat at the table for a few minutes without talking. John swirled the last of his beer in its bottle, both of them pondering what they were getting mixed up in.

The music started pumping loudly which prompted Lisa to say, "I think the music's too loud. I'm going to get going, but let me know as soon as you know what's happening." John said "OK," and winked at her. He then wondered, why did I do that?

29

The next day John felt compelled to meet with Dr. Duretts, to separate fact from fiction, and to determine how much input Lisa would have in their business. While Lisa seemed like a poised young woman, he wondered why she was involved at all, and how she would fit in.

At 5:00 PM, John sat in his car outside the Geneteka building. He was waiting for Dr. Duretts to leave the parking lot. He waited 45 minutes, but it seemed like much longer. He could feel the sweat roll down his back, and thought he hadn't experienced that sensation since his final in physical chemistry in grad school.

Finally, he saw Duretts' Volkswagen pull out of the garage and exit the parking lot. John followed him a few blocks onto First Street, then flashed his high beams a few times to get Duretts' attention. Dr. Duretts signaled, turned down a side street and pulled over to the curb. John drove up beside him on the quiet, empty avenue.

John opened his window and asked, "I need some directions." He decided to be funny, "I'm lost. I saw Lisa Street and I'm trying to figure out if I want to take it to Easy Street. Are you familiar with Lisa?"

Duretts grimaced and replied, "John, are you certain that no one is out here? Anyway, I do know Lisa and she is someone that must be involved. It's how I am going to get paid, and that's all you need to know. By the way, what steps have you taken to move forward?"

John responded, "I've talked with my friend," then John lied, "and soon we should be meeting with some of his banking friends."

Duretts began to wonder if this enterprise was going to succeed, whether working with this impertinent upstart was a good idea. He then moved on to wondering if John's friend would be able to pull this off. Duretts smiled and thought that he would be patient and let things play out, before taking things into his own hands.

John looked ahead at his windshield and said, "I could use some direction on exactly what the business plan should be. I look forward to getting some input from you. When I need anything more, I'll call you on the burner. Let me get going, now."

Duretts considered what John said, shook his head and said, "Fine." John put his car in gear and started to drive off. Duretts did the same a moment later.

30

As John drove home, he resolved to nail things down with Artie, because he was uncomfortable lying to Dr. Duretts. After fifty minutes in bumper-to-bumper traffic, John finally arrived at his apartment. The traffic on Connecticut Avenue confounded him and he vowed to learn alternate routes to getting around this town.

When he entered the apartment, Artie was on the couch, and his eyes were trained on the big screen. John asked, "Hey, what's going on?"

Artie said, "Just watching ESPN."

John said, "I really want to sit down to go over the plans for presenting my business plan to bankers real soon."

Artie responded, "There's no time like the present. You want to go to IHOP and talk it over? I have a two for one coupon for dinner."

"Works for me," John said. Artie went to the bathroom, threw some water on his face, combed his hat hair and left the apartment with John.

On the way to IHOP, they started to discuss the business plan. Artie said, "I need to know what kind of equipment you'll need and how expensive it is. We can probably go on the Internet and find the costs for specific equipment. We also need to know how many employees you'll need, how much space you'll need, where you'd like to set up the business. Particularly, the types of employees and their skill sets – obviously a PhD will be more expensive than an unskilled worker. We'll need to put together a budget for the capital outlays, the rent, and the payroll costs."

Artie continued, "I also want to know what my cut is. I'll be honest,

I don't think this can work, but I'd like to help you out, and I happen to have the time. Since I'm a gambler, as payment, I'd like to get some stock in your company. This endeavor can be set up as a close corporation which is a fairly simple process, but it costs about $100. Do you have the cash to lay out?"

John said, "I'm sure I can scratch up a little money, but you've already lost me. What's a close corporation?"

Artie thoughtfully responded, "Oh sorry, neo. It's a company that has stock which is held by a few people, like a family-owned business. It's different from a public corporation that's traded on a stock exchange, where people can buy the stock on, for instance, the New York stock exchange or the NASDAQ. A close corporation can go public, and start trading on one of the exchanges, and usually when that happens, the owners make a boatload of money."

Artie continued, "Don't expect that to happen. It requires that the company have tremendous capitalization or intellectual property rights – like owning the rights to an operating system. It has to be something that everybody wants, and it has to be such a safe bet that the public wants in on it. It's what Martha Stewart Living did, enabling her to make a fortune."

As John parked near the IHOP on Fourteenth, he started to get the picture. He said, "I'm not thinking that big, but I have some ideas that would make the company viable." That was the second lie he told today, which was totally out of character for him.

They walked into the IHOP and there were two couples in front of them. After a short wait, a young Hispanic woman walked them to a booth. They slid in. The waitress came and they ordered breakfast for dinner.

After a few minutes John began to disclose his idea to Artie. He began, "I think that the new company should have two parts to it. The first would be more commercial and do DNA testing for the public, to let them know about their ancestries and backgrounds, do paternity tests and court cases against criminals where DNA is part of the case. The other side will be for CRISPR DNA research."

Artie, pleasantly surprised, appreciated what he was hearing. John seemed to have come up with a good idea.

Artie said, "Sounds good. Do you actually know how to do that kind of lab work?"

John confidently responded, "Of course. I've done some research on it and all you need is the right equipment, protocols and lab techs to do the procedures in accordance with those protocols. Then you send the information to the client or, if it's for a court case, you have someone like me testify about the results."

Artie, excited by what he was hearing, jumped in, "That could be a good thing. You have part of the business doing straightforward labwork, generating easy money, then a more complex element with the CRISPR research. The research can be the hook for getting someone interested – the pitch is simple, you can make money on a safe bet and the research could potentially bring in the big bucks, if it pans out."

John thought, Amen, brother, if he only knew.

Artie asked, "What do you need to do the tests?"

John responded, "All I need are two pieces of equipment, an ABI Prism 310 Genetic Analyzer or possibly an HP 610 Gas Chromatography apparatus, for doing DNA forensic work. I also need a lab tech to do the work. A lab tech can also do the research under my direction, so maybe I should get two techs."

"Anything else?" Artie asked.

John said, "Yeah, we'll also need a website to be set up to sell the tests online. Then there's the equipment we'll need for the research. I'd like a CEQ 8000 Genetic Analysis System. Also, I think we need a specialized supercomputer, which we could probably get used."

John continued, "Finally, I think we'll need to get an office manager to keep track of bills and other things. I actually met someone who I think might be perfect for the job," John said, without offering more.

Refusing to be sidetracked, Artie teased, "What do you mean you 'met someone?' Where, serving coffee at a Starbucks? She must be hot. She must have a great resume. Why is this the first I'm hearing about her? It has to be a her."

"We can't all be as impressive as you Artie," John said, then added, "I met her in a bar."

Artie cocked his eyebrow, crumpled his face and said, "You're kidding, right?"

Ignoring Artie's judgmental commentary, John continued, "She's a college graduate, seems very bright and besides, this is my show isn't it?

Artie shook his head, then said, "OK, we can discuss this later, but I hope your thinking with your business head and not the other."

Their food came, they ate, and then they instructed the waitress to keep their coffee cups full. Finally, they rolled up their sleeves and started drafting a business plan.

31

Over the last three days, they were men focused on a mission. They worked at the kitchen table for hours at a time, only leaving for bathroom breaks and to open the door for food deliveries. They crafted a fourteen-page document, complete with a mission statement, market analysis, sections on financial strategies, the competition, their competitive edge, operating requirements, how they would meet market needs and a budget. Also featured prominently was a section on CRISPR research and its potential commercial applications.

John was impressed with the end product. He appreciated the bland but descriptive way that these business plans were written; they had perfect grammar, no awkward phrases, were matter-of-fact and concise. John knew he couldn't have written it without Artie's help.

Artie reviewed the pages on the computer. They'd both expended considerable effort on this masterpiece, and he hoped it wasn't just a big waste of time and energy. Though he wouldn't admit it, he too, was surprised by how well it had turned out.

Artie was also amazed at how inexpensive the CRISPR equipment would be. They'd gone online for price quotes for the equipment they needed and included it in their calculations. They also checked online resources to find out how much good lab technicians earned.

They then moved on to their own compensation and figured out what each of them would be paid from the initial investment: John as the chief scientist and Artie as the marketing and financial guy. John would be listed as the President and CEO, and Artie as the VP of Marketing. These figures were included in the overall calculation. The numbers looked good.

Artie's prose may have artfully exaggerated CRISPR's potential and John's knowledge of DNA evidence, but it made a compelling case. The embellishment carried over to John's experience using the equipment, his education, teaching fellowships and the two seminars he presented relating to CRISPR, the analysis of DNA for use in identifying individuals from small samples of skin, saliva, hair or bodily fluids. As further enhancement, they added a section about Internet testing for latent genetic problems, or to determine one's heritage, proven moneymakers, since other websites already offered the services.

From talking to John, Artie learned that there was a new technique, discovered by a research team that permitted the analysis to be done much faster. This would be their marketing hook.

However, what intrigued Artie most was the section that most attracted his attention. This was the section on potential research projects and goals, and the equipment they would purchase to do the research. It seemed like *Andromeda Strain* stuff, using gene mapping, CRISPR, and computer algorithms, to locate and counteract the genes that cause sickness and disease.

There were a number of big banks already gambling a ton of money on CRISPR research. It could very well be like the tech bubble, where money was thrown at anyone with any feasible business plan. At least he hoped that's what would happen, but bankers could also be skeptical, after having been burned a time or two.

They both looked up at the same time, over the top of Artie's laptop, and realized that they were finished. John said, "I believe it's time to get turnt."

Artie with a satisfied grin said, "Yeah, I think we can probably wait 'til tomorrow to put this in the mail. The bankers can probably survive another day before they get their teeth into this. I need a shower and feel like celebrating in Bethesda. Maybe we'll get lucky and meet another office manager tonight."

"Screw you," John laughed, as he walked toward the other bathroom to take a shower.

32

It was a torrential downpour and Alan Duretts was on his way home from work. He turned on the radio, perpetually tuned to WTOP, and heard the traffic report. What a surprise, another tractor trailer had jackknifed and crashed on the Beltway.

As he pulled out of the lot, he noticed John's car parked in the same place he'd seen it the last time. Duretts, annoyed by John's disregard of the rules he'd set, passed him then turned onto a side street and drove to a secluded cul-de-sac, pulled over and stopped. John pulled up beside him, then lowered his window. Without saying a word, John passed an envelope with the business plan to Dr. Duretts and then drove away.

Dr. Duretts drove away a moment later, but not before opening the envelope. He was pleased to see that progress had been made, even if it was only on paper.

Later that evening, Duretts read through the whole document several times. It was certainly long enough, seemed to have the right amount of puffery and swagger, but his experience told him that no responsible banker would touch this with a ten-foot pole; unless, of course, that responsible banker was a friend of his who had been tipped off.

33

Glen was sitting in the kitchen eating cereal when John came back to the apartment after a snail mail run to the downstairs box. John glanced at him, and Glen said, "Hey man, long time no see."

John said, "You don't look so good. Anyway, where have you been hiding, we were beginning to think we'd lost a roommate."

Glen said, "I didn't move out, I've been trying to decipher this new language called 'the law.' What's going on with you guys – get something interesting in the mail?"

John responded, "Good guess, Counselor. Artie and I put together a business plan and sent it to a few banks and a couple of what Artie called 'venture capitalists.' Anyway, one wrote back and wants to have a meeting. They're in New York City. Artie's gonna lose his mind."

Glen asked, "Would you mind if I looked at the document sometime? I took a lot of business classes in college and want to practice corporate law. Anyway, right now I've gotta go, I have class soon and I try to sit near a girl named Renate who's smart and good-looking. I want to get in early and try to lock it down."

As Glen was leaving, Artie came into their living room. John looked at him and said, "You won't believe it, but we got a bite." John held up the letter and Artie snatched it from John's hand. Artie skimmed the letterhead impressed – it was from Hunt Manhattan.

After he read the contents of the letter, Artie said, "Well amigo, I think we need to book Amtrak to New York, the sooner the better. Artie proceeded to call Hunt Manhattan and they agreed to meet a week from Thursday.

34

John and Artie awoke early as they prepared to embark on their momentous Thursday in New York. They'd splurged and were taking the Acela from Union Station into Penn Station. They both donned their best suits and ties, Artie's suit was blue; John's was dark brown. Artie was carrying the Coach briefcase that his father had given him when he graduated from Hofstra's MBA program, and it contained extra copies of their business plan. After they finished the 2:00 PM meeting, they'd stay overnight at his parent's house in Long Island.

John was surprised at how well Artie cleaned up. He looked very professional, but a little young. Artie had his game face on and looked serious – a look that John hadn't recalled seeing before. He couldn't tell if this bespoke of nervousness or confidence. They didn't say much as they walked down Connecticut Avenue during rush hour. They saw many other people scurrying to work, looking like them, carrying briefcases, and trying to get wherever they were going, without being late.

They made it to the Metro and stepped up to the ticket machine, which took dollars. They weren't sure how much it would cost to get to the Union Station stop, so they just fed five dollars each onto their Metro cards.

Then they took an escalator down what seemed to be a never-ending tunnel to the bottom of the station. Their escalator was especially crowded, since one of the others was under repair. The workmen, nowhere to be seen, had removed the steps and when John peered over, he could see the escalator's inner workings, its gears and belts. What stood out to him was that there was no one around to work on the equipment.

He and Artie waited on the end of the platform, then saw the lights on the floor near the tracks start to flash on and off. He'd never seen anything like it before living in Washington. He'd learned that it meant a train was coming.

When they entered the Metro car, they had to stand. Artie finally spoke. He advised John, "When we get on the Acela, we'll go to the cafe car, where they have booths and we can go over everything again." John nodded in agreement, but felt a little peculiar because they were so tense and barely talking.

When they arrived at Union Station, John was happy to see that they had enough money on their cards to exit without paying extra. When they came off the escalator into Union Station, John could see that its floors were gleaming and it was lined with stores and restaurants. It was crowded for the early hour. They checked their phones to make sure they could access their train tickets.

Their train was scheduled to leave in fifteen minutes so they ran through the station, and down the escalator to the designated train platform and into the train. It was crowded, mostly with business travelers, but they were able to get their own booth in the cafe car.

John was surprised that a line had already formed for refreshments. Artie said he was getting in line to get coffee, John said, "I'll take one too, with cream." John glanced over at the line and noticed a guy in the front of the line getting a beer. He just shook his head, wondering what that guy did that stressed him out so much that he needed to drink so early in the morning. Time to change jobs, John thought.

Artie returned to the booth and told John, "You'll be surprised at how good the coffee tastes." John took a sip and agreed, "It's almost as good as Dunkin Donuts." Artie's solemn veneer cracked for the first time all day, he smiled and said, "We're trying to move up to the big time, so maybe we should aim a little higher, like Starbucks." They both finally laughed when John said, "I think I'll keep some of my plebian tastes, I like Dunkin's coffee better."

Artie pulled the paperwork from his briefcase and concentrated on reviewing the finer points of the new business plan with John, so that any question asked could be confidently answered. For the rest of the ride they studied the numbers, talked about potential profits and discussed ways of trying to explain what CRISPR was and why it was on the cutting edge of biotechnology. They would conclude their presentation with why it was a worthwhile investment, and how a few million dollars directed at their unproven enterprise could return great dividends.

35

By the time they arrived at Penn Station New York, they should have been tired. Instead they were juiced, experiencing such a level of adrenaline rush that it made them feel invincible. John had almost forgotten the smell of the New York City subway, with its layers of grime. He remembered his father's warning when they went to ball games at Yankee Stadium to always check the seat before sitting down, because a bum might have used it as a toilet. He quickly examined the seats, then they sat down. They rode the subway downtown to the Wall Street stop.

When they arrived at the stop, they only had to go half a block to 14 Wall Street, to the offices of Hunt Manhattan. They were meeting with Frank McMillan, 47, and Ben Harris, 29. Artie had looked them up on the corporate website. McMillan had graduated with a joint MBA and law degree from Boston College. Harris had an MBA from Wharton, a well-known business school world-wide. The company controlled assets totaling 11.2 billion dollars.

They showed their identification to security and rode the elevator to the 12th floor. The doors opened into an impressive space. The company had the entire floor. The floor was of a honed granite and the few walls were beautiful wood paneling which matched the reception desk. The artwork was refined, if understated. The view from the surrounding windows overlooked Wall Street. Looking out the window you could see the New York Stock Exchange. The receptionist was an appropriate fit. She was attractive and tastefully dressed. The air smelled clean. The place reeked of wealth.

They walked over to the receptionist, Artie smiled and announced, "Hello, we're here to see Mr. McMillan and Mr. Harris. We have a 2:00 o'clock appointment." The receptionist flashed a perfect smile and said, "I'll let them know you're here. Would you like something to drink?" Artie said, "Coffee would be great." John declined.

The receptionist offered them a seat as she pushed a button on the phone and told someone on the other end that "Mr. McMillan's 2:00 is here."

John and Artie sat on a leather couch that undoubtedly cost more than all the furniture in their apartment, and possibly even their cars. Another woman, slightly older with an equally perfect smile as the receptionist, came over, gave Artie his coffee and then ushered them into a large conference room with 15 seats surrounding the table. She introduced herself, "My name is Barbara, I'm Mr. McMillan's assistant. He's on a conference call. Someone will be with you shortly." She left and closed the door to the glass enclosed room.

John looked around and wondered if he could ever be comfortable in this setting. Was he capable of performing in a way that would convince people such as these, whom he never really understood or rubbed shoulders with, to give him money to support his fledgling idea? He was out of his element and he knew it.

However, the overriding question in his mind was, is Artie up to the task? Or would they just crash and burn and embarrass themselves? Well, no matter, they were here. If they didn't make a deal with these guys, the likelihood of ever seeing them again was nil. The larger consideration was how much a failure would disappoint Dr. Duretts.

36

As John and Artie waited in the conference room, admiring the room's appointments, Frank McMillan was reprimanding Ben, a fairly new hire who didn't seem to be able to do anything right. He had recently missed an important conference call, arrived late for work a number of times and never seemed to timely prepare reports or respond to client emails. He also thought that Ben's analysis and writing style left much to be desired. Unfortunately, you couldn't always tell from their resumes who had talent and who didn't.

Frank chastised Ben, "I looked through the business plan from these two and I'm not exactly sure why they're here. They have no track record to speak of, the scientist doesn't look like he has any experience working in private industry. Aside from a wish and a prayer, these guys are nobodies. I'm not even sure what they're talking about with this CRISPR thing, and the other stuff is only remotely interesting to me. So, again, I have to ask, are you kidding with this garbage? Does my time mean so little to you?"

Ben was nervous and scared, but defensively responded, "I was going to get more information from them, but I got tied up in the analysis of the Durgin Food deal for Jonathan and I didn't have a chance to follow-up. I told Sheila I thought it was interesting, and she took it into her own hands to schedule the meeting. I didn't realize it was so soon, or I would have called them and obtained more information, or canceled the appointment."

With visible disgust, Frank just rolled his eyes. He didn't want to hear more excuses from Ben, or to listen to him blame others. He decided to meet with the nobodies for a few minutes, then he'd deal with Ben later.

They walked down the spacious corridor, past rows of smaller offices of lower level associates. Despite their high-tech gear, the small offices were strewn with open books and voluminous paperwork.

Frank and Ben finally got to the end of the hall, where one of the more modest conference rooms was located. With Ben trailing, Frank entered and quickly assessed the two young men in the room. He felt like he should, at the very least, lend them some money so they could afford decent suits. What they were wearing looked like it had come straight off the rack from Men's Wearhouse.

Frank shook their hands and said, "Thanks for coming down. We wanted to have a brief initial meeting with you to go over some concerns we had and to get a better understanding of the business plan you forwarded to us. This is my associate Ben, he's one of our top people."

Ben smiled weakly, shook their hands, and said, "Nice to meet you guys. I hope you had a good trip up from DC."

John, focusing on them, couldn't help but notice that both were dressed in suits that were perfectly tailored and fit like a glove and that the fabrics had an unfamiliar richness that screamed, 'This guy's made of money,' and 'I have money and you don't.' Frank was perfectly groomed, with an expensive haircut and shave, a tan and nails that looked like they had clear polish on them. At least his associate, Ben, looked a little scruffier. He was probably the worker bee that made Frank look good.

They sat down and Frank graciously asked if they needed anything else. They declined his offer because they just wanted the meeting to get underway.

Frank started by saying, "I want to be upfront with you guys. After reviewing the plan, there are a number of concerns that have come up. Foremost among them is that it does not appear that either of you have any real experience in industry, outside of academia, and neither of you have directed a lab, or have a track record of keeping clients happy or even getting clients. Frank paused before continuing, "As my Dad used to say: 'there is no substitute for experience.' In addition, my colleague, Ben, here told me about some type of a patent fight going on between UC Berkeley and MIT and Harvard which muddies the waters even further."

As John and Artie listened to Frank, John's face began to reveal disappointment, while Artie remained poker-faced. It was clear to both, from the start, that this meeting was not going well.

Frank looking at the more handsome John, didn't have the heart to go on much longer. Frank thought, what is the point anyway, other than torturing these kids for a mistake that Ben made.

"Anyway," Frank continued, "the amount of capital you would need would be significant. The equipment you referenced in the plan would be fairly expensive to acquire. There are also issues with the most expensive component of your proposal, that is, whether or not you would be able to make this gene technology pay off, or even if you wouldn't, if you'd be encroaching on a patent exposing all involved to lawsuits."

Frank could see that he was deflating these youngsters' balloons, and so he decided to give them a little hope. Frank went on, "I'd like to have you go over more of the specifics with Ben. He can also give you some helpful pointers on business development and planning that could change your situation and possibly help you alleviate some of our concerns. We don't like to give any prospective client short shrift."

Smiling at Ben, Frank thought it serves him right. Now Ben will have to waste a few hours with these two – and he'll probably have to work several late nights or on the weekend to make up the time. Next time, he'd be more respectful of Frank's time. Frank then said, "I'll leave you in Ben's capable hands." Frank then rose to his feet, shook both their hands and went back to his office to check the price of the stock for a recent IPO they had underwritten.

Ben spent the next 3 hours with John and Artie going over their business plan. He explained what he'd found out about the patent question, and generally tried to make them feel better about their endeavor, with a smattering of free advice.

He delicately reminded them of what they lacked, a track record or collateral to interest real money managers, both points of which they were fully aware. They seemed like nice enough guys. Ben felt sorry that his free advice really couldn't help. He was reminded of an old adage – free business advice is only as valuable as what you paid for it.

John and Artie exited the plush offices, rode down the elevator and walked out the revolving door thinking this had been a disaster. They had been in their meeting with Frank for less than thirty minutes and the other guy just told them what they did not have.

Even though it was 5:30, John was surprised that the street was so crowded. There were people walking fast, pedestrians scampering on their long treks home. There were also a lot of cars driving on the boulevards and there was a sooty smell in the air, probably from all the traffic which had just passed by. What were they thinking, coming here to talk with guys that earned more in a day than they had amassed in their combined young lives?

John wondered when he should call Dr. Duretts with the bad news. He decided that he'd wait until he returned to DC. He hoped that Dr. Duretts would know what to do to help get this train back on track.

37

Tai Tan visited the compound for Xian Corporation. He liked everything about the facility, which had been specifically designed to facilitate the company's CRISPR research. He liked all the newness, the way the just-laid carpet and freshly painted walls smelled. He liked its remote location out in the countryside, where his people could be focused on their research and this important mission without distractions. This also made it easier to keep their work secret.

Tai's expertise was genetics, and he had been tasked with putting together a team of scientists and technicians who would give Xian the best chance of succeeding with their mission – to safely genetically engineer animals, then humans, using CRISPR. He had unfettered access to the best Chinese talent available, and he recruited scientists from universities and labs throughout the country.

He knew that his government had also directed their intelligence network to keep their ears to the ground for any information, from any source that could be useful to his project. In the meantime, he was to accelerate the research and produce results.

If Xian accomplished its mission, he would not only gain recognition from the people who mattered, but would also be rewarded with great wealth. He could not afford any mistakes, so he devoted his complete focus and attention to this enterprise. He knew that difficulties abounded in using CRISPR, but was convinced that with the right team, and enough funding, any problems could be overcome.

There had been unintended consequences which needed to be

avoided in future trials. One such setback involved changes to the DNA in areas where it shouldn't have occurred. Thus far, it had been a trial and error process, and the errors weren't pretty, but necessary to advance the research. Another problem encountered was that even within a species, some test animals were changed, and other test animals didn't respond to CRISPR in the same way, resulting in a lack of predictability in outcomes.

Despite these obstacles, Tai wanted to believe that they were close to a seismic breakthrough that would justify moving to the next level – human trials. The thought of proceeding without such a breakthrough was repugnant to him, but he knew his superiors would brush aside ethical considerations and insist that his team move forward with human testing because they believed the ends justified the means.

He had already spent considerable time rounding up willing human test subjects, to supplement the test paddocks full of chimpanzees, bonobos, mice and lizards, down to the simplest organisms, like amoebas. With everything ready to go, it was time for his team to get to work to produce the results he was sure were just beyond their grasp.

However it came, Tai was hoping for a discovery that would eliminate the dangerous unpredictability of the process, and ensure that CRISPR could be used safely in human beings.

38

It was Saturday and John woke up happy to be back in DC. He put on a shirt and sweats then exited the apartment, rode the elevator downstairs, walked out the front door, and crossed the street to the National Zoo.

He pulled out the burner phone and called Dr. Duretts from the panda exhibit. He tried to muster as much tact as he could, but he wasn't sure what to say. Maybe this was just too hard to do. He autodialed the number to Dr. Duretts' burner phone, as the earthy smell of the animals wafted through the air.

Duretts answered the phone, "Hello, Alan speaking." John began, "It's John. I need to let you know that the meeting did not go well. We need your help."

Duretts anticipating this, had already taken the liberty of calling his lifelong friend, Joseph DeBerg, at the firm of Kolb Kravath, LLP, which had an arm that invested solely in biotech companies.

Duretts had already had lunch with Joseph a couple of weeks before, and told him on the QT that he knew of a young man who was attempting a potentially viable start-up. Duretts had coyly let it slip that he believed this young scientist, who had interviewed with him at length, had some ideas to tweak the CRISPR technique. He might hit it big in the biotech field, and what he was working on could be an excellent investment opportunity.

Duretts confided in his friend, "I don't want this to go any further than these four walls, but I feel so strongly about this that I would almost guarantee that he will be a big moneymaker." Joseph considered what his friend, who winked at him, had to say.

He had never known Alan to be anything but trustworthy, and he'd never mentioned anything like this before. Reading between the lines, it was pretty apparent that Duretts had some inside information – exactly what Joseph was on the lookout for. It had to be that the good doctor knew something that the public did not.

Duretts mentioned John's name and said he'd ask him to send Joseph the business plan, if he was interested. To add an extra measure of intrigue, he advised Joseph to be very discreet about any meeting he might have with John. Also, if he thought the company had legs, to take a smaller than usual equity position, and never disclose to anyone what Duretts had said about John.

Joseph didn't have to be told twice. A guarantee from Duretts was all he needed. He figured that when he returned to his office, he'd have one of his associates close the deal promptly after he received the materials. Still, he was curious and wanted to meet the wunderkind.

Later, Duretts dialed up John from his own burner and was recounting the highlights of his conversation with DeBerg. He said, "Let me give you the name of the banker and his address and you can send him a business plan."

He added, "Practice your pitch before you go in, I don't want you and your friend to embarrass yourselves, again. If this doesn't work, I might not be able to help you further. Joseph DeBerg is a very old and trusted friend who is, for the most part, our best possibility to secure the necessary funding." Duretts still had some tricks up his sleeve, but didn't want the younger man to squander this opportunity.

When they hung up, John, once again, began feeling the pressure squeezing down on him.

39

John opened the door to the apartment to a familiar sight. Artie wearing sweat pants, a shirt emblazoned with 'I survived Mardi Gras' and a Jets cap, was sitting in front of the TV watching sports. John's first impression was, 'This, is my partner. God help us.'

He shook off that thought and said, "I have the name and address of a hot shot investment banker, at Kolb Kravath, LLP here in town. I've been told he's open-minded, has deep pockets and is pretty loose with money. We need to send him a cover letter and our business plan ASAP."

Artie said, "I've heard of that company, but I think you've gotten some bad intel. They're not particularly loose with money, and they're heavy-hitters in the investment banking biz. I doubt they'll be any easier than the last time around. Who told you that anyway?"

John replied, "It's not important who it was. I think we need to move on it fast. Give it the old college try, at least one more time." Artie, with nothing to lose and only marginal confidence in their enterprise, decided to go along with John's hail Mary.

Artie said, "All right, you win. This game's pretty much over anyway." He grabbed his laptop, entered the new information and printed out the documents. John asked him to make sure it was addressed to Joseph DeBerg, and that the cover letter had John's name on the signature line. Artie, annoyed at this point, responded, "Aye, aye, mein capitan."

40

On Wednesday, Artie slept in because his only plan for the day was to get a run in. When he finally awoke, he put on his compression shorts and the wrinkled Navy tee shirt, purchased on a trip to Annapolis specifically for the purpose of working out. Before going out for his run, he stretched, then went downstairs to the mailbox, and turned the key as he breathed in the familiar musty smell of the first floor.

He flipped past the junk mail and spied an envelope with the return address of Kolb Kravath, LLP, addressed to John. Sweet Jesus, he thought. That was fast, it has to be a rejection because they'd never be able to react this fast. Well, at least they had the courtesy of sending a response. Most of the time, like unsolicited resumes, they didn't bother responding at all.

No point to being let down in the lobby, he decided to delay the disappointment a few minutes more, until he returned to the apartment. Breaking his habit of taking the elevator, Artie walked back upstairs. He unlocked the door and entered.

Even though he knew John wasn't there, he couldn't wait any longer. He finally tore the envelope open and pulled out the fine, watermarked piece of stationery. As he read the first sentence he thought, "And so it ends." He prepared himself for the form response.

The letter began, "Dear Mr. Ordell, thank you for your interest in doing business with our firm. As you know, we receive inquiries from many business ventures and we are selective in the types of projects we consider to pursue." And, here it comes, Artie thought.

The next paragraph almost knocked him off his feet. It continued: "After careful deliberation of your submission, we have determined that it may be mutually beneficial to meet with you and your partners to go over the details of your venture. This will enable us to further explore the possibility of our working together and whether or not we will be able to provide you with the level of financing you are seeking. Please call my secretary, Emily, to schedule a mutually convenient time."

Even more amazing, the letter was signed by Joseph DeBerg himself. Shaking, Artie thought, I must be better at writing these business plans than I thought. This is the real deal – this guy is major league.

He instantly called John's cell phone, which went straight to voicemail. He then sent a text for John to return home immediately.

John walked into the apartment a half hour later and Artie handed him the letter, without speaking but wearing a huge grin on his face. John read its contents, and a moment later began jumping up and down and hugging Artie.

Artie said, "This is incredible. I can't believe we did this. These guys have almost $9 billion in assets in their venture capital fund and some of it could be ours. Even if we don't get it – we gotta get it – this is huge. You must have a guardian angel or something."

John said, "Yeah, or something."

With Artie beside him, John called Emily and scheduled the meeting. It would be on Friday, a mere two days away. Artie was stunned by how fast things were moving and advised John, "We have to brainstorm. We gotta go over how we handled the last meeting with a fine-toothed comb, what we should have been more prepared for, what we could have done better. We have to close this deal."

Artie's run would have to wait. He changed into sweatpants and John changed into his sweats and tee shirt and they both left for the neighborhood coffeeshop where they would hunker down and plot their course.

41

Less than 48 hours later, they were on their way to the firm of Kolb Kravath, LLP, on Connecticut Avenue, a few short blocks from the White House. It was a bright, sunny Friday morning.

They stood as they rode the Metro downtown a couple of stops to Farragut North. They were riding with the tail end of the rush hour crowd. John and Artie saw that most people looked sleepy after a full week of work. Still, others wore angry expressions. Those were the ones who likely felt overworked and underloved.

The train stopped at the Farragut North station. They were in the cluster of riders that thrust forward and out the doors, as almost half the train emptied at the stop.

As they rode up the escalator to exit the station, John looked up and noticed a cute girl in blue jeans and a red top. He continued to look at her until Artie turned and reminded him, "Now, remember what we talked about. Don't look nervous, whatever you do, because these guys can smell fear."

"Don't worry," John said, "I hear what you're saying and I'll picture them wearing their underwear. Not to be perverted, but I get it."

Artie, pleasantly surprised, thought John looked much calmer than the last time around. It almost looked like John was getting ready to do something routine, like going to an ATM to withdraw money with a bankcard.

Anyway, John thought to himself, you're the one who needs to chill and take it easy. After going over the proposal so many times, you've made yourself crazy. If only I could tell you the whole story, including Dr. Duretts' involvement, you'd be cool as a cucumber.

Since it was a beautiful morning and they had time, they decided to walk to their meeting, and proceeded down Connecticut Avenue. After the second time walking up and down the street, they became alarmed.

"Where the hell is this building?" Artie wondered. "I can't for the life of me find this address," he continued.

John countered, "We're supposed to be these sophisticated businessmen and we can't even find a simple address. Let's try the map app."

Instead, Artie in full panic mode went to the company's website and called them. Artie didn't like this one bit, it wasn't good luck. He liked things to go smoothly and did not want to be late. He looked at his watch and they had only 10 minutes left to find the building and get up to the suite. God damn it.

The receptionist answered on the first ring and said, "Kolb Kravath, LLP, how can I help you?" and it sounded like she said it all in one word. Artie said, "Hi, I have a meeting there soon, but I can't seem to find the building on Connecticut Avenue." The receptionist, who sounded like she was in her late twenties, said, "Don't worry, it happens to everyone. The entrance is really on K Street. It's at 1717 K Street. Over the entrance it also gives the Connecticut Avenue address."

Jesus, Artie wondered, why can't anything be easy? "Thanks," he muttered and they turned toward K Street and quickly found the building. Artie couldn't shake his bad feeling; John, on the other hand, looked like he didn't have a care in the world, that poor naïve sap.

The glass doors to Kolb Kravath, LLP, opened, into a sleekly modern setting. A strikingly beautiful, well-dressed blonde sat behind an impressive glass and granite desk framed by a simple but expensive looking arrangement of flowers on one side and an impressive modern sculpture perched atop a pedestal on the other.

The receptionist, with perfect white teeth smiled at them and asked,

"Can I help you?" John and Artie, smiled back. They were both thinking the same thing, that this girl who looks like a model should be on the cover of a magazine, not smiling for every guy who walked into an office. Artie thought, interesting how very attractive women and money always seem to go together.

Artie, still smiling, approached the desk, and said, "We're here to see Joseph DeBerg." "Really?" the receptionist asked, almost as incredulous as if they were there for an audience with the Pope. "I'll ring his secretary. In the meantime, would either of you like a water, coffee, or tea?" In tandem they said, "No, thank you." Artie, in an effort to remain composed, kept repeating in his head, 'Focus, focus, focus.'

After a short wait, DeBerg's secretary, Emily appeared. She was a middle-aged woman, slender with good looks. She told them that Mr. DeBerg was concluding a conference call with London, and would be with them in a few minutes. She asked them to follow her to a conference room

As the glass door to the conference room closed, John looked at Artie and said, "The receptionist was a babe and I'm starting to have a good feeling about this. Lighten up, and have fun. I feel lucky today."

Artie said, "Luck has almost nothing to do with it, we have to be on." John said, "I guess you're right." Only Artie didn't know how right he was; luck wouldn't have carried the day, but hopefully having the inside track would.

Artie, in the process of pulling out the prospectus and a flow chart he had developed, looked up when in walked an older, distinguished looking man, accompanied by a middle-aged woman. The man held out his hand to shake first Artie's and then John's hand, as he said, "Hello, I'm Joseph DeBerg, and this is my associate, Betty Rhoads."

Mr. DeBerg stood 6 feet two inches tall, had a head of thick dark hair peppered with silver, and looked exactly like one would expect a successful banker to look. He had a pleasant demeanor, but an unflappable air about him.

DeBerg continued, "Betty does a great deal of the legwork in the process of assessing these types of transactions. At this point, we will be the only people involved in this application. I would also like you to know about our group and what we do."

"On a personal note, I've read and studied much regarding the biotech industry. I believe there is a lot of promise in this particular area of the economy, and possibly with your company. I have been faithfully following developments in the industry and issues with CRISPR."

As he listened, John couldn't help but think that if Dr. Duretts had painted even a small picture of what they were up to, that DeBerg must be salivating.

DeBerg, for his part, didn't mind overplaying his role for these two young men – particularly ones connected to his old friend. The key was not to let on that anyone actually knew what was going on. It was something that came naturally to blue-bloods like himself.

Any unpleasantness should be swept under the rug. Just turn your head and ignore it, and if you made stacks of money in the process, so much the better. He needed plausible deniability, a term he recalled an attorney once having used in another matter. If the shit hit the fan, he had to make certain that Betty had written it up correctly, so it would pass muster with his partners and they would be compliant when he pitched the loan.

If this venture worked out like his old buddy Alan expected, DeBerg would bring a ton of money into the firm, which would cement his stature. His section hadn't been doing so well recently, and he needed a big score to knock down some of the younger upstarts, particularly McQue, whom he never liked anyway.

He seethed thinking of the last partner's meeting where McQue, after pointing out that his receivables were 45% higher than any other partner, started acting like he owned the place. DeBerg thought how great it would be to land this or some other big fish and then put McQue in his place – maybe even freeze him out completely. McQue would not have been anything but for the promotion DeBerg gave him a few short years before.

DeBerg continued to his rapt audience, "In this new era of globalization, only high-tech companies with intellectual capital will be immune from ravages of cheap labor and competition from abroad. That is why I am so intrigued by your proposal. Also, as a closely held company, you're right up our alley. We typically don't get involved with public companies."

He said, "What we can offer you is access to capital, management experts, and office and technical support. Since you do not have many assets, we would expect to take a 51% stake in the company. The two of you can divide the remaining stock as you see fit."

He went on, "The capital can be used to set up an office, procure any people and equipment you may need and to set up labs. Betty will be the point person, and we will have to approve all purchases and hiring but we are somewhat flexible in that regard."

Then DeBerg said, "What happens after today is that you make your decision if you wish to proceed to the next step. After you inform me, I would then present my partners with a recommendation. We then vote on which businesses we like to go forward with. I must say even before you begin, that I was impressed with the documentation. I love biotech companies and am inclined to recommend to my partners that we back your enterprise."

Betty, surprised, quickly thought back on her 13 years working for DeBerg, and couldn't remember a single instance when he'd ever before approved a proposal before the presentation was made. He seemed almost over-accommodating to this team of young men, but then he did like biotech, even if he didn't really understand the intricacies, and lacked a certain depth of understanding. She dismissed her concerns since he's the boss, and with so much money flying around the firm, this amounts to small potatoes.

Betty had reviewed the same prospectus as Mr. DeBerg and was confused by it – she did not think it at all well-written, or thought out. The essence of the project seemed to be that the company could do DNA ancestry and forensic work, while the 'scientist' who looked more like a football player, did more cutting edge and potentially lucrative research on something called CRISPR.

It could work in the right hands, that the core business might support the more lofty aspects of the other part of the venture. Her firm could help set up websites to sell the ancestry assessments and provide some connections with law enforcement.

Artie stood and gave a presentation that was very similar to the one he'd made the first time. John thought, he's nervous. DeBerg and Betty were politely attentive, but asked no questions when he finished.

DeBerg then looked to John for a brief synopsis of his research while working on his PhD. DeBerg closed by asking if they had any questions for him, then suggested that they think about what he'd said, and to please get back to Betty with their decision, one way or the other. The meeting was over. The next step was theirs.

42

After the meeting, Betty followed Mr. DeBerg to his office. He closed the door and said, "As you know from other projects I've backed, I like this high-tech stuff. After that remarkable presentation I will strongly recommend we do this deal – even though these two are rather young. My gut says that this is something worth pursuing. With the right person keeping an eye on it, I like the odds."

DeBerg continued, "I was never great at science in school, and I have the Fun-gin matter that is taking up a lot of my time, so I'm not going to get overly involved in this. This is a perfect opportunity for someone to get noticed, and I'd like that someone to be you. I think it's time for you to break out and show what you can do, which could lead to your becoming a director in our company. I can't promise you anything, but I like what I've seen so far, and I think you deserve this. Think about it."

DeBerg believed what he said, for the most part. Hard-working Betty Rhoads was pleasant, more than competent, experienced and tough minded. She was an average looking forty-something, with less impressive academic credentials than most of the other assistants, but she did have staying power. She also had few distractions from her work.

She never married, had no demanding kids to pull her off task and was good on the fundamentals. It was unlikely that she would ever make director, even if this project worked out as he hoped, but it couldn't hurt to get her fully invested in the project.

His careful management of her expectations would narrow her focus so that she would be motivated to keep a lid on any major problems, while at the same time acting as a buffer between him and the project – making it look more like business as usual until either a big payoff or a total bust. He could easily take credit for the former and cast blame for the latter.

He shifted his thoughts back to a successful outcome and smiled. He believed in Dr. Alan Duretts. His long-time friend was a brilliant scientist, not rich, but a person who was rarely, if ever, wrong. He indulged himself with the daydream of how sweet future partnership meetings would be, if only he could get rid of McQue.

43

As Betty walked back to her small cubical after the meeting, she mulled around what Mr. DeBerg had just said.

Now, forty-four years old, she had started at Kolb Kravath, LLP, right out of Fordham with a joint MBA/Law degree, 13 years ago. She had been thinking about leaving and doing something else that didn't take up all of her time. She wanted more out of a life. Not one to envy others, she was tired of being passed over for promotion by co-workers who didn't work nearly as hard. After all she had sacrificed, she was tired of it.

Despite her years of hard work, she felt disappointed by her lack of progress at the firm. She earned just over $230,000 a year, but was barely making ends meet. She was still paying off student loans, helped support her widowed mother and had purchased a small condo in a less desirable suburb, commuting with the rabble each day. She hated it.

Oh, but she would love to be a director in this company. They had assistants who handled all the drudgery, and weren't harried as she was. They had their own well-appointed offices with expansive views, not cubicles. They earned well over a half million dollars a year, not to mention significant executive bonuses, and other perks like golf club memberships and executive level healthcare that wasn't provided to lower level employees.

If you made your mark, after a few years, partnership was on the table. However, very few women became directors at Kolb Kravath. To get that far, one needed a partner to go to bat for her. Would Mr. DeBerg do that for her? Despite his words, she had her doubts.

When she sat down at her laptop, she noticed several new emails, one from Mr. DeBerg. It read, "As you and I agree, the presented project has great potential. I plan to recommend it at the next partnership meeting. Since you were at the meeting and appeared enthusiastic about its prospects, I would like you to take a more substantive role should this project be approved by the partnership. Let me know your thoughts."

Betty thought he was jumping the gun, since she hadn't even received a call from the principals they met with. Also, after their years working together, Betty was astonished by how often he misread her. She couldn't imagine how he'd gotten the impression that she was in favor of proceeding with the project. But rather than challenge him, she thought, I've spent 13 years of my life here, what's another 6 months, or so, when it could get me what I want?

Besides, always the optimist, she wanted to believe the best in people, so she decided to take DeBerg at his word. She replied to his email, "I am happy to assist in any capacity you need." She hit the 'send' button.

She then turned to a file that had been on her desk for 3 days, certain that if she didn't review the documents and get them out today, the partner who sent them to her would be all over her. It never ended, more fun and games.

44

At the quarterly partnership meeting 2 weeks later, Howard McQue was smug as usual. He had driven in from his McLean home in his new Jenson Interceptor, which he had rewarded himself with a few months before. He handed it over to the parking attendant with a derisive scowl, communicating that it had better not come back with as much as a fingerprint on it.

McQue entered the Willard Hotel and proceeded directly to the Crystal Room where the meeting was to take place. He had reason to swagger because, once again, he had brought in more profits than any other partner in his firm.

He had been especially lucky with one particular investment. An Internet startup that had achieved record profits because it had developed a new software program licensed to Sun Microsoft. His analysts had undervalued the software, but he decided to take the gamble, and it had paid off handsomely. For him, the bottom line was the only thing that mattered.

The mood at the meeting was boisterous – it had been a good quarter. Everyone was congratulating each other. Life was good in the boardroom. They controlled about 9 billion dollars of investments in their hedge fund. They received a 3% fee just for managing the fund. They also received 20% of the profits received from the investments – and the returns were good.

The meeting began with the opening of a wet bar in the corner of the luxuriously appointed room. The Macallan's and Blue Label scotches were flowing freely, as were the artisanal beers and specially selected wines – many of which were picked by Howard McQue himself. They also had a choice of the finest cigars, a tradition that most of the partners loved, to be smoked later. After getting their drinks and appetizers, the partners took their seats and the meeting began.

The Secretary of the corporation, the only non-partner present, read the prior meeting minutes and issues raised at the last meeting. The partners, however, were more interested in hearing the Treasurer's assessment of the fund's finances, than this particular formality of the meeting. After the Secretary finished, the Treasurer presented his report and the financial outlook for the firm.

DeBerg didn't really have to listen, since he already knew the pertinent facts. Thus, he was more interested in the glass of Blue Label that he held in his hand. As the meeting dragged on, he looked around the room and saw the eyes of his colleagues light up as the topic of dollars and cents were discussed in great detail. He was biding his time until new business opportunities became the subject under consideration.

DeBerg had placed an item in the new business agenda and sandwiched it about two-thirds of the way into that portion of the meeting. By then, the partners would be in no mood to question any small investment, and instead would be wondering when they were going to eat. He was careful to place his item after a $725,000,000 request by a junior partner, so his new business would seem insignificant – the type of thing hungry partners, who were just told their bonuses would be quite fat, would not question.

As the Secretary went through the new business line by line, the partners' eyes glazed over and the investments were being rubber-stamped, until they got to Gill Franks' proposal for the $725,000,000 investment. After a few questions about the fundamentals of the investment, and whether he really needed the full amount, they approved his request, but only for $200,000,000, with the ability to obtain more financing at the time of the next meeting, if necessary.

They then arrived at the item which DeBerg had placed on the agenda. The Secretary went through the particulars of the transaction, indicating that AlgoGene was a biotech start-up, no capital contribution from the individuals involved, and that KK would keep an equity stake of 51% in the company.

The amount sought was an initial investment of $4.6 million which would be maintained in a capital account and disbursed on an as-needed basis by a partner or director, who would be monitoring the company. The sponsor of the enterprise was Joseph DeBerg. An update on the status would be on the agenda for the next meeting.

None of the partners even seemed to notice the modest request. For the most part, anything under 10 million dollars barely registered as noteworthy. Moreover, DeBerg had been around for a while, and no one wanted to get on his wrong side, even if his project seemed a little light on the details.

The motion to allocate the funds was passed and the Secretary quickly moved onto the next order of business. DeBerg continued sipping his scotch, as he smiled his best Cheshire cat smile at Howard McQue, and privately toasted his old friend, Alan Duretts, who had never steered him wrong.

45

The next morning at 8:02 AM, Betty received an email from Mr. DeBerg. It was short and said, "The Partners approved the funding of the biotech company we discussed. $4.6 million has been allocated to Bank of America account number 3455324. More may be allocated, if required. Please further analyze the specifics, and meet with me prior to the close of business today. Thereafter, please schedule a meeting with the principals."

Betty was surprised that the partners so readily agreed to fund the project because the business plan was obviously weak, and the principals lacked both experience and collateral. Then again, she had never been invited to a partners' meeting and had no idea how deals were approved or denied. One thing she was sure of, however, was that the conference room would smell of cigar smoke when the meeting was done.

She was always a little disheartened around the time of the partnership meetings. Decisions made in that room affected the lives of her and her co-workers – without any thought about, or input from, the people who would be affected. Now she had to prepare herself to call that guy from the meeting, what was his name, Artie? She couldn't believe she hadn't already heard from him.

Betty pulled the file and called the number listed in the business plan. The line rang and she heard, "Yes," from a voice sounding just awakened from sleep.

She said, "Good morning, am I speaking to Artie Cohen?" When he replied, "Yes, who's asking?" she continued, "Mr. Cohen, this is Betty

Rhoads from Kolb Kravath, LLP. I know I haven't heard from you, but I have some good news regarding the business plan you submitted, if you're still interested. There was a partnership meeting last night and the financing for your venture was approved. Could you and your associate come in to meet with me today to go over the arrangements?"

Artie almost dropped his cell phone. He'd fallen asleep on the couch last night and must still be dreaming. He stammered an apology about not calling her, then asked Betty to hold for a minute, muted his phone looked at John, in his pajama bottoms and T-shirt, sitting at the kitchen table and asked, "Hey John, are you around this afternoon?" He nodded in the affirmative. Artie unmuted his phone then said, "Would 2 PM be OK? Great, thanks, see you then."

John was wondering what he'd agreed to when Artie said, "You won't believe this, but we're in business, paaartna. We're meeting with Betty Rhoads at 2 o'clock to talk about our project."

John thought it had to be one of Artie's friends helping him pull a practical joke on John. He looked at Artie and warned, "You better not be shitting me." But the shocked look on Artie's face told the story. John knew Artie wasn't putting him on. Artie then said, "We go there, we play it low key, and we negotiate." John couldn't do anything but nod in agreement.

46

Artie and John arrived at Kolb Kravath, LLP at 1:55 PM, and were greeted by the same receptionist, dutifully at her post. She smiled and stated, "Ms. Rhoads is expecting you." They smiled confidently, realizing that their stature had been elevated in her eyes. She directed them into a small conference room right off the reception area.

Betty joined them at exactly 2:00 PM. She said, "Congratulations, we're pleased about your decision to work with Kolb Kravath. Let's go over the details, shall we? The partnership has agreed to your initial funding request, that is $4.6 million. I have been assigned to be your liaison, to review the transactions for the new company, and possibly access additional funding if warranted."

She continued, "Our in-house attorneys will set up a close corporation for you and will file paperwork with the state of incorporation. They think it would be beneficial to set you up as a Delaware corporation for tax and other reasons, and they are aware of the allocation of the shares in the company. As Mr. DeBerg told you, since Kolb Kravath is putting up the money, we will get 51% of the shares in your company, AlgoGene Corporation."

Betty then asked, "So can you please tell me who should be listed as officers of the company? I must be listed as Treasurer, but you can decide who will be the President, Vice President and Secretary. We also need someone to act as the CEO and possibly a CFO, although initially, I will act as the money person and perform the duties of CFO."

She then said, "You may also want to get your own lawyer to review the incorporation paperwork, and to counsel you on any other issues that may arise."

She looked at Artie, then John. Both looked as if they had been unprepared to hear what she had said. Amateurs, she thought.

She continued her spiel, which she'd given so many times it was automatic. "I will review all purchases, all hiring decisions and all salaries that are to be paid. I think you need to get a better handle on the purchases you need to make. I would like cost estimates for the equipment, and/or other documentation from the sellers before you buy anything costing more than $500."

Finally, she ended with, "Why don't you two take a day or two to absorb what I've said, then come back with your ideas, based on what you've heard. Please take this time to contact a commercial real estate agent to begin looking at office and lab space, I would suggest somewhere off of I-270, where you can get a good amount of space for a fair rent. If you'd like, I can call a real estate agent I know who could assist you. Based on your business plan, I think that we need about 5,000 square feet of space. What do you think?"

Artie and John were several steps behind and could not believe their ears – did she say $4.6 million?

John could barely formulate an answer to her question. He knew that Dr. Duretts had some pull, but he didn't believe it would be enough for them to pull this off. Did she know that this was a fraud? He doubted it. Did she suspect something? Probably not. He quickly shook it off, he couldn't believe it, knew he had to try to play it cool.

"That sounds great," John said, "a lot of the material for CRISPR can be purchased right on the Internet, using my cell phone. Thermo Scientific is one company that sells the CRISPR technology, and it's reasonably priced."

Betty asked him, "What is the technology exactly? What did you call it, CRISPR?"

John, now in his wheelhouse, was back in control of his faculties and said, "It's truly one of the most incredible technologies ever to be conceived. It's in practice already. Researchers have used CRISPR to change the genetic code of plants and animals, for example, to create wheat which is resistant to crop diseases, and to grow mushrooms that don't turn brown."

He continued, "Since it actually changes or edits the genetic code, it also has the potential to cure diseases like cancer and AIDS, or could theoretically even change the genes effecting the way you look, or how smart you are. We are also working on AI programs to help with the application of CRISPR. The only reason I say 'theoretically' is because we can't do it safely in humans yet."

Betty's eyebrows shot up and she was unable to prevent the look of disbelief showing on her face. She smirked and breaking her professional demeanor, said, "Are you joking? That sounds like a really bad sci-fi movie." She regained her composure and asked, "I'm sorry, but have labs already done this type of work and successfully changed the genetic code in animals?"

As John began to nod in the affirmative, Artie interjected, "It has been done, and there are two different groups, one from UC Berkeley, and another affiliated with Harvard, who did the basic research. Both groups independently have been trying to patent the technology. As far as I know, the case is still pending. There is big money in this and it is my understanding that a company named Editas, who has licensing agreements with one of the groups, filed a $100 million IPO."

John jumped in and said, "I'm 99% sure that everything he just said is true."

Betty then said, "Well if it's all tied up in a patent fight, and there will ultimately be a patent, how do you plan to create a company without getting the licensing rights? The cost would be tremendous, wouldn't it?"

John adeptly fielding her question said, "Yes, but we could still work with the technology. I have done some research and some theoretical work that uses a different methodology to generate the same result. If I'm correct, then we may have something that falls outside of the patent, or so I've been told."

He continued, "I've also discussed some computer models with a programmer I want to hire. These models might be able to isolate specific genes, or at least discern through the proper algorithms, which specific genes control particular expressions."

Betty thought these two young men were selling her a bill of goods, but time would tell, and it wasn't her call because she had her marching orders.

She continued, "I'll look into this further. In the meantime, here's a letter from Kolb Kravath, accepting your proposal, with my email address on top. Before we meet next, email me a list of websites which have pricelists or prices for the equipment. I'll email you when the paperwork is complete, so that you, and possibly your attorneys, can review and sign it."

With the meeting concluded, Betty stood up to shake their hands. John rose to his feet, but Artie's legs were rubbery, and he struggled to stand. In unison they said, "Thank you, Betty," as they shook her hand, then left.

After they left the building, they finally felt like they could breathe again. John said, "Can you believe it?" He felt like hugging Artie and shouting for joy, but didn't want to act the fool on Connecticut Avenue. Instead he said, "Let's celebrate. I feel like a beer and some Buffalo wings, but let's walk a few blocks." Artie gave him the thumbs up, and they walked over to Rumors on M Street.

The aroma of the bar was a pleasant mixture of beer and bar food; a smell that both recognized. They sat at the bar. John ordered a Sam Adams, then Artie ordered a Coors Lite. They sat silent until the bartender brought them their beers. They both took big swigs then finally relaxed.

Artie began, "I can't believe it. I did it. I finally put together a plan that worked. I have to tell you, I didn't think we could do it. 4.4 million dollars."

"4.6 Million," John corrected him, and thought, Artie doesn't know the half of it. Hmm-m, pretty big ego for someone who had little to do with this turn of good luck. Anyway, John having no desire to fight, take credit, or ruin the moment merely said, "I estimate the cost of the equipment we'll need to be about $50,000 dollars, with the exception of the supercomputer. How many people do you think we need to hire? Anyplace you have in mind for our office? Did we overreach for our own salaries?"

Artie said, "Whoa, boy, one question at a time," as he considered the possibility of being an executive of a well-funded company. Visions of him flying the corporate jet back and forth from DC to New York or London, or even Tokyo, danced through Artie's head. $3,000 suits, thousand-dollar shoes and season tickets for the Nationals, the Redskins and even the Wizards would be sweet.

He lifted his beer, and with gusto clinked it against John's mug. As they toasted, John had a different train of thought and that was that he needed to talk with Dr. Duretts ASAP.

47

John felt giddy with enthusiasm as he pressed autodial on his burner phone to call Dr. Duretts. Duretts picked up on the second ring, saying "Hello, how can I help you?" John said, "It's me. I have good news. Your very good friend came through for us. He got us our initial funding of $4.6 million. It's starting to move fast."

Dr. Duretts thought for a moment, then asked, "Have you ever heard of a place called Bedford, in Pennsylvania? You drive up I-270, past Frederick and after that take Route 70 to Route 30, or the Turnpike. There's a restaurant, called Hoss's, which sits at the end of the highway, where it ends in a T-intersection. I'd like to meet you there tomorrow at 7:30 PM. No one will know us there. Can you do it?"

John said, "I don't know the place, but I'll be there. I'll make a list of some of the questions I have." Duretts wondered what those might be, but responded, "Tomorrow at 7:30 PM. It's a 2 hour drive, don't be late."

48

John exited the Pennsylvania Turnpike leading to the T-intersection and couldn't miss the large sign announcing, Hoss's. It was only 6:45 PM. He'd made great time despite the traffic. He saw several gas stations, a few fast food restaurants, and not much else. This place was Nirvana for truckers.

He wondered why Dr. Duretts picked Hoss's. He was surprised while driving up I-270, at how quickly it became rural so close to DC. As he looked around, a calmness descended on him as the slow pace of being in the rural area affected him. He was certain that here, off this remote exit ramp, no one would know him or Dr. Duretts, no record of the meeting and they could get down to business. Good choice, John thought.

He turned into the lot and had to go 4 rows back to find a spot. He exited his car and walked into the restaurant.

It was a family style place, with a large salad bar/food station. It even had a soft serve ice cream machine, which he noticed when a young kid walked by with a cup of ice cream covered with jimmies. He waited in line for few minutes, and then saw Alan with Bob and David.

They got in line and he noticed that you ordered before sitting down. He wondered if this was what it was like in the 1950s.

Dr. Duretts smiled a grandfatherly smile at the hostess, and she smiled back. He said I'm with my friends and we will be 4. Dr. Duretts advised them, "Don't order too much from the menu because you need to leave room for the salad bar. I recommend the burgers, they're my favorite."

John ordered the half-pound cheeseburger with onion rings and Dr. Duretts ordered the regular burger with a baked potato. The hostess seated them at the last booth in the corner, farthest from the salad bar, at Dr. Duretts' request.

Dr. Duretts began, "You know Bob, and David Goldblum. I've told you very little about David. He is a master programmer, and we are lucky to have him working with us."

As Dr. Duretts paused, John looked at David. He was the epitome of an engineer. He was pale-skinned and reed thin, wore thick dark framed glasses, and appeared to have long sticks for arms and legs. He wore pants that were slightly shorter than they should have been, perhaps because he was so tall. He seemed detached or aloof and wouldn't look directly at John. He looked at the floor when he mumbled, "Good to see you again."

John wasn't put off, because this was the kind of guy he'd interacted with most of his academic life. He could relate to David. He imagined that David was probably into the same types of things he was, although more heavily into math, while John was more into biology. John shook his hand and said, "Likewise. Glad to have you on board."

David stammered, "Yes, me too. I was very intrigued speaking with Dr. Duretts. I had other opportunities as a data scientist, making better apps or Internet advertising, and this seems much more interesting, challenging and important."

John shook his head in agreement and said, "What can be better than developing a computer algorithm to translate all biological information, or as you might put it, animal source code, into usable information? It doesn't get better than that."

David became visibly more relaxed, which made them all feel comfortable. David's face broke into the slightest of smiles when he said, "Yes, as you probably know the human genome consists of approximately 3.2 billion base pairs, that literally comprises a person's genetic code. That creates a file that is approximately 300 gigabytes. With the right algorithm and a powerful enough computer, I think all things are possible, including cracking the code of which genes do what." David glanced at John then looked back to the floor, without saying anything for a moment.

Dr. Duretts interrupted, "To give you guys some background, David here is an expert in what they call machine learning and data science. He worked closely with the best minds in statistical machine translation, which creates programs that generate translations based on patterns found in large amounts of written text or other material. The computer then is used to discover rules based on statistically significant patterns in the data."

Duretts continued, "It is my understanding, and correct me if I'm wrong, David, that he spent a couple months by himself developing an algorithm designed to apply this technique to the genome. The algorithm can isolate patterns of genes that determine various characteristics of plants and animals. He believes that it can determine the genes that make someone good in math and music, make them a gifted athlete, have a high IQ, give them a long life and even things as mundane as whether they have high cheek bones. It might also be used to determine what diseases they might get."

Duretts went on, "A number of computer scientists are working on deciphering the genetic code, but as far as I know, none have also connected artificial intelligence with CRISPR. But, gentlemen, this is exactly what we will do."

Dr. Duretts turned to David and said, "You will need to go to John's office for a perfunctory interview for the position. The job is yours, as you know, and this is just a necessary formality."

Dr. Duretts then said, "Let's eat. I recommend the soup, it's homemade here and the garlic bread is passable."

John asked Duretts, "How did you know about this place?" Duretts looked over his shoulder as he said, "I had relatives in Pennsylvania, and used to drive there from time to time. My kids loved this place, and I hate to admit it, but I liked it too – especially the desserts." They waited behind a family with three young kids and finally got their chance to load up their plates and bowls with salad, bread and soup.

When they returned to their table, Duretts switched topics and said, "The research at hand regarding a cure for baldness was accomplished partially by using the algorithm created by David. Using his algorithm, and a statistically significant number of test subjects with varying dates of balding onset, or no onset at all, we figured out the two genes that effect balding. If you get rid of those genes, a person will not lose his hair."

Duretts continued, "Consequently, you, Dr. Ordell, will go down in history as the man who cured the ravages of balding." He had difficulty keeping a straight face when he said ravages. He went on, "This small group of fellows dedicated almost all of their personal time to doing this work, and now it will be yours to give to the world."

Duretts continued, "We were also able to test it topically. Our inspiration for topical application came from early work done by Aacuity Pharmaceuticals. They developed RNAi, which shuts down genes for new blood vessel growth. When it's injected into the eyes of age-related macular degeneration patients, it causes a blockage to prevent vessel overgrowth. This effectively stopped the progression of the disease. It wasn't injected to change every cell in the body through the bloodstream. Instead, it just changed the cells in the patients' eyes."

He said, "That is what prompted us to test our formulation by applying it topically. And it worked. As I told you earlier, based on the tests, some of our techs agreed to be injected with CRISPR. And that worked too, although no one can know that. I am confident that there will be no side effects – partially based on the computer models. Also, unlike current treatments, ours will work 100% of the time."

Dr. Duretts continued, "Our goal for the future is that a patient will have two options – topical application, which may need multiple uses, or an injection if you want it to be permanent and to genetically transmit the trait to your kids. Voilà, you have a head of hair like a 20-year-old, and your descendants won't have to worry about premature balding. It may seem superficial, but it's a moneymaker. After all, hair restoration is a multibillion-dollar industry."

Dr. Duretts paused, then continued, "During our research, we made another discovery. When we looked closely at CRISPR, we found another compound that acts like Cas9, to cut DNA. Others have come up with variations of Cas9, but I am confident that ours is innovative enough to be protected by a patent. We will not publish our findings, so that AlgoGene Corporation, your company, John, can announce the discovery and capitalize on it, in due course."

He went on, "All of our data logs have been removed to a safe place – a storage locker in Kensington Maryland. When the time is right, you will be patenting this new compound."

Duretts said, "I have the notes from our work on this new product and made a copy for you on a zip drive. Read through it, transcribe it onto your own computer, as if it's your own research. Make certain that the notes are made using your method of expression and are dated into the future. After you finish retyping the notes, destroy the zip drive. I compiled a list of the equipment we used, which you will need to buy. Call me if you need to, but I urge you to limit future contact with me and Bob."

Just then the waitress came with their food. When she left, Duretts continued, "We need to discuss how 'you' will go about protecting the trade secrets which you will invent soon," Dr. Duretts actually put air quotes around the 'you.' He continued, "We have a friend in the security division of our company and we picked his brain over the potential for industrial espionage. He's not involved with our little endeavor, but he was helpful and got us thinking."

Duretts went on, "Apparently, there are a number of companies that hack into computers, to keep tabs on the competition. Our friend indicated this year alone there were 6 incidents where our Internet IT personnel were able to intercept hackers and stop them before infiltrating our company's server. It's called phishing and we must be very careful."

After taking a deep breath, Dr. Duretts continued, "It may not be a bad idea to let some people gain access to your server. If someone, maybe a competitor or even a friendly investment banker, gets wind of what 'you' created with its potential profits, they may become motivated to buy your company. But we must maintain some computers with absolutely no Internet connection, including the supercomputer which will have the algorithm on it."

Duretts said, "The offline computers will be the ones with the new process on them, and will be the ones with the results of the notes inputted into them, so that no one can copy the new process or the algorithms. You can have plenty of online computers, which will have just enough information – emails and other materials – to whet their appetites, so hackers would be able to understand what we're doing, but without the ability to re-create or steal David's and Bob's, I mean 'your,' idea."

John said, "I'll be meeting with the computer contractors soon and I'll be sure they dedicate several computers, and particularly the supercomputer, with no Internet access."

"Don't pick the most competent group," Dr. Duretts advised. He added, "You may even want to figure out who might be less careful with Internet security, so that hackers can gain entry. We don't want anything in the program that would warn us of hackers. This is so potential investors who want the inside scoop before they invest can get a snapshot of the tremendous capacity of our technology and know-how."

Duretts suggested, "We may even want to float a few memos to suggest that the company is closer to breakthroughs than we are. This could be very persuasive when seen by the right eyes. Don't make it too obvious, but some understated white lies can be very enticing and lucrative for us. It's just something to think about."

John said, "I know what I have to do. It's a lot of work coming at me all at once, but I'll get it done. I've already finished transcribing my, I mean, your notes."

Duretts said, "Good boy. But don't forget to hire Lisa. I don't think she's heard from you yet."

John said, "Don't worry, it's already in the works."

Duretts nodded and said, "Also, we need someone else on the inside, like your friend Artie, to be in a position to do certain things that may not seem too smart, but which will serve our purposes. It makes sense to appoint him as a manager of some kind, you can even give him a small piece of the company if you want, but it will have to come out of your share. Do you want to use him, what do you think?"

John was flattered that Dr. Duretts cared about his opinion. He liked Artie, but he too was completely in over his head. Not so different from John, himself.

John said, "Yeah, I think he would serve our purpose. He seems a bit dull at times, but I think he would work fine." John felt guilty as he said it, remembering back to a time not long ago when he wasn't so judgmental. Being swept up in this whirlwind, with all its possibilities, was having an effect.

Dr. Duretts continued, "He seems the right choice, because believe me, we don't want someone analyzing what we're doing, asking all the wrong questions. We need a guy with a bit of an ego, who is a little out of his element, but believes that he isn't. From what I've heard, your Artie is just what we want."

Duretts said, "Also, please remember, I want Lisa to get stock options of at least 33% of your shares. However, you have to do it, make it happen."

John nodded, curious why a third of 'his' 49% should go to this person unknown to him, hoping that this part of the plan would go smoothly.

They then got up to get dessert and shop talk ended for the night.

49

John saw that it was just past 10:30 PM by the time he returned to the apartment. Artie was sitting on the couch with his laptop. John said, "I think we really have something here. I don't want to seem like a jerk, but please don't disturb me. I'm going to continue putting together the acquisition plan for the equipment we need, and I really need to concentrate, so I'm gonna work in my room. Don't even knock unless the apartment's on fire."

John leaned on the back of a chair, "I want you to know I appreciate all that you did for me, and I'll be speaking with Betty to make sure that you get a good job in the new company, if you want it. You deserve it."

Artie responded, "Thanks, but I think I already knew you'd do that."

John with a smirk said, "Maybe you could be our in-house exterminator, or one of our test subjects. Hmmm, you do make good coffee, you could be our team's gopher – driving us around and getting our dry cleaning – like Turtle on 'Entourage.'"

Artie flipped him off. He knew John was trying to be funny, but without him, John would never have gotten his company off the ground. Artie, after all, had been instrumental in persuading the bankers to offer all that cabbage. John should stick to the science, and leave the business to him.

Artie closed his computer, and stated impertinently, "I hate to do it, but to quote Sean Penn from *Fast Times at Ridgemont High,* 'you d-i-i-i-ck.' I have a great idea, maybe we can inject you with something to change your DNA so you won't be such an asshole. So close your door and get to it." That should put him in his place, Artie thought, as John left the room.

John had been wondering if his contact with Dr. Duretts hadn't already changed his DNA in some profound way. Stealing someone's property, even if it was intellectual property, wasn't something that would have ever entered his mind before. But no matter what the law said, wasn't it Dr. Duretts' property, created from his hard work? And John did not want to disappoint Dr. Duretts.

John went into his room, found the paper with Lisa's information and called her on the burner phone.

She answered, "Hello, this is Lisa."

John said "Hi, hope it's not too late. It's John Ordell. Remember me?" Lisa said, "Mm-hm." He continued, "Just wanted to let you know that our venture is a go and we're going to put an ad on Monster.com and Indeed.com for an administrative assistant. Send your resume to the email address and in your cover letter write that 'you are seeking an opportunity to be on the ground floor of a new enterprise.'

Don't call me, we'll contact you to set up an interview and hire you. It will take a few weeks, but don't worry, it's just a formality." She said, "I'll send a resume as soon as I see the ad and we can work out the details later." John said, "Great, talk with you soon. Bye," and he hung up.

Next, John called Betty's direct dial number and, despite the late hour, she picked up on the first ring. He set up a meeting with her for 10:00 AM, on Monday morning to review all the material he'd put together. He hoped she'd be easier to deal with than Artie, who was beginning to rub him the wrong way. Was this what he could look forward to now that real money was involved – that he'd get to experience the worst in people?

John read the articles Dr. Duretts gave him on gene mapping and CRISPR RNA technology. He moved on to reading Duretts' notes on an old tablet that he had, so they couldn't be traced to his computer. He needed a break, so rather than brew a pot of coffee, he decided to walk to Starbucks. He knew he had a long night of work in front of him. His goal was to finish reading and transcribing all the logs over the weekend so no one would stumble onto them, or become suspicious. When he finished, he'd destroy the flash drive. He didn't expect to sleep much in the next few weeks, but the rewards would be worth it.

On Monday, at 9:55 AM, John arrived at Kolb Kravath for his meeting with Betty. He hadn't invited Artie to join them, since his gut said go alone. He wanted the opportunity to get to know Betty.

John approached the receptionist and said, "I'm here to see Betty Rhoads." So this must be the guy that Betty mentioned, she thought. He looked pretty ordinary for a soon to be millionaire, and he was really young. "I'll let her know you're here," she said.

John barely sat down before Betty's secretary arrived to shepherd him to the same conference room as the last time. Betty, wearing a conservative navy blue suit, walked in a few minutes later. They exchanged pleasantries, then she said, "I told you there would be a few papers to sign. We'll get them for you in a few minutes."

She said, "These are the corporate documents that must be signed so that we can proceed. You can have your lawyer look them over, if you wish. We'll need to insert the names of who will be President, CEO and Secretary. We also need to revise your business plan, since we know the amount of the initial investment."

Before she could ask, John handed Betty the equipment list he'd rewritten from Dr. Duretts' notes, including their projected costs from the Internet, with asterisks beside those items he might be able to get 'used.'

Betty said, "Thanks, I really appreciate how fast you put this together. The total outlay of $280,000, is a good number. It's workable. I can get my secretary, to begin purchasing the items on the list and I'll issue the checks as the company's Treasurer. If there are some items you need to purchase yourself, let us know. I've already opened a new account and the funds should be wired in shortly."

Betty continued, "Also, if you haven't had been able to look into anything yet, there's some office space in Gaithersburg, off 355, that might work for you. There's large open space for a lab, and turn-key office space, all for just under $100,000 for the first year."

John said, "This all sounds great, Betty. I also have a lead on a used supercomputer we need. But do you think I could get a cup of coffee? I've been working pretty late since we last met." Betty said, "Please, help yourself. It's the third opening on the right, down the hall."

As John walked away, Betty was pleased that he had come here to play ball, a development that surprised her. His diligence reminded her of a prior client who started with a pipe dream and, through sheer drive and determination, turned it into a company with earnings well over $50 million a year.

She thought of the closing line from her favorite classic movie, *Casablanca*, where Humphrey Bogart tells the French police captain, 'I think this is the beginning of a beautiful friendship.' She loved that old movie. And she hoped that this new business relationship would work out likewise.

She felt a palpable change in John. He was calmer, more confident. He even seemed more mature. Perhaps it was because his colleague, Artie, wasn't with him, or maybe it was the newfound wealth coming his way. A couple of million dollars could do that to a guy.

When John returned, coffee in hand, he looked at Betty and said, "I'd like to hire an administrative assistant to begin working within the next month. I also want to start interviewing people for the tech positions soon, too."

Betty nodded her head in approval and said, "Very good. You may be able to poach one or two people from the competition and I'll get a good technical headhunter on it. I'd like to meet any prospective employees before you actually hire them," she added.

"I will prepare a projected payroll, which reminds me, we should prepare a spreadsheet with the first year's earnings projections."

John nodded in agreement, then blurted out, "What about my compensation?" Betty held back her urge to laugh and thought he's not as self-possessed as I thought. This wasn't a good sign. Most entrepreneurs in his position weren't so interested in the initial salary, but instead, were looking at the big picture. Most were just chomping at the bit to get started, when they succeeded, the big payday would come.

Betty looked directly at him and said, "We can discuss it, but I was thinking $145,000 per year. That, of course, doesn't include your interest in the company, or cash outlays for company business, like travel or other related expenses. Is that acceptable?"

John's face was flushed with embarrassment that he had brought up his personal compensation so early in their conversation. He quickly agreed, saying, "That seems fair, and my title, should it be President, or CEO? Do I get stock options?" This conversation was becoming even more awkward.

She looked away, then down at her notepad as she said, "Let's not decide on titles just yet, but you will be responsible for all the labs and R&D. You also have a 49% stake in the company and you can distribute the shares as you see fit, to entice good people to join the company, as long as you retain at least 50% of your shares."

She explained, "As for stock options, they do not apply to you because you already control a considerable proportion of the shares in the company – 49%. Some company founders do get stock options later, after they take the company public, but we frown on it. We look at it as a way to steal equity from the public investors that the company's founders had originally taken on as partners. The bottomline, no stock options."

"OK," he answered, unsure of what she'd said and what he'd agreed to, he suddenly found himself wishing he'd brought Artie to the meeting. Betty continued, "For the first year you cannot sell any shares, but you can give them to essential employees. I urge you to do this sparingly, but it is up to you."

John said, "OK, thanks. So, I was wondering whether I could hire the guy who helped me with the business plan? I think he'll be a great help to me and seems well-versed about the business end of things. What do you think?"

Betty said, "He didn't create that impression with me, but if you're comfortable with him, I'm sure we can find something for him to do. You're going to be very busy starting this up. You should develop an employee flow chart, a reporting structure for the various positions, areas of responsibility and pay range. Then we'll figure out where to go from there. And yes, you will likely be the President of AlgoGene Corporation."

Just then a secretary knocked on the door. On Betty's OK, she walked in with the stack of documents which needed to be signed to set up the corporation, including the articles of incorporation, bylaws, application and other documents. Betty asked if he wanted to take the papers with him for attorney review. He told her it wasn't necessary, that he would just sign them.

After he finished signing the last form, John meekly said, "Thanks. See you soon." He then picked up his stack of documents and walked out the door.

50

John was sitting in his room for hours with the door closed, alternating between looking at apps on his phone and transcribing the remaining pages of the notes Dr. Duretts had given him. Betty called and asked, "Can you get up to Gaithersburg in the next hour, or so? The real estate agent is available to show you the space we talked about. After that, maybe we can grab a quick bite and talk about the next steps."

John said, "Sure. I'll meet you at the property." Betty gave him the address. John entered the address into his phone's app and a little over a half hour later he was standing in front of a building a few blocks off of I-270.

It was a small two-story office building with an extension, probably the warehouse. He saw Betty pull up in her Subaru Forester and behind her was an Audi A8, probably transporting the real estate agent. They all shook hands, he was introduced to the agent and they went inside.

There were 10 offices and a kitchen on the first floor, in the two-story portion of the building. They next walked into the adjacent warehouse area that reminded him of an airplane hangar. It was comprised of three open spaces with a high ceiling. This place would work well for the lab.

Finally, they walked to the upper floor which had fewer offices and a conference room that could comfortably hold twenty people. On each side of the end of the hall were two corner executive offices.

John walked into the one on the left, which had a view of a small man-made lake, complete with swimming geese. The room was large, with built in book cases. The agent said, "It could easily fit a desk, a small table and couch, and you have your personal bathroom behind that door. Can you picture yourself behind your desk over there?" The agent was smiling, happy with her use of the oldest trick in the book, as John thought to himself, yes I can.

The agent shared that the space was in move-in condition because a deal had fallen through for the intended tenant, who had paid for the build-out.

Betty asked the agent to meet them on the first floor, so that she could speak with John in private. She asked him, "Will this fit everything you need, or not?" John considered the list for a moment, then said, "With exhaust hoods, I don't know if we need a ceiling this high, but the floor space is right. And I do like the corner office."

Betty smiled and said, "You're thinking like a CEO already. Before we sign a lease, why not go through the dimensions of your equipment to make sure it all fits. We'll ask for a blueprint that shows the building's layout and dimensions. You can tell her you'll be making a decision fairly quickly."

John said, "Great, let's get the plans from the real estate agent and I'll call you tomorrow." Betty nodded in agreement, and after concluding their meeting suggested Dogfish Head for a casual dinner. She said, "They have decent food, a superior beer selection and it's only a few miles away."

John approved and was looking forward to his first perk. He would enjoy this dinner, which Betty assured him would be a tax write-off for the company.

After they were seated at the restaurant, John looked at Betty and said, "I'd really like to thank you for everything you've done." Betty hoped she'd soon be saying the same to him, although for now her fingers were crossed.

Curious about Betty's background and wanting to know what made her tick, John asked, "So where'd you go to school and how did you get into the world of high finance?"

Betty responded, "I got a joint JD/MBA from Fordham, and found that I especially liked business law and international trade. I also have a subspecialty in tax law. During summers I worked for the World Bank, which convinced me that I needed to move into the private sector."

John asked, "Why not stay at the World Bank?"

Betty answered, "The World Bank isn't exactly what you think it is. I became disillusioned in my short time there; it became apparent to me that their mission isn't to help the people in developing countries, but rather to protect monied interests. I was such an idealist back then, but I figured it out fairly quickly."

She continued, "It still bugs me when the news outlets report about protests against the World Bank, because they never explain why people are protesting." As she paused, John thought that she was much more liberal than most bankers should be, but he liked it.

She continued, "The World Bank, in my opinion, is an arm of big business and multinational corporations. It lends money to countries at a steep price and they are supposed to open up their markets to American and other multinational companies."

Betty went on, "To participate, countries must agree to privatize many of their industries, which are then purchased by the multinationals who were let into their country. For example, when I was there, I saw a case where a multinational purchased recently privatized water companies and utilities, and then dramatically increased the price of the commodities. Suddenly, the locals weren't able to afford something as basic as water.

There are also instances where they destroy the small local stores by buying them, or forcing them out of business. Once competition is eliminated, a monopoly market is created and prices are increased with no regard for the people's ability to pay. In a nutshell, that's why I'm no longer at the World Bank."

John admired her frankness, how perceptive she was, and then asked, "So how do you like the private sector?"

The beer was affecting Betty, like a truth serum. She confided, "If you can't beat 'em, join 'em. The pay is better, I work with gifted people, and at least there are no pretenses as to what we're doing. Truthfully, it's not all it's cracked up to be. I guess I make a lot of money compared to many people, but structuring business deals, like IPOs, doesn't help anyone except management and shareholders, who usually get rich. But that's what we are trying to do for you.

Anyway, I have some experience in emerging markets too, but I don't think this will ever be your problem since it's highly doubtful you'll be doing business with emerging markets. What we are hoping for, is that there is some interest by a large pharmaceutical company to purchase your company in an IPO, or by licensing your technology. That would make you a millionaire and advance my humble career."

When they finished eating, Betty handed him his first paycheck drawn on his fledgling company, AlgoGene Corporation, and a freshly minted corporate credit card.

John was staring at the credit card when Betty advised him to keep detailed records of his expenses, who he met with and why, and that he should keep receipts for everything. She handed him a paper memo that outlined what expenses were permitted, how and when to use the card and what to do with receipts. She said, "I'll also email this to you, since you might want to reference it from time to time." She then pulled out her own AlgoGene credit card to pay the bill.

51

John drove to Brooklyn, up 95 North, over the Verrazano Bridge onto the Belt Parkway. Out of habit he looked over the left side still expecting to see the World Trade Center. In its place stood the Freedom Tower, which his father said could never take the place of its predecessor, the World Trade Center.

He took the usual exit, 11N, to the familiar road home. He pulled up in front of the low-rise garden apartment where his father lived, but had to look for a parking spot. He was not surprised he had to walk 5 blocks to get to his father's unit.

He walked up the stairs, onto the stoop where he used to hang out, and rang the doorbell. His father yanked the door open and stood there stone-faced. He didn't move to hug John, but extended his arm and shook his son's hand with a vice-like grip, saying, "Don't just stand there, come on in."

He asked John some cursory questions about the drive from DC to New York. John said it was OK, not feeling like complaining, even though an accident in Staten Island added an hour to the trip.

His father's apartment looked the same. Everything in its place. He guessed it was a residual effect of military service. The furnishings were spartan. John wasn't sure if it was because his Dad couldn't afford to change it, or because he preferred it that way.

His father directed him to sit down on the couch, as he went to get a beer. As an afterthought, he asked John if he wanted one, too. John said, "Sure." His father came back, handed him a beer and parked himself rigidly on the edge of his Barcalounger. He then grabbed the remote control and said, "Don't tell me you turned into a Nats' fan, especially now that the Yankees are playing pretty good ball."

John needled his father by responding, "Oh yeah, for sure – they have the best starting pitching rotation in the league, not to mention the second coming of Mickey Mantle, in Bryce."

His father grimaced, as if in pain, from this betrayal, then admitted, "They do have a pretty good team. How come they didn't make the playoffs last year? Where do you think Bryce'll be playing next year?" now smirking at his son. With the tension finally broken, John laughed because he knew his father, a die-hard Mets fan, could recite the names of all the '69 Mets, their stats from that year, and even some of their birthdays. His father was a purist, with a true love of the game.

John, tired after a long drive, didn't want to hear a lecture about the players back in the day and how much better they were, or what phonies today's players were. He hated when his Dad droned on about Barry Bonds' transgressions and how Hank Aaron was so much better and did it the real way, with integrity, no cheating, no drugs, no BALCO, just old-school talent. He'd heard it so many times, and didn't want to hear it again.

Still unable to resist, John said, "Yeah, and how about that A-Rod? He was doing great, until he retired and now he's a fantastic announcer." His father gave him a look of disgust and said, "Don't be stupid. Everyone should hate that guy. Dating Madonna, now that Lopez woman, doesn't change anything. He was a cheater, pure and simple. And cheaters shouldn't prosper. It's just not right."

John's father wore a look of disgust on his face, despite knowing that his son was just busting on him. John felt uncomfortable. He hated his father's characterization of A-Rod's success as cheating. After all, A-Rod did make a quarter of a billion dollars in his first contract and was a hell of a good player, at least statistically.

Changing the subject, his father said, "I know you can't get decent deli in Washington, so I figured we'd go to Mill Basin Deli by King's Plaza."

John said, "I could eat." He lugged his suitcase down the hall to his old room. When he returned to the living room, his father said, "I hope you don't think I'm paying." John considered the statement as they went out the door, and thought when it came to eating red meat, like most other things, his father was serious. John just said, "OK, I'm buying."

As they walked the six blocks to the deli, John could almost taste the hot corned beef on a club roll, his usual order. When they entered the restaurant, John breathed in the smells of an authentic New York deli. You could smell the sour and half-sour pickles, the coleslaw, the hot dogs on the grill and the hot pastrami and corned beef. He felt like one of Pavlov's dogs, drooling in anticipation.

They sat down and John said, "I have some good news for you."

His Dad said, "Let me guess. You finally got a job with those fancy diplomas I helped pay for."

John ignored the comment and continued, "You're in the ballpark. I actually started my own biotech company."

His father looked at him, waiting for the joke to be over and said, "Wait a minute. You, without any money, not even a pot to piss in, started a company? Let me make another guess, you need some money from me. Sorry, but the well is dry. I'm not exactly in a position to be your bank anymore. You're grown and on your own on this one, bud."

John paused for effect before saying, "No I don't need your money. I already have investors. The financing's in place, we already picked out space and will be moving into the office in the next few weeks. Like I told you, tonight dinner's on me."

His father's face revealed a look of doubt as he considered what John had said. That expression meant one thing, his Dad's B.S. meter had tripped. He was analyzing what John had told him and it ran counter to his common sense. He could almost hear his father's wheels spinning. How does this kid have the balls to think someone would back him in some crazy venture? Why would any legitimate businessman back a kid with nothing but an idea – no track record, no credit history, no real history of any kind, other than a history of going to school?

His father, incredulous, said, "Tell me more."

So John did. He went into the details about Artie's involvement, the meetings with the financiers, and about Kolb Kravath's offer, without discussing the specific dollar amount of the commitment. He also told him about Betty.

John told him most of the incredible story. What John left out were all the facts pertaining to Dr. Duretts' involvement and Geneteka. He didn't mention the misappropriated research that was guaranteed to work. What John felt most guilty about was that he couldn't disclose that he would be misrepresenting Duretts' research as his own.

John explained CRISPR to his Dad, almost exactly as he had to Glen. Like Glen, his father couldn't believe what he was hearing, and at one point John pulled out his phone and typed in 'CRISPR' to show his father that what he was talking about was real.

His father just took it all in, much like when he was a Green Beret in the field – assessing the facts on the ground, and the practical aspects of what he was hearing to figure out if a plan could work or not.

After John finished, his father said, "You know, there are always things that happen, that you don't expect, to mess up the best plan. What do you suppose could muck things up when you're tampering with the genetic codes of living things? Have you given a thought about who's the one that's going to make the decision on who gets the good genes, and who doesn't? Put this in the wrong hands, and there are a lot of wrong hands in this world, believe you me, and I'm very afraid. And I don't scare easily. If what you say is right, and scientists in other countries, like terrorist countries, can use this CRISPR, then I wouldn't be so all fired up about being part of it, if I was you."

John was not surprised. Even if someone else told his father about CRISPR being the greatest thing since sliced bread, he probably would have disagreed. His father, was guided by common sense, a strong moral compass and both feet planted firmly in the past. He didn't think all the changes he'd seen in his lifetime were for the best.

His father's predictable reaction gave John some pause, but then he already had a deal with Dr. Duretts, a brilliant scientist very knowledgeable on the subject who wouldn't steer him wrong.

John's father's arms were folded across his body, when he asked, "Tell me again, why would anyone back this hare-brained scheme of yours?" Before John could answer, his father said, "Whatever you're up to, it stinks to high heaven and I hope it doesn't get you in trouble. You might think you're smarter than everybody else, college boy, but don't be so sure."

John reverted back to his high school self and said, "Whatever." But his father's words got him thinking maybe this wasn't such a good idea. Would Geneteka figure it out and sue him for every penny he made and more, and could he go to jail? Would his father read about his downfall in the newspaper and be able to say, 'I told you so.'

John thought to himself, it's not like he didn't do crazy shit when he was in the Green Berets, it's just that he never talked about it. But what if his father was right? John was unsure. He wondered, does Dr. Duretts really have it under control like he said? Again, unsure. Who to believe? It was unclear to him.

The only thing John was certain of is that the guy sitting across from of him with the mustard smear on his chin could never know the whole story. John had almost lost his appetite, but didn't want his father to grow any more suspicious. John managed to say, "You know, Dad, it's a funny thing, but biotech is like computers, investment bankers love it and anyone with even a hint of a good idea can get seed money. There are a lot of people out there with money, and they're looking for projects just like mine to make a big score." John stopped talking, and hoped his father would do the same, distracted by the food.

John thought he was in the clear a moment too soon, because his father winced and said, "Son, I hate to say it but you're not making sense. I just hope you're not going to do anything dangerous, or something that gets you into real hot water, or even prison 'cause you'd be on your own. I'm in no position to help you." John just looked away. He was confident that Dr. Duretts had his back.

52

Artie walked into Betty's office at Kolb Kravath, said, "Hi, Betty," and shook her hand. He reminded Betty of the company's summer interns. He was young, not particularly polished, and in desperate need of a new suit. Unlike those interns, his academic background wasn't very impressive, and she doubted that he'd even get an interview at Kolb Kravath.

As the office manager, he probably couldn't cause too much damage, and he might be able to minimize any anxiety John felt, so what's the harm. He could also take some of the heat off her; get the office up and running and handle the administrative part of the start-up.

Betty began by saying, "John thinks highly of you. Since you assisted him with the business presentation, and he trusts you, we want to offer you the job of Chief Administrative Officer. There will be no well-defined responsibilities, at first. Everyone will have to pitch in and do whatever is necessary."

She continued, "For the initial transition period, we would like to compensate you at a rate of $80,000 per year, based on your educational background and your limited experience. Not to worry, you're getting in on the ground floor and we will revisit everyone's role and compensation after the first 6 months."

She told Artie, "This is your chance to show us what you can do."

Artie thought he should ask for more, but decided to bide his time and do it in 6 months, like the lady said. He then said, "I accept your offer and like the title, thanks. I look forward to working with you. I'll hold you to the 6-month reassessment."

Betty thought he probably has no idea what the Chief Administrative Officer does. She smiled and said, "Go to the new office tomorrow. Talk with John and find out what needs to be done. The office still requires computer and lab equipment installations. The lab equipment should be delivered shortly. I'll see you at the office in the next few days. And remember this is a start-up, no prima donnas."

Artie said, "It's all good. Thanks." He stood up, shook her hand, and walked out of Kolb Kravath, already a richer man.

53

Betty was typing furiously to meet a deadline for the due diligence report. About an hour later, Mr. DeBerg popped his head into her office. She looked up trying to conceal any look of desperation on her face, though she could feel perspiration on her forehead.

"How are you doing, Betty?" DeBerg asked. She looked up and said "I'm trying to finish the due diligence filing for Robert." DeBerg responded, "Oh, OK then, I don't want to bother you, I just wanted to check up on that special project you're handling for me. Remember, it's high priority, I don't want it to be back-burnered."

Betty said, "Of course not." He responded, "I don't want to be disappointed on this one, so make sure you give it your full attention. If need be, let me know and I'll make sure you're freed up from any other distractions."

Hm, Betty thought, I didn't think he cared. Great, just what I need, more pressure. Even buried under her workload, she still managed to fake a smile when she said, "No problem."

54

The following day found Artie busy in the lab directing equipment installers and signing for deliveries. John was about to begin the first interviews for the various positions he needed to fill. He looked at the stack of resumes and placed Lisa's and David's on top. As for the others, he felt like just throwing them into the air, taking the ones that landed faceup, confident that all had been vetted by Betty, without a slouch in the bunch. All of the tech candidates looked qualified, and some even had some relevant experience. The office workers also looked good, at least on paper.

He grabbed a cup of coffee, then looked at his interview schedule. Betty had loaned them Camille, a secretary from her office, to assist with the start-up work. She was a middle-aged woman with two kids in college. She was no nonsense and efficient, and had booked him solid for the whole day.

Knowing he probably wouldn't remember one candidate from the next after the first few interviews, Camille emailed him the resumes, in order of their interviews, and provided him with a place for notes on each one. She also gave him a list of suggested interview questions and tips.

John wondered if he could just steal Camille as his assistant, but thought better about biting the hand that was feeding him. Then he remembered Lisa.

After the first three interviews, John felt bad that some of the candidates weren't going to make the grade. One was older and disgruntled at the current job, another couple were unemployed victims of downsizing and some were just looking for their first job. John drew a smiley face on the resume if the person might be a fit, and a plus if they had a special skill that could be helpful, then he wrote a brief descriptive note to try to remember each of those people.

The seventh interview was with Lisa. He had a few minutes before she arrived and he actually felt nervous when he refilled his coffee in the break room. As he poured the coffee, he thought to himself, she should be the one that's nervous, not me. He'd already marked her resume with a smiley face, a plus and a note, 'must hire.' He returned to the conference room and waited. Camille finally escorted Lisa into the room. She wore a navy suit and a crisp white blouse and looked professional and attractive.

Camille left and closed the door. Lisa flashed a smile and said, "Hello." John waited to respond until Camille was out of earshot, "Nice to see you again," Lisa then said, "I thought you were going to blow me off, and as you know, that would have made you-know-who unhappy."

John said, "I didn't think that you-know-who was ever supposed to be mentioned here, right?"

Lisa, embarrassed, said, "Sorry, I won't make that mistake again."

John said, "Just be careful, it's important that we be discreet. The idea is to take care of you, with shares in the company, and you work out his compensation with him. Let's try to never discuss him again, especially here."

"Anyway, I'm going to insist that you be the Administrative Assistant just below Artie, who is the Chief Administrative Officer, and above others in the office. I'll pay you a good salary with benefits. What are you making now?"

"At the coffee shop, I make $10 per hour with benefits." Lisa said.

John responded, "How does $52,000 per year sound?"

"OK," Lisa said, "but what about bonuses and the stock options I was told about?"

John glanced at the glass wall to see that no one was there and said, "Let's not talk about that either. I've been doing some research about tech companies before the bubble burst, and how they distributed pay. Just leave it to me. I'll paint you as essential to the company's operations and make sure you get those options."

Lisa looked at him and said, "Don't worry you're not going to have to cover for me. You'll find that I can carry my own weight. You have my resume in front of you. I graduated cum laude from college. Anyway, if this thing you've got going on doesn't work, I'll still gain some valuable office experience."

John hadn't actually reviewed Lisa's resume, and was surprised by her education and the honors she received. Dr. Duretts may have done him a favor, and John had likely misjudged the situation. He'd try to use her in the operation of the company. Smart and pretty, but not really his type, is a good combination, he thought.

John laughed and asked, "Why did you decide to get a high-powered job in a coffeehouse then?"

Lisa answered, "Because both of my parents were killed in a car accident my junior year of college, and I needed time to ease into a real job."

John immediately apologized, "I'm so sorry. I shouldn't have made fun of your job. Anyway, the job is yours. Call this number, ask for Camille, and tell her you'll take the job." John knew he'd broken Betty's rule, that she had to approve all hires, but he'd make a case for the exception later. He continued, "Can you start a week from Monday?"

Lisa said, "Thanks, I'll call her before 5 PM, and yes, I can start then."

After Lisa left, John walked over to Camille and said, I just made my first hire. I offered Lisa Stanley the administrative assistant position." Camille asked, "Don't you need to call Betty first?" John said, "No, I already offered it to her. When she calls back, tell her I'd like her to start a week from Monday, if possible."

Camille said, "Fine, Mr. Ordell," as she thought how much he reminded her of the men at Kolb Kravath, and all men for that matter. John had chosen the first piece of eye candy to walk through the door. He'd have to live with the consequences of that decision, not her. She wouldn't be here much longer, so let boys be boys, she thought.

The next interview was with Mr. Goldblum. He was sitting in the waiting room without much of an expression on his face. He looked even paler than the last time John saw him. John escorted him into the conference room and began with, "So why did you leave Silicon Valley?"

David matter-of-factly said, "Well, I was working as a coder when my friends and I found out that all the big tech companies colluded not to pay us any raises. They also agreed not to poach any coders from each other, so they could get away with paying us less. We sued. You might have read about it in the news. The managers said that the coders didn't know their asses from their elbows."

He continued, "Turns out, they were dead wrong. In the suit, they were caught red-handed, through various emails which they stupidly wrote to each other, agreeing not to poach each other's best and most talented engineers – thus keeping their pay below market rates. Well, anyway, I did OK with my settlement and decided to move on, and that's what brought me here."

John had heard something about it, but didn't know the specifics, or that David had been involved. Anyway, with Dr. Duretts' endorsement, it was pretty clear that he had to be a top-flight coder, and now was to be involved in John's enterprise. And John liked him, even with his quirks.

John said, "That must have sucked, but I'm glad to have you. We won't screw you like that. You'll be on the ground floor of this business. My door is always open."

David didn't react with any emotion, but said, "Thank you, I am happy to work with Dr. Duretts and you. It is challenging work, but I can tell you the results were shocking, even to Dr. Duretts."

John glanced at the door to double check and make sure it was closed. He asked, “What do you mean, the results?”

David said, “Yeah, the results with the mice. We were able to fine-tune the algorithm so it was very good at predicting the results of the CRISPR injections. It was able to determine what genes controlled what traits. The algorithm also could identify other genes on chromosomes where the CRISPR RNA would form an unwanted bond. Dr. Duretts thought this could alert us to unwanted mutations at genes we do not want to change. That is what he liked most of all. He thinks it could be able to predict effects on humans.”

David proceeded, “We were able to engineer mice in a number of ways, like to change their color, their size, their ability to learn mazes, and we even have some mice that don’t show signs of aging. Anyway, I am still tinkering with the algorithm. But Dr. Duretts is one of the most brilliant people I have ever worked with.”

John said, “Don’t worry, we’ll hire you and intend to pay you commensurate with your contributions.”

Then John gently admonished David, “I’m sorry, but please remember, never mention or talk about Dr. Duretts. He’s not supposed to have any connection with this company, or any project we work on here. OK? And never, ever use his name again, unless you are 100% sure that we are by ourselves, and even then, only if it is necessary.” John then wrote must hire on the resume and shook David’s hand.

55

John tried to reach Artie on the new office phone system. The seemingly never-ending candidate interviews were over, and now he wasn't sure if he knew how to use his phone to call someone inside the office. He called out to Camille for help and she showed him which buttons to press to make an interoffice call.

Artie answered and said, "Hey. What do you need?" John said, "Can you come to my office? We have to meet with the Internet security guys."

Artie said, "I'll be right up."

As he walked into John's office, Artie said, "I like the new digs." John said, "Did you square everything away with Betty for your employment?" Artie shook his head yes, and John responded, "Good."

John changing course said, "These IT guys will be arriving shortly to discuss setting up our computers, servers, Internet and security systems. Do you know anything about this stuff?" Artie, a little hesitant said, "Sure."

John said, "Great, give me a minute and I'll meet you in the big conference room, we're meeting with three companies today. Can you get the list from Camille?"

Artie saw Camille. She said, "Good morning," barely able to hide her feelings about him. She thought he looked like a baby in a $150 suit. It was hard to take him seriously, but one never knows, maybe these two would fumble through and make a go of it. She gave Artie the list of IT security companies he and John would be meeting with, and who would be representing those companies.

Artie walked into the conference room. He sat at the side of the table and waited. John joined him about 5 minutes later. Artie gave him the document Camille had prepared. John said, "Listen, I've had to deal with a lot of problems the last few days, I interviewed a number of candidates, hired two already and I sure need your help."

Just then, Camille came to the door and announced, "Mr. Thompson and his team are here to see you." John asked her to bring them in.

Dan Thompson was accompanied by two associates. All three looked like IBM clones. Thompson was clean-shaven with a recent haircut and wore a blue suit with a white shirt and rep stripe tie. The other two guys, a couple of decades younger, looked like carbon copies, dressed in grey suits, white shirts and rep stripe ties.

After introducing himself and his colleagues, he said, "Before I begin the presentation, I'd like to tell you a little about IT Select Services, Inc. We treat each of our customers like they're our only customer. Big or small, we give you the personal touch. Betty Rhoads provided me with information about your company so I have a good idea of the systems you may need, and I fashioned my presentation accordingly."

Thompson knew that the packages he sold were tailored to the size of the company and what it could afford to pay. His company sold a great product and it was reputedly the best on the market, so he continued with his time-tested pitch, which he knew by heart.

Thompson began his presentation, "We have installed systems at the Pentagon, for the Federal Government and numerous multinational corporations throughout the world." He continued, "We can guarantee that our firewalls will hold back the most sophisticated cyber criminals, the best hackers your competitors can muster, and will protect you from industrial espionage."

That's all John needed to hear. He zoned out even before the lights were dimmed to begin the powerpoint presentation. He recalled the conversation he'd had with Dr. Duretts, and his comment that a little industrial espionage wouldn't necessarily be a bad thing. Anyway, these guys were out – way too professional.

John accepted their claim that they were the best. When the presentation was finished, he and Artie asked a few questions, thanked them for their proposal and John told them he'd let them know when he made a decision.

After the first dog and pony show, Artie visibly impressed said, "Those guys really know their stuff. What did you think?" John said, "Pricey and a little too corporate, if you know what I mean. I hope the next group's more our speed, but I won't make up my mind until I see what the others offer."

"OK," Artie said, "but I still think those guys had the juice. We have 45 minutes 'til the next group gets here."

The next IT group arrived on time but couldn't have been more different than their competitors. The leader, Matt Reid, looked like he just graduated college. His two associates looked even younger. The female associate looked youngest of all, and was dressed in a conservative top paired with a skirt that was just a little too short. She wore large dark-framed glasses, which made her appear intelligent, as well as good-looking. Was she a model hired to accompany these guys to drum up business, or did she really know something about the product? John wasn't sure.

While John and Artie knew Reid's company was pretty new, they didn't know everything about its short history. Reid had worked for IBM for 16 months and hated every minute of his tenure. When he quit, his uncle bankrolled him with $80,000 to help with his start-up. Reid supplemented the investment with his own savings and the earnings from a few odd jobs, until his college buddy from Dartmouth began working with him.

His buddy's uncle was a Congressman, and helped them obtain a contract to provide IT help to Federal government workers. His buddy lost interest and decided to pursue other opportunities, and Reid subsequently won other projects providing small DC law firms with tech advice.

Reid introduced himself and his associates, Kim and Josh. He said, "I began IT Factor Solutions a year ago. Since then, we've grown into a company with a number of contracts. Though we specialize in smaller operations and have set up a number of companies from inception to execution, the Federal government is among our clients. Our software engineers are from top schools and are current with the most cutting-edge technology. We give high quality personalized service for a fraction of what you'd pay our competitors."

He continued, "We offer different packages for different levels of security and can tailor our services to meet your specific needs. We require information about the computer systems you'll be using, how many people are involved and how they'll be using your system, as well as who should have access to what information. My associates will take the information you provide, and we'll customize a plan for you.

Reid had read about firewalls, had set one up as a classroom exercise, but hadn't done it professionally. His associates had limited experience as well, but he was confident that they would be able to come up to speed sufficiently to implement an effective firewall for John's fledgling company.

John was glad that Betty wasn't at this meeting because Reid's group would have been out from the get-go. She would have thought they lacked experience and more than likely would have disliked Kim, based on her attire alone. John thought they were probably capable of setting up an adequate security system to pass muster. He hoped it would be good enough, but not too good.

John answered Kim's questions about the business, its needs, search engine requirements and other rudimentary issues, necessary for IT Factor Solutions to be able to provide an estimate for the work that needed to be done. Artie and Josh sat in the meeting, almost as observers, without adding anything.

Finally, Reid said, "We have enough information to analyze your needs and will follow up in the next day or two with a quote containing all the particulars. I'll call you after that to answer any questions you may have." Kim has your email address. Is that where we should send it?" John said, "Yes, I look forward to receiving your proposal."

They stood up and all shook hands, then the meeting was over. After they were gone, Artie looked at John and said, "I don't know about Matt and Josh, but I could certainly see working very closely with Kim. She looks like a tall glass of water." Even though John couldn't agree with him more, he reminded Artie, "This isn't a frat house, this is a business and you really need to act that way."

Artie, annoyed at being dressed down by John, said, "OK, I was only kidding. I guess you're right, boss," as he thought to himself, this guy is too much. Artie revisited his doubts about the enterprise. Heck, even with serious backing, the place would probably fail. Artie thought if things got bad, he could just leave. In the meantime, he couldn't believe how full of himself John had already become. He acted like the place was already a booming success.

John said, "I liked this group better than the earlier guys. They seem competent and more in sync with us. I have another meeting I have to get to. Do you think you can handle the next group by yourself? I really don't think we need to talk with anyone else, but if you think I should see them, call me on my cell phone and I'll join you."

Artie said, "It's under control," although he didn't like being ordered around, especially not by an ingrate who would be nowhere without his business plan.

Betty was happy to take a break from Kolb Kravath and called John. She was relieved that things were well underway, that the office and lab were pretty much set up, and John was in the final stages of staffing his operation. Betty said, "Like I said when we talked, I had a few minutes and wanted to talk to you to see how it was going."

Pleased with his progress, John smiled and said, "We're making headway. Most of the equipment's been delivered, and I think we can get most of everything else we need in the next couple of weeks. Once you authorize all the hires, and the computers are delivered we should be in business." Betty was pleased and said, "Thanks for the good news," then hung up the phone.

56

John and Artie were in the apartment watching the Wizards on TV when Glen came home. He'd just finished his last final in Contracts. He was tired, but still had adrenaline buzzing through his system.

John said, "Haven't seen you in a while. How's it going?"

Glen answered, "I'm done, just finished my last final. I feel like I've been living in the library the last few weeks."

John got up to go to the bathroom and Artie noticed that John was wearing new Cole Haan loafers, without socks. Until now, he hadn't thought of John as the kind of guy who was brand conscious, or one to follow the vagaries of fashion.

John asked Glen how his tests went. Glen answered, "Hard to say. In law school, it's very subjective. If you think you did well, you've probably done poorly. I have a friend who's a second year who told me he was sure he failed contracts, and he ended up with one of the highest grades in the class. He told me another guy who always had the right answers in class, got a C+. So, I'll just have to wait until grades are posted."

John said, "That sucks. In science classes, if you learned the material and got the right answer you could count on an A. It didn't matter who was grading your paper."

Glen said, "In law school, it's more fluid. There doesn't seem to be an exact answer, or there's usually more than one answer – and persuasion and presentation means everything."

Glen went into the kitchen and got three beers, one for each of them. Glen immediately chugged three-quarters of one of them. John and

Artie were struck by the same idea, that Glen might just become a great lawyer; he was already on the road to drinking like one.

Glen asked, “So what’s the deal with your new company?”

John said, “It’s going pretty well. The financing’s in place, Artie’s set up the office and lab and I’ve been doing non-stop research.”

Glen looking into his beer, like a crystal ball said, “So are you going to be engineering six-foot flies, or bus-sized amoebas any time soon? I’m envisioning something like DrugCo’s ape-opotamus from the Drew Carey show.”

John replied, “Yeah, coincidentally, look out for the giant amoeba taking a swim in the bathtub and the ape-opotamus snuggling under your bedsheets.”

“All joking aside,” John said, “I think that there’s some promising research on mice and rats. There have been some experiments with mice where we change their characteristics and others where it doesn’t seem like they are aging. Time will tell for sure.”

Glen, intrigued said, “Bet you could bank some serious money if you found the cure for aging; although it’s not like you’d be finding the cure for not being able to get a boner – someone already beat you to that.”

John laughed and said, “There’s some research on CRISPR that we’re doing to reverse or at least slow the aging process, by turning on and off genes that make it happen. Imagine living to be 200 years old and at the age of 180 being as healthy as today’s fifty-year-old.”

Artie chimed in, “If you do that, you’ll have every billionaire investor in the world begging to give you money. I don’t know a person on the planet who wouldn’t want to buy what you’d be selling.”

Glen said, “I don’t know about that. Maybe it’s the Catholic in me, but if God, or whatever you believe in, wanted people to live to be 200, they’d already live that long. I don’t think it’s right.”

Artie, in a ball-busting mood, said, “Isn’t everlasting life what the

Catholic Church has been selling for 2,000 years? I think they converted a lot of lost souls with that promise."

Glen replied, "Artie, you'll probably burn in hell for that comment, but if something goes wrong with John's research, prayer might be your only option."

Artie continued and said, "You're just sore that he didn't find the cure for a small dick, so he could help you out."

John laughed and thought Artie's idea might be even more lucrative than a cure for aging.

Glen said, "Speak for yourself, a-hole. I just believe that you don't need to mess with these things. After all, why would living so long be a good thing? But I think you're right, many of the baby boomers would jump on the opportunity to be immortal. They're not called the 'me generation' for nothing."

John reflected for a minute. Maybe he was onto something. If they could convince investors with a lot of money that they had viable research on the cure for aging, the investment potential would be limitless.

So, that's what Dr. Duretts was getting at, when they discussed the weak firewall – this would be a perfect way to maximize the asking price for their company. A cure for aging could dovetail well with the concept of a cure for balding – and greatly increase any takeover offer.

57

Artie was in his office looking at the calendar, in disbelief that AlgoGene was already six months old. They had four scientists, fourteen lab technicians and two salesmen and a functioning website to sell their wares and services online.

A short year ago, he couldn't have anticipated that this is what he'd be doing and where he'd be. Funny how you could never be sure of what twists and turns life had in store for you.

Although he had a role in the company's inception, he hadn't foreseen the company branching out in this new direction, collecting people's genetic information by mail and analyzing their genealogy for a fee. Their ancestry would be traced and they would be tested for genetic diseases. Customers were assured that AlgoGene would protect their personal information.

Artie's job now included developing a privacy plan for the company. This made it his responsibility to hire an attorney to look into the issue and determine what guidelines would be appropriate.

The lawyer he retained charged $400 an hour and advised that the Food and Drug Administration could regulate genetic tests but chose not to; the Centers for Medicine and Medicaid Services could require proficiency testing for labs, but did not; and the Federal Trade Commission had some power over the regulation of false claims and could assert power over the genetic testing industry, but did not.

There wasn't much of a regulatory scheme to deal with now. Maybe later, but the only thing to do, if you had enough money, was to hire lobbyists to make sure any new rules would favor your business model and wouldn't be too intrusive. And it paid to do it now, to build relationships for later. Artie would let John and Betty know, but they would have to decide.

Artie occasionally thought about Lisa's role at AlgoGene. She was cute, but he wondered how she'd moved into the inner circle so fast. She wasn't instrumental in getting the place up and running, didn't come up with any brilliant ideas like offering the gene profiling services to the public (that had been Glen's idea), and really hadn't made any significant contributions as far as he could tell.

So why did John spend so much time with her at the office? She was attractive, and reasonably intelligent, but nothing so special. And her personality wasn't that great. Anyway, John insisted that their relationship was purely professional, and Artie took him at his word.

Artie dismissed his negative thoughts about Lisa as he considered how John had generously given him a 2% stake in the company, something he was sure Lisa hadn't gotten. This meant an even nicer bonus at year-end. So let Lisa have her tete-a-tetes with the boss-man. Artie was confident that he'd gotten the better end of the deal.

58

Artie was developing friendships with some of the technicians and scientists from work. When they went out for drinks after work one night, they told Artie that they couldn't believe how much theoretical research was pouring out of John's brain. He had been providing them with very specific notes to follow. Initially, they didn't exactly grasp the direction of the research, but lately it was becoming abundantly clear.

The research involved some very specific mapping of genetic information they received from clients who paid them to analyze their genes and heredity. Clients received a 50% discount if they were willing to fill out an exhaustive five-page questionnaire, providing a lot of personal information and a color photograph, for verification. Not surprisingly, almost everyone took the discount.

All a customer needed to do was swab their cheek, put the swab into a plastic tube and send it to the company. AlgoGene would then determine if the person had genes for a multitude of different diseases and conditions, such as cancers, MS, diabetes, and heart disease.

The tests were so precise that they could even discern a person's ability to taste bitter food, whether they had wet or dry ear wax (though most people could probably figure that out on their own), and Artie's favorite – whether you had restless leg syndrome.

Artie knew they weren't making a fortune on this market, but it provided data for their talented programmer to fine-tune his algorithm for analyzing genes. When this was accomplished, the next step would be to complete the CRISPR research which was the most promising and profitable area of their work.

David was cross-referencing the information acquired from their customers to perfect the gene mapping ability of his algorithm using AlgoGene's supercomputer. His time was dedicated to constantly reviewing and tweaking the algorithm. He thought it might be worthwhile to purchase data from Internet companies to supplement the customers' profiles, but they hadn't done it yet.

They were moving ahead with utilizing the computer program to analyze mice and plants and employing CRISPR to edit their DNA to affect specific traits. The lab techs and scientists had been required to sign NDA's before they began working, swearing them to secrecy, but they were still able to discuss the company's R&D with Artie, since he was part of the management team.

One fascinating aspect of the research that they were able to share was that David had been able to locate eighteen different gene sites which affected mouse intelligence. They had actually created super intelligent mice by editing those gene sites using CRISPR.

The negative outcome of the process was that it changed the mice brains so that they forgot what they knew before those gene sites were edited. The positive outcome was that they could learn tremendous amounts of new information quickly. The altered mice could learn a maze in just one run through, which typical mice could not. And that was just one of the areas where they were editing the genes of mice.

It sounded like science fiction to Artie, but if this same technology could be applied to human beings, priceless wouldn't begin to describe its value. At the same time he wondered, were these scientists prepared for the consequences of playing with this kind of fire?

59

John liked to start his mornings with a Starbucks' coffee, ESPN and Yahoo news on his phone. Often Lisa would join him in his office and they would discuss 'his' research. He explained what CRISPR did, how it could be applied, and the potential application to all types of potential maladies including balding. They began emailing back and forth about what they talked about in his office, as the research was slowly bearing fruit.

Their emails also discussed the problems with the patent fight between the two scientists who'd both claimed they invented CRISPR. John specifically mentioned that hundreds of millions of dollars was behind each side of the ongoing patent dispute, and added that the new technique that he developed shouldn't be subject to the current CRISPR patent dispute, according to AlgoGene's lawyers.

John's emails contained precise details of the progress, sometimes exaggerated, about techniques and computer models they discovered on how specific genes expressed themselves in plants, mice and people. They discussed commercial applications for food or for curing diseases.

They discussed their brilliant programmer, David, who had written a software program able to identify specific genes in mice that dovetailed with CRISPR, that could soon be applicable to human beings. They frequently discussed the use of his algorithm, and how it was being perfected over time. John made sure his emails contained too little detail for any of the techniques to ever be reverse-engineered, or tested by anyone else.

Lisa's emails discussed Internet research she did, regarding their cure for balding and the competition. John responded that the toxicity testing was coming up negative. She calculated how much profit the company stood to make as she compared market shares for products, which didn't always cure hair loss, that were already on the market. She proposed marketing ideas, including possible commercials.

It was mouthwatering stuff, especially if it fell into the right monied hands.

60

Bill Moore was sitting in his office reviewing market research on potential targets for hostile takeovers. He wasn't happy with what he saw. The markets were tanking, he'd had some bad luck and was overdue for a big score.

An 80-inch flat panel 4K TV was positioned over his credenza. Bloomberg News played all day. To his left was a handcrafted bookcase with a number of first editions which he'd probably never bother to read. He was content with the words and numbers which flowed through his computer monitor. His only break in the workday was his occasional peek at golf.com to check how his favorite, Jordan Speith, was doing, to see the latest golf toy, and to get the tip of the day from a pro.

Today, there would be no solace from golf.com. Instead, he had the itch he usually got when something big was about to break.

Bill got up and started pacing the length of his corner office in his custom Alan David suit, with a light plaid pattern with a hint of blue. His impeccably matched silk tie was tied in a perfect Windsor knot. He barely noticed the mug his son got him for being the world's greatest golfer, the photographs of him and his third wife – whom he jokingly referred to as his second trophy wife – and the sign in his bookcase that said 'the beatings will continue until morale improves.'

He asked his secretary, "Can you find Azim and bring him into my office?" The secretary responded, "Yes, sir" and promptly located him.

A moment later, Azim walked through the door. Bill liked Azim. He had a mathematical mind, with limited people skills, so posed no threat to Bill's position in the company. Azim was a serious numbers cruncher and knew a lot of people in the economic trenches – people at the Fed, at commercial banks and at investment banks. He knew how to get information from his sources, often friends from his days at MIT, where he had been an engineering student.

Azim's story was similar to others Bill had heard. He'd begun as an engineering student but later became enamored with business after taking classes in business law and economics. His natural aptitude for mathematics was as helpful in business analysis as it was in engineering, but Azim found a certain allure in the elements of risk and, sometimes pure luck, that went into forecasting what the markets would do in the future. That passion effectively ended Azim's parent's dreams of his becoming a doctor.

Azim also had the gift of being in the right place at the right time. He always seemed to have the inside track on information that no one else could get, and effectively used it in his complex models. Bill relied on Azim's work and it had paid off handsomely.

Azim's forecasts were critical to someone like Bill. A guy's guy with unremarkable mathematical skills, but an uncanny ability to make money on trades and to follow his gut feelings about distressed companies ripe for takeover. His analysis of companies was rarely wrong; a skill he traced back to when he was an associate at one of the biggest bankruptcy law firms in New York.

He, too, loved the element that luck played in his work. He was a gambler at heart and loved to play hunches. As a kid he enjoyed going to the track where he evaluated the jockeys, the horses and the track and won more than he lost. He had a fondness for poker and played it when he had time. He recalled junkets to Atlantic City, when it was still good. He remembered spending more than one all-nighter playing Texas Hold'em in a casino before leaving in the early morning to play a round of golf, and afterward collapsing in a state of bliss. But now he needed to focus because he had that 'can't lose' feeling again.

Bill said to Azim, "I was reading about biotech companies that were using something called CRISPR technology to come up with new ways of fighting diseases and curing, God knows what. My gut tells me that the hard work funded by the government in the human genome project is already over, and some of these smaller biotech companies may be in a position to make a killing."

Bill continued, "Can you take a look into which companies might be profitable with low market capitalization. I'm interested in companies considered best in breed, you know the drill, low operating costs, good management, but a great deal of upside potential. I'd like to take a hard look at these companies. Be sure to leave no stone unturned."

Azim said, "I'll get on it tonight and keep you looped in on my progress. Any particular companies, or specific areas you want me to concentrate on?"

Bill thought about it for a moment, then decided it was best to give Azim free rein and said, "No, I trust your judgment."

Azim liked when Bill left it open ended. He enjoyed working with Bill, a down to earth guy who was very good at what he did, and not a pretentious prick like a lot of the guys in this business. Azim said, "I'm on it. Let me know if there's anything else you need."

Bill said, "That should be it for now, but that reminds me – great work on the Semotech merger. Your input made all the difference." Azim nodded and walked out of his boss' office with an extra bounce in his step.

61

Azim was sitting in the Star Café on 32nd Street near his apartment in Manhattan. He liked lounging in a comfortable chair, coffee within reach, and Internet access.

He turned on his computer and accessed the public Internet connection. He then changed his mind and switched to his company MiFi. As he got online, he watched two girls sitting at another table. One was a blond and the other had black hair with deep blue eyes. He couldn't decide which one he preferred.

His focus shifted back to work once his connection was made. He began a Google search for biotech companies. Most seemed like old, established, stodgy, highly capitalized, pharmaceutical firms without much upside potential. He knew they weren't what his boss was interested in. One or two had been taken over by huge conglomerates after they began the FDA approval process for selling one drug or another. Azim thought that's the absolute wrong time to enter the fray.

To maximize earnings, you needed to know when a company was on the verge of a breakthrough. That is when they're most vulnerable and in the greatest need of money, and are willing to sell out for what they perceive as big bucks, but before they actually hit the big one. But how could he lay his hands on that kind of inside information, the only kind of information likely to pay off?

Azim continued searching the web for all things biotech. He saw many ads for a variety of products, and finally found a website for

AlgoGene Corporation, a place that would test your DNA and tell you your genetic predispositions.

Azim was afraid what this would show about him. His family was a hodgepodge of genetic detritus from around the world. One grandmother had been chased across Europe before making her way to America. One great grandfather left Ireland to escape the potato famine. Other relatives were from places in the Middle East.

His DNA might possibly break the machine.

As he read further, customers had to swab their cheek or spit into a tube and mail it to the lab, which was located somewhere in Maryland.

He continued clicking into parts of their website until he found information on the company and its personnel. The employees were all young, perhaps a good sign. They were branching out into areas including gene mapping and medical applications for genetic research, and CRISPR. It definitely warranted a closer look.

Azim had been an accomplished hacker in his college days, and thought it could be the only good way to get the inside scoop on the small company. He was a little rusty, but he'd give it a try. If they had an effective firewall then he might not be able to hack their system. Worst case scenario, he'd call on his friends, who prided themselves on being able to hack into almost anywhere.

He ordered another caramel latte and then accessed the software his friend Jason had given him for just such an occasion. He remembered Jason using the software to take over a professor's computer to steal the midterm test, and then getting an A on the exam. The software allowed him to type commands to the business' computer remotely. He didn't need to do that, but he was curious to see what this band of young people were up to. He had done it in the past with great success, making him look almost prescient to his bosses.

Azim found a list of email addresses for the employees, and then sent a phishing email to each of them. It would only take one scientist, one executive, one employee to open up the attachment to launch the software virus. Incredibly, it took less than a minute before his email caught the eye of an employee, who clicked on to see the pictures which infected AlgoGene's whole system.

The program then attempted to use different permutations to unlock passwords allowing access to the entire system. With two strokes of the computer keyboard, Azim gained entry to AlgoGene's server which permitted him to view the email account of the founder, a guy named John Ordell. It couldn't possibly be this easy. He started getting the feeling that it was amateur hour at AlgoGene.

He noticed that the girls at the other table were still there, and he glanced over every now and then.

He looked more closely at the emails to see what was actually under the hood of this fledgling startup. He picked an email from two months ago to someone named Lisa. He clicked it open and began reading. Jesus Christ, he felt like shouting as his latte nearly went flying across the room. He squinted his eyes as he thought that this must be a joke.

The email staring him in the face seemed to suggest that they had determined the genetic site that caused baldness. He read from John, "Using David's algorithm, I have located the site for the genes that cause balding using CRISPR technology, I can stop the gene from expressing itself and obtain a complete reversal of the balding process. I believe that the cure can be applied using my new Cas9 technique, which we will patent. We may be able to use it topically before we make it in an injectable CRISPR format."

Azim read a newer email, sent a few weeks later, that stated they were doing trials to check the toxicity of the particular gene using CRISPR on mice and it appeared OK.

He moved on to a series of emails in John's in-box from someone named Lisa. They discussed the potential market for balding products and the profits to be made, estimated in the billions of dollars, especially if the product worked 100% of the time. She also noted that if it was done topically the product would have to be purchased over and over again, which would create a limitless stream of profits.

Azim jumped to a more recent email from Ordell, which was longer than some of the others. John was closely following the market trends for their gene test kits and with the information collected from those kits, they were better able to isolate genes connected with plaque build-up and heart disease. Since those diseases typically presented in people in their fifties or sixties, it stood to reason that, like balding, the onset was also controlled by genes that could be effected by CRISPR technology.

Ordell hypothesized that if they could locate the genes for traits which were brought on at a certain time in a person's life, those genes could be turned off, and the heart disease or other malady would be prevented. Even more astounding, he suggested that by turning off various genes as someone ages, one could possibly reverse the aging process, thereby allowing someone to live to the age of 150 or more, especially if the person's physical weaknesses were accurately assessed.

Azim actually exclaimed out loud, "Holy shit." He said it so loud that the blonde girl actually turned to locate the source of the outburst.

Next, Ordell wrote he was compiling a list of genes, which specifically related to old age, and was in the process of identifying their sites, including breakdown of muscle mass and tone, calcium absorption, heart disease, macular degeneration, hardening of the arteries, deterioration of the immune system, and an array of other health problems.

Ordell mentioned he was also curious about telomeres. He wanted to investigate the possibility of editing telomeres, pointing out that as people age, the length of their telomeres typically shortens, and people with longer telomeres outlive people with short telomeres. Ordell had written, "This may also bear fruit in a search for a slowing or a cure for some or all of the aging process."

As Azim perused the private emails, the same themes were repeated.

They had a cure for balding and were hot on the trail for more breakthroughs. He read an email from a lab worker to someone named Artie, stating that John was producing so many experiments using a new CRISPR process that it was hard to keep up. He described Ordell's detailed notes on the research as 'incredible.'

Azim was now copying portions of the emails furiously. He knew he'd have to do some research on his own and follow-up with independent scientists to corroborate what he was seeing, before he could share his treasure trove with Bill Moore. Azim also knew he had to move fast, because he couldn't possibly be the only one looking into AlgoGene Corporation. He was also in disbelief that this naked gem was just out there with no real protection from prying eyes. Well, Ordell wouldn't be the first scientist who was positively brilliant, and incredibly stupid at the same time. Anyway, Azim would have to hurry if he hoped to impress his boss.

Azim snapped his computer shut, smiled at the girls he had previously been ogling, and then walked out the door.

62

Wang Wei was the deputy secretary of science and technology for the Chinese government. He had been deeply involved in the Chinese CRISPR program from its outset, although now he was with the clandestine group outside the public eye that did not publish their findings.

He recalled that publicizing research findings had not gone well in the recent past. A team of researchers at Guangzhou Medical University tried to genetically modify human embryos but the result was horrible unexpected gene mutations and the embryos were all destroyed. Another study, appearing on YouTube, reported findings that gene editing made a child HIV resistant, but it was unclear if the results could be reproduced. Human testing of gene editing generated a lot of condemnation on the international front, and there was much negative publicity.

There were some good outcomes in university experiments where animals were test subjects. There was success when specific genes in monkeys were altered, but only a few of those experiments worked and the results were published. There were too many unknowns about the consequences of using the technology in such a way. So the decision was made to conduct further experiments in secret.

There were many technical issues to be worked out before the technology should be applied to humans, but Wang Wei was feeling a lot of pressure from those in charge. There was talk of testing on criminals or peasants. There were ongoing discussions about using the technology for military purposes, to make soldiers faster and stronger. A number of important people were interested in curing health problems or even curtailing aging, which the scientists theorized could be addressed by the new technology.

Up and coming younger party members saw the technology as a vehicle for producing offspring with exceptional abilities, even better than their own, so the next generation of rulers would be better and smarter. But the scientists in China, no matter how well trained – even those schooled at prestigious institutions in the United States or Europe – were still unable to devise techniques for safely using CRISPR on humans. But Wei knew his superiors were not patient.

They were emboldened to push the technology to its limit when they learned about successful research on animals, like the beagles with double the amount of muscle mass. A Harvard University professor postulated that the same gene editing technology could be used to further enhance the dogs, by making them smarter or extending their lifespans.

Such theories only amplified the expectations of party bosses. They demanded more of this kind of useful research and not excuses. Further, because the research was being conducted worldwide, it shouldn't be hard to discover if anyone was on the right track to discovering the answers.

Wei was admonished by a high-level politician to, "Use whatever means are necessary, including PLA Unit 61398." That fifty-five year old politician didn't want to meet his father's fate, to die of early onset Alzheimer's. So, Wei met with the head of PLA Unit 61398, and asked them to hack companies in the USA, Europe, and Japan to uncover any secrets that could jumpstart their knowledge of CRISPR technology and how it could be applied to human beings.

Wei doubted the existence of any such data, especially from those countries, since their governments opposed human testing unless safety could be all but guaranteed. Otherwise, they would consider it unethical and/or illegal for companies to experiment on people. In those places, testing CRISPR technology on human beings would likely end up in criminal prosecution.

The PLA unit had hacked into Northrop Grumman, Yahoo, and Dow Chemical for much smaller stakes. So, it should be a piece of cake for them to breach the security systems in place to protect smaller, less sophisticated businesses. The question was, would they find anything worth the effort?

63

John and Lisa stood in the security line at BWI airport. He was wearing new slacks, an expensive sweater and carried a Burberry trenchcoat. He looked like he just posed for the cover of GQ magazine. He had an expensive looking haircut, which was probably part of a purposeful makeover.

Both carried their computers as carry-ons. John's bag contained one of the offline computers, as well as the one he used to connect to the Internet. Lisa's bag also held her old Nook tablet, which was loaded with magazines and an e-book. John's laptop was loaded with research papers and some of his 'own' research that he was going to read on the plane. Lisa figured it would be a long process to get through security, especially since they were going to China.

She recalled how happy John was when he was invited to speak at the CRISPR convention in Macau. She was pleased when he asked her, rather than Artie, to accompany him. Most of the authorities on CRISPR would be in attendance. If the technology wasn't so interesting, it would've probably been a snoozefest. But this was more like a Star Trek convention only with real science, and without the wierdos in costumes.

Lisa expected the hotels in Macau to be beautiful. She'd read that the biggest and best hotel companies had built there, and it had been a gaming capital since the 1800's. They were staying in the Grand Lisboa Hotel, which was centrally located. It was not the new Winn hotel, or the Ritz-Carlton, but it looked good and had all the amenities, including a gym.

They'd be there for four days. The whole thing was comped by the Chinese government since John was giving a presentation on developments in CRISPR. It seemed strange, but why look a gift horse in the mouth? Anyway, there were many Chinese scientists doing CRISPR research and so far they had done research on dogs, monkeys, and embryos. When she was working at the coffeeshop, she couldn't have foreseen that she'd soon be traveling business-class to China. It could have been the fortune inside a fortune cookie. Thank you, Cousin Alan.

They would be taking an Air China flight out of BWI airport. Once on the plane, they settled into their seats and fastened their seatbelts. The flight attendant, a petite Asian woman in a tailored uniform, glanced at them and thought that they were a good-looking couple. After the safety demonstration, John and Lisa started reading. Lisa was reading Cosmo on her Nook. John was organizing research related to the DNA sites predicted by the algorithm that dealt with medical disorders associated with aging, such as muscular breakdown and lowering of steroid levels, elevated cholesterol, hardening of the arteries and Alzheimer's.

John entered notes in his offline computer regarding theories and potential research for DNA sites suspected of causing autism, muscular dystrophy and activating the aging process. He extrapolated to other animals from the findings predicted by the algorithm for the mice, which was able to successfully anticipate their diseases, size, color, weight and even ability to run mazes.

He described a protocol to test his theories and algorithm on higher level animals, most notably chimps, which share about 98% of their DNA with humans. With the primate research protocol complete, he expected testing to begin soon.

John's notes reflected great confidence in David and that he was on the right track to perfecting the algorithm that was so productive. The raw data had been entered into the computer and the results were obvious, even if not yet peer reviewed.

Their research strongly suggested that they would be able to locate the genes for thousands of human traits using the algorithm. Moreover, the heredity testing offered by AlgoGene generated hundreds of thousands of test subjects who willingly supplied their genetic information so they could save a hundred bucks.

John highlighted that the computer program could check all the base pairs on the 25,000 genes to see where else the particular Cas9 molecule might connect to other DNA sites. It was a way to predict potential unintended consequences, which would make the testing and treatment undoubtedly safer.

He further enhanced his notes with log entries concerning the use of CRISPR to cure balding, how the algorithm found the site, but without giving up the actual formulas or the algorithm. It all made for interesting reading, particularly for someone with money to invest.

A couple of days before John and Lisa left for Macao, IT Factor Solutions, AlgoGene's Internet security company, advised them that their system had been breached. Hackers had gotten into AlgoGene's server and viewed emails and PDFs. Obviously, someone was watching and might try to get a closer look at his research.

For these reasons John was glad he'd brought the offline computer and that he was beefing up the details on the research, so that any prying eyes would be amply rewarded. A trip like this would provide the perfect opportunity for someone attempting to steal intellectual property from AlgoGene.

Throughout the entire plane ride John and Lisa didn't speak much. She was absorbed in her Nook, and John was writing on his laptop and reviewing printouts in his bag.

It didn't matter to John, that they were in their own worlds, but he still preferred traveling with someone. As he worked, he would occasionally glance at Lisa, reading magazine articles or sleeping sweetly, like she didn't have a care in the world. If all goes as planned, she probably won't, he thought. She knew she owned a pretty good share of AlgoGene, since she signed all the paperwork transferring the stock.

Before the plane touched down, the flight attendant walked through the aisle a final time before she gave instructions on disembarking. As she passed John and Lisa, she thought, even though they look young, they must have been together for a long time because they barely spoke a word to each other during the lengthy flight.

64

When the airplane's door finally opened, the passengers started walking down the jetway to customs. Most passengers had been warned that they were traveling to a communist country and in the post 9/11 world it could still be a hassle, even in Macau.

John and Lisa were unaware that the head of security for the Advanced Persistent Threat Group, Wang Jie, was monitoring their Air China flight. Wang knew their arrival time and gate number; he even knew what they were wearing when they boarded the plane.

From Wang's years in military intelligence, he knew to leave as little to chance as possible and that there was nothing like intel directly from the source. He liked what was happening at this fellow's biotech company, at least as reported by Wang's hackers. He also needed access to the information contained on the laptops which were not connected to the Internet. As of now they were opaque to him, and likely held the code for the algorithm.

His sources told him the scientist was traveling with more than one computer, so the possibilities seemed good. Wang also wanted to meet the young scientist, size him up with his own eyes, and get him talking about his work.

He transmitted photographs and descriptions of John and Lisa to the customs officials, and told them exactly what he needed. Wang estimated ten minutes with the bags and computer to download everything on both the girl's and scientist's computers, and to copy anything else that was relevant. He even paid a small 'tip' to the people on duty at the customs station. This was to ensure they wouldn't screw it up.

John and Lisa waited for what seemed like an eternity before the bag carousel started to move and the bags came in to view. It felt good to be standing after the long flight. As they looked around them, they appreciated the beauty and newness of the Macau International Airport. It was good to see where all the money from Americans' 'made in China' purchases was being spent.

Finally, they both saw their bags and John pulled them off the carousel when they got to them. "Now we need to go through customs," he said.

A porter helped wheel their bags over to the customs area. They had their passports out and proceeded to the next customs officer that became available. He began by asking them, "What is your purpose for traveling to Macau?" They both answered, "For business and tourism." He asked them, "Where are you staying?" and both said simultaneously, "The Lisboa Hotel." He said, "That is a very nice hotel, near excellent shopping and good for sightseeing."

Just then, a supervisor walked over and said, "We need to do a spot check of these passengers. If you will come with us, we must scan your bags and carry-on luggage. Please hand the luggage over to Customs Officer Xoa."

Concerned, John said, "These are computers, what type of scan are you using?" "Don't worry," Officer Xoa said, "we conduct these inspections all the time and it is really quite routine. It will not damage your computer in any way." He then added a little white lie and said, "Just three or four months ago, we were able to catch a terrorist as a result of a random inspection."

Lisa said, "We were hoping to get to our hotel quickly. We're only here for four days." The supervisor responded, "It should only take five to ten minutes, and then you can be on your way. Madam, please follow that officer over there. Sir, if you would follow the officer over to the left, we'll try to get you on your way as soon as possible."

John shrugged his shoulders and went with the officer. Lisa pouted because she was tired and wanted to get to her room, but she complied, too.

Officer Xoa took the bags into the supervisor's office where two computer technicians were waiting with hard drives and flash drives to copy the computer files. Lucky for them they had previously obtained the passwords for the computers that connected to the Internet through a simple phishing exercise. They got even luckier when they discovered the password for John's offline computer was the same as his other computer.

As the techs were copying the computerized information, Xoa was copying paper documents and everything that was handwritten in John's bag. The techs then transferred the information through an encryption software developed by Wang Jie's team to their Chinese cloud account.

The Customs Office had recently gotten a high speed color copier, even though they did not normally do a lot of copying, but it was certainly helpful on this occasion. Xoa ended up copying almost everything except the material in the Nook, which they quickly assessed as containing unimportant personal information. Within the first five minutes they had copied the contents of both computers, and before the next five minutes was up, all of John's notes. As they left the office, all the participants were already figuring out how they would spend the extra cash they'd been given for their trouble.

Separately, in the other rooms, John and Lisa were being asked a similar series of questions. They were gently interrogated about their educational backgrounds, prior travel, occupation and exactly what they would be doing in Macau. Inquiries were made about where they were staying, what places they planned to visit, and how long they planned to stay. They were asked about military service. After ten minutes, they were thanked for their cooperation, and their bags were returned to them.

John walked back over to the line and saw Lisa picking up her bags. He was surprised at how fast the stop was, but figured some multinational company or sovereign fund paid off the right customs official and likely now had the contents of the 'cooked' computer books.

When Lisa noticed John, he said, "It could have been worse, we could have had to submit to a full cavity search." As they walked away, Lisa said, "Why would they pick us? We don't fit any terrorist profile." John responded, "We're just lucky I guess."

65

Deng Ngo was in a conference room on the highest floor of the building on Avenida Commercial. He could look out and see the black beach and the South China Sea from where he sat. This was the office rented by a shell company of the Chinese government. He loved the view, but knew that there was work to be done.

With a 170 IQ, Deng was one of the most exceptional students to come out of his province. He studied finance at Harvard, and at the ripe age of 36 was rumored to be on the short list for membership in the Politburo. He undoubtedly had the ear of the most powerful men in the country.

Deng ran a front for an investment company that owned the Xian Fund, specifically created to advance CRISPR to the next level, before any other government.

He assembled five scientists to review the materials pilfered at the airport. The scientists would also attend the conference, befriend the young scientist and then take the appropriate action – whatever that would be. Deng also added a young female military officer, Li Na, to the mix. She was in prime physical condition, looked almost too good to be a scientist, but had studied chemistry at university and had basic understanding of CRISPR technology.

Deng had the full, if not covert, support of the government and was authorized to do whatever was necessary. He hoped to accomplish his mission the easy way, but the hard way was also an option.

Deng moved deliberately, spoke in measured tones with the

confidence of somebody who had deep connections with people who mattered. He was the go–to guy in finance, understood biotechnology and had a tightknit group at APT to engage in cyber espionage, under the direction of Wang Jie.

His operatives were skilled at acquiring secret information from American and European companies about the results of clinical trials for new drugs, drug registration applications, and specific formulas. Up to now, it had been enough to get a leg–up for their emerging pharmaceutical industry.

That all changed with the advent of CRISPR technology. The leadership viewed CRISPR as a probable gamechanger. As such, the leadership was no longer satisfied with what had been an acceptable level of infiltration.

These leaders believed that CRISPR could be a turning point in human history. Whoever controlled the technology would take control of evolution, cure diseases, but more importantly, create a new breed of humans. As debatable as this seemed to Deng, he learned early on not to question those in power, but to simply deliver whatever it was they wanted. And they wanted this desperately.

Deng had been ordered to get his hands on whatever documents were out there, obtain any scientific corroboration and then report back on Mr. Ordell's CRISPR research. What he had initially seen was very impressive.

The notes indicated that young Mr. Ordell had already made great progress in the field of hair restoration through a process patent pending. Although his people didn't know the particulars, a contact at the US Patent Office confirmed that Ordell's company, AlgoGene had applied for a patent due to be granted at any time.

Deng's technical advisors believed it was possible to use CRISPR technology to do what Ordell claimed, however, there would be a lengthy delay bringing it to market in the US due to the FDA approval process. Deng could only imagine what would happen to a bureaucrat who was an obstacle to making such technology available in his country, especially if there was data from animal studies proving it was safe.

According to an internal email, one of the scientists at AlgoGene actually tested it on himself with excellent results. Although it was unorthodox, and probably wouldn't be publicly disclosed, the fact that it worked was very exciting if you liked the idea of making billions, possibly even trillions of dollars, but Deng's bosses wanted more, much more.

Deng was more surprised by the other avenues of research being explored by Ordell that dealt with life extension and manipulating physical characteristics, including intelligence. He was stunned to learn of a programmer on Ordell's team, who had developed an algorithm that could compare the DNA of tens of thousands of mice, and with reasonable accuracy predict how the genes would express themselves in individual mice. It did this by comparing specific nucleotides, the structure which held the base pairs, and determining how a specific base pair sequence in a gene would express itself.

Deng's scientists advised that it was feasible, but could be slow going due to the complexity of the DNA molecule. What Deng knew was that their government had one of the fastest computers in the world, and would grant Xian access to it, which would be a game changer with the right algorithm.

Deng sat at the conference room table with his scientists and hackers. Seated beside him was Li Qiang, his right-hand man who had already reviewed the material on Ordell's off-line computer. Li Qiang, typically calm and subdued, looked unusually tense and his lips formed a tight line.

Li Qiang began, "In reviewing the materials with our experts, it appears that Mr. Ordell has progressed further in his efforts to isolate specific traits and characteristics associated with aging than initially thought."

Li Qiang continued, “The material still must be fully vetted, but it appears that Ordell’s company, AlgoGene, created an algorithm which can be used to determine which genetic traits are created by specific sequences of base pairs in genes.

It can also locate the transcription factors in genes, which turn the gene on and off – which ensures the genes are expressed at the right time and in the right amount. This could be a way to locate and target genes that turn on and cause someone to age or to turn off genes that cause age related diseases.”

He went on, “In the mouse experiments AlgoGene conducted, they used CRISPR Cas9 to slow the aging process in the mouse’s circulatory system, to resist heart disease. They were also successful in affecting the endocrine system so it continues to generate hormones of a much younger specimen.

Now they’re trying to map and explore the possibility of switching specific genes on and off that become activated through the aging process, which if successful could slow or halt those processes. Using this data it appears they have had some success in retarding the degradation of the immune system in mice.”

Li Qiang said, “Our scientists believe that the notes on changing the genes related to the immune system are especially promising. Many age-related deaths are caused by the breakdown of the immune system because as humans age, they cannot fight off diseases. If the genes could be edited to restore the immune system to act like it did at the age of twenty, then diseases such as cancer might be placed in check in elderly people.”

Deng purposely asked Li Qiang, “Our researchers have had difficulty with the unintended consequences of the CRISPR technology. Do you believe that Ordell and his computer expert can control the technology adequately to ensure reasonably safe testing in humans?”

Deng asked the question because, unknown to many in the room,

Xian Corporation had many problems with 'unanticipated consequences' relating to CRISPR testing and it was slowing the research.

Li Qiang's voice wavered when he said, "We cannot be absolutely certain because we do not possess the algorithm. It must be located on an offline computer which Ordell did not bring with him to China. The offline computer, which we were able to access, discusses how they were able to check various CRISPR formulations for other areas where they might inadvertently cut DNA, and therefore they can predict unintended consequences. We assume this to be factual since there is no reason for them to be deceitful on the offline computer."

Deng, considering his aide's comments, was expressionless, but for an almost imperceptible smile. He looked directly at Li Qiang and said, "Good work. Your team should make contact with Mr. Ordell to assess the situation further. I would also like to have a six-man secret police team following him at all times while he is here." The meeting was over.

Deng left, pleased with what he learned in the meeting and decided this deserved a closer look from his friends in the US. Back in his office, Deng called Jim Fox, at the law firm of SimpsonLevin. Fox was tuned into the biotech market and was an expert in mergers and acquisitions.

Fox's secretary answered his line and Deng Ngo asked to speak with Jim. She said, "Oh, hello Mr. Deng, I'll see if he's available, please hold." Deng, the face of a multibillion dollar fund with its true source hidden behind a number of shell companies, appreciated the instant access to the best and most connected lawyers and financiers that money could buy. These same people wouldn't give him the time of day if he couldn't make their receivables double in a few transactions. As they say in America, money talks and BS walks.

True to her word, the secretary got her boss on the phone in less than a minute. He said, "Hi Ngo, it's Jim, sorry it took me so long to get to the phone, I was on a conference call. What can I do for you?"

Deng Ngo asked, "Have you heard of a company called AlgoGene

Corporation? I believe it's near Washington, DC I've heard some interesting buzz about it."

Jim had recently heard something about this company, too. Others had inquired about it, but none of them were players as big as the fund Deng represented. Lucky for Fox, they hadn't formally entered into a retainer agreement for his services.

Many banks nowadays didn't have the instant access to money that was needed for a takeover bid, but he knew Deng did. And Jim could definitely use the business. He was also friendly with one of the principals holding an ownership interest in AlgoGene, Joseph DeBerg with the investment bank Kolb Kravath.

Fox said, "There's definitely some buzz about the place. I actually know the investment group that holds a large stake in the company, it's called Kolb Kravath, and I'm well acquainted with one of its principals. I can make some inquiries if you'd like, about its valuation and whether it's in play. I know it's a closely held corporation, and therefore the shares are privately held. If you're serious about acquiring this company, you'll need to move quickly. Shall I make some inquiries this afternoon?"

Deng said, "I would appreciate if you did."

Jim responded, "I'll do my best to get the information you need as soon as possible. It may take me a day or two to get in touch with the right people, but I'll call you tomorrow at the latest to let you know my progress. If necessary, I can come and meet you in your offices."

Deng said, "That sounds great, speak with you again soon," and hung up the phone. He liked working with Jim Fox. He kept the small talk to a minimum, got to the point in short order, and wasn't one to waste time. And in this case, time was of the essence.

66

It was a gray day at Kolb Kravath. How could this have happened? Joseph DeBerg met with the Auditing Subcommittee of the Board of Directors for Kolb Kravath, and they found something disturbing – the firm had write-downs of three billion dollars, maybe more. It appeared that that punk McQue had destroyed all DeBerg had built for the better part of his life.

DeBerg couldn't believe the idiot had taken short positions on commodities just before the Chinese stopped buying raw materials. McQue had committed the cardinal sin, he bought high and sold low. He also leveraged the stakes with a derivative program that actually bet on the continued strength of commodity prices. McQue didn't see the commodities crisis coming, and could no longer hide his mistake.

Sadly that wasn't the case for the hedge fund speculators McQue dealt with, who were either better informed or guessed right. They now wanted their payoff.

This situation reminded DeBerg of the problem that arose around the last crash with mortgage default swaps. Like people who'd gotten burnt then, McQue had taken very aggressive positions and held many of the contracts at the company. He relied on his quants who assured him that the derivative contracts weren't as dangerous as the ones sold by AIG during the great recession, but it appeared that the 'geniuses' were, once again, wrong.

Joseph DeBerg was not feeling charitable. At this stage of his life, he didn't have the time or inclination to reconstitute himself again. He'd survived a number of close calls in the past, including potential bankruptcies, but nothing as bad as this. He would need a fast infusion of cash if he was to save Kolb Kravath, but at least he could throw the punk out. He hadn't liked McQue for a long time and would finally be rid of the smug prick; nevertheless, it didn't take the sting out of what had happened.

Joseph DeBerg, a second-generation Wall Streeter, still couldn't shake the feeling of doom and was disconcerted by it. Too late now, but he should have kept a closer eye on the fool. Instead, he left McQue to his devices and now the firm was at risk.

Not that DeBerg would be depleted, he would still have his house, the great apartment in Manhattan, the beach house in Miami and the ski chalet on Aspen Mountain. He also had more money than he could spend in his lifetime, but it still amounted to a setback.

He was suddenly glad that investment banks were allowed to be organized as limited liability corporations. It was something unheard of in the 1990's, when all the big investment houses were partnerships, and each partner's assets could be at risk and would be needed to pay off any debts of the partnership. Not so in an LLC, where his assets were shielded.

Thank God for the lobbyists. They pushed the legislation through to make it easier for investment banks to change to the limited liability corporation structure, which made all the difference in the world. Even with his personal assets protected, DeBerg's ego made him want to fix this. He wanted to be rid of McQue and for Kolb Kravath to be still standing

Unable to control his wrath at McQue, Joseph DeBerg called in his chits and made his case to the subcommittee. He wanted to blast McQue the hell out of his company.

The lawyers for Kolb Kravath who attended the meeting blathered on, but clearly assured the subcommittee that even a shareholder with his name on the door could be dismissed for an infraction of this magnitude. In addition, the bylaws permitted the company to deduct losses from the severance package of the departing officer, and it could even support a suit for additional funds if there was a breach of fiduciary duties.

DeBerg thought, serves McQue right. It might teach him a lesson, especially if he finds out that his golden parachute had its strings cut. He'd love to see the look on McQue's face if he even thought his personal assets were at risk and not covered by the company's directors' and officers' insurance.

After everything was decided, DeBerg walked into the conference room on the top floor to give McQue the bad news. When DeBerg entered, McQue was already there. He observed McQue looking calm as could be, like nothing amiss had happened. McQue even wore that permanent smirk on his face that drove DeBerg crazy. He intended to finally erase that look from the jerk's face once and for all.

Joseph DeBerg put on his best concerned look as he approached McQue. He put out his hand and they shook. DeBerg then said, "I can't believe this happened. It will create a huge write-down for us." He was looking straight into McQue's eyes and couldn't believe there was no glint of shame or remorse for the precarious position he'd gotten the firm into.

DeBerg tried to look sympathetic as McQue began blathering, "It wasn't my fault that the Chinese stopped buying raw materials from emerging markets. How was I supposed to know that Brazil and some of the other countries in my portfolio would stop selling to China, and that China didn't want to buy anymore? I bet the Chinese will start buying more soon and if we can renegotiate some of the terms of the derivatives. We can get one of those quants to analyze them a little better, then I think we'll be OK. Anyway, I still have a few deals cooking. You know me Joe, I always land on my feet." DeBerg, who hated to be called 'Joe,' had to make a concerted effort to prevent himself from rolling his eyes and correcting McQue.

Instead DeBerg responded by saying, "Certainly you know, don't you, that the company has to write-down almost three billion dollars in losses – because of your derivatives, regardless of what you or your quants think."

DeBerg's sympathetic concern transitioned to a smirk of his own, as he began the process of getting his revenge. "You may not be aware, but the partners are very perturbed by your actions, and the reckless positions you took. I must tell you, it is hard to control their anger." He left out the part that he, himself, was one of the partners to whom he was referring.

McQue then blurted out, "I am a top shareholder in this company, a top earner, and I don't care what they think – who do those bastards think they are?"

DeBerg looked right into McQue's eyes, and was about to lay out his cards. He said, "As you are aware, the bylaws are very specific about how a shareholder can be dismissed for cause, and even for no cause at all." He watched as McQue finally showed a tinge of desperation in his eyes, if not on his face.

DeBerg found it almost amusing because he had seen McQue dress down so many underlings over the years. He appeared to delight in embarrassing them, and holding their jobs over their heads. McQue even once laughed with glee as he described how he made an ex-jock employee cry when he fired him for some minor infraction.

But now the shoe was on the other foot. DeBerg wondered if it would make McQue reflect back on his actions. DeBerg doubted it. McQue was only about McQue. He couldn't care less about anyone or anything else, not even the company responsible for providing his wealth and creature comforts. So McQue deserved what he had coming; and he wouldn't be bothering DeBerg any more, or threatening DeBerg's control over the company. Good riddance to bad rubbish, he thought.

DeBerg said, "Unfortunately, I don't really have control of the board and you may want to consult the bylaws. Because the write-down is quite significant, the subcommittee will want someone's head to roll."

McQue's look changed to one of being startled. Had he heard it right, did DeBerg say heads will roll, as if referring to him, McQue? DeBerg appreciated McQue's change in demeanor. It suited him more than his usual smugness.

DeBerg continued as he placed his hand on McQue's shoulder, "You had a good run, but now you'll need to bow out gracefully. It was agreed that you will need to surrender your keys and leave the building at once. You can schedule a time, preferably on a Saturday, when you can come in to get your personal effects. As I understand it, the protocol is that you will be escorted by security at that time."

McQue pointed his manicured finger directly into DeBerg's chest as he said, "After all I've done for this place, you can't do this to me."

DeBerg thought isn't this rich, I made him, and he now thinks I can't break him – just watch me friend.

DeBerg, with an air of seriousness, then said, "I'm sorry you feel that way. Your incompetence made us all lose a lot of money, not to mention the damage you caused to the credibility of the firm. I again suggest you look at the bylaws, and shareholder agreement. I'll paraphrase them for you – you can be removed for cause and you may have to forfeit your right to some, or all of the golden parachute you negotiated. You also may have civil liability to our company for the losses. Some of it may be covered by insurance, but there is an exclusion for dishonesty."

"I'll call my lawyer and sue you for everything you have," McQue blustered.

DeBerg just shook his head and said, "We don't take kindly to threats, no matter how idle. Just get out and we will send a letter to you detailing your discharge and providing the appropriate documents. I trust I will not have to call security."

McQue walked toward the door – the swagger gone from his step and the look on his face was now one of trepidation. DeBerg smiled to himself when he finally saw humiliation creep into McQue's eyes.

67

Joseph DeBerg went back to his office to figure out what he would do to right the ship. They needed some cash fast, and he was weighing the options; the obvious one was to call friends overseas to get a feeling about how much liquidity was out there. He was rubbing his nonexistent beard when the phone rang. His secretary was on the line and said, "James Fox is on line 2."

DeBerg liked Jim Fox, so he said "I'll take it," and he picked up the phone.

"Hello, Jim. To what do I owe the pleasure?"

Jim said in a cheerful way, "We know each other pretty well, so I'll cut to the chase. I know you own a large position in a company called AlgoGene Corporation and the word on the street is that it's in play."

DeBerg wanted to go slowly. He didn't have a good grasp on the situation, because of everything else going on, and he wanted to get a better handle on the landscape before discussing anything of substance. So he said, "It's one of the really interesting ventures I've been involved in and I'd like to talk with you, but how about meeting over lunch later at Bourbon Steak?"

Jim was pleased by DeBerg's suggestion and said, "OK, but only if I'm buying." DeBerg said, "Agreed, see you at 12:30," and then he hung up the phone. He immediately dialed Betty's extension and asked her to come into his office.

Betty showed up three minutes later. She didn't know what was happening, but was leery about the rumors she'd heard and the sudden departure of Mr. McQue. She had spoken to McQue's assistant, who was confident that her boss was going to stay and see them through the troubling times, but the most recent rumor contradicted this.

If the guys at the top didn't know what was happening, then how could the people like her, at the bottom, have a clue about what was going on? As she walked into her boss' office she had a wary look of someone who could be getting pink-slipped herself.

DeBerg said, "Please, sit. Make yourself comfortable. I want to discuss AlgoGene with you."

Betty relaxed a little, relieved he was asking her about something for which she was the bearer of good news.

He said, "I received some inquiries about the company and I wanted to get a briefing on its progress."

Betty nervously cleared her throat and said, "Well, I'm happy to report on the progress of the company. John, the young guy in charge, really has been prolific in his research. They're already making a profit in the gene analysis area. They also have filed some patents with the Patent Office for a new method of hair restoration. He's also working on some other projects concerning cures for various diseases, especially those that afflict aging baby boomers."

Mr. DeBerg looked pleasantly surprised, didn't really care about the details, but said, "That sounds promising, but why is this the first time I'm hearing about all of this?" That should put her on her heels, something he should've done much earlier with McQue.

Betty cleared her throat again and stammered, "Well, you were so busy, and I was so busy that I just didn't get to it yet."

DeBerg shook his head and said, "I need you to get copies of all documents you have in the office, especially any patent applications, and meet me in the large conference room. Also I'm going to need you to come to a lunch meeting today with a friend of mine who is interested in the project."

Betty nervously shook her head yes, and decided against asking Mr. DeBerg about the current state of their investment banking operations and the company's viability. She thought it was better to deal with one crisis at a time.

68

Dr. Duretts was in his office when he received an email from the Director of Research and Development. It said that there was a mandatory meeting for all Geneteka R&D Department employees in conference room 1, in fifteen minutes.

He was surprised because they rarely did a meeting of the whole department, and certainly never on such short notice. Maybe it was another one of those ridiculous inspirational gatherings that the company set up periodically. They would hire some motivational speaker to spew well-rehearsed, inane lines to make the rank and file feel like their business wasn't just a money-making enterprise. After you were told that you were part of something special, you were supposed to graciously accept the paltry raises they doled out, without complaint.

He hoped this wasn't one of those meetings because they not only bored him to tears, but they also angered him. Employees were expected to drink the Kool-Aid and be satisfied with meager 2% raises, when clearly the same did not apply to management, with their stock options, platinum insurance policies and golden parachutes.

He got up, walked through the entire building to the conference room, along the way saying 'hello' to some of his colleagues and asking them what this was about. None of them seemed to know.

He sat down next to one of the other research scientists who he was friendly with and waited for the presentation to begin.

After the room filled with scientists and technicians, he saw Michael O'Donnell, Geneteka's CEO, enter the room. He never liked Mike; he was pompous, a mediocre scientist at best and Duretts could never figure out how he moved into management. As far as Duretts knew, he had never published any papers of note, or had any original ideas worth mentioning.

Mike was flanked by his Assistant Directors and the CFO of the company. Duretts couldn't have guessed what was coming next.

Mike walked to the microphone which reverberated with high pitched feedback, when he was assisted by a technician working at the sound board. Mike looked stern as he began speaking, "I wanted to address the entire group because of some disturbing trends we've seen recently. Our business analysts have found that some upstart companies have recently made great strides in biotechnology, currently in the process of being patented. Frankly, these developments put you guys to shame."

He continued, "These new companies, and one in particular named AlgoGene Corporation, do not have the resources – neither the money, nor the personnel – that we have. Yet they seem to be doing your jobs better than you are."

Mike then said, "We have the best technology, state-of-the-art labs and I'm certain that no request for equipment has ever been denied. We have an obligation to our shareholders. Our stock price has gone in the toilet since rumors of AlgoGene's activities got out."

Exasperated, Mike said, "Why don't you people get it? My God, we've recruited the best and the brightest, and the amount we pay our scientists is sky high." Although he didn't mention that the highest paid scientist made less than 1/100th of what he earned.

He paused, then continued, "AlgoGene has a millennial 20-something owner and has a patent pending for CRISPR technology to cure balding."

Sounds familiar, Duretts thought as he smiled to himself. He must be a very bright young man.

Mike continued, "I am exceedingly disappointed that our scientists have been shown up by this upstart. I was expecting a lot more from all of you. We have recently contacted the principals of the company to look into a merger and purchase of the AlgoGene tech business, but it doesn't look promising. We should never have been in this position. We should have been a leader in this area, not a follower."

Bob Daniels glanced at Duretts and when their eyes met, he had to look away because he didn't want to burst out laughing. Duretts thought about Mike, and who was following the leader now; although it would be ironic if the company that never took care of its intellectual capital might ultimately pay him and Bob for their idea. Well, anyway, only time would tell.

Mike, scowling, said, "Things are going to change around here. We are going to reassess the organization and reevaluate all positions, including those of senior scientists, to determine which employees are pulling their weight and who is not."

Anxious tension filled the air, but neither Duretts, nor Bob, was particularly troubled. They were thinking how it would be poetic justice if the company they worked for purchased AlgoGene. Money from such a merger could pay for all manner of things to ensure their families' futures, and a comfortable retirement. It was even sweeter that Mike and his cronies might be the ones paying for it, in more ways than one.

Meanwhile, Duretts and Bob would bide their time as they strained to keep the smiles off their faces, because after all, heads Would roll.

69

After Betty's briefing, Mr. DeBerg was pleased by what he heard and quickly grasped the implications of the research and its profitability. He made the tactical decision to make Jim Fox wait a little while at Bourbon Steak – nothing says I'm in control like being fashionably late, he thought.

He felt like the cavalry coming to save the day for his poor little investment bank. It would probably be written up in a *Business Week* article which, in all likelihood, would be very flattering to him. He and Betty went outside and as he hailed a cab to Bourbon Steak, DeBerg hoped the New York strip steak was good that day.

They arrived at Bourbon Steak about fifteen minutes late and saw Jim Fox already seated at one of the 'good' tables. DeBerg could see that Fox was anxious to have the meeting. Fox clearly knew a good thing when he saw it, and he might actually know more than he let on, if there was any truth to what goes on in industrial spying.

Mr. DeBerg smiled, moved in for a handshake as he said, "Well, if it isn't Jim Fox."

Fox stood up, shook DeBerg's hand and said, "Joseph, it's been too long. How's the golf game, you still an 8 handicap?"

DeBerg laughed, impressed that Fox remembered and said, "Sometimes I think my handicap is 'wheelchair' because recently it feels like I'm sitting down when I hit, but yes, officially, it's still an 8. How about you? Do you still get out to play?"

Fox said, "Yes, I was at Hilton Head about 3 weeks ago and on one course I shot a 77. That's the only round I care to talk about," he laughed.

DeBerg then introduced Betty. He said, "This is my associate Betty, she is assisting me on this project, and is more familiar with the day-to-day operations, so I thought it would be helpful to bring her along. I also brought some documents with me, just to whet your appetite. But first, I'd like to know who you're representing, even if it's off the record."

Fox didn't want to disclose his client, especially not this well-financed whale. But this deal could mean tens of millions of dollars in fees for the offering, and an increased stature for him in his firm. His law firm would likely get the work for the due diligence, for obtaining bridge loans, preparing the purchase documents, and otherwise working out the fine print details. He was even looking at a finder's fee bonus. Although these transactions were routine and once you'd done one, you'd done them all – the firm could still collect huge fees.

Fox coyly said, "For now, let's just say it's a very large institutional fund, along the lines of an overseas sovereign fund."

As DeBerg fought the urge to ask more, Betty's expression gave away her piqued interest. They both knew that the sovereign funds of the Middle East had dried up with the falling price of oil, and that they usually didn't invest in high tech as much as they should. Neither was quite sure which sovereign fund Jim was talking about, but there were two possibilities: China or Russia. No, most likely it was China, with its much larger economy and biotech industry.

Jim Fox looked right at DeBerg and said, "Since you suggested it, let's go off the record. I have a principal who is very interested in this particular company and asked me to take a hard look. He's ready to move fast on the acquisition and is willing to leave some equity in your hands – although the price goes down precipitously as the number of shares you retain goes up. What type of equity arrangement do you have – is your firm the only shareholder?"

DeBerg said, "No, we're not the only shareholder, but we hold a very strong position and the other shareholder is the scientist we bankrolled, with whom we have considerable influence. I must mention that according to our records, the business is actually making a profit. It also has a very high upside potential. Betty can better address the personalities of the staff and the owner, John," he paused for a minute to remember his name, "Ordell."

Betty smiled and said, "Yes, I spent a lot of time with John, his scientists and technicians and he is extremely prolific. He already has a patent pending for a hair restoration product."

DeBerg, interrupting Betty, said, "Betty, what he really wants to know is two things – if the employees who own shares will be willing to sell, and if they'll be willing to continue working at the company as intellectual capital. I can fill him in on the boring details of the company, or he can get it from the materials I brought. Of course, Jim knows he and those he represents will need to sign confidentiality agreements."

Betty, somewhat deflated answered, "Yes, I think they will all sell their shares," as she sat back in her chair.

Jim Fox was thinking that DeBerg could have brought a younger, prettier assistant, but he smiled anyway and said, "Thank you, that's good news and of course all this will be kept confidential."

Just then the waiter came by and asked to take their orders. Fox ordered a $140 bottle of wine, but Betty didn't catch the name or year of the vintage. She also heard Jim say the meal was on him. Betty then just sat back, wasn't asked and didn't offer any additional comments. She just ordered, ate and drank while they talked about trips to exotic places she had never been and golf courses she would never play.

As she ate her filet mignon, she wondered: why is this always happening to me? I do all the work and someone else takes all the glory, or at least all the money. She had a sinking feeling that her hope that this project would be career-making was quickly evaporating. It was obvious

Mr. DeBerg was not going to give her any credit at all. Well, she thought, I might as well enjoy another glass of expensive wine, after all, I give so much for so little.

Before the dessert cart came over, Fox finally got down to business. He looked through the documents that Betty prepared for DeBerg. One was a corporate ledger, showing a healthy profit, and another was a patent pending. He also had some information on other projects that were in the works. It all looked like a lesser version of what he had already seen.

Fox asked DeBerg some questions about the future projects which DeBerg faked his way through, without Betty's help. It didn't seem to matter, because Fox appeared to have already made up his mind. At the end, Fox asked, "Can I meet Ordell and his employees, and get some more information as part of the due diligence?"

DeBerg replied, "Yes, but come on Jim, there's a great cigar bar across the street, let's go over and get two for old time's sake." DeBerg turned to Betty and gave her $25 for her ride back to the office.

The men left the restaurant, as Betty stood outside by the entrance, pulled out her cell phone and ordered an Uber. As she waited, she watched DeBerg and Fox cross the street and disappear into a shop with an old-fashioned wooden Indian out front.

70

The cigar bar wasn't very crowded so they just took a seat at an out of the way table. Fox started talking first, and said, "Look, we've known each other a long time, and now that we're alone, I want you to know that we can get this done and I assure you there will be serious money involved."

He continued, "I know about your firm's problem and this could be great for both of us. As you know, with the Internet, very little about companies 'in play' is secret for very long. My principals are confident that with a little more information, and a meeting with the key employees, they could move ahead quickly."

DeBerg said, "I'll level with you, Jim. You know Bill Moore. He also called me to express some interest in the company. I believe it's one or more Russian oligarchs who are interested in investing." He left out the part that he hadn't yet returned Bill's innocuous voicemail from this morning, and that he had no idea who, if anyone, might be interested in making a deal.

DeBerg continued plying his streak of misinformation, "I've also received a number of calls from other investment houses, so what I need to know from you is who your principal is, just to be sure we can do business as quickly as you indicated."

Fox replied, "Deng Ngo, who is a principal in, among other funds, the Xian Fund." This time DeBerg didn't try to put on a poker face.

DeBerg responded, "You understand that this company has intellectual capital which can be tapped now and very significantly in the future."

Fox shook his head in agreement and said, "Off the record, old friend, we knew about the patent and if you extrapolate from the sales of Minoxidil and other products, the value of the company exceed the losses your firm recently incurred. Plus, the company has trade secrets and proprietary information, such as computer algorithms, which my client finds extremely interesting."

He continued, "Finally, there is additional value in the potential new biotech products and the profitable portion of the company can be sold to help raise additional capital." DeBerg appeared out of his depth about the biotech aspects of the company, and had little knowledge of any algorithm, but smiled as he shook his head yes.

They shook hands and DeBerg said, "Let's get this done. I'll be in touch early tomorrow to set up a meeting with you and the employees." They then left the bar without ever ordering cigars and went their separate ways.

As Jim Fox walked down the street, he held his cell phone and called Deng Ngo. He reached voicemail and said, "Hello, Ngo, it's Jim Fox. I've met with the controlling company. I think we have the inside track, although it won't be cheap – nothing of value ever is. I know your people will meet with Mr. Ordell soon, and I will keep you posted as well. Enjoy your evening," and he hung up, not knowing whether it was night or day wherever Deng might be.

71

Lisa and John rolled their bags through the airport and were surprised by its size. They were both tired so they stopped in a coffee bar, called Pacific Coffee, for a quick pick me up. They sat at a circular table, finished the coffee, and then left to get a cab. As they walked through the airport, Lisa liked the Chinese writing on the signs, which gave the place an air of mystery. She noticed that the airport was cleaner and more modern than the few she'd been to in the States.

As they left the airport, there were numerous cabs waiting to transport tourists to their hotels. Their cab was yellow with bright red lettering on the side. They were surprised to see people driving on the left-hand side of the road, like in England. Most of the roads were one-way, presumably to help ease congestion. The coffee was kicking in, but they both wanted to get to the hotel as soon as possible so they could relax.

They had to go over the harbor to get to the hotel. They took the Ponte Da Amizade Bridge, which was fairly ordinary. It reminded Lisa of the Bay Bridge in Maryland, that crossed the Chesapeake Bay and went to the Eastern shore. It didn't appear to be as long, but as you drove on the bridge their hotel sat directly in front of them. As John and Lisa watched the impressive skyline they were unaware that a dark sedan was following them the entire time.

In the sedan were six ex-members of the Advanced Persistent Threat – APT – Group. One of them was Wang Wei. The other five were ex-members of the military and military intelligence. They had been briefed, that these two targets were of high value and if the operation was successful it would be remembered. The team was well-acquainted with the hotel where the targets were staying, and had been informed that the targets had no reason to believe that they would be followed; they could approach the targets as friendlies, but try to make limited contact. There was already a contingency of scientists at the hotel who would establish primary contact with the targets.

Wang Wei would coordinate between both groups for maximum effect. Essentially, they had been advised that these two individuals had commercial and scientifically necessary information which could be vital to their government. It had something to do with genetic engineering, and the six members in the car, along with the scientists, were tasked with attempting to persuade the American targets to work with a Chinese company called Xian.

They were permitted to detain and use minor psychological pressure only if necessary. Only on further orders from higherup the chain of command where they allowed to use force.

Wang Wei was a veteran at this type of work. He had negotiated with CEOs of large American companies, like Boeing, and knew how Americans thought and how personal greed controlled their actions. In most cases, CEOs gave away the fort – they agreed to build products, such as planes, in China without considering the long-term consequences.

American CEOs would endorse technology transfer agreements that gave away important intellectual property. Their companies even lobbied the Federal government to permit deals to go through, so the stock price and their stock options would go up, without a thought about the long-term consequences. Long-term meant nothing to them, since they were usually long gone before anything could go awry.

In order to gain access to their market, the Chinese government required plants be built in China, that they use Chinese workers, and contract with Chinese companies for ancillary goods and services – so all the money and jobs stayed in China.

The CEO's didn't seem to care that at the end of the day, when the contract was over, in their wake would be left a large factory that could effectively compete with their American counterparts. From Wang Wei's viewpoint, the CEOs he dealt with seemed to only care about increasing the value of the stock, and consequently the CEO's stock options.

All a multinational company had to do was announce a contract and immediately the share price skyrocketed; then tens of millions of dollars went directly into the CEO's pocket, with no consideration for the long-term effect on employees. He mused at how different this was from the Chinese way.

It was shocking to Wang Wei that the US government allowed this to happen, but as Churchill once said: Americans always do the right thing only after exhausting all other options. In this case, he felt they might've been too late and exhausted the options.

He also remembered a conversation with a high-level executive during a negotiation who said something startling: he'd rather bring three Chinese people out of poverty so he could sell his goods to them, even if it put one American into poverty, because ultimately it would produce two extra customers to sell goods to.

The executive knew there were 1.4 billion Chinese, and only cared about how he could sell more product – even if it hurt his own countrymen. He didn't care if twenty years after the contract that China was a competitor – by then he would be on a beach in Maui or a golf course somewhere, maybe even in China, teeing off.

Although Wang Wei had no illusions about the Chinese leadership, he knew they took a long-term view. His country's plan was to sell cheap goods throughout the world, especially in the US while working to create their own middle class. Once the Chinese middle class market was large enough, China would no longer be beholden to foreign trading partners – instead able to focus on selling to their own people.

This was coming to fruition more quickly than he or anyone else could have expected, since now only twenty-two percent of the economy was based on foreign trade. Only a few short years ago the percentage had been forty percent. It made him proud of his leaders, and that the US government and American CEOs played right into China's hands, with the US owing them $2 trillion to boot.

But for some reason, this assignment seemed different to Wang Wei. It was now time to focus on the task at hand – with an opportunity to put a feather in his own cap. All he needed to do was get to know the targets, understand what made them tick, and then complete the objective.

72

The cab ride only took fifteen minutes. When they pulled up in front of the hotel it looked like a large reflective egg, with a pillar sticking out the top. The sides of the building were not straight, but flared out in an unusual way. There was also a dome on top with something else sticking out. John liked its odd appearance. He paid the driver in MOP, and asked for a receipt.

John and Lisa rolled their luggage through the front entrance to the check-in area. It was a round room with a remarkable granite floor. It was inlaid with a large eight-pointed star. He picked up the aroma of garlic, but thought it might have just been the people there.

At the check-in desk, a clerk wearing a Lisboa uniform greeted them. He asked if they were involved in the scientific symposium. John said, "Yes," and was handed a packet of information including a brochure listing the various speakers and the topics. He felt a sense of pride as he flipped through to find his name and picture in the handout, beside more prominent scientists in the genetic engineering realm.

He and Lisa walked to an elevator, which had two gold patterns on the floor with a black circle and a black square inside of it. They were too busy soaking up the sites of the hotel to notice the six individuals who came in after them.

The six men had four rooms – one directly above and below John's room, and one directly above and below Lisa's room. Their bags contained state-of-the-art surveillance equipment, which could easily penetrate the floors and ceilings of the rooms in this hotel. Their eavesdropping devices could hack into cell phones allowing them to listen to conversations on the phone through its microphone even if the cell phone was off. They were also able to view what was on the cell phone through the two cameras on the front and back. The six men went through the check-in process without saying much, and proceeded directly to their rooms.

John opened the door to his room, decorated with bold blue carpet, brown walls and brown curtains, and a graphic designed bed cover. It looked inviting, and he started to unpack. Just then the room phone rang. He picked up the phone and said "Hello."

Phil Vandecamp, a college friend who was attending the conference, said, "Hi, it's Phil. I got in a couple of hours ago. I spoke to the bellman who told me about a decent bar nearby, called the Whiskey Bar. You want to meet me there?" John paused for a second then said, "Sure what's it called? The Whiskey Bar?" Phil responded, "Yeah, that's it, and it's only 3 blocks from the hotel. How's 8 o'clock?" John said, "8's great. Do you mind if I bring a colleague?" Phil said, "Not a problem. See you then," then he hung up.

This assignment seemed almost too easy to Jaing, who was assigned to monitor John's phone. It took him all of three minutes to hack John's cell phone and he was already listening in on a conversation through his headset.

Jaing preferred the challenge of penetrating firewalls created by the best security people on the planet, not the pedestrian task of hacking cell phones. But it wasn't up to him, and like a good soldier, he did what he was told. He turned to his cohorts and said in Cantonese, "It looks like they're going to the Whiskey Bar, so we need to be there by 7:30 pm. That means you too, Li Na, and your dress is in the closet." Na looked back at him and nodded her head in agreement. He said, "It's for tourists, and only a short walk down Avenida da Amizade. We'll leave at 7:15 sharp. We should purchase drinks to blend in, but only pretend to drink because we are on duty. Na you can drink, but if you have an opportunity spill your drinks because we want you to be clear headed." She again nodded in agreement.

The cell phone monitor lit up again, indicating John was on the phone again. This time he asked the woman to meet him in the lobby because he wanted to do some sightseeing. Zhang, another newer operative, prepared to leave and follow the two when Jaing said, "I'll stay here so I can monitor the phone and listen to the conversations. I will text you with a heads-up on their possible movements."

Jaing looked at his screen, and with a few keystrokes was listening to whatever John's telephone was picking up in the room. The sophisticated program that he was using to hack into phones didn't activate the phone's lighting mechanism, so the person was unaware that anything was going on with the cell phone. He could also turn on a phone's cameras, but did so only when necessary. This was the same technology they used to eavesdrop on high-level heads of state.

He had to tip his hat to the programmers for the People's Republic of China. Some of those guys were educated at not only the best Chinese institutions of higher learning, but also some of the best academic institutions in the US and Europe. One of his buddies, a programmer with the government had even worked for the NSA in America for a short time before returning to China.

As Jaing listened, he heard John's off-key rendition of a Lady Gaga song, as he opened and closed drawers while he unpacked his suitcases. Jaing had watched enough American television to recall the phrase 'don't quit your day job.' A moment later, there was a knock at the door and someone entered the room.

It was Lisa, and she said, "I was thinking of just relaxing, but if you want company, I'm game." John said, "I want to go to Senado Square, it's only a short walk up the street according to GPS, and we might as well do something before we go to the Whiskey Bar." John always liked to rush around whenever he went somewhere new, to see everything he could;

Lisa, on the other hand, preferred a more leisurely and relaxed pace of touring.

She asked, "You're ready to go right now?" Before John could say yes, Jaing turned to the Zhang and said, "They're going to Senado Square." Zhang nodded and headed for the door. He figured to get in front of the two, stop in a store, and then follow them over to the Square. According to their files, they had no background in surveillance, so this should be a piece of cake. It was a lot easier than some of the dissidents he followed and then detained, because they were paranoid – and these two Americans looked self-assured without any suspicion of being followed.

While John was still talking with Lisa, Zhang immediately left the room. He caught the elevator, went down to the street level and exited the front door of the hotel. He crossed the street, and waited in front of a building which had pillars that were easy to stand behind so he wouldn't be visible from the hotel exit. The sidewalk was narrow, flanked by streetlights, but he was familiar enough with the area that he knew the direction John and Lisa would go.

He only had to wait a few minutes before they left the hotel in the direction of Senado Square. The incoming text from Jaing said that they left the hotel and were on their way to the Square. Zhang shook his head as he thought about Jaing stating the obvious, although in their line of work, precision was more important than Jaing being annoying.

As they walked down the street, they saw a vendor selling Pearl Tea. They bought two cups. Lisa was surprised at how much she liked it and she thought she would probably be drinking a lot of these on the trip.

As they walked, John was surprised at how quiet it was on the street. It also appeared that the traffic was very orderly. John had a tendency to walk quickly and Lisa pushed herself to keep up. As they walked Lisa asked, "Are you nervous about giving your speech to all those highbrow scientists?" John smiled and replied, "No, because we know more about CRISPR than they do.

What I'm looking forward to is talking to some of my colleagues about work done by a guy named Stanley Qi at Stanford. One of my buddies at the conference worked with him for two years and I'd like to get more information on his work." Lisa was breathing a little heavy at this point, but asked, "What's so different about his research?"

John liked Lisa's inquisitive nature, and said, "He did research on activator molecules that regulate and switch genes on and off. He was able to isolate activator molecules, and repressor molecules, and using CRISPR he could control genes. Using techniques he pioneered it could be possible to turn off genes that fuel cancer to grow, or turn on genes that may have been turned off by old age, like genes that slow down the production of testosterone and human growth hormone in men, the weakening of the immune system in older people and the decrease in muscle mass. Or in women, suppressing the gene that causes a decrease in estrogen and osteoporosis. This gene regulation technology does not change the genes, it merely fuses with it.

The other type of CRISPR work we do, cuts the genes so that new genes can be installed – like ones that people have who live to be a hundred years of age or more." He turned his head, then looked back at her and said, "David said he could have a field day with this research and his algorithm. I may try to poach one or two of the scientists with intimate knowledge of this technology to work with us."

Lisa's ears perked up as she considered what he was saying. She had heard a lot of surprising things, but until now, the ability to turn genes on and off was only a theory. This was definitely less disturbing than changing the genetic code of a person so they could be faster, stronger, smarter, or taller. Anyway, as they walked down the narrow sidewalks, she smelled something amazing. There was a street vendor selling little cakes, and as she glanced at his wares, John turned to the vendor and asked what they were.

In English the vendor replied, "Almond cakes." John bought two and they stood on the street enjoying the delicacy, which tasted even better than they smelled. They had read that this was a treat not to be missed in Macau.

They continued walking and John started talking about the research again. "I can't wait to talk to scientists in other labs about our research. I wonder if there will be any tech experts who could be useful. We have a number of traits which we've been able to nail down in mice, but I'd like to find more so we could find ways of avoiding the unintended consequences and be better at predicting multiple genes with the potential to affect particular traits in humans."

Lisa asked, "Can't you just use animal models as, dare I say, 'guinea pigs' to figure out where the genes are located?"

John shook his head and said, "I wish it were that easy." They turned the corner and entered Senado Square. The fountain in the center of the square looked like a gyroscope in the middle of a pool of water. More striking was the black and white tile on the ground of the square. The black tiles came in waves that undulated around the fountain. There were three-story buildings surrounding the square that looked very old with interesting architecture. There was little else around the square except for a post office, a hotel, and some kind of flea market, but John wasn't much of a shopper, and Lisa didn't seem interested, either.

As he and Lisa stood in the middle of the Square they saw a vendor selling Pasteal de Nata. Lisa had read about them online and was getting hungry again, so they stopped and bought two. They were almost like a soufflé, made of eggs and were sweet and fluffy. Lisa thought these would be good with the pearl tea.

As they were eating, a tall slightly built Chinese guy approached them and meekly asked, "Are you John Ordell?" John squinted at the guy, and said, "Yes, I am. Do I know you?" The guy smiled at John with teeth that looked a bit too big for his mouth, and said in passable English, "My name is Li Ming, and I'm here for the conference. I recognize your picture from handout. I'm junior scientist from Chinese delegation. I very much look forward to the conference."

John smiled back and asked, "Are you one of the presenters at the conference, because you look pretty young." Ming answered, "No not speaker. I lower level researcher on team. I was with Broad Institute. Now I working with Institute and Xian Corporation."

John's interest was piqued at that point because the Broad Institute was a modern biotechnology palace. He thought it odd, however, that the scientist was also working jointly with a company.

John smiled at Ming and said, "We should get together for coffee and compare notes. I like talking with researchers in the trenches, the people actually doing the work. They're usually better informed."

Ming seemed pleased, gave another toothy smile and said, "I would like very much get together." The smile suddenly evaporated from his face when he looked up and noticed a tall Asian man walk past them. Ming bowed his head, having recognized one of his handlers, Zhang, who glanced at him with a menacing look. Ming quickly walked away saying, "See you at conference."

Zhang was not happy. These scientists were hard to control. Often they didn't follow orders and they were socially inept, so they'd say too much to make someone else like them. This young scientist should have been briefed not to make contact with the Americans. Too late for that, but it didn't appear that any damage was done.

John noticed the tall Asian man, and saw his eyes lock with Ming's for an instant. He also noticed Ming's sudden change in demeanor. John saw the face of the Asian guy as he walked by, and he never forgot a face. The encounter seemed odd.

He was glad that his Dad had ingrained in him the special forces skill of noticing what was going on around you. It was one of the games he'd play with his father after his mother died. Whenever they went out, he and his brother would either follow people, or try to remember everything from a particular situation. Later, his father would test their memories for everything they saw. They called them reconnaissance missions, but it was really just a way to bond with their uptight Dad. But sometimes it came in handy.

Lisa finished eating her pseudo-soufflé, looked at John and said, "What a peculiar guy." John nodded in agreement and said, "Maybe we'll see him again, but we better get back to the hotel to get ready to go to the Whiskey Bar."

He then scanned his phone to see what else he wanted to see before they left Macau. There was the Venetian Hotel, with its gondolas and gambling and he also wanted to see the Guia fortress, which overlooked the city and had a great view of his hotel. He wondered what Lisa might want to see.

Their main purpose at the conference was to meet people and to see if there were any potential financiers interested in his work. Still he was hoping that these side excursions would fit into their schedule.

As they walked back to the hotel, John felt tired which he attributed to jetlag. They passed another aromatic coffee shop and he told Lisa, "We gotta stop, that smells too good to pass up." Lisa nodded in agreement and they went in and saw a plump Asian man, with a welcoming smile, and happy looking eyes, behind the counter who said in broken English, "Can I hep you with someping." John said, "Yes, two of the largest cups of coffee you have with cream, and some sugar on the side." They walked to the front of the shop, coffee in hand, and perched on tall stools overlooking the street.

As they sat sipping the delicious coffee, they engaged in some people watching. John recoiled when he saw the same tall Asian man, who he saw lock eyes with that scientist, standing at a nearby kiosk. When John looked over to watch him, the guy furtively looked around for a second, then ducked into a market stall. John had an uneasy feeling in his gut. He didn't know why.

John practically chugged his coffee, and told Lisa, "Let's get out of here, I want to get back to the hotel to take care of some things before we go out for the evening." Lisa noticed a strange look on his face, but it had been a long trip and he was likely feeling some stress because, face it, he wasn't the greatest public speaker she'd ever seen. They walked a different route back to the hotel, on a long Boulevard, then some side streets around the circle, finally arriving back at the main lobby of their hotel.

As they were walking back to the hotel, Zhang called the command post to advise what had occurred on their walk and to learn about their conversation from the eavesdropping transmitter.

He was told that the superiors liked what they heard about the gene regulation research, and the potential cures for combatting old age. Zhang, who was normally as tense as an overwound watch spring, was able to relax a little because if this job produced good intel, it could advance his career, and he could get out of the field, at last.

73

Jim Fox was sitting in his office, bored while reviewing paperwork on a recent merger between two small players. The associate on the paperwork had been sloppy, leaving out a few key phrases which were in all the forms, and would require a stern reprimand, maybe more.

As he thought about how to handle this unpleasantness, his private number rang and he picked up. On the other end was Deng Ngo. Jim sat back and said, "Hello Ngo, I didn't expect to hear from you so soon."

Deng got right to the point, "Good morning. I've spoken to the principals and they've done the preliminary review of the materials you provided. Although the vetting is not yet complete, they have indicated that they wish to go forward with this bulk sales transaction and purchase the entire company. We would like the company to be purchased by one of our subsidiaries run out of Switzerland. The new company will be called Xian Corporation. We wish to come to the United States to discuss terms.

We also want you to look into the issue of technology transfer related to biochemical and computer coding, but I don't think it should present a problem. We do not want to run afoul of United States laws, even if we do not identify Xian Corporation as a Chinese entity." Deng paused, then continued, "Make it known to the principals that we are willing to pay a fair price for the company and its intellectual property, as well as the personnel piece of the company."

Fox, not wanting to overstep with this prized client, asked, "What price point are you thinking?" Deng replied, "A few billion dollars. We are willing to pay for discretion and a smooth transaction process without wrinkles. I emphasize we are willing to pay a premium for having this transaction done discreetly, outside the purview of the news or government regulators."

Deng's directions to Fox were crystal clear, and both men knew this was Fox's forte. Deng then said, "I'm in New York, so all you need to do is call me on my cell phone, I am available to meet the personnel and close the deal as soon as you can make the arrangements." Fox smiled to himself and said, "I'll try to do my due diligence for you and make it happen within the next three days." Deng responded, "Excellent." After cursory farewells, both hung up.

Jim Fox felt his heart race as he contemplated this deal. When the Chinese wanted something, they had no problem paying for it. This could be thirty-five to fifty million dollars in fees for him. He was curious, however, what Xian meant. Googling it, he learned it was a Taoist word that meant, 'spiritually immortal or superhuman.' He thought it an odd choice to name a company, but his fee did not depend on such decisions. After all, business is business.

Fox decided he should call his friend Joseph DeBerg. He looked up DeBerg's number on his cell phone and called from his office phone.

He preferred using the office phone because he'd read somewhere on the Internet that overuse of a cell phone may cause brain cancer. Uncertain if it was just an urban myth, he acted on the premise that it was better to be safe than sorry. This came with the territory of being in your late fifties and not completely trusting of technology, or those who were responsible for its regulation, especially when large sums of money were at stake. Ironic, considering how he made his fortune.

The phone rang twice before DeBerg's secretary answered, "Mr. DeBerg's Office." She seemed harried when he said, "Hi Sarah, James Fox. I need to talk with the chief right away. Is he in?" Sarah, at ease, laughed and said, "I will see if he is available, please hold, Mr. Fox." She buzzed DeBerg and relayed, "James Fox is on the line, should I put him through?" DeBerg said, "Yes," and she did. Jim, jovially asked, "How's it going over there? I heard you might need to vet your partners a little better in the future."

DeBerg, slightly annoyed by Fox's jab gruffly replied, "We're taking care of the problem. What's on your mind?"

Fox took the cue that DeBerg wasn't in the mood for ribbing, good-natured or otherwise, and continued, "I have some great news. My principal wants to meet with you ASAP and I'd like to set something up right away. It could be a big break for you. Even better, I don't think my principal is going to try to leverage your position, or insist on any write downs, and is willing to give you a fair valuation for AlgoGene."

DeBerg suddenly felt as if a weight had been lifted from his shoulders. "That sounds good." He threw a curveball to up the ante, and said, "I have no problem with meeting, especially with your track record, but in case you don't know, we do have some other suiters, including a group of Russians. My team can be ready by tomorrow afternoon at 1:30 PM. How does that sound?" Fox merely said, "Done. I'll see you then at your office."

DeBerg then called Betty, and said, "I set up a meeting tomorrow for 1:30 PM for the sale of that little company in Maryland you've been working on, AlgoGene Corporation. It's the first step in the negotiations, but I want you to produce a market valuation of the company and pull some draft contracts, revise them, and run some of the numbers for us. I appreciate your diligence and discretion, and remember this is a big step in your career." Betty sat in her office, surrounded by papers, and as she surveyed her domain she said, "OK, I'm on it."

She asked herself, why can't I ever say no. She was sure Mr. DeBerg never had that problem, and he never had any papers on his desk, either. Anyway, she braced herself for another all-nighter. She suddenly remembered that John Ordell was out of the country and could not meet.

She called DeBerg back to apprise him of the situation, and he said, "It's OK, we own the majority of shares and can sell whenever we want, but I appreciate the call. Anyway, leave it to me, I will call John to get him on board." He dropped the handset into its cradle. Betty had hoped he'd tell her to cancel the meeting, so she wouldn't have to work all evening, but that was not to be. Her time was his, and after all was said and done, money trumped all.

74

John and Lisa walked the short distance to the Whiskey Bar. It was crowded with tourists, pretty young women, and a larger than usual number of nerdy looking people who were obviously in for the conference. The scientists may not have been physically attractive, but they were mentally irresistible, and John was comfortable around them. The bar had an open contemporary decor, with backless stools located around a circular glass divider. The rich purple color was appealing.

There was also a long bar and a small stage. As a group was getting up to leave a table, John and Lisa made a bee-line for it, entering the carpeted area behind the glass enclosure and sat down, as they waited for Phil. John was perusing the large area as a waitress came to take their order. Lisa chose a white wine from a list with a number of Chinese vintages, and John ordered a Johnny Walker Black.

As he looked around the room, he noticed a cute young blonde woman who looked like she was there with her friends on a gambling junket or a bachelorette getaway. He also noticed more than a few cute Asian women. From the conference brochure he recognized one of the other presenters sitting at the bar, deep in conversation with two other nerdy looking guys, probable scientists. He didn't feel like engaging with them right now, so he gazed past them.

As he looked around the room, his eyes abruptly stopped on a tall, familiar Asian guy. He instantly recognized the guy as the one he saw on the street earlier that afternoon. He didn't mention anything to Lisa, but noticed the guy turn to look at him and quickly look away. Something just didn't feel right to him. Before he could think further, a young Asian woman was at their table introducing herself, saying, "Hello, my name is Li Na. Are you John Ordell? I recognize you from the picture for the seminar."

John smiled at her as he, for the first time, thought he was glad that they included his photograph in the brochure. He was in disbelief that this striking woman, who was more than a little physically attractive, was a scientist attending the seminar. Well, you can't always judge a book by its cover, and he certainly liked the cover.

He smiled at her as he said, "Yes, that's me. And if you don't mind my saying so, you sure don't look like the typical scientist I meet at these types of things." Lisa looked away, as she began to feel invisible to these two.

Li Na returned John's smile. John continued, "Allow me to introduce my colleague, Lisa. Would you like to join us?" She nodded yes as she shook Lisa's hand, then pulled out a chair and sat down. John noticed her beautiful white teeth, and that she had surprisingly good muscle tone for a geneticist. She looked directly into his eyes as she said, "I've read some of your papers and thought they were most interesting. I cannot believe how fast the technology is changing and how much it could impact the world. I'm privileged even to be a small part of it."

John looked back at Li Na and asked, "What lab are you working in?" She responded, "I'm just a very low level technician at Sichuan University." John became a little excited because he knew that they had recently done human clinical trials on lung cancer patients to extract T cells, snapped off the proteins called P1, and then reinserted the modified cells into the patients. The new cells, presumably, would not stop the immune response from identifying the cancer, so T cells can kill the cancer.

John said, "You're involved in some cutting-edge stuff," realizing she had been modest about herself and that she had to be particularly well-qualified to get a job there. Li Na blushed a little, not because she was embarrassed that he was impressed, but because it was not at all true and her military intelligence background made her a skillful liar.

The waitress returned with John and Lisa's drinks and asked Li Na for her order. Li Na ordered a Mai Tai.

John immediately felt at ease with this intelligent, attractive girl. It was unusual for him to feel this level of comfort so fast, especially around women he considered to be good looking. Maybe it was because she spoke his language – the language of genetics. Anyway, he wanted to impress her, so he said, "I'm familiar with Dr. Yu's work. It's exciting that he put together a protocol for testing on humans. How is that research going?"

Li Na had been briefed on how to respond to questions like this. She smiled sweetly as she said, "It's going very well, but until we publish, I really can't talk much about it. The research has to be completed, then peer-reviewed."

John nodded in understanding and apologized, "Sorry, I guess that was a stupid question. Anyway, where are you from? Do you have any brothers or sisters?"

Li Na cocked her head slightly and smiled when she said "I am from Shanghai, and I do not have any brothers or sisters, because of the one child policy in China." John was sorry he'd relied on standard questions in this interaction.

Zhang had positioned himself at the bar behind the post, out of line of sight with John. It looked like Li Na had John's full attention, which was very good. He was hoping that Li Na would get some valuable intelligence from this first contact then maybe, if necessary, get more through 'pillow talk.' He trusted that Li Na was prepared to do whatever was required. He could see that their conversation was flowing, they were both talking to each other intently, and it looked like everything was going according to plan.

John said, "I have a brother and I grew up in New York. Now I live in Washington, DC." Li Na looked genuinely interested and said, "I don't know if I would have ever left New York, at least from the magazine articles and books I've read. What made you move?"

He replied, "Just outside of DC in the State of Maryland is the National Institutes of Health and there's a tech corridor. The job prospects are what prompted me to move. It's mellower than New York, I liked it, and decided to stay. I ended up starting my own company, and the rest, as they say, is history."

Li Na said, "Yes, that is a very American story. It is not as easy in my country to do things like that, although things are changing. Anyway, I read the synopsis of your topic and thought it would be very interesting to hear your presentation."

John felt his face warm and wasn't sure if it was because of the drinks or the attention from Li Na. Anyway, he proceeded with his effort to impress her said, "We have done some interesting work, but the most compelling is our work with algorithms.

I found a computer scientist who is incredibly skilled at computer coding. He's experimenting with algorithms using the genomes of large mouse populations to locate the genes for particular traits. After we locate the genes, we use CRISPR to insert an edited gene to create a new trait in a mouse which it didn't have before. So far, we've been successful in determining the location of the gene for large ears, and then re-creating a mouse with large ears by changing its DNA.

The algorithm was also successful in locating three sections of genes which affect color. We have been able to change the color of mice from white to brown, and brown to white. We did it with other traits, too and are testing it for genes relating to intelligence. We created mice that can learn a maze incredibly quickly, and do other exercises that require intelligence. We found 14 genes that effect their intelligence.

The computer can locate other areas where the Cas9 system could make unwanted cuts in the DNA. This is a great way to figure out if the Cas9 will attach to other base pairs and affect other genes which express themselves in unintended ways. It seems to work seamlessly in mice, and should make testing safer. Soon we hope to begin a trial on chimps. We still have a way to go, but I have great faith in my computer guy, although it would be nice to have a faster computer."

Li Na's eyes widened slightly which made John feel good. She asked, "Is your computer engineer with you at the conference?" John replied, "No, but I don't think you would have liked him, anyway. He's not really a people-person. He prefers to remain behind the scenes."

Li Na unaffected, then asked, "Will you discuss these findings during the seminar?" John said, "No, because it's something we're still working on. I'll touch on it as possibilities for the future, but that's not the meat and potatoes of my presentation." She laughed, then he joined her, when she asked, "Meat and potatoes?" For a moment there was a pause between the two of them as they just looked at each other.

What John did not know was that the Chinese were listening in on their conversation through his phone. They were pleased with what they heard – that unintended consequences were the obstacle, otherwise the research was moving forward. Also, they couldn't believe how easily Li Na was able to extract this information from John. This young scientist prematurely ejaculated his secrets to the first pretty face he encountered.

Li Na looked to her left, toward a tall thin, mop-headed Chinese guy with thick, rectangular glasses who was urgently waving to her, and she said, "It looks like my research team is getting ready to leave, and I need to go with them. I hope to see you again at some of the seminars." She said good-bye, bowed her head to Lisa, and then shook John's hand. As she walked away, John was struck by a waft of her perfume, which he found to be intoxicating.

75

The salesman in DeBerg decided he could be more persuasive in convincing John to sell his part of the business if he was engaged face-to-face. He thought Facetime would sufficiently constitute a personal touch. He checked the time in China to make sure he would not awaken the young mogul. He dialed John's phone.

When Ordell picked up, DeBerg said, "It's been too long since we last talked. Betty's had a lot of positive things to say about you and your little shop. I have some very important news for you," DeBerg paused for effect before continuing. "We have had some inquiries about your business and I want you to know how impressed we are with what you have built here. Yours is a top-flight operation. The new products in development and those already patented have created quite the buzz. Sometimes, exciting translates into investor interest."

John had a nervous smile on his face as he listened with rapt attention. He was very nervous because of all the uncertainty. He didn't know why DeBerg was contacting him, instead of Betty. He didn't know what Dr. Duretts wanted him to do, and didn't know how things would pan out. Initially he thought that the meeting may have been set to pull the plug on his operation because Artie had told him that Kolb Kravath was having some money problems.

DeBerg continued, "We've set up a meeting with James Fox, an investment banker, who represents a significant and well-heeled client. His client is very interested in purchasing your shop and its intellectual capital, meaning you and your staff of scientists and computer experts. He or his client may need to speak with you and other key employees. Are you on board to sell your interest in the company?"

John was biting the inside of his cheek to contain his feelings. He had hoped that this day would come, but he was in disbelief that it happened so quickly. He answered, "If the price is right."

DeBerg cleared his throat and kept talking, "I need you to go over the various projects you have and the use of, what is it called – CRISPR – to impress our friend Mr. Fox, can you do that?"

"Yes, I can," John responded in a way that DeBerg liked, because it demonstrated confidence. Investors liked perceived confidence.

DeBerg said, "Great, that's what I hoped you'd say. Also, not to worry, he and his principal have signed confidentiality agreements covering the period of their due diligence." DeBerg was comfortable that he'd said enough. If this young talent thought that everything was OK, that was good enough for him. He'd learned early on that you don't oversell.

Before they signed off, John asked, "Mr. DeBerg, what kind of numbers are we talking about for the purchase?" DeBerg smiling like the cat who ate the canary said, "Numbers it would be difficult to say no to, possibly five to ten million per share. I'll get you a better market valuation after I speak with Betty. Anyway, so we can get a secure encrypted line, let's plan a business Skype call for tomorrow. Let's say 8:00 PM your time, 8:00 AM our time." As John looked into the screen of his cell phone, he said "Yes," and nodded as DeBerg hung up.

After the call, DeBerg called Betty to check on the status of the valuation. When she picked up her cell phone he said, "Hello it's me, how is the corporate valuation going? If this works out, I will be sure to bring it up to the compensation committee, and there should be a nice bonus in it for you."

Betty responded with a tepid, "Thank you." She had seen some of the papers they were drafting, and knew the numbers for the purchase of this business were in the billions, while her bonus would be likely in the tens of thousands, if that. She also noted the glaring omission of any mention of partnership. She felt like crying, but there would be no tears.

Betty then said, “Good-night, Mr. DeBerg,” she squeezed some eye-drops into her dry, aching eyes and turned back to the computer screen to finish the valuation.

76

After he finished the phone call, John took the card out of his wallet where he wrote down information from the corporate book, mostly just the number of shares and who had them. He remembered when they issued the 200 shares of equity stock, ninety-nine shares were issued to him, so the investment bank would have a majority of the stock. He then took great pains to have forty-nine of his shares properly issued to Lisa, with all the necessary signatures attached. That left him with fifty shares. He also issued two shares to Artie, because he'd made the commitment, which left him with a grand total of forty-eight shares.

As he stared into the air as if he was looking at his shares, it was hard for him to grasp that each could be worth five million dollars or more. Christ, he thought, that's a lot of money. He did a quick calculation in his head – at that rate the purchase price would be a cool billion dollars. That seemed unbelievable, but it could possibly be even more than that, given the value of the hair restoration product alone. He thought, Dr. Duretts is going to be one happy camper, or so he hoped.

Half a world away, in her office, Betty zoned out a little as she looked at the corporate book. She didn't believe in counting their chickens before they hatched. Still, she had work to do.

She reviewed the corporate book to ensure that it was in order. She was happy to see that her company had its 101 shares, but was shocked when she saw that Lisa owned forty-nine shares and two shares belonged to Artie, leaving John with the remaining forty-eight.

Betty Facetimed with John a moment later. He picked up on the second ring, and she said, "Hi, it's Betty. I was just working on the valuation and when I looked at the corporate ledger was surprised to learn that Lisa is going to be a very wealthy woman." She furrowed her brow and asked, "Did you sleep with her?" Betty instantly regretted saying it because it was none of her business, and moreover she was certain that there was nothing between the two.

John, taken aback, said, "No, I didn't, and I don't appreciate the inference. But you said I could distribute my shares however I wanted – and I stayed within the parameters you gave me. And again, there's no funny business going on. She actually helped me a lot when I bounced ideas off of her. She's kind of a muse for me. Just look at our emails back and forth. She's been invaluable to the company and as you know, she was one of the first hires. I couldn't pay her a lot, and I also had no idea that the company could ever be this profitable and would ever be worth this much."

"Unbelievable! I work like a maniac. I put in all the hours that are necessary, have no personal life and earn a whopping $230,000 a year, with my bonus, not to mention incredible stress, and Lisa come-lately is a serious millionaire in less than a year," Betty blurted out, again surprised that she hadn't stopped herself. All of a sudden, she began laughing uncontrollably.

John said, "Listen, I want you to know how much I appreciate your help with all of this. I'm new at this kind of thing, but I'm surprised that DeBerg didn't take care of you. I only ask that you don't make a big deal out of this. What's done is done, and if Lisa comes out OK, I'm good with it. I'll also make sure you do OK too."

Betty thought that comment was odd, but it was her nature to believe him even if it was improbable. Anyway, she wasn't in the mood to argue with this potential multimillionaire and they had a lot of preparation ahead of them.

77

John had a funny feeling in the pit of his stomach, and he didn't think it was because of the food. He felt unsettled, that something was not right. He couldn't put his finger on it, but after sitting in seminars all day and with the important phone call coming up that evening, he felt like getting away from the hotel and going out into the warm air. He hoped to clear his head of the pressures of the meeting, the money, and the butterflies he felt in his gut.

He instinctively raced out of his hotel room, down the stairwell and out to the front of the hotel, where he caught the first in the line of taxis. His destination wasn't far, but it was fairly hot outside and he didn't feel like walking. He put his hand on his back pocket, hoping to feel his wallet which, thank goodness, was there. He noticed, however, that he didn't have his cell phone.

He quickly decided against going back for it, and asked the cabdriver to take him to the Guia Fortress. The driver gave him a big smile, with 2 missing teeth and said, "Yes," without letting on that he thought, 'What a lazy American, who can't even walk the short distance to the fortress.'

The trip was over almost as suddenly as it began. John paid his driver with the local currency. He then exited the cab and walked up the steps into the fortress.

Meanwhile, at the hotel, all hell was breaking loose. The target had left in such a big hurry that they lost him, and when Zhang and his team pinged John's cell phone, it wasn't with him but was in his room. That put everyone in a state of panic, because they were under strict orders not to let the target out of their sight. He had left so quickly that they couldn't get a tail on him.

What made matters worse, was that when Zhang spoke with Wang Wei last night, he learned that the downloaded computer hadn't contained any formulas for specific uses with the CRISPR system nor any algorithms, either – only emails describing how great their research was going.

Also, they hadn't recovered any formulas or algorithms when they hacked John's server. They were aware from some emails that John had a second computer which was offline. For a guy whose company had such an ineffective firewall, it was surprising that he had a separate computer that likely contained the most important information. Though, in this day and age, it was an excellent way to maintain secrecy.

In any event, Deng Ngo, the money guy, and Wang Wei, his boss, were unhappy with this development because it meant they'd actually have to proceed with the purchase of the business. They could not simply rely on having their own scientists reverse engineer the information from hacked materials. Zhang did not want to be the bearer of more bad news, that John had escaped them and was off the grid.

So he decided not to call. Instead, his team would just sit tight and wait for John to return. Zhang would then employ their secret weapon – Li Na.

Meanwhile, John was at the top of the fortress and when he came to the spot where the cannon faces his hotel, he decided to sit down and think. When he found a bench, he looked to the left and noticed the scientist that he had encountered earlier – Li Ming. He gave a friendly wave and the scientist walked over to join him. John noticed some birds singing in the trees around the park, and thought how similar it was to Washington.

John asked Ming, "Did you enjoy the seminars today?" Ming responded, "Yes, very much."

Ming watched a bird as it flew into a tree and then said in imprecise English, "It is interesting time to be a scientist, particularly in our field. My country is very eager in this kind research. A reason for host this event."

John shook his head as he said, "Yes, I agree. But I have a big telephone conference call with the financial guys from my company tonight, and I'm getting nervous, which seems to happen every time I talk about money. I also forgot my phone, which makes it harder for me to get back to the hotel without the GPS. Anyway, how did you get your position at the Broad Institute?"

Ming's smile widened a little when he found out that John did not have his phone. As he looked at another bird in the tree he asked, "I feel naked without connect to phone, do you?"

John smiled back and said, "Yeah, me too, a little."

Ming went on, his English much improved, "I graduated third in class at University and went a semester at MIT and then got Phd. That is how I got assigned for work at Broad Institute. You should know that here, our government spends a lot of time following people using their phones.

Actually, some time ago, American companies sold the Chinese government software which allowed them to track people and keep track of where people are located at all times. The companies also helped with the Chinese firewall. It's hard to believe that your country's companies gave my government the ability to crush political dissidents and protestors for democracy.

I know firsthand from my friends, that government can and does listen in on your conversations using your cell phone. Government agents watched one of my friends through his phone. So, forgetting your phone not bad thing sometimes."

John then looked at Ming differently, as if for the first time, and felt that his intense intelligence had been masked by his slight build, funny looking haircut and glasses. John continued, "Yeah, you're probably right, but I'm just a scientist and not very political – I can't imagine that anyone has any interest in me."

Ming continued, "I studied in America, and liked it. Anyway, if you ever need lower-level scientist without much experience in field, I would be honored to work for you. I was lucky to get position with the Broad Institute, but I don't come from politically connected family so it unlikely that I move up. My family is Christian, and that doesn't help, either. I am also involved in some research which goes against my conscience."

John said, "Your English is pretty good, and I may be able use someone like you." As he looked directly into Ming's eyes he asked, "But what do you mean, that goes against your conscience?"

Ming looked troubled, and furtively glanced around the park before quietly saying, "Some leaders are impatient with pace of research and have no qualms about accelerating breakthrough by allowing testing of all kinds, no matter how bad outcome, or how they could adversely affect other people. They do not understand the limits on the scientific method, they only want results which cannot be forced. Some of the research into cures for different diseases is publicized, but they conduct other research which is not – which is, how do you say, under the radar."

John, taken aback, thought that he had to be misinterpreting what Ming was telling him. Were the Chinese following him? Had they engaged in espionage to get information from him through his computer at the airport and hacked into his server? After all, they were in a communist country, and the government could jail people for minor infractions or for nothing at all.

He now questioned the wisdom of laying it on so thick in his emails when referring to the algorithm. He hadn't realized he'd been playing with fire, and on their home turf he could get burned. It was ironic that Ming desired to get a job so he could leave China, and even if John granted that wish, the CRISPR product could, ultimately, still be made in China.

Ming then said, "I better go," and then implored with a nervous look: "Please tell no one that we talked, or what we talked about." John, still looking at Ming, responded, "You can trust me. Maybe we can talk again, later." Ming nodded yes, and as he walked away hoped he wasn't noticed for this contact with the American. From everything he'd read about John, and their brief encounters, Ming felt John could be trusted.

After Ming left, John sat in a shaded area for another half-hour, thinking about the upcoming conference call – who wanted to buy the company, and for how much. He didn't know what to do, was uncertain about what Dr. Duretts wanted him to do and what the bankers expected. He couldn't get past the feeling that something wasn't right, especially after the disturbing meeting with Ming.

It was still light outside, so John decided to walk back to the hotel. He looked through the parapet, saw the hotel in the distance and just began walking in that direction. He went down the steps and was back at the hotel quicker than expected.

As he entered the hotel lobby, Li Na just happened to be walking across the lobby heading toward the adjacent Starbucks. She offered him a warm smile and said, "Hello again. I was just going to get some coffee. Would you like to join me? You could give me a preview of your talk tomorrow."

John felt like going back to his hotel room to relax, but he just couldn't say no to Li Na. He returned her smile and with a slight tilt of his head, said, "Sure, you can help me by giving me some feedback."

A smile returned to Zhang's face, as he listened through Li Na's phone when he heard John acquiesce. He thought that Li Na was a perfect solution to his problem; a young guy like John could not resist her. Zhang had given her a list of questions to ask, but told her not to push to make him suspicious.

As they walked out the door, Li Na asked him, "Did you see anything interesting while you were out?"

John, a little distracted by Li Na's perfume, said, "I went to the Ghia Fortress," as he pointed toward the fortress and said, "I like it up there. The views are great and I needed to clear my head for a phone call from home this evening about the possible merger or acquisition of my company. There's a lot of money at stake." He didn't know why he was opening up to her like this, but it weirdly felt like he was bragging to impress her.

Once in the coffee shop, Li Na ordered in Chinese and he ordered in English. He preferred when she spoke English, but it was nice to be with someone who easily blended in and belonged. Li Na got her drink first and walked over to a set of chairs. John watched as she walked away. After the barista handed him his coffee, he joined her.

Li Na asked, "So what will you say in your seminar tomorrow? Will you begin with a joke?"

John said, "That's not a bad idea. If you have a good CRISPR joke, I'm all ears. I was planning to discuss my thoughts as I devised a new type of CRISPR process and the method I used to locate the balding gene. I also planned to talk about how I even did some of the initial calculations in my head, and assisted my tech guy in doing the calculations which are the foundation for the coding."

Li Na, seeming impressed, asked, "What is 273×127?" John quickly said, "34,671." Her face lit up with the immediacy of his response. She said, "You may not believe this, but my father used to be able to do that, too. When I was a little girl my mother loved asking him crazy math problems, which he could always do in his head."

Li Na then got back to business, although the lines between business and pleasure seem to be blurring. Anyway, she was still smiling when she said, "I know I asked you this already, but are you going to discuss the algorithm that you used to select the proper location of the gene for balding? To me, that is the most fascinating part of all."

John responded, "My prodigy programmer, an expert in statistical machine translation technology, uses the information we received from customers who send us samples to check their DNA profiles. We input it into a computer using his algorithm and it learns from the different profiles where specific genes for different traits are located. That's how we found the gene for balding.

The programmer loves repeating to us that the entire genome of each person is only about 300 gigabytes. Since the DNA series is essentially four letters, it is tailor-made for computer analysis. It's even better with mice because we can test the results against whole generations in much less time.

The computer has become very accurate in calculating which genes affect which traits in mice. It's also proficient in tracking changes in genes as mice age, and the changes in their genes which are turned on and off as the result of their aging or disease."

Li Na looked captivated by what she was hearing and then asked the billion-dollar question: "Who is this mystery programmer that you're talking about?"

Without hesitating, John said, "David Goldblum."

Zhang, of course, had been listening intently during the whole conversation and thought, 'Good girl.' He would run the name through Google and their own special databases to find out all there was to know about this super programmer. Zhang couldn't wait to talk with his supervisor, and immediately dialed Wang Wei.

78

John sat in his hotel room with Lisa. He was drinking a Diet Coke and was deep in thought. She was scrolling through her phone and had been on Snapchat until 7:55 PM, when she hung up in anticipation of their scheduled conference call. She would sit out of view of the camera and John had asked her to remain silent. Still, she was representing her own, as well as Duretts' interests, unbeknownst to any of the other players in this drama. So she stayed in the room for moral support, if nothing else.

Finally, the phone rang at exactly eight o'clock. It was Mr. DeBerg, on an encrypted Skype business line. He had boasted to John that it was the best encrypting software money could buy, and his IT guys had assured him that even the NSA could not penetrate this particular software. Regardless, DeBerg was in high spirits, the way you feel when money problems are about to fizzle away.

John, by contrast, was feeling unsteady. He sat in front of the screen and pressed a button on his phone so the call was on speaker, so that Lisa could hear the conversation. He wasn't sure who was offering the money. Whether they were legitimate or spurious business people, and whether they were reputable or dangerous. He recalled reading an article about Russian oligarchs, who bought sports teams and expensive homes around the world, to preserve their wealth beyond the reach of the Russian government, in case they fell out of favor with their ruler.

DeBerg knew by the amount of money involved that the group of investors was serious about obtaining this company and using its technology. He didn't completely understand why, or exactly what this new technology might do, but he didn't care. When this deal went through, he would be elevated as the miracle worker who saved the financial day for his company. Once again, he would be revered as a financial genius, a position he felt he deserved.

DeBerg cleared his throat and said, "I have wonderful news – the company my friend represents is very interested in buying our company and made an initial takeover bid of $750 million. I used to be an excellent poker player." With a wink and a smile he continued, "The bid is now $5.35 billion, with an initial payment of $2.2 billion."

John's jaw dropped as he couldn't believe what he just heard. He wondered if Mr. DeBerg had mistaken him for someone else involved in another deal, or maybe he'd simply misspoken. DeBerg probably accidentally added a few extra zeros. John actually thought he heard Lisa swallow hard. This was money at a level beyond his comprehension. As lacking in business savvy as he was, he realized that this amount of money would come with serious strings attached.

Suddenly the phone signaled that other parties were joining the conference, and DeBerg continued, "Please allow me to introduce Deng Ngo. He is working with Mr. Fox, an attorney and a friend, to put together the paperwork for the deal. We also have a team of lawyers, with some outside counsel, who are reviewing the tender offer. All parties concerned are eager to have this deal completed as soon as possible. To that end, they want you to retain some equity in the company as well as to continue working as the head of research and development." DeBerg paused to allow Deng to speak.

In confident, measured tones, Deng said, "I've been looking forward to meeting you. I represent a private company – Xian Corporation. We are enthusiastic about your groundbreaking research and believe it has potential for improving the human condition. We also have some scientists who would like to work with you and review your methods and computer capabilities."

The screen shifted back to Mr. DeBerg who smiled and advised John, "Because things are moving so very quickly, I've taken the liberty of hiring a lawyer for you to go over the details of the transaction, to make sure your rights are protected and that you are familiar with all the ramifications of the deal, including the way the payments for your equity are allocated to your accounts."

John still dumbfounded by the price they were willing to pay, thought that they could have had it all, including Mr. DeBerg and himself, for much less. But if they'd gotten hold of some of his emails and other materials which were accessible on the Internet, then they clearly were investors on a mission. Whatever their motives, this deal would make him richer than he would have ever thought possible. His portion alone would net him A-Rod type money, and it wasn't a multi-year deal.

Mr. DeBerg still had that big smile plastered on his face when he said, "At this time, I just wanted you to give our friend Deng some assurances about the processes, the IT abilities, and the viability of our new product to reverse balding. They've signed nondisclosure agreements, so you can speak freely."

John looked into the camera as he began to describe the capabilities of his algorithm, how the CRISPR technology was directed to the proper location of the genes, how it cut the genes and then repaired them with coded genes to permanently prevent hair loss in the subject. During parts of the presentation, he became extremely technical, and DeBerg had no idea what he was talking about. Deng had a better handle on it, but was not exactly following it all. It was impressive nonetheless. Finally, John talked about the presentation he would be giving the next day.

Deng shook his head, approving of what he was hearing, then said, "We would like you to stay on as the president of the company, and your IT team as well, to continue using the algorithm, possibly even improving upon it." He continued, half-jokingly, "I just hope you don't teach the other scientists at the convention so well to permit them to steal our ideas." He turned serious again, then said, "I'd like to see you in our corporate headquarters in the immediate future, so that we can finalize the deal. When will you return from the conference?"

John, still looking at the camera, stated, "I do appreciate the offer. I'm going to be finished here in two days and will fly back to Washington, where I'll meet with my key people. After that, I can fly anywhere you want me to be to meet with the principals. If you don't mind my asking, who are the principals, and what are their backgrounds?"

Deng stated, "I believe they will soon make their identities known to you. I am glad that you are now on board. I look forward to meeting you in person very soon. Thank you for taking this call on such short notice."

DeBerg then said, "Thank you, and take care everyone." John also said, "Goodbye," and then the screen went blank and the conference call was over. John had just become a multimillionaire, at least on paper; it remained to be seen whether he would be one in reality.

79

Deng Ngo was shocked when he received a call from a member of the central committee. He knew that the CRISPR technology he was dealing with was a high priority, but he didn't realize its import until that moment.

Deng had heard that the higher-ups felt that it was their duty to harness this technology for the 'better good' or at least their own good, and they owed it to the next generation to use the technology. But he knew better – that they wanted it for themselves and their families, and certainly didn't want the Americans or others to be the first ones to harness the power of CRISPR.

The member said, "We are particularly interested in acquiring the technology from John Ordell's company, who our intelligence tells us has made great strides in both the AI side and the biological piece. We want his breakthroughs on the use of CRISPR that may have military applications, or be able to cure diseases or even extend life." The voice raised slightly as he said the last phrase.

The speaker said, "I would like us to see Mr. Ordell and his programmer, one way or another. Understood?"

Deng said, "Yes. We have Ordell under surveillance and we can get the programmer."

The speaker was pleased that Deng was on top of the situation. The speaker said, "I would like us to make sure that Xian purchases the company and there is no leaving anything to chance. I also want to make sure we have his programmer. Are we clear?"

Deng said, "Yes. One problem, though. Mr. Fox indicated in a roundabout way that there appears to be a group of Russian oligarchs who may be trying to buy Ordell's company out from under us."

The speakers' eyebrows raised slightly when he said, "I do not want that to happen, and if it does, it will make many people unhappy." Deng knew what that meant.

The speakers' eyebrows raised slightly again when he said, "I do not want others to acquire the company's technology and innovations. I think you agree that no one wants to see leadership unhappy." Deng again said, "Yes."

The speaker then offered, "As you know we have identity cards, facial recognition and perform collections of DNA from millions of our citizens. We have culled massive amounts of data from social media. Our access presumably will allow the algorithm to perform and unlock the potential of CRISPR. We will be providing access to the most sophisticated computer we have, which was the best in the world until recently."

The speaker, barely moving a muscle said, "As you are aware, we authorized up to $5.5 billion to purchase the company, if we are unable to get their secrets and algorithm by other means. Until this is done, Ordell is not to leave China, and I want the programmer here, too.

Let's see what we can do to get the technology either before the sale, or release partial funds and convince them to provide the algorithm and other trade secrets. As you know, I do not like paying full price, so see what you can do."

Deng, simply said, "Yes, sir."

80

John was ready to leave Macau. He wasn't a big gambler, had seen the sights, and even though the city was exotic and exciting, he was looking forward to getting home. A high point for him was meeting Li Na. Anyway, there was only one more day of seminars, with time in between to be spent talking with business-minded friends and acquaintances. He'd already gotten Li Na's contact information and hoped that he'd see her again before he departed.

He picked up the room phone and called Lisa to ask if she wanted to get dinner. She responded, "Why not? I'll meet you in the lobby in ten minutes." He responded, "Uh-huh." When he went down to the lobby, he saw Lisa sitting on a comfortable looking couch with her legs crossed as she looked at something on her phone.

When he approached and stood over her, she looked up, and asked, "So where should we go for our last dinner in Macau?" He responded, "I made a reservation at Clube Militar de Macau. I heard it's supposed to be pretty good." She said, "Fine by me."

The doorman hailed a cab for them, and the driver looked disappointed because it wouldn't be a big fare. As they rode to the restaurant, John looked at Lisa and said, "Our trip is coming to an end, but it looks like we have a deal for the purchase of the company, and I think both you, and Alan, will be happy with the outcome. I know I am. This whole thing happened so fast, and seems to have worked out for all of us. Now, we just have to start finding cures for all that ails humanity." Lisa just shook her her head, rolled her eyes and looked at him the way an older sister would look at an annoying little brother, although there was some truth to his joke.

They got out of the taxi and as he looked up at the pink façade of the restaurant, he noticed the same Asian man he'd seen at the bar, and then later on the street. For a split second he dismissed it as coincidence, but then decided to mention it to Lisa. He said, "Lisa, I'm getting a bad vibe from that tall Asian guy over there. I think he might be following us." Lisa cautiously peeked at the man standing in front of the entrance to the restaurant. She thought she recognized him.

John then led her by the elbow away from the entrance onto the sidewalk, and noticed that the man started to move with them. He glanced again at the man, who never made eye contact with him, but kept moving with them as they walked. John remembered his father telling him to always follow his gut instincts – because your instincts were almost always right.

John said, "You know what, I'm going to run across the street. Why don't you walk down the street a couple of blocks, then take a cab back to the hotel."

Lisa kept walking, while John turned and ran across the crosswalk which was painted with white stripes. Just as John began to run, Lisa glanced over her shoulder and saw the tall Asian trying to keep up without calling attention to himself. Out of the corner of her eye, Lisa noticed another guy on the other side of the street, about a quarter of the way down the block, also starting to move in John's direction. Lisa hoped she was wrong, and speeded up her pace, though it was difficult in heels. When she glanced behind, she didn't notice anyone following her, much to her relief.

Zhang couldn't believe that he had a runner on his hands. He was surprised by how fast John was running when he crossed the street. With his special forces training and athletic abilities, Zhang felt certain that he would catch his man. However, to ensure that they wouldn't lose him, two other agents were stalking their valuable quarry, as well.

John made it across the street and turned left toward a parking lot. He made a quick right into the lot and saw a large number of scooters, where a young man was getting on a scooter. He was short and skinny, and John, running at full speed, easily knocked him down and grabbed the scooter with his left hand. Briefly, he thought how lucky he would be to be able to drive out of this. He swung on top of the scooter and hit the gas.

Unfortunately, Zhang ran into the entranceway of the lot just as John started moving forward. Although the entry was fairly wide, John was looking back over his shoulder at the guy from whom he'd boosted the scooter. Zhang extended his arm and clothes-lined John, knocking the wind out of him. The scooter slid out from under his body. John was surprised that the guy who hit him used his arm to cushion John's fall. What was this guy up to, was he trying to kidnap him for a ransom? He had no idea, but didn't want to find out.

John scraped one of his elbows and tore his shirt when he landed flat on his back, with the other guy's hand and arm beneath him. A moment after he landed John sprung to his feet. The man looked surprised, when John swung with his right hand trying to punch him in the face. The man ducked, then John swung with his left hand and made contact with the assailant's stomach.

Zhang was surprised by the second punch and, although he had been hit much harder in the past, it was a decent blow. Through sheer instinct, Zhang swung and hit John slightly below the eye. John's eye would probably blacken, but Zhang hoped no one would be too upset about him striking the scientist. Unfortunately, it had to be done.

At that moment, the other agent sprinted into the lot and surveyed the situation. John went down onto the pavement, but again sprung up looking directly at Zhang. The two Asians were unhappy with how this was unfolding, but when John hesitated for a moment, the second man pulled back his jacket to disclose an Uzi in its holster. John's eyes widened and he stopped moving. At that moment, a van pulled up in front of the lot entrance and the side door slid open. The person who clothes-lined him, then grabbed John, and placed the hood over his head. He then guided John to the side of the van and placed his hand on John's head, so he would not bang it, as they forced him inside. John was still in shock as he felt the van accelerate and speed away into the night.

81

Lisa kept walking for several more blocks, until she was able to flag down a cab. She was actually shaking when she entered the cab. She told the driver her destination, then checked her phone to see if John had texted her. It was unclear exactly what had happened, but she wanted to get back to the hotel ASAP. The cabdriver dropped her off at the hotel, she paid him, and then swiftly walked to the elevators and up to her room. She wasn't sure what she should do, so she decided to call the police.

The person who picked up spoke Chinese, and Lisa began having second thoughts about getting the police involved. Lisa then asked, "Does anyone speak English there?" The operator immediately switched to English, and said, "Yes. Is there a problem?"

Lisa quickly began, "I was with my colleague, and someone was following us. I think something might have happened to him."

The operator stated, "I will send an officer to meet you, are you staying in a hotel?" Lisa said, "Yes, I'm staying at the Lisboa." The operator said, "An officer will be there shortly." Lisa felt reassured by the calm voice of the operator.

Less than an hour later, two officers arrived who were fluent in English. She explained, as best as she could, what had transpired. One of the officers asked, "Did you see what happened after your boyfriend ran across the street?"

Lisa did not like where this was going, and said, "He's not my boyfriend, he's a colleague. And no I did not see everything that happened, but it looked like two men were chasing him." The officer looked quizzically at her and asked, "Did you see any contact between them, any violence?" Lisa shook her head as she said, "No," and the officers appeared satisfied. The officer continued, "Look, in this city, guys ditch their colleagues all the time because there is so much to do. Don't worry, he probably found something more interesting to do. If you get any more information, or if he doesn't show up within forty-eight hours, then you can call us." They then handed her a business card.

The officer in charge didn't bother to make a written report, and called into the dispatcher. The dispatcher asked him to hold for the deputy police commissioner who wanted to speak with him.

After a brief pause, the deputy commissioner came on the line and said, "This matter ends here. The investigation relating to the call you just took is going nowhere, and you are not to pursue it any further, understood?"

The response was equally clear: "Yes, sir."

82

John felt the van finally slow and then come to a complete stop, for what felt like a long time. He then heard voices speaking in Chinese. With the hood still on, he was led from the van into a building. A moment later the hood was removed by the man who chased him. The man had a look of contrition on his face and said in passable English, "I am Zhang. I am sorry that I had to strike you, because I did not wish to do so. You left me no good choice."

John surveyed the room and realized it was a well-appointed office with bookcases filled from top to bottom with interesting looking books. It didn't strike him as the kind of place he'd be secreted to by a terrorist organization or someone involved in gangland kidnappings. Also, his captor seemed calm and relaxed. Consequently, John asked, "Who are you, and what am I doing here?"

Zhang said, "I am Zhang. I am not the best person to answer your questions, however, I will tell you what I am permitted to tell you until that person arrives. I work for a company that wishes to buy your company."

John, trying to remain calm, said, "Then why not just approach me and talk with me. And why was there the guy with the hardware – what was it, a machine gun? That's a funny way of making someone feel comfortable."

Zhang nodded and said, "That was regrettable. However, principals of our company thought there were other potential buyers and decided to take control of matters. You can understand that, can't you?"

John nodded yes, but still felt something else was behind this.

Zhang asked, "Would you like something to drink, tea, water or coffee?" John said, "Yes, please, can I have some water?" Zhang left the room, then returned a few minutes later with water and a platter of rice and cooked meats. Zhang said, "Please, help yourself." He took some food and then sat down at a table across from the desk in the office.

Zhang looked up at John and said, "I expect the company chairman to appear any time now. I see you have a bruised eye. Again, I am sorry about that. I have asked someone to bring ice for it." A moment later the door opened and a manservant arrived, with an ice bucket and towels.

They sat in silence as John held the ice compress against his eye. John was trying to make sense of this bizarre situation. Zhang remained mum, since he had been directed only to make the prisoner feel less uncomfortable.

A few minutes later, the chairman entered the room. He walked in with a confident air as he made his way to where John sat. The man was dressed in a navy business suit with a bright red tie. He had thinning gray hair and a round plump face with a serene mien, the look of someone who always expected to get his way.

The man reached out to shake John's hand and said, "Hello Mr. Ordell, I am Liu Wei. I am the Chairman of Xian Corporation. It is a pleasure to meet you and I hope our friendship leads both of us to prosper."

John was finally beginning to feel at ease. They both stood silent for a moment, then Zhang excused himself.

Liu Wei sat down directly across the table from John, and softly said, "It is truly my pleasure to meet an exceptional, young scientist like yourself. As you may know, our country is embarking on a new path which combines communism with capitalism. We are serious about being at the forefront of new technologies, including renewable energy, IT and, of course, CRISPR DNA technology. That is what brings us here today – the reason we are so interested in your company, the people in the company, and the technology which you bring to the table."

Liu paused for a moment, then continued, "As an old man, I am personally intrigued by a world without cancer, heart disease, schizophrenia, Lou Gehrig's disease, and many other diseases that are too numerous to name."

Chairman Liu continued, "I have heard rumors about an algorithm to uncover what the various genes do. This technology, combined with our best supercomputers – and we have the best – hopefully will eliminate mistakes in the research. How could we allow this opportunity to advance humanity to pass us by?" The chairman was smiling broadly.

As John nodded, he thought, this guy sure did his homework. He even knew about the algorithm. This made John glad that they'd gone to the trouble of protecting the algorithm in the other offline computer.

John, trying to make the best of the situation, said, "I agree in principle with everything you've said. I planned to devote my life to this type of work, but as you know the Achilles' heel for this research is the fact that we cannot in good conscience test our hypotheses or computer-generated data on humans, which makes the research painstakingly slow."

The Chairman cocked his head slightly and said, "It might not be an insurmountable problem. That is one of the reasons we wanted your team to come on board with us. We wish to accelerate the research and to advance the technology in the immediate future. I know about your mother, and how she died. No one should have to endure the agony of cancer and this technology can stop a great many people's suffering." He paused before changing the subject to lighten the mood, then said, "I also know that you have developed a therapy to end balding, an affliction that I am familiar with," as he rubbed his own bald head.

John then said, "As desirable as it may be to want to advance the science quickly, most of the international community opposes human testing, and in the US, it is a criminal offense and is completely out of the question."

The chairman nodded and said, "You might not be familiar with our business practices, but I can fill you in. You are the CEO, right?" In a quivering voice, John stammered, "Yes," which made Liu confident that he was the one in control.

Liu continued, "We usually enter into licensing agreements with American companies, sometimes called technology transfer agreements. We are proposing this kind of deal to buy your company, although we are purchasing your company and its technology, unlike in transfer agreements which occur when the American company invests in China. Anyway, the lawyers can explain better than I can.

When we go through with the sale, your products will have access to a market of over a billion people. We will, of course, pay you well for the licensing of the technology."

Liu strategically paused to provide John a moment to mull this around. It was the same line they used to hook CEOs since the 1990s, and it usually worked like a charm. Much different than the Chinese way, short-sighted Americans were looking for quick profits, and they didn't get bogged down with the long-term ramifications of sharing technology with their biggest competitor. If nothing else, the Chairman understood the psychology of people and their primary motivations.

Liu continued, "We will enter into a technology licensing agreement with your company, something called a joint venture where we make an initial payment and then, over time, make additional payments for the licensing rights for the technology. The CRISPR technology is not very difficult to use and that is not a critical part of your research, although we like your new method of CRISPR that was recently patented. What we are more interested in is the algorithm."

The chairman continued, "We would like our people to collaborate with your staff to fine-tune the computer program. Your country has some of the best programmers in the world, and we look forward to working with your esteemed computer professionals," he said humbly, though he actually believed his team of Chinese professionals to be superior to their American counterparts. But Liu was willing to supplicate, because he desperately wanted to get his hands on the algorithm technology.

John said, "Unfortunately, you may be too late. We already have a deal in place with a group that offered a fair price."

The chairman nodded and said, "We are aware of that offer. It is from my company, Xian. I am sorry, I thought you knew. Anyway, I am speaking with you off the record because your team has signed a confidentiality agreement. Here is a copy of one for you to sign. Take a minute to read it and then sign it." John scanned it, and signed it to move along whatever was happening here.

Liu said, "Thank you. This means you have no choice but to keep what we discuss secret. Now, we are both bound to keep our talks secret."

John merely shook his head in agreement.

Liu's voice became lower when he said, "I will deny what I am about to tell you if it is ever disclosed, and I will sue you, too. We already have two levels of CRISPR research going on. One is public, the other is confidential and private."

John, once again uncomfortable, said, "I'm not exactly following you."

Liu did not want to spell it out, but felt he had to in order to close the deal. He said, "It is in the best interests of our people that we get this technology into a usable form as quickly as possible." He intentionally omitted the fact that elderly influential party members, who had very little time left, were demanding help now to relieve their maladies, and to possibly extend their lives.

Liu took a deep breath and continued, "In China, we believe that the good of the few is subordinate to the good of the whole – society at large. That being said, for public consumption we have traditional research that is reported in scientific journals. You may have read about our recent use of CRISPR to target a specific gene in monkeys without any ill effects. That was well-publicized."

The chairman went on, "Still, we have other research which is not public, not peer-reviewed, and which we are not prepared to disclose to the outside world, at least not yet. That research involves testing our hypothesis with animals, chimpanzees and even human subjects." He looked at John to assess his reaction.

A stunned John asked, "What, exactly do you mean by testing on animals and humans?"

Liu looked at him and said, "I'm sure you heard of the work our scientists have done with embryos, that didn't work very well, until now. That is the type of research I am talking about, but we were not actually involved in the recent work on embryos, which was conducted by a rogue scientist. More to the point, our scientists are experiencing difficulties with the unintended consequences of changing DNA material, and that's where your algorithm comes in. Please tell me about it."

Though John was becoming more uncomfortable with the direction of this conversation, he was at the same time intrigued by the possible application of his technology on humans. Perhaps he was destined to become the father of modern-day genetics. Although the algorithm appeared to work well with mice and other animals, occasionally there were serious problems. Terrible mutations or death were always possibilities. There was no certainty that new genes would successfully translate well in humans.

John decided to provide a thumbnail on how it worked. "We were successful in using mice with various genetic diseases and traits and input the information into a computer. We did this first with 1000 mice, and our computer was excellent at identifying particular genes. We used a computer program with statistical machine translation technology.

We were able to inject mice using a variant of the CRISPR/Cas 9 with material targeting the genes identified by the computer, and were able to change white mice into black, and short-tailed mice into long-tailed mice. We were even able to identify one mouse, particularly good at navigating a maze and created others similarly skilled at navigating the maze."

John continued, "In all honesty, I must say, that we had some issues with the mice embryos; some died, some were born with hideous mutations, and one appeared to be brain-damaged. Overall, I would say we had a good success ratio, like the Chinese scientists who experienced success in using CRISPR to create muscularly enhanced beagles."

John went on, "My program has actually identified numerous genes in people, although they have not been tested, and we know which genes control eye color, hair color, balding, height, muscle tone, muscle efficiency, strength, speed, as well as a number of genes that affect intelligence and a whole lot more. Again, full disclosure, it was not tested on people and the amount of genetic information we have from our ancestry business is statistically significant, but limited."

John continued, "When we did the tests on mice, we had the computer isolate other areas in the mice genome to make sure that there were no areas that the CRISPR/Cas9 would improperly attach to and to be certain it did not cut at a wrong or unintended spot."

He further stated, "The computer was also used to assess the viability of CRISPR-blocking proteins and perform calculations to target a precise spot on the CRISPR-Cas9 molecule. This has the potential for blocking changes in DNA that cause manifestations of disease or old age. It was based on the work by a postdoctoral fellow in Jacob Corn's lab. Using the supercomputer we have, it took a very long time to perform these calculations."

With a sense of pride, John said, "Using our system, we were also able to track when certain genes in mice turned on and off, to effectively determine how mice mature and age."

Liu shifted in his chair and said, "This is exactly what we were searching for. Now I am certain that I want to meet your programmer. He continued, "When our scientists conducted research on animal subjects, there were issues because they were unable to locate the correct genes, and even when they thought they had, they were wrong and there were those unfortunate unintended consequences. Your computer program seems to eliminate that problem."

The chairman then lowered his voice to almost a whisper and confided: "I shouldn't tell you this, but our successes have not only been with the beagles, but also with changing certain characteristics in primates. Certain genetic issues are straightforward and deal with one gene for a particular characteristic, and it is easy to identify because very few animals exhibit that problem – like for some genetic diseases."

Liu continued, "As an example, one of the easier ones to locate relates to people born with a genetic defect that makes them mute. The portion of the gene controlling speech is located on a specific portion of a specific gene in human beings, and people without this gene were not able to formulate speech."

Liu went on, "What has not been made public is that our scientists tried adding that gene into the DNA of capuchin monkeys, and the ones that survived were able to speak." He added gleefully, "It's really something to see. That is an example of Xian's off-the-books research." The chairman decided against reviewing the history of testing done by Xian which had gone horribly wrong.

He leaned back to gauge John's response. John had an inquisitive look on his face, so Liu continued and said, "That's one of the reasons we're interested in obtaining your company, and the input of your valued employees to help us advance in our endeavor. We hope that your programmer can tweak the algorithm to eliminate the guesswork and needless suffering of animal and human test subjects. We hope to speed up the research to eliminate suffering from all types of maladies. As a scientist, I am sure you see the value of what we are trying to do."

John appeared interested, but remained skeptical and leery about what he was hearing, given the aggressive way they had abducted him. He looked over at the chairman and said, "Your motives may be pure, but was it really necessary to kidnap me?"

Liu appeared sympathetic, and with a concerned look on his face, said, "I think our man was perhaps a little overzealous. I am sorry about your discomfort, but our culture is different than yours. Sometimes our actions appear as aggressive behavior, which is at odds with Western sensibilities. I apologize for our transgressions, but with the potential for such groundbreaking advancements, I think we owe it to humanity to get past this misunderstanding. Only in this way can we move on to the important work that will benefit all mankind."

Liu wanted to close the deal and said, "We have already contacted VIP clients in China and abroad for purchasing of our product, and that is why we have provided your team with such a generous offer. They are people for whom money is no object. I'm expecting that they'll love to pay to alleviate diseases in themselves and their progeny, and pay to change their health, bodies, minds, and maybe their life expectancies. We foresee prominent individuals willing to pay for CRISPR. Indeed, a number of Chinese party members have already indicated a desire to use the technology."

Excited, the chairman took a deep breath and continued, "Like your balding cure, we want to take it to the next level by allowing people who are willing to test the CRISPR treatments to do so. I'm certain that we will have no problem finding volunteers. It is a patriotic and selfless act, a way to help your fellow man, especially if we can learn to cure diseases, or enhance human beings by making them smarter, faster or stronger. Most test subjects will likely be criminals or peasants, and if there's a bad outcome, their families will be compensated. Isn't that the American way?"

John said, "Before we go further, I need to speak with my partners and our attorney to review your proposal."

The chairman said, "That is understandable."

"My banker knows the attorney's name. I suppose your representatives have already spoken with him," John said.

The chairman paused for a minute. He knew all the attorneys in the States who purportedly were experts in Chinese law. Although most of them demonstrated some level of competency, a neophyte to Chinese law would be a very good development. He hoped that was the case.

The chairman returned to one of his most important objectives and asked, "When can I meet your programmer? We can have someone pick him up in the US and bring him here."

John, concerned about David's reaction to being told that he would suddenly be whisked away to Asia for a meeting with a high level corporate executive, said, "OK, but I need to speak with him privately to get him on board."

83

The programmer, David Goldblum, was sitting in his $400,000 condo on Georgia Avenue in Wheaton, Maryland. He was engrossed in solving a coding problem for his friend, Frank, who was developing a new app. David, however, was quickly unraveling a solution. For David, it was like looking at a whiteboard with an intricate tree of information that had a few gaps to be filled in. It seemed quite simple to him. He was upset when he looked at the clock, and two and a half hours had burned past him. He wondered to himself, am I slipping?

When he texted Frank that he finished, the immediate response was "Great. Thanks!" David couldn't help smiling his goofy smile to himself as he sent a quick text back, "Remember, I get 10% of sales."

He decided it was time to grab dinner at a local favorite, Los Chorros, just up the street. As was his habit, he grabbed his tablet and headed out.

Like most nights, he would be eating alone, which he preferred, since he didn't like engaging in small talk. His pursuits were rather narrow, and he typically wasn't interested in the same things as others. In social situations, he would often find himself tuning out during conversations, and that frequently made for unnecessary discomfort for all parties concerned. It came down to the simple fact that the only people he could relate to were those who talked shop. Anyway, he was looking forward to reading an article about 5G, between the salsa and chips and his vegetarian chimichanga.

When David entered the restaurant, the owner recognized him and stated, rather than asked, "Table for one." David nodded yes. As he walked into the main dining room, he noticed two deuces of Asians seated at separate tables. This struck him as odd; usually there were Hispanic families and blue-collar workers and a smattering of more adventurous Caucasians. Who knows, with property values going sky high, maybe the neighborhood was changing again and causing a new surge of regentrification.

He sat at the second table on the right. He immediately turned on his tablet and his MiFi. A moment later his business skype app opened and it was John Ordell. David answered, "Hello, I didn't expect to hear from you. I thought you were in China." John responded, "Thanks for picking up. I am in China."

As John looked at him, David looked away but, always to the point, asked, "How is my software? Do you need any upgrades?" John replied, "No, it's nothing like that. I'm with investors who are eager to meet with essential team members, especially you." David then asked, "Why me?" David didn't want to meet with anyone. He liked to think his work spoke for itself. He did not know anyone in China, did not want to know anyone in China, and hated trying to explain his work to people who didn't understand it.

John smiled at him and said, "I know, I know, you're not exactly a people person, but these guys are serious. Before they are willing to do the deal, they need certain assurances about your algorithm." David glanced at John on the phone and said, "OK."

David was on board because he trusted John as a science guy like himself. John didn't strike him as judgmental, and he didn't get hung up on David's vibe. John then continued, "I think someone named Dai will be picking you up to bring you here. All the arrangements have been made. You only need to bring the algorithm." Almost expressionless, David said, "OK. Bye," then hung up and returned to his article.

When he was finished, he asked for the check. He was startled when one of the Asian men sitting closest to the entrance came over and in an unassuming voice said, "Hello, my name is Dai. Have you spoken with your CEO?" David looked perplexed and was instantly on edge. He said, "Yes, I was told about you. I did not expect to see you this soon."

Dai had only been in the US for a few days, awaiting instructions. He was surprised that his mission was to ensure that this slight, awkward young man be brought to China as soon as possible. Dai said, "I would like to assist you so that you can go tonight. We have a private jet on standby at the FBO at Reagan Airport."

David was friends with some of the best hackers around, and had a sinking feeling that he had been hacked and tracked. He had either heard of, or seen firsthand, all manner of corporate espionage before he accepted the position with John's company. Without a secure link to John, he thought the best course of action would be to take matters into his own hands.

He told Dai, "I want to leave tomorrow morning. I have to fulfill an obligation with another colleague before I leave. What time tomorrow morning, maybe sometime after 10 AM?"

Dai made a snap decision that this guy would be easy to follow, and his instincts told him to do this the easy way. Dai said, "I will pick you up at your condominium at 10:30 AM," David agreed, "Yes, that will be fine." Dai left the restaurant with the man he'd been sitting with. A few minutes later, the two Asian men from the other table left as well.

David then pulled a burner phone from his pocket that his hacker friends insisted he use when he contacted them. He dialed Jason Norton, the best malware programmer he'd ever met. Their friendship went way back to their college days when they studied coding.

He hoped to reach Jason quickly, given the short window of time he'd been given before he'd be leaving for China. Jason picked up on the third ring and said, "Hi David, what's shakin'? It's been a while. Have you changed the world yet?"

David tersely replied, "Not yet. Can you meet me tonight?" Jason said, "Sure, at our usual watering hole," referring to McGinty's in Silver Spring. David said, "Thanks. See you there at nine o'clock and please bring your new friend," referring to the most recent malware Jason wrote. Jason said, "I'm sure he'll be pleased to make your acquaintance." They then hung up simultaneously.

David left his usual generous tip, and without so much as a word departed from the restaurant. He took a left to Georgia Avenue and another left back to the condo. When he got home, he changed clothes and put on a hat before taking the back entrance to the Metro, and riding it two stops from Wheaton to Silver Spring.

In the meantime, Dai held a conference call with his extended team. He told them, "We will pick up the target from his home at 10:30 tomorrow and transport him to our jet at Reagan National Airport. Between now and then we must follow him at all times. No one is to engage him unless it is absolutely necessary." Dai then hung up the phone to let the team take care of the business they knew so well.

Dai was unnerved because he was unable to hack into the target's phone, probably because he was an expert programmer. He consoled himself with the knowledge that his team of skilled human assets would be more than sufficient to cover this 90-pound weakling, who appeared to have no intelligence background.

One team watched David's condo and two teams worked to track him – a pair in a car, and another pair on foot. The two on foot were on the opposite side of Georgia Avenue from his building, with a clear view.

They observed David walk out the front door of his building. The teams were connected by phone. The team in the car rode southbound on Georgia Avenue. The other team began walking southbound as well. They figured if he was on foot, then he must be heading toward the Metro.

They called ahead to two additional operatives who needed to be in position inside the Metro. They were positioned at the bottom of the long escalator pretending to look at the Metro map. When told that David entered the Metro station, they split up, one standing next to the northbound track, and the other the southbound track. They thought it more likely that David was going southbound, toward DC, so the other agent went down to the left and sat on one of the stone benches. The other agent stood right by the opening that connected the two tracks so that he could move to the southbound track, if necessary.

The agent standing by the opening observed David all the way up at the top of the escalator. He said, "Here," to the other agent in Mandarin, lifted the Chinese newspaper which he pretended to be reading when David made his way to the tracks. The operative at the northbound track moved closer to the track area to be less conspicuous, but stayed near the opening so he could determine which direction David was moving when he got off the escalator. They were used to following professionals and did not know what to expect from this amateur. They found out soon enough.

David rode the escalator to the bottom, then turned right toward the southbound track. He walked about a quarter of the way down the track when the lights on the floor began to flash. The train came into the station with a 'wooosh' sound and a rumble before stopping, the doors slid open and David entered the train.

The agent on the southbound side, was in the car next to David's. He walked to a seat near the door closest to David's car. The other agent had also entered the southbound train, but was in a car approximately four cars behind where David entered. The operatives were glad this had been such an easy assignment, but couldn't imagine what made the skinny guy such an important target. They reported David was on the southbound train, and would tell their counterparts where David would exit the train.

Two stops later, in Silver Spring, David exited the train. From the platform, he took a short escalator ride to the south side of Colesville Road. He walked up the hill towards downtown Silver Spring, crossed

Georgia Avenue, and then walked south to Ellsworth Avenue, the heart of downtown Silver Spring. The two agents on opposite sides of the street followed David until he entered McGinty's bar. They decided against entering the bar, but instead took turns walking past the bar monitoring the patrons that went in and out. They also posted an agent at the back exit which went into a five – story mall.

Jason had arrived at McGinty's about 30 minutes earlier, waited about 20 minutes at the bar and then took a booth on the second floor in the back corner. It was a good vantage point and would be a good place for a serious conversation that would remain confidential. When he saw David's highly perturbed facial expression, he thought he had guessed right – this just might get heavy.

As he approached the table, David looked nervous. Without any formal greeting, Jason said, "You look pretty damn serious, what's this all about?" David looked discomforted when he responded, "I'm not sure, but like the saying goes, something is rotten in Denmark."

Jason, still uncertain of whether David was engaging in hyperbole said, "What do you mean? What's going on?"

David said, "Something is just not right," then continued, "I'm not really sure. You know, I took a job writing code for a biotech startup. Then, all of a sudden I'm sitting in a Salvadoran restaurant and these Chinese guys are approaching me, wanting me to take a private jet to China. What are they doing at my restaurant in Wheaton and how did they know I was there? They wanted me to go tonight. And it was right after my boss called me for a video chat."

David proceeded, "I know from some of my tech friends in San Francisco that the Chinese like to steal software and not pay for it. I developed a code that reads DNA, maps it and figures out what different genes do. It works better than the scientists even realize, and with better hardware it should be even more effective. Anyway, I'll be damned if I let other people rip-off my idea. I swear it's not going to happen that way again. Don't think I'm nuts, but I'm sure two Asian guys followed me when I left the Metro."

Jason got the gist of what his friend was saying and knew well the bitter pill of having someone pilfer your idea for their own gain – even if David might seem a little paranoid. David knew first-hand how companies screwed with, and took advantage of coders. If memory served Jason, David had been a plaintiff against the tech companies, who colluded to artificially depress engineers' pay.

Just then a waitress came to their table and asked if they'd like refills. After she walked away, Jason looked directly at David and said, "I think I know where this is going, my friend. I do have a new malware program that I brought with me which should be virtually undetectable."

He then leaned into David's space and whispered the details of the code, what made it so hard to detect, and the finer points of its method of attack. David had a glimmer of a smile on his face, occasionally nodding his head as Jason spoke, and the reason why everyone thought Jason was a genius coder became, once again, readily apparent. Jason had even thought to bring a fake gold necklace that could hold the zip drive without it being detected. David had become much less concerned by the time they finished speaking.

They stayed at McGinty's for another half-hour, and Jason entertained David with the most recent hacking escapades he knew of, while a content David listened. When they downed the last of their beers and David paid the tab, they parted company. A more confident, relaxed David, was on his way back to his condo to pack a few things, wearing his new necklace under his shirt.

84

After packing his bag with the basics – a couple of shirts, an extra pair of pants, socks, underwear and a few toiletries – David drank a cup of coffee to prepare to embark on the next task at hand. There was still work to be done before he went to China. For him, installing the malware into the code would be a walk in the park. However, to do it, he had to go to the office. He would then transfer the algorithm from the offline computer to his souped-up Allenware computer. It would be a hassle going through all the security in the office, but it had to be done in order to get access to the algorithm code. He figured to be done by midnight, and back home no more than an hour later.

As he was proceeding on the Metro back to Wheaton, he had already decided where he was going to insert the malware, so it would be virtually undetectable. As a failsafe, he would set it to completely meltdown all software on the infected computer on a date certain. That way, if anyone stole the software, they wouldn't have it when that day came. Anyone who inserted it into any computer would also lose all software on that computer, too. He also knew how to disable the malware, if need be. He was happy with his well thought out plan. And for those who dismissed computer geeks as lacking in common sense, they were just plain wrong.

85

John Ordell was unsettled because he was confined to a compound. His suite had everything but a window. They were treating him well, but it didn't change the fact that he was a prisoner. He knew they had already contacted Kolb Kravath, and hopefully Betty and DeBerg would soon arrive at the compound. He was actually looking forward to seeing the always level-headed Betty.

He had been introduced to the Xian scientists, who seemed genuinely interested in his research, and shared with him tidbits about what they were working on, and problems they were encountering. They described the projects that went wrong, which resulted in stillborn animals and animals with other defects which ultimately killed them.

John brought up published research done in the US on 'mutant ants.' The American researchers used a particular type of ant, called the clonal raider ant, which reproduces asexually. They used CRISPR to change the DNA to remove the ant's ability to smell pheromones emitted by other ants. This completely changed the ant's social behavior, and they no longer interacted the same way.

The really interesting part of the ant's biology is that the worker ant can, if the colony loses its queen, become the Queen. If the worker ant that became a Queen is later exposed to pheromones of the original queen, it reverts back to a worker again. This is interesting because the Queen's lifespan is normally four years, while worker ants only live seven months. If the worker ant that converted into a queen is exposed to the original queen's pheromones, it reverts back to a worker ant, and only lives for a few more months before it dies. This means that there must be a reversible genetic switch that controls the ant's lifespan. When the queen's pheromones make contact with the worker, it changes the lifespan.

John told them he thought his algorithm could take this research to the next level. He explained that he was in the process of using the algorithm to track the changes and analyze what happens to increase the lifespan, and then find ways to harness the biological pathway. The scientists agreed that it looked like a promising avenue of research.

He also told them about the newest research scientists had reported, that they were able to change the colors of butterflies' wings, which was the result of editing a single gene. Still, the research the Chinese scientists were most interested in hearing about dealt with gene expression and John's own experimentation with mice.

The Chinese scientists had their most prized achievement to share with him – their talking Capuchin monkey. He was told there were problems with the first hundred attempts, but they finally got it right with this monkey. They weren't really sure why. Anyway, when they finally showed it to him, it spoke in a high-pitched squeaky voice and its head seemed larger than those of other Capuchins. He only got to see it for a few minutes and it spoke Chinese. The scientists joked that it asked him for a banana.

It was the first time he came face-to-face with the reality of the technology; the sights, the sounds, and the smells of biology being manipulated. This new reality was scary and exciting at the same time. He wondered if the computer would have been able to figure out why this monkey was receptive to the CRISPR technology, while many others were not. Maybe the computer algorithm would be able to tweak CRISPR to make it possible to successfully alter all the Capuchins. But, John wondered, would that be a good thing?

86

John didn't know it, but David Goldblum already sat in his own suite, three flights above in the same compound.

In accordance with the banker's orders, David had not given the algorithm to the Chinese and kept his laptop close to him at all times. He had also taken the time to encrypt a password so it would take an eternity for an unauthorized party to gain access to the program if they tried. If the laptop's software felt its password was being compromised, it would meltdown the algorithm. Anyway, David was sure it would take time for the Chinese to test it, understand it, and make sure it was authentic. He also felt confident that they would not be able to detect the malware.

Wing Shu walked into the compound's conference room number 4 and David was ushered in five minutes later. Wing, who had already heard a lot about David's algorithm, greeted him with a pleasant smile.

Wing was forty-five years old, and had studied at Carnegie Mellon University and did his PhD at Cal Tech. That was a while ago, but he managed to move up the hierarchy quickly, working as a hacker for his government. He specialized in espionage – obtaining and analyzing commercial secrets from competitors, including multinationals.

Still smiling, he reached out to shake hands with David. In perfect English, he said, "My name is Wing Shu. It is my distinct pleasure to meet you. I hope you had a pleasant trip to our compound, and that your accommodations are satisfactory? I, too, am a programmer. I studied in the US, first at Carnegie Mellon, then at Cal Tech, but enough about me. Please, tell me about yourself."

David meekly reached out to shake Wing's hand. Wing continued, "We looked into your background, and particularly your expertise in statistical machine translation, that's enabled you to develop such a powerful algorithm. With information culled from our population, I think we could make great strides combining it with your work. I must say, David, I find your work to be a stroke of genius. You are a very impressive young man."

David was unaccustomed to such high praise, and met Wing's words with a simple, "Thank you," as he looked down at his own feet. After a too long pause, David added, "but we still need to revise the coding as more data is provided and faster computers are available. Our company's hardware, despite being a supercomputer, processes pretty slowly." He used air quotes when he said the word super, and felt that this fellow software engineer would appreciate the dig at the hardware.

Lightheartedly, Wing said, "I am happy to tell you that you're in the right place. I have access to the 93 Peta Sunway computer. It was the fastest computer in the world, until very recently. It should be fast enough to handle your algorithm."

David was familiar with the computer and his interest piqued at the possibility of using it. The computer was rumored to be able to perform 93,000 trillion calculations per second and had 10.5 million cores. It was ultra-fast, and shockingly, until recently was faster than any computer in the US. David began to feel embarrassed that the Chinese technology surpassed that available in the US; it was even more surprising than the ultra-modern airport he arrived at that seemed light-years beyond Reagan National, which he'd flown out of.

Wing couldn't miss David's enthusiasm at the prospect of using this state-of-the-art tool. Wing continued, "Our scientists did not come up with using AI and learning software to approach the problem of gene interactions. I must say, David, well done." After taking a deep breath, Wing asked, "So have you and John applied any of the information to the human genome and its expressions?"

David, now in his wheelhouse, began feeling comfortable talking shop with Wing, and said, "Keep in mind, that the entire human genome is 300 gigabytes of data per person. In mice it is far less. My AI algorithm learns from large numbers of genetic data in a species gene pool and finds statistically significant patterns in their expression. It can run through the genes, match them up with the traits expressed in large numbers of individuals, and then catalogue them for targeting by the Cas9 molecule. Even better, it can theoretically go through the billions of base pairs and check other areas where the Cas9 may attach, which should eliminate unintended mutations. It's a challenge but doable with my algorithm and the right computer."

Wing looked extremely pleased, but he didn't want to push David too far. Still, sooner rather than later, he hoped to review the algorithm and install it into the 93 Peta Sunway computer. With a little help from this young coder and the CRISPR experts at his disposal, they would be able to expedite the greatest experiment in human history.

87

A few stories above David's floor, John had been waiting in a conference room for approximately 10 minutes, not knowing what or whom to expect. Suddenly, the door opened and in walked David, Betty, Joseph DeBerg, and his new attorney, Bob Walker, an expert on Chinese transactions. John eagerly stood up to shake hands with each of them. He noticed that they looked jetlagged and harried, but DeBerg was in good spirits.

John spoke first, asking, "Can you fill me in on what's happening, because I'm not entirely comfortable with what's gone on here."

DeBerg put his hand on John's shoulder to calm him and said, "We were in contact with the Chinese and their deal is very good, but we do have some reservations – which is why we brought Bob with us. He has considerable experience in these matters and knows most of the players. The Chinese also agreed to permit us to go to Bob's office, so that we can discuss the deal in private and not in one of their conference rooms which could be bugged." DeBerg looked up at the ceiling as he said it. Bob also nodded in agreement.

DeBerg went on, "They've graciously offered us a lift to Bob's office, which is about 20 minutes away. Anyway, I know this has been tough on you, but I like what I'm hearing from the Chinese. We'll discuss it more when we get to Bob's office."

Just then two Chinese officers in uniform opened the door and one said, "We are here to take you to your lawyer's office." The two officers silently led the group to their SUV and they became part of a motorcade to the lawyer's building. They were somewhere in the middle of the high-speed procession. It seemed over the top, but it punctuated this as a very important deal for the Chinese – maybe a little too important.

When they arrived at their destination, they disembarked from the SUV. The Chinese motorcade remained parked in front of the building to await their return.

As they rode the elevator to Walker's office, he asked them to remove the batteries from their phones. Nothing more was said until all the batteries had been removed. DeBerg then asked, "What was that all about? I know they're willing to pay a lot for this company and its technology, but don't you think that was a little crazy? What do you think, Bob?"

Walker looked at DeBerg, and then at John, and said, "In the twenty-plus years I've been doing deals in China, I've never experienced anything like that before, nor have I heard any of my colleagues speak of such a display. It was unusual, to say the least. In case you don't know, there's a lot of industrial espionage that goes on here. That includes everything from hacking phones to bugging rooms and everything in between, so I wanted to make sure that we had our privacy."

Walker looked at each of them, before continuing, "When dealing with the Chinese, it is imperative to get as much money upfront as you can. They have a poor reputation for making deals and not following through. I've seen deals where they agree to pay a large sum of money, but renege once they get technology, then all of a sudden all bets are off and it's a fight for every nickel."

Walker went on, "The laws in China are difficult to navigate and often the agreement will be between a company and your company, then, and at the last minute the Chinese change the deal so a subsidiary is substituted, which has no assets. Consequently, you can't recover from them through the courts if they decide to take the technology and not pay you. Another shady tactic I've seen employed is that their courts permit them to get out of deals if the agreement is not properly translated into Chinese."

Walker continued, "I have also seen them try to leverage a client's desire to get the deal done, where the client thinks that they need you more than you need them. Most of the time, however, they want your technology and don't really need you. So, again, I cannot overemphasize that you need to get payments upfront. Under no circumstances should you give them the technology before payment clears."

Walker proceeded to educate them, "With the demonstration of force that they just made, I think we will be able to get them to bite on the upfront money being wired to a joint account before the actual exchange of technology occurs. I have a general idea what your technology does, and they apparently urgently want what it does, so this transaction may well go off without a hitch."

Walker then informed them, "I've spoken with your prior attorney, and he's already transferred all of the relevant information regarding the deal to me. The Chinese seem willing to pay you a premium to close on the deal within a narrow timeframe, which I think is extraordinary. I've also done some research on the Xian Corporation you are dealing with, which is a subsidiary of a subsidiary. Like most of the companies here, I guarantee you they are at least loosely connected with the Chinese government. The Xian Corporation appears to have access to large amounts of capital, and can easily cover the cost of this deal. As such, if you wish to proceed, I believe you can succeed if you do so with caution. I will go over the paperwork, but the critical issue is the concurrent timing of the transfer of the funds to your accounts with the transfer of the technology to the buyer."

Walker then focused on what might be a sticking point, when he said, "It also appears they want both John and David to continue working for them in China for a two-year period. They are each to be paid a salary of $1 million a year, which is over and above the amount that they get from the transaction. From my experience, that's a lot of money to make in China if your family is not connected to the party."

Before John or David could respond, DeBerg said, "How exactly is this going to work? Will their company purchase all the stock in our business, and is that legal under American law?"

Walker said, "Yes, although China does limit market access for US companies in China, the Chinese basically have full access to purchasing American companies. And if, for example, you were going to open up an arm of your company in China, like Ford Motor Company, you'd be required to do a joint venture with another Chinese company in order to operate there. In this case, though, because they are buying you out entirely and will take total control, a joint venture will not be necessary."

Walker continued, "I had my associate do some preliminary research and we do not believe that your technology is subject to closer scrutiny by the US government. From the Chinese government's standpoint, they seem to be in favor of this transaction, which is always a plus in a country like this, where, how should I put it, the laws are somewhat malleable."

Walker smiled when John started to raise his hand, like a schoolboy, and Walker queried, "A question?" John replied, "Yes, what if David or I don't want to stay in China for two years working with them?"

Walker responded, "We may be able to work something out in the purchase agreement, though I am fairly certain that they'll want you to be on board at the beginning to help them navigate the new software and technology. We can put in a liquidated damages clause if you want to leave earlier. This is a challenge, but not an insurmountable obstacle."

Walker then added, "Another thing we can do is ask for additional stock options in the new company, which would make it worth your while to stay, should the new enterprise make it big. It's very likely you will have to agree to an anti-competition clause, which is fairly standard. Some equity in the company might be the best way for you to go. What do you think?"

At that moment, John wasn't sure what he thought. What was clear to him, however, was with so much money at stake, no one in the room wanted to nix the deal. He merely responded, "I guess it sounds OK to me." He then glanced at Betty, who looked back. It was clear to her that John wanted her opinion, since they'd gotten close as colleagues over the past year. She gave a little nod, acknowledging that she would talk with him later.

In a further effort to rewarm cold feet, Walker continued, "I think this is a great opportunity for you on many levels. You're poised to become rich, to possibly learn Chinese, to make invaluable contacts and to be at the forefront of DNA research. It seems like the opportunity of a lifetime. Keep in mind, it's a market of 1.4 billion people. Most CEOs would kill for entrée to this type of market."

Mr. DeBerg, momentarily concerned by John's seeming reluctance, now wore a giant smile on his face, as he moved to adjourn the meeting, "Wonderful work and congratulations everybody, I think we're done here." DeBerg thought to himself, like the Phoenix, he would, once again, rise from the ashes through this crazy deal. This transaction would put him on top again.

DeBerg clapped John on the back as he shook his hand, then proceeded to shake hands with David and Betty, and then did something totally out of character. He hugged his lawyer, who appeared to have effectively navigated through this course of landmines.

88

Mr. DeBerg, Betty and Mr. Walker stayed at the office to go over the terms and conditions of the prospective deal. Walker began by reviewing with them the voluminous document the Chinese had provided for the bulk sale transfer of the business. It contained the usual boilerplate language, including the transfer of the technology prior to payment being tendered.

Walker advised them his counterpart, a prominent Chinese lawyer, agreed to a change in that provision without much negotiation, which surprised him. In fact, the lawyer representing Xian was agreeable to almost everything Walker wanted. It was clear, someone had been given marching orders, and that was to get the deal done. The Chinese didn't engage in the usual pretense, they simply wanted the deal to go forward.

Under his counterproposal, a number of initial payments were to be made, which included $2.2 billion being transferred prior to the proprietary information being exchanged. Walker disclosed much about the business to them after the confidentiality agreement was signed and firmly in place, but the guts of the research and computer algorithm's coding had not been disclosed.

Experience told Walker that once critical information was disclosed, further payments would stop. All initial payments needed to be made and wired to the appropriate accounts before the entirety of the technology was turned over. He'd previously discussed his concerns with Mr. DeBerg, who concurred. They were both of the opinion that obtaining an initial payment of $2.2 billion was the way to go. This would guarantee they received sufficient payment. They might even get a little more, but $2.2 billion would work. They were unlikely to ever see a total payment of $5.35 billion, but they were OK with that.

Walker added to the agreement that both John and David would be employees of the new Xian company, and part of their compensation would be in stock options in the company. They would relinquish all stock for cash and pay back 10% of their share of the sale, if they did not remain as employees for at least one year. Moreover, the full stated purchase price was $5.35 billion, although Xian Corporation had them for $2.2 billion.

Bob Walker, Mr. DeBerg and Betty rode the elevator down to the lobby and when the doors opened their Chinese handlers were ready to whisk them back to the compound so the documents could be signed. Five black SUVs sat in front of the building and Walker, Mr. DeBerg and Betty were led to the middle SUV while their security detail entered the other vehicles.

They arrived back at the compound without much fanfare, and were ushered into yet another conference room where three lawyers representing the Chinese entity shook hands with Mr. Walker and Mr. DeBerg, ignoring Betty. The Chinese made some minor changes to a few paragraphs, which were of little consequence, and indicated the new purchaser of the company was called the Xian Gongsi, which meant the Xian Corporation. Walker didn't know the translation for Xian, and it didn't matter, but he thought maybe later he'd Google it. This had all seemed too easy, Bob Walker thought.

Once all the paperwork was in order, they had John join them in the conference room so that both he and Mr. DeBerg could sign the multiple documents. Both had already signed a confidentiality agreement, whereby if they violated the agreement, provided any proprietary information to other companies, or in any way described or explained the activities and work performed by Xian, they would have to pay back all of the amounts they received under the contract and be subject to punitive damages. But no one was thinking along those lines at this happy time, and both of them signed and initialed without giving it another thought. There was another Chinese man in the conference room who signed on behalf of Xian Gongsi.

When all documents had been signed, the most senior attorney on the Chinese side of the table stood and said, "Congratulations the transaction is complete. Xian will be wiring the agreed upon monies to the account provided by Mr. DeBerg. As per the stipulations in the contract, Mr. DeBerg's bank will act as a fiduciary in distributing the funds to the appropriate shareholders. Thank you for your professionalism, and we look forward to a long and fruitful association." There were handshakes all around as everyone awaited the transfer of funds within the next five minutes.

After confirmation that the transfer had occurred, the Chinese attorneys left the conference room, wondering why their negotiating skills had not been tested and why the payments were made so quickly. After they were out of sight, they shook their heads as if to say this is not how deals should go, but orders are orders.

After the room cleared, John approached Mr. DeBerg and said, "Since I'm going to be here a while, I was wondering if it would be possible for Betty to stay and help me with the business end of things?" Although DeBerg didn't consider Betty to be irreplaceable, he said, "I don't know, Betty is an integral part of my team and even for a short period of time will be sorely missed." He looked to her and asked, "What do you think of Mr. Ordell's request?" Betty smiled and said, "I'd be happy to stay to help."

DeBerg said, "OK, I'm sure we can work something out, and hopefully our investment bank won't have to close down without her." Betty smiled again, but was thinking how overworked, underpaid and unappreciated she felt working for Mr. DeBerg. It made her decision an easy one. At this point in her life, she had nothing to lose by staying.

DeBerg grabbed his coat and said, "Consider it settled, Betty will stay as long as you need her. I'll have my assistant get you folks set up in a hotel, but until then you'll be staying at the compound, while you're getting acclimated."

DeBerg still had one piece of outstanding business to attend to before he left for home. He called the banker controlling his wire transfer account, who confirmed that the $2.2 billion had been received. DeBerg then texted John, 'Payment received, let them have the algorithm.' With a huge weight lifted, DeBerg left the compound with Bob Walker. This time, however, there was no motorcade, just one SUV that drove them back to their hotel.

At the hotel, DeBerg asked their concierge where the best steakhouse in town was located. He invited Bob to join him for a celebratory dinner, complete with the best vintages and cigars money could buy, all to be expensed to Kolb Kravath. DeBerg had more than the deal to celebrate; he'd gotten rid of his nemesis, Howard McQue, and he'd also single-handedly managed to save his company from the brink of financial ruin. Yes, indeed, life was good.

DeBerg reconsidered his planned side trip to Beijing. At this juncture, it would be much better to revel in his success with his partners, to let them know he was still the Big Dog.

89

Meanwhile, John was feeling anxious and constrained, and not at all like someone who was in control because he had just become richer than he ever imagined possible.

He needed to talk with Betty and David. Maybe that would make these feelings disappear. But he was scheduled to meet with one of the Chinese CRISPR scientists. So much for the idea that money gave a person his freedom.

Just then there was an almost inaudible tap at the door. John slowly opened it to reveal an Asian man wearing a white lab coat that made his light-yellow skin look even paler. He had a hint of a mustache, which looked like it hadn't grown in completely. He struck John as the most unassuming person on the planet. The man said in a soft voice, "My name is Tai Tan. Congratulations on being purchased by Xian. I look forward to working with you on this fantastic venture."

Tan continued, "I was assigned to accompany you to our labs to share with you our latest research." He looked at John and said, "What you are about to see is confidential proprietary information." John was surprised by Tan's command of English and even more surprised that the scientist cared about the proprietary nature of the research. What were they afraid he would reveal, John wondered?

Tan handed John a white lab coat, then said, "Follow me. We are going to the lower levels of the complex."

They walked down a long corridor without saying anything and finally came to an elevator with a security device. Tan stared into a facial recognition camera. He hit the elevator button and the doors slid open almost instantly.

He then turned to John and said, "I'm going to show you the work performed by the Xian scientists. What you are about to learn is not for public knowledge, and I ask that you keep an open mind. Our research is not for the faint of heart. But I think you'll agree, as a scientist, you are viewing a seismic shift."

As Tan said these words, he was carefully studying John's reaction. He didn't know if the message was getting through, but he felt that he was laying the proper groundwork to prepare John for what he was about to see – softening the blow to a certain extent.

Tan continued, "What you're about to see are the changes we were able to make in animals and even some consenting humans." John shot an incredulous look at Tan, then asked, "Did you just say humans?"

Tan matter-of-factly stated, "Yes, I did."

John, staring at Tan, then said, "Surely you're joking. That violates maybe a half dozen international norms and rules." Tan didn't miss a beat when he said, "It is a small price to pay to alter the destiny of human kind – to be able to improve our species."

The curious scientist in John took hold, and he asked, "But how do you get subjects for the human experiments, and how do you limit side effects?" Tan replied, "We use criminals and the poorest of the poor. They are happy to make the sacrifice and understand it is a small price to pay for the good of the rest of us." John doubted the 'happy' part of the argument, but was still intrigued.

There was something exciting being on the cutting edge of this research, well past where other scientists dared to tread. It made sense for the people who would benefit, but it wasn't necessarily so good for the guinea pigs who made the sacrifices.

The elevator door opened and John was reminded of a line from a movie where one character says to another, 'Oh, so now we're going toward the creepy.'

They walked through another corridor to a steel door. Tan stared into another retinal scanner and John heard the latch click open. Tan offered, "I urge you, please remember, with your expertise and the software you developed, some of the more problematic outcomes hopefully will be avoided in the future. Since I need to get back to my research, I'll give you a quick tour of the eukaryotic organisms, including the mammals, first."

Tan walked over to a cage with what appeared to be a 4-foot-long chameleon – the kind that John had when he was a kid, only about 100 times larger. On the door it said chameleon, number 1,538. Tan explained, "This is a simple pet store chameleon which was injected with CRISPR DNA targeting the size of the chameleon. We inserted the DNA from a crocodile to elongate the chameleon. There were 1537 misses until we finally got it right."

John was fascinated by this creature, which reminded him of his childhood, but asked, "What were the misses? And, what happened to those animals?" Tan shook his head and answered, "We killed them if they were not viable."

Then they walked over to the cage that held the talking Capuchin monkey. John wanted to know more about this animal and asked, "What was the inspiration for this monkey?"

Tan said, "I read an article about a group of people who were mute, and scientists were able to isolate a gene that was not present in their DNA sequencing. Everybody who exhibited this problem was born without that particular DNA sequence, so it seemed logical that adding this DNA would enable those people, or primates, to speak. We first applied it to the Capuchins, and it finally worked after 1,812 tries. Don't ask about the ones that did not work because it was pretty nasty business."

They walked over to the next cage, which was empty, but labeled:

Subject number 28. John asked, "Why is this cage empty?" Tan responded, "It held a test subject who had autism. We tried to reverse the autistic gene but it did not work. Apparently, there are a number of genes controlling autism and the CRISPR technology we used wasn't successful because we didn't address all of them. The subject, who was not cured, was released." John said, "That's too bad, was he OK?" Tan responded, "Sure."

They turned the corner and saw three dogs in a cage. The tag said, Dogs, number 792. John looked to Tan and asked, "What's with the dogs? They look like ordinary dogs." John couldn't resist saying, "What did you genetically engineer them to be? Dogs with colder, wetter noses?"

Tan said, "Not exactly," but thought it a good sign that John could joke about the research. He continued, "Watch this," then hit a button that activated a mechanical arm about 20 feet over the cage which held some dog treats. John and Tan watched as one dog after another jumped the 20 feet to get to the treats, then landed safely on the floor of the cage. Tan explained, "We analyzed the genome of wolves, and other related animals to develop a dog which has ultra-efficient muscles. They can jump higher and run faster than any dogs you've ever seen."

Tan continued, "We got the inspiration for this change from reading about muscle efficiency. Human muscles are only about 12% efficient, which is the reason they are slower and weaker than other animals of similar size. Dogs also have less efficient muscles, but as you can see, we successfully altered these dogs to change that." Tan beamed as he said, "With CRISPR, there may yet be hope for you and me that we will one day be able to play shortstop for the Yankees."

John returned Tan's smile, as they continued the tour. They reached another door, with another security device that Tan looked into. Again, the door unlocked and they went through. They began walking down another long corridor, toward another group of cages. Suddenly, they heard a scream and a loud, pulsing buzzer went off.

There was then an agonizing wail, which had a blood curdling effect on anyone who heard it.

Tan looked at the horror on John's face and said, "We should leave this corridor. Either an animal escaped, or one of the animals attacked its handler; we should allow those who are equipped to deal with this problem. Also, I must get back to my work." They rushed back through the doors to a bank of elevators which returned them to the upper floors of the compound.

John's need to talk with Betty and David had become urgent, because what he'd seen and heard pushed him far beyond feeling uncomfortable.

90

When John got back to his room, the phone was blinking. He picked up and dialed the number to retrieve his messages. The operator said, "I have a message from Betty. She would like to see you. We can arrange for a conference room on her floor. Would you like me to do that?" John responded, "Yes." The voice then directed him to, "Take the elevator up one flight, turn left, proceed down the corridor until you reach conference room number eight, on your right." John then hung up the phone and left his room to meet Betty.

John knocked twice before Betty opened the conference room door. She had arrived just a few minutes before, and was in the process of pulling a bottled water from the refrigerator. She really wanted coffee, but wasn't exactly sure how to operate the machine on the counter, and though there were a variety of pods to choose from, the packaging was all in Chinese. When she opened the door, she could tell John was glad to see her, and she greeted him with a little hug.

Betty began, "Since I'm staying, I want to be completely up front with you. Xian's made me a generous offer, too. Like you and David, I had to sign their 25-page nondisclosure agreement."

She continued, "Between you and me, I've seen a number of these NDAs that other people have had to sign during business deals, and you should know they are ironclad. If you disclose any of the information you learn from Xian, they will be able to sue you and get back every penny that you earned from the deal. You could also imperil payments to everyone else involved. So, if you don't want to go back to square one, you can't tell anybody about what's going on here. We have to play ball with Xian."

She went on, "There's really nothing new about what the Chinese are doing. They like to buy hightech and biotech companies. I remember reading somewhere that in 2016, China purchased $40 billion worth of US companies. That's billion with a B. That being said, I think Xian is already getting funding from other rich investors who want first crack at their products."

Betty paused to take a breath and said, "In this part of the world, officials turn a blind eye to all kinds of activities, including black-market stuff. In this case, there is little likelihood of scrutiny of Xian and no regulators will come swooping in to save the day. I can't imagine the company will encounter any blowback from testing on animals and possibly even humans, which is a commodity in no short supply in China."

This revelation hit John like a ton of bricks. With Betty's help, John had finally put two and two together, and now it was clear to him what was going on, and how his algorithm would be used. The computer program, if it was successful, was the missing piece to their puzzle – particularly with their supercomputer.

Now he understood why there were only a few cages in the bowels of the compound. Xian's plan was to get him and his team to help as much as they could, then forever hang the thought of losing everything over their heads, like the proverbial Sword of Damocles. And he had given them the keys to the castle – a program that David had written to speed up the research and limit, or altogether eliminate, unintended consequences.

Betty was silent, to allow time for what she said to sink in, then continued, "In a communist country with a command economy, there's a lot that goes on off the grid, if it's sanctioned by the right people. Most of the capital is concentrated in the hands of a few people, and what they want goes."

She said, "Paying a few billion dollars to retard the aging process, to cure their own diseases, or to give their children a leg up is a no-brainer for them. It's something that these old guys would be very interested in. Especially since CRISPR is like the gift that keeps on giving. Most people would pay just about anything for that, and these people have already demonstrated that they have the means."

John, loathe to what he was hearing, decided to end this discussion, since he knew that the walls had ears. He told Betty, "I'd like to meet with my team to go over a few things. Can you set it up?"

91

John asked to see David Goldblum, and it turned out his room was on the same floor of the compound as Betty's. They talked for a while about the trip to China and the conference, then discussed the compound and their accommodations. When they were done with the pleasantries, John asked, "Did you turn over the software to Xian?" David said, "Yes, only recently because Betty told me that under our contract we had to."

David then put a finger to his lips, indicating he didn't want to speak, while he put his other hand in his pocket to pull out a piece of paper. He then palmed the paper to John. The note said: 'There's a meltdown virus embedded in the software.' David surreptitiously took the note back from John and then made a move like he was wiping his mouth, but he was actually eating the slip of paper. It felt like an amateur maneuver, but was probably effective if they were being listened to or watched.

John didn't want to do anything to cause suspicion, so without batting an eye said, "Yeah, she was right, you have to give them whatever they need. They own us now." David nodded in an obsequious way, then said, "They also asked me to sign some kind of confidentiality agreement. I don't really understand why they needed it from me, since I'm not one of the suits, although I know in Palo Alto it's not uncommon, so I signed it."

John shrugged his shoulders and said, "Looks like they made us all do it. It's really no big deal, though they should have paid you for it. Did they?" David shook his head yes.

John then said, "I'm feeling a little antsy and would like to get out of here for a while. I'd like to do some teambuilding exercises, maybe all of us can go for a hike. I'm going to go see if there's someplace we can go." John told David he'd call him as soon as he knew anything.

John then went to the cafeteria, located two floors below. He had been told he could expect the arrival of members of his US team and was hoping to see a familiar face – either going to or coming back from lunch, but no such luck. As he walked through the corridors, he saw only Asian faces.

Then as he turned the corner he recognized Li Ming, whom he met in Macau. It took John a split second to remember his name, and then Li Ming came over to him and said, "John, very nice to see you again. I heard they purchased your company and I was glad to hear it." He then made a strange face at John, which suggested something was up.

Ming said, "I need to use the bathroom which is just down the hall to the left. The bathrooms here are very clean and nice. You might be surprised." Ming kept making strange faces as he looked at John. John thought it an odd conversation to be having with this peculiar guy and said, "Yes, I've noticed that. Hopefully we can have lunch in the cafeteria one day."

Ming responded, "That would be very good." The whole time, however, he continued making weird faces at John. Ming left for the bathroom and John walked to a water fountain and took a drink. John decided something strange was afoot and he decided to ask Ming about it.

Once in the bathroom, his first thought was that Ming was right, it was nice and it smelled clean. He saw Ming leaning against a stall door to hold it open, as he extended his arm and beckoned John to come toward him. John cautiously moved toward Ming and discreetly took a folded sheet of paper from him.

John entered a stall two doors down and read, 'I would like to talk with you privately. They do not have video in the bathroom, but they may be listening through your phone. On the fifth floor there is closet D. It is a dead zone not under surveillance. Meet me there in 15 minutes. Nod if you agree. If yes, remove battery from your phone before you leave here.'

John exited the stall, and saw Ming looking at their reflections in the mirror above the sink as he washed his hands. John said nothing, but nodded yes, so that Ming knew they were on. Ming then left the bathroom. John walked over to the sink and washed his hands. He waited to make sure no one else was in the room before quickly pulling the battery from his phone. Then he walked out and returned to the cafeteria as if nothing had happened

John poured himself a cup of tea and sat down pretending to read a recently published CRISPR paper on his tablet. About 12 minutes passed by the time he finished his tea, and he began making his way to closet D.

When he exited the elevator on the 5th floor, he turned the corner and noticed that three-quarters of the way down the corridor a door was slightly ajar. He looked up and thought he saw a camera, but proceeded to walk until he got next to the door and noticed it had a Chinese symbol on it and also an English translation – closet D. Ming was already inside when John furtively looked up and down the hallway before slipping into the closet. A bare bulb hung by a wire to illuminate the space. John said, "I think I saw a camera outside." Ming said, "Don't worry, that camera is not working, it only has a loop of the hallway."

John, with a quizzical look, asked, "So what are we doing in a closet in an office park in China?"

Ming leaned in and whispered, "I thought you needed to know what was really being done here. It is very 'top secret,' and on a need-to-know basis, but almost nobody in China is on that small list. I've been involved in the research, and have seen it firsthand. You may find this hard to believe, but they have been injecting a number of peasants from the countryside using gene altering CRISPR technology. I've seen things that haunt my sleep."

He continued, "I saw one docile test subject who was injected with a genetic cocktail which was supposed to increase his intelligence, but he experienced severe headaches, saw hallucinations and ultimately became psychotic. I had to run to the bathroom to be sick when I saw the condition of that person, who finally had a stroke and died." Ming paused for a moment as if reliving the event, or in remembrance, John couldn't be sure which it was.

Ming proceeded, "I saw a boy injected with a genetic combination to increase his muscle efficiency to that of a great ape. He ended up developing an unusual liver cancer and dying a painful, horrible death at a young age." He shook his head with a look of disgust on his face. John saw there was more to Ming than met the eye.

Ming was not finished and confided, "I am afraid for my safety and that of your team. I know that those in control are deadly serious about harnessing and unleashing the power of this new technology. They have read your emails and see promise in what they saw – particularly with the technology that controls genes to turn them on and off. They also see great potential with your computer program. Without it, they would have great difficulties doing the research, because it is too dangerous, even for them."

Ming, becoming emotional said, "You are empowering them even further, and I beg you to do something about it before it is too late. I have been in contact with people from your government because the research is so alarming. I am from the region where most of the test subjects were taken, many of them remind me of my own family."

John looked at him and asked, "So what can I do?"

Ming was disappointed by John's response but said, "You may not believe this, but a number of the scientists here are unhappy with the research being performed and are appalled by the human suffering. Many researchers here feel that we are moving too fast and are being pushed by people with their own agendas."

John finally said, "I think you are justified in your concerns. I, too, was shocked by what I witnessed when I toured Xian's labs. It's possible that my brilliant computer coder may have provided us a way out of this mess. But that's all I think I should say for now."

Feeling some sense of relief, Ming said, "I'm happy to see that someone took precautions. I think you'd be well served to see the research for yourself – it is how you say it in the United States: mind blowing," and Ming even made the 'pchhh' sound like his head exploding, with the corresponding exploding hand gesture.

Ming leaned in a little closer before whispering, "You may be surprised at how this plays out and by the other powers that may be involved." John was taken aback, but in this day and age, with hacking, satellites, facial recognition and other ways to track people, nothing was out of the realm of possibility.

John was glad about the embedded malware in the computer software, even though David had done it without his authorization. As he carefully crept out of closet D, he wondered who else at the compound was on board with Ming.

At the same time John was walking down the hall toward the elevators away from closet D, a man in a military uniform turned the corner and was walking toward him. A moment later, Ming stepped out of closet D. John then turned the corner to the elevators and began thinking of ways to get back into the research bays where he could confirm what Ming had told him.

92

Back in his room, John saw the phone was flashing. He dialed into the voice message system and heard Betty say, "Hi John. I just wanted to let you know that the staff has arrived at the facility and are being checked into their rooms. Call me when you get this message."

John called Betty's room phone and when she answered he asked how everyone had settled in. She responded, "The usual complaints about the long flight, but it went fine. By now everybody should be in their rooms. As you asked, I set up the teambuilding thing – a hike for tomorrow morning to reconnect with the staff and bring everyone up to speed on what's going on."

John asked, "8:30, right?" She said, "I don't know if the staff will agree that it's right, especially after their long flight, but 8:30 it is." After they hung up, John lay in bed worrying about what to do, until he drifted off to sleep.

The next thing he knew, he got a wake-up call announcing it was 7:30 AM. John quickly dressed in a golf shirt, jeans and Nikes, and then went down to the cafeteria for a quick breakfast before the scheduled hike. He met two employees on their way out of the cafeteria as he was walking in and one said, "Betty told everyone to meet at the compound entrance, so we'll see you there."

A half-hour later, John went up to the main entrance to rally the troops. When he went outside, he saw the 13 people who were selected, and he knew they had picked the right people. Lisa, of course, was there. He also saw Harry Reid, one of his shining star genetic engineers. There were also a number of technicians. He wasn't 100% certain, however, that Xian wanted his employees doing the research. If Ming was right, John highly doubted that the Chinese executives wanted any more people in the loop knowing what was actually going on. For whatever it was worth, they were all there, and he would go out in the woods with them and do whatever he could to push the project forward.

John stepped into the courtyard in front of the building and all the employees stood around him.

Immediately to his right was Lisa, who seemed a little distant. On the other side, was Betty who seemed happy with her new situation, where she no longer had to deal with the stress of pressure-packed deadlines, or the crushing demands of unreasonable partners.

John began his speech, saying: "I guess you all have a lot of questions about the acquisition of our company, your role, and why you're in China. Hopefully, I can explain it all, and then we can go on a short hike in the Chinese woods, where I can answer any other questions you may have."

He continued, "First, I want everyone to know that we were purchased by Xian Corporation. This should not change our mission and goals to move forward with CRISPR technology at the fastest pace possible. The new company that acquired us has the same goals and wants to support us in this endeavor – particularly with their high-powered computers which are not available to us in the United States."

He said, "This might come as a surprise to some of you, but China has some of the best computers in the world, although I've been told the US recently built one that is slightly faster than the one we will use. Anyway, we'll be working with Xian's scientists and hopefully we'll make great strides together."

He went on, "As for the work, we'll need to begin by going through the new labs, to determine if we need any additional equipment." He paused, feeling more self-confident than usual, then looked around and continued, "In this compound you can work with very little distraction and I foresee many genetic diseases being cured within these walls. I want to welcome all of you to this important endeavor."

He added, "One last thing, each of you will receive a signing bonus of 30% of your annual salary, so that you will feel rewarded for the hard work we expect from you."

Everyone applauded.

Then John said: "Now for the fun. We can commune with nature, before we attempt to control it." With the last line, he heard a few groans. He said, "Now, since I don't want any distractions, and as Betty would say, this is a teambuilding exercise, I want everyone to leave their cell phones here – no exceptions. OK everybody, we're off on our 5-mile hike to ground ourselves before we roll up our sleeves and get to work."

John noticed two soldiers sitting on the porch in front of the entrance to the compound, and figured they were eavesdropping. He also expected that they would track the group, and have field operatives nearby attempting to eavesdrop whenever possible.

Two members of the group went back into the compound to get appropriate footwear for the hike while the rest of them stood around either stretching or simply enjoying the view. A few were interested in the differences between the forests of the US and those of China and wondered if there was any chance that they might see a wild panda.

When they finally began walking down the wide path cut through the woods, one of the technicians approached John and asked, "So I was just trying to understand why we agreed to be purchased at all, and why we had to come to China."

Betty, who was walking near John and the technician said, "I can take this one. The reason why we are doing it is because of financing and technology. Xian Corporation is an independent company with very significant resources and the ability to acquire computer technology which is vastly superior to that available in the United States. You will have tremendous backing by Xian executives and also the assistance of some of their best scientists. I think you'll all be surprised at this opportunity to be biotech pioneers. Plus, the bonus they offered was also great – so even if something happens and the job doesn't last, you'll have a cushion."

As they came to a turn in the path, an out-of-place unusuallooking flowering plant was growing between two downed logs. Most of the group walked over to the area to get a better look. They were guessing its genus and species. John, however, stayed on the path watching his curious scientists engaging with each other.

Harry Reid also stayed back for the express purpose of privately talking with John. He asked, "So what are we doing here, Boss? Is this really what you wanted?" John looked at him as he answered, "Well, you know there are always financial issues. Like you, I'm more of a purist when it comes to the science and I've seen some things here that concern me."

John went on, "Harry, before we continue, it's OK to ask these questions out here, but remember, you never know who's listening or when they're doing it in a communist country, so be careful. That's the reason I asked everyone to leave their cell phones in their rooms."

Harry then said, "I don't know, I just have a bad feeling about all of this. I can't put my finger on it. Anyhow, I just wanted to let you know that when performing the most recent calculations with the computer models for humans, we came up with a gene that can alter a subject's sperm count to make it very low so they cannot reproduce. This could counteract CRISPR's ability to pass genes to subsequent generations, and could be useful if the Chinese want us to do something which we consider to be unethical. I'm just saying." John smiled but didn't say anything as he thought about what his clever colleague said.

John then said, "I really appreciate your telling me that, and if you could write the formula down on a piece of paper, without noting what it's for, that would be even better. Like you said, it could be useful later."

Based on this conversation alone, John didn't feel the need to bring up any of his concerns with anyone else during the hike. Although unburdening himself to other members of the team would have probably made him feel better, he quickly dismissed the idea. He figured he could always manage to have a secret exchange with Betty or Lisa later, after he got a better idea about the testing that was being done by Xian.

93

John wanted to return to the research area of the compound. He doubted his handlers would be accommodating, but he still wanted to try. He pressed the button for the elevator. A few seconds later, he heard the familiar 'ping' when it got to his floor. He entered, then hit the button for the lowest floor on the keypad and hoped he wouldn't need an access card for the doors to open once he got there.

The door opened and he walked to the left. He heard his footfalls, which sounded especially loud. He turned toward Tai Tan's office, and saw his secretary sitting behind her desk. She smiled and greeted him, "Hello, Mr. Ordell."

He asked her, "Is Mr. Tai in?" She replied, "I'm sorry he's taking someone on a tour of the entire facility. You can wait, but it might be some time before he returns." John stood there as he contemplated his next move. A second later, the phone rang and when the secretary picked it up and he heard her say, "Certainly, I will get it for you in 10 minutes." As she got up to leave the suite, she nodded at him and said, "Please sit down if you choose to wait. I will be back shortly."

John sat silently for a moment, considering what he would say to Tan when he saw him. He was also curious about who the VIP was. As the minutes passed, his curiosity got the better of him, and he decided to take a quick look around the inner office where Tan might've been sitting.

When he opened the door, he saw a suit jacket hanging on a hook and noticed a lanyard with an access card attached. He knew that most of the locks were controlled by facial recognition software, but he also remembered seeing one visitor use a card, which looked exactly like the one he was staring at.

John wondered, is it possible that this key card was for some high level official, who didn't want his face to be in a facial recognition database? Maybe it allowed full access to the facility. He decided to find out.

John walked over to the hook and carefully removed the lanyard with the card and shoved them into his pocket. Before leaving the office, he wrote a quick note to the secretary, 'I'll come back later. Thank you, J. Ordell'

What John didn't know is, indeed there was a high-level official visiting the facility. The facility's entire staff, including scientists, support staff, and all but a few security personnel, were at that very moment in a closed-door meeting with him. In fact, almost everyone at that meeting wanted to be there, in the presence of this VIP. Consequently, John benefitted from either good timing or good luck.

John nonchalantly walked down the corridor to the first set of security doors. He could already smell some of the animals. The thought of the talking Capuchin monkey brought a smile to his face. Had he not seen and heard it with his own eyes and ears, he wouldn't have believed such a thing was possible.

He knew the facial recognition scanning device wouldn't work for him, so he took the card and touched it against the card-reader, and incredibly the door opened. He quickly noticed that no one was around, which surprised him, but he still looked over his shoulder to double check. After passing through the door, he made a hard right and then saw sign in Chinese, which he recognized as the word for 'human.'

John followed the direction of the arrow, wondering what he would find. He came to another door and again touched the card against the reader, which caused the lock to click open. He pushed the card back into his pocket and then entered this section of the facility. He was sure that he had never been in these research bays before.

He approached the first tank, which had bars and a large cutout window. As he peered into the cell, he saw a creature that looked like a person sitting on a bench in the corner. The creature had a reddish tinge to his skin and appeared to have a lot of hair on his body for a human being. The startled creature looked up at him for a second, then jumped off the bench, and in a flash climbed a tree to a platform above. The creature seemed spooked, and moved with lightning speed, like some kind of wild animal. It peered down at him with curiosity.

John instinctively looked up and put his hands out with the palms open. The creature then shouted something in Chinese, which John vaguely understood to mean, 'Leave me alone.' The creature was a man. Suddenly, John remembered the word for, 'help,' in Cantonese, and said it. The guy cocked his head and cautiously climbed down the tree, looking at John every inch of the way.

The guy came right up to the edge of the bars to the window, and John could see fear as he looked into the guy's eyes. The eyes were wild, with the look of someone in turmoil. John used the few words of Cantonese he knew, and the caged man just kept repeating, "Help me." John also thought he recognized the word for 'army,' though he couldn't be sure. Regardless, he hated what he saw.

These were paddocks for CRISPR experiments. What had they done to this guy and why was he behind bars? It did not compute. John needed to think. Without warning, the guy began emitting a high-pitched squeal that made John's skin crawl.

John jumped back and stepped away from the opening. With all the commotion, he began to fear that he'd be caught. It was then that he thought of Li Ming's warning.

But then he looked down the hallway and saw rows of rooms, and he couldn't stop. He heard what sounded like many human voices. Some were talking, some were moaning, still others were yelling. It felt more like a prison camp than a lab.

John walked to the next cell and saw a man uncontrollably shaking in the corner. Was it Parkinson's disease, or something else? He looked decrepit and his skin had a green tinge. As John got closer to the cell, the man came over to the bars and mumbled something. He, too, used the word 'help' and pointed to his head, indicating hurt or pain.

The desperate look in the man's eyes caused John to feel queasy. It was the vacant look of someone who knows the end is near, and is preparing to check out. The look was vaguely familiar, something he'd seen before that made him feel uneasy and sad. He wanted to help, but he felt powerless. He hated this feeling. He wondered, how many more people were down here, and what were they doing in this horrible place?

John knew exactly where he was. This was the CRISPR experimental wing for human subjects. These poor souls were experiments gone wrong, terribly wrong. He thought, oh my God, this can't be. There are supposed to be laws and ethical guidelines to prevent this kind of thing. You simply cannot do it, it's criminal. These people didn't look like willing participants, not at all.

John was about to leave the paddock because he felt such a sense of revulsion, when he experienced a sudden urge to go back. He walked toward another cage, where he saw a man asleep on a bench. The man was lying on his side with his face exposed, and John was able to see that his skin was an unusually pale, yellow color. The man was completely still, and as John got closer to the cage, he recognized him. It was his friend, the young scientist, Li Ming. What the hell was he doing here?

The last time he saw Ming, was when they met in closet D, and he was a respected member of the Chinese team. Who was the army guy John encountered after leaving closet D? Did that guy see Ming leave the closet and figure out what they were up to? Was that guy responsible for putting Ming in this cell? John's heart was pounding as he grasped exactly what he was looking at.

After a moment's hesitation, he turned and ran down the hall and rode the elevator back to the floor where Tai Tan's office was located. The coast was clear, the secretary was still away from her desk. He slipped into Tan's office and rehung the lanyard on top of the jacket.

John then raced out of the office and made his way back to his room. By the time he closed the door, he was almost hyperventilating. He had to do something, though he didn't know what. He knew he had to talk to someone he could trust.

94

Larry Pan finished the last of his Starbucks coffee as he sat in his Langley office watching his computer screen. He was recruited directly out of George Washington University because he had graduated with honors with a degree in computer science and was fluent in Mandarin and had passable skills with Cantonese.

His duties at the CIA included hacking, monitoring and listening to mid-level Chinese operatives. Some of them were business people from prominent families, or the children of cronies who had risen to the level of multimillionaire or billionaire. Larry had his dream job. He was allowed to do what he loved, which was to hack into the lives of and listen to the secrets of the people he was assigned to follow.

His latest target was Deng Ngo. According to his file, it appeared he was educated in the US, was pretty smart, a Chinese entrepreneur of sorts, and on the short list to become one of the ruling elite.

Larry had managed to obtain Deng's personal cell phone number and was able to read his emails and text messages, as well as listen to his conversations. Larry had even turned on the cameras – both front and back, without Deng's becoming aware. Until further notice, Larry was expected to surveille the target, and determine if escalation was warranted.

Larry was perusing the emails and text messages, while in the background the sounds the cell phone picked up yesterday were playing. He was looking through yesterday's deleted emails when he came across an unfamiliar name. The email was to someone that he didn't recognize. He entered the name into the COMINT and ELINT databases showing on his second computer screen and discovered it was an assistant to a deputy of a Politburo member.

The email said that Xian had purchased an American company for their computer models which are used to alter the DNA in their subjects. Further, the American and his team had been taken to a Chinese CRISPR research center. It said that, 'research would be unshackled now and could move forward.'

As Larry read further into the email, it said that the deputy could 'advise others, without leaving a paper trail, that the research on curing diseases, life extension and military applications was now able to proceed at a breakneck pace.'

Larry had to stand up to look over the cubicle wall at Ryan, who sat in the adjacent cubicle to make sure that he wasn't being punk'd. He didn't think so, because intelligence was serious work, and none of the possible pranksters would've been able to write Chinese. Just to be sure, he walked down the long row of cubicles to see if anyone was laughing and giggling. When he saw that everyone was somberly focused on their work, he then went back to his cubicle to do some searches on the Internet.

The first thing he did was look up CRISPR. For the first time since he worked at CIA, he was shocked. For some reason, he'd never heard of it before. Also, he couldn't remember it ever being discussed in any of their intelligence briefings.

It looked like there were some articles about it in the *New York Times* and *Washington Post*. From what he was able to glean from those articles, CRISPR had the potential to do exactly what the email suggested. The next thing he needed to do was look up who they could be referring to, when they said the 'American and his team' and finally, where they were, and what to do about it.

He decided to cross-reference some other emails for the names of more Chinese officials and targets, to see if they could shed some light on what their friend Deng was up to. Larry was also able to restore four more emails about CRISPR technology, which Deng had attempted to delete. They had the same assistant contacting Deng.

They discussed the purchase of an American company by Xian Corporation. He then did a simple Google search and found an article about an investment bank that was selling a biotech company to Xian Corporation, and that the CEO of the company, John Ordell, visited China to sign the paperwork and was going to work in China.

Larry sensed that this was something that had to be immediately moved up the chain-of-command, for at least his boss' input. It would be her call whether it should go higher than that. So, Larry called Janet Marino, the Assistant Director of his unit, and she asked him to meet her in their conference room in fifteen minutes.

Larry didn't like one-on-one's with Janet. He thought that in addition to being no-nonsense, she was incredibly formal. The office's corporate casual dress code suited him just fine. But he couldn't think of a single time that he saw her dressed in anything other than a business suit. Also, she was always straightforward and never joked around with the staff.

He barely knocked on the oak door when Janet, said, "Come in." They both had high-level clearances, so she was able to discuss most matters freely with him. Marino, in her upper 50's, was a lifer at the department and had risen through the ranks to management. In addition to a Master's degree in computer science, she had a law degree. Early on she had been in the JAG Corps. Even though she thought that she could make more money on the outside, this job suited her just fine.

Marino looked at this young hotshot programmer, and felt good about the quality of people selected for the nation's important work. She asked, "Hello, Larry. What was it you needed to see me about? It sounded pretty urgent, so I rescheduled another meeting to fit you in."

Larry respected Janet and how she supported her team, even if she was a little too straight-laced. He began, "I was looking at some emails when I came across something a little strange. The emails were talking about something called CRISPR. After I did some quick research, I found it to be some pretty incredible technology."

He went on, "It looks like a Chinese company, Xian Corporation, purchased a US CRISPR company, AlgoGene Corporation, started by a young American entrepreneur. However, it also looks like the Chinese do a lot of this type of work already, so why would they purchase this particular company? Then, after they bought the company, they almost immediately brought the American, named John Ordell, and a dozen or so people who worked for him, to China. Something about the whole thing just didn't feel right to me."

Larry continued, "Several emails contain vague mentions of 'special research' with high levels of interest shown by the Chinese elite. From my brief time working here, I am aware that the Chinese try to pirate certain technology or enter into technology transfer agreements, but I don't think this technology is on our radar when it comes to protecting national secrets. Maybe I'm wrong, but I thought it was important to bring it to your attention. It could be worth pursuing."

Janet smiled at Larry. She liked that he had good instincts and showed initiative. Some people bought the rampant politicized line that government was filled with incompetents and was worthless, but she knew better and this young member of her team was only one of countless examples of proof that refuted such wrong-headed thinking.

Janet said, "Thanks, that's excellent work. I think you could be onto something. Let me make a call to the field office that covers the area where Mr. Ordell will be living, and see if there's any information that may shed some light on what's going on over there. I'll get back to you if it's warranted. Again, good work. That will be all for now."

Janet picked up the secure line, and contacted the American Embassy in China. She was then transferred to a local consulate, and after speaking with the receptionist, was put through to the right guy – a CIA operative who had previously been with Delta Force.

She only knew the guy from his codename, "Wyatt Earp" and his credentials were stellar. Jesus, she loved those guys, and wished she could have been one herself, but it was not an option open to women when she would have been the right age.

She began, "This is Janet Marino at Langley. I have some information that I'd like to vet with you regarding someone named John Ordell and something called CRISPR technology. It may be about cutting-edge research. I'd like to know why Ordell is staying in China and what the Xian Corporation, that purchased his company, is working on."

'Wyatt Earp,' paused for a moment, then said, "Your call is timely, and it's funny that you ask. We have been investigating the Xian Corporation for a while now. We had a scientist on the inside who provided us with some information, but it's become increasingly difficult to make contact with him. Over the past few weeks the situation has become complicated because communications with our informant went dark. We are unsure why."

He continued, "It's been hard for us to connect all the dots, and it's an ongoing investigation, but there appears to be some research going on which is outside the norm at the Xian Corporation. Before our asset went dark, he advised us that there was human testing going on and a computer program that could fast-track the Chinese research."

The agent continued, "Our asset told us some things that made us believe that the genetic research being done could have some military applications, particularly in enhancing soldiers' physical abilities. It was our understanding that research was too dangerous to continue because the genetic modifications were unpredictable and dangerous."

'Wyatt Earp' proceeded, "It was unclear to us exactly how the American company fit in, but it had something to do with the computer program. With our asset dark, it's hard to say what's happening now, but they're likely still doing research and it might be further along because of the American. There's also intel indicating that the American may not be a willing participant, although we did trace payments made to an investment bank and Mr. Ordell's share is in the millions of dollars. Anyway, we've been investigating because of the military implications."

Janet then said, "Thanks you've been very helpful, and we're going to mount our own investigation. Can you send me an encrypted file with all the information you have on Xian and the participants from Ordell's company?"

'Wyatt Earp' said, "No problem, you'll have it today. If that's all you need, I'll sign off." When Janet said, "That's it for now. Marino, signing off." The line went dead and Janet sat to collect her thoughts before calling Larry into her office.

Larry didn't know what to expect when he returned to Janet's office. After she closed the door, she told him about the conversation she had with the CIA operative, then said, as a result, "I want to put four analysts and the full brunt of our capabilities on it and I'm assigning you as the group leader to dig deep into this issue. I want to know exactly what CRISPR does, what it has the potential to do, and what the Chinese acquired by purchasing this company. I also want to know everything about everybody involved in the American company before it was sold. Particularly those who are currently in China. I want a report from you before week's end, and sooner if you learn something that you think I need to know about before then. And I just want to say again, Larry, good catch."

Larry smiled and said, "It was nothing that my colleagues in a similar situation wouldn't do." He left the office, feeling a sense of pride, thinking to himself that this was the reason he'd signed up with the beleaguered agency.

95

John Ordell was still shaken by what he'd seen in the underbelly of Xian's labs. Those in charge meant business. When they felt threatened, they had even harmed one of their own scientists, Li Ming. He wondered what kind of CRISPR experiment they were trying on Ming and what would become of him. John was unable to erase from his mind the fear and disorientation in the eyes of the test subjects he'd seen.

He took the elevator back to his apartment, where he carefully emptied his pockets. He saw the piece of paper he was looking for, the one that contained the scribble with the CRISPR formula to make a test subject sterile.

John then heard a knock on his door. It caused a sick feeling in his stomach. He wondered what would be next in this horror show. Since there was nothing else he could do, he answered the door.

He opened the door rather abruptly, expecting to see Xian security personnel, but instead he had a pleasant surprise. Standing at his door was Li Na. A smile began to form on his reddened face, and he stopped shaking and thinking about anything but this lovely young woman.

His nostrils welcomed her delicate perfume, and his eyes were even more receptive to her appearance. As he was overcome by this welcome surprise, she asked, "Are you going to invite me in?" He responded, "Of course, please, come in."

As she walked past him, he wondered what brought her to his apartment. He followed her into the living room and they both sat next to each other on the couch. She began, "I hope you don't find this too forward, but since we met, I have been thinking about you a lot," and, as she blushed slightly, she said, "Actually, I haven't been able to get you out of my mind."

John just sat dumbstruck. This had never happened to him before, and he was unsure what he should say. He felt the same way about her, even though he'd been distracted by everything going on at Xian. Whenever he wasn't thinking about Xian, he found himself thinking of Li Na.

John confessed, "I feel the same way." And they both looked at each other for a moment before she leaned in and kissed him. He could not believe it, he finally said the right thing to a woman, and a great-looking one at that.

What Li Na didn't want John to know, was that Zhang had instructed her to do whatever was required to gain John's trust. It was within her discretion as how to accomplish the mission, but when John opened the door, she knew that she had real feelings for him. This made her job both much easier and much tougher, and she could not reveal her true feelings to her handlers.

She felt comfortable with him, almost like they knew each other for a long time. As they sat on the couch kissing, he moved his hand to her leg and then her butt. When she didn't resist, but reciprocated by putting her hands on his face, and then his shoulders, their pulses quickened. Both became lost in the moment.

John was not thinking about CRISPR or genetics anymore, although he was thinking about procreation. Li Na, likewise was not thinking of her handlers or her duty to her country, but instead about this man in front of her, whom she had powerful feelings for – so strong that she didn't want this moment to end.

When John finally thought things were moving too fast, he said so, then moved away from her. He sat back on the couch and she put her head in his lap as he played with her hair. She had long, thick straight black hair, which he found to be very sexy.

Li Na began telling him about her childhood and what it was like growing up as a little girl in a country that prized boys, and how the country had changed in the last twenty years. He liked how she explained things, and that she was apolitical.

He asked, "Would you like to go for a walk outside?" She agreed, and they left the apartment walked down the hall, rode the elevator to the main floor and then they were outside where the sun was shining, and the birds were singing. Neither had brought their cell phones.

When they were a fair distance from the main building, Li Na said to him, "We must be careful at the compound because the state has a long reach. We don't have the same privacy like you have at home, in your country. I think you might know, I am good friends with Li Ming. I know you are friendly with him, too. I have not seen him for some time, which makes me sad."

John looked at her, wondering whether he could trust her. He instantly made his decision, then said, "I know what happened to Ming." John said, "They're experimenting on him. He's in a cell in the paddocks."

The shocked look on Li Na's face was real. Maybe he should have made the revelation more gently. He did not like putting her in distress, but he continued and said, "Yes, I saw him myself when I went down to the lab. I couldn't believe my eyes when I saw him there. Did you have any idea about what's going on here?"

Li Na felt suddenly exposed and said, "I know that Li Ming was suspected of contacting your government, and they even believed he had contact with you, so they must have done something horrible to him. He was a great person, extremely smart, and much shrewder than you would expect a young man from the countryside to be. It upset me when I learned that he was on the outs with our team of scientists. I suspected that he was in big trouble, but I guess you just confirmed that."

The die was cast, so John continued, "I sneaked back into the lab, into an area I wasn't taken to before and I saw many human test subjects there. They looked like they were in agony – the kind of pain that no one should suffer. The kind of pain that our research is designed to alleviate. The type of pain that is so deep that I could feel it myself. It made me scared, but it also made me angry. I hate that they are purposely causing people pain. But I may be able to do something to stop this atrocity." When John said that, he reminded her of her uncle, a dissident who passionately fought for peasants' rights against all odds.

Li Na then whispered, "I knew about that, and I was shown documents relating to the testing. Unfortunately, they had a very poor record. I even saw subjects given genes to increase their intelligence, and almost all of them died with the exception of one subject who became psychotic. He kept screaming, seeing hallucinations and hearing voices, and every few hours had debilitating headaches until he finally died of a heart attack." John said, "I never trusted the people here, but what could one person do to stop this?"

Li Na looked disappointed by the statement followed by the rhetorical question. But John had no solution. He wondered what his father would do; even if he could be judgmental, he was also a man of action, who made the tough choices that mattered. John wanted to be like that, especially for Li Na.

Li Na then said, "I can't believe someone like you, who started and then sold a company for billions, really doesn't know what to do."

John felt the dig of her comment. He again thought of his father, who always saw things in black-and-white, and didn't overthink the consequences, or survey others for their opinions before taking action. While still looking at Li Na's face he knew that he had to follow his instincts, do what was right, and not care what Dr. Duretts, Artie, Lisa, Betty, Mr. DeBerg, his father, or anyone else thought.

Now was his time to make a choice, and he had to take action.

He said to Li Na, "There is a solution. My team and I have taken precautions just in case the time came and we needed to take matters into our own hands. The algorithm has a failsafe, and if we don't disarm the malware, it will meltdown in the next day or two. Also, I have a formula for a CRISPR compound that will make everybody who has the injection sterile. I may try to use that, too and then return to the states with the money Xian paid me. I will continue to work on genetics and related issues, but now I can focus on pure science and not just making money."

Li Na was pleased by what she heard. She believed him, and liked the empathy he exhibited. It was a trait in short supply with the people she worked for.

Li Na, torn between John and her duty to her country, knew she had a choice to make. With John's description of Li Ming's debilitated condition, and what she had seen in the paddocks with her own eyes, she instantly decided she would not compromise John. She would leave China for good, hopefully with him. Li Na couldn't believe that she felt this way, but she did.

Li Na said, "I admire you for that, and I too don't like seeing CRISPR subjects cruelly mistreated. I know that the common people, like my family members will never reap the benefits of all this suffering. I do think, though, that your algorithm could make the difference."

John said, "I bet that if the big shots had to endure the uncertainty of testing, that would slow the pace of research."

This was Li Na's moment to come clean, "I have a confession to make, and it's not easy. I am in the Chinese military. I have some scientific training, am a good linguist, and was a plant to spy on you."

John momentarily taken aback, thought to himself, if she's telling me this, she has to be on my side. He reached out and pulled her to him, hugged her as he said, "From the first time I met you, I thought I might be in love with you."

Li Na was almost crying, as her emotions overwhelmed her, and she said, "I know this means I'll have to leave China, but I'll help you anyway I can. It's the right thing to do, especially with what they did to Li Ming. And, I'm in love with you, too."

As they embraced, John kissed her lips, before grabbing her hand. He said, "We have to go back. If you want to talk again, just ask me to go for a walk. If I want to communicate with you, I'll write on a piece of paper or napkin and show it to you. Also, if you're serious about leaving China, I would love to make that happen, too."

As they walked through the door into the rear of the complex, they gave each other a serious look, then parted to return to their own rooms. John was anxious about having opened up to Li Na. Li Na, on the other hand, felt a sense of freedom she'd never before experienced.

Zhang and Li Na's other handlers always thought of her as their ace in the hole. She was their reserve player, called in to finesse whatever was required, and although the thought of the Caucasian touching Li Na made them feel uneasy, it went with the territory. Soon enough they would be doing their own computer enhanced targeted studies on their 'subjects,' and there would be no further need for any of the Americans.

96

John got into the apartment and put his hand in the pocket of his pants and took out his key. He felt the crumpled piece of paper in his pocket with the CRISPR formula for sterility.

He decided to go to the lab and try it. He walked five doors down the hall and then knocked. His best technician, Frank, was there and John said, "Let's go down to the lab, I want to do something."

They quietly proceeded to the glistening new lab. Frank was not a big talker, but he was extremely proficient in the lab which made him well-liked. John said, "I want to make a change to the base in which we place the CRISPR compounds made in the lab. Here's the formula, it's a CRISPR compound as well."

Frank looked it over, didn't question anything, and began combining the elements that would alter human DNA. Initially, John was looking at his phone and occasionally watching Frank work. Then John began to help Frank to make the process go faster.

After the compound was completed, John and Frank measured and placed it into saline solutions. It would be a base saline solution tainted with whatever it was that the gene changing compound did.

Frank, satisfied with his status as a technician, did not want to know more. Others on the team would sometimes make fun of Frank for being like Sargent Schultz – he sees nothing, hears nothing, and knows nothing – but Frank preferred it that way.

John believed that this was all the saline there was in the lab. He was confident that if anyone wanted to inject CRISPR, they would have to use one of these tainted bottles of saline.

97

John back in his room, had already taken a shower, and was drying his hair when the phone rang. He picked up the line and a voice told him, "The leaders at Xian want to have a meeting to brief you and your team on some developments. Could you email everyone to meet in the main conference room on level 3, at 4 PM?

John agreed to do so, then asked, "Are you sure you want everyone, or just the geneticists and computer scientists?" The voice on the line said, "Just the higher-end talent," then hung up. John then sent his short email.

At 3:50 PM, John started walking to the meeting. He had spoken to Betty about this, and she wondered what it was all about. She speculated that it could be to coordinate the efforts of the Chinese and American workers.

John arrived at the room at 3:58 pm, and he saw Betty standing outside. He walked over and shook her hand. He also saw David Goldblum, and nodded at him. There also were a number of Chinese scientists standing around looking at them. As they began with introductions, a man in a well-tailored suit asked everyone to go into the conference room so the meeting could start.

The man in the suit introduced himself as Mung. He had a smile on his face and his bald head shined under the lights illuminating the podium. With a slight accent, he said, "I'm glad to see all our new friends. Please take seats in the front of the auditorium and we can get started."

He paused for a moment, then continued, "I want to thank everyone for coming. As you all know, we will be working together on this important and necessary work. This could be the most important work that humankind has ever endeavored."

Mung went on, "I also believe that we are at a crossroads of this technology – it may be the end of evolution and natural selection and the beginning of a mankind-controlled evolution – what I like to call re-evolution."

He continued, "I envision cures to all the maladies that afflict mankind, and the ability to make mankind better, to eliminate genetic weakness and replace it with strength. There are people afflicted with diseases, like autism, congenital heart disease, and muscular dystrophy. It is awful to hear their stories.

We are here to make these problems a thing of the past. We may even be able to prevent the aging process. The human condition that the Buddha weeps for will be vanquished to history, assuming we are successful. These are all the challenges we have and the challenges which must be met, one step at a time."

Mung wiped his brow with a handkerchief, and then continued his motivational speech by saying, "In that regard, I would like to explain how we will go about our task. I have decided to split the group into two teams, the Chinese team and the American team. Each team will have its own labs, data, and test animals. The teams will be separated and the results will be evaluated by a team of senior scientists who will peer review the work and liaise between the two groups.

The team of computer scientists will work with both CRISPR teams to facilitate the creation of the formulas used on the test subjects – mostly primates. I note we have downloaded the software into our supercomputer. We ran an experiment where we inputted data from an experiment with mice that went well, and we determined that the computer got the outcome correct. We are writing experimental protocols for mice and chimpanzees to further assess the algorithm's abilities.

I want to offer my compliments to the computer team and David Goldblum, for his ingenious software. It will take our scientists a few weeks to grasp the intricacies of the software, but we believe it is truly an ingenious program. David will be working with our computer engineers to educate them and help them understand and possibly even improve upon this wonderful program. It may be the integral key we've been searching for. We're happy to have you on our team."

Mung then bowed his head slightly and asked, "Any questions?"

John, curious, decided to ask an obvious question, so he stood up and asked, "Why are you splitting up the teams, wouldn't it be better to integrate the thinking of two different teams, or mix-and-match the teams?"

Mung, unaccustomed to being challenged, responded, "At the beginning we think it best to have two teams with disparate outlooks making decisions on research with a group of senior scientists keeping track. If, after additional research, it appears that the groups should be re-integrated, we may do so."

John then sat down, thinking that the Chinese would be permitted to do research on whatever they wanted, without the need for any prying American eyes to be involved. It would also put a crimp in his plan to implement the CRISPR formula that would assure sterility in its subjects.

With no other questions, Mung concluded, "Thank you for your attention. We will meet in our separate groups tomorrow. Now there is an early dinner for all of you in the dining room next door. It is a good opportunity for those of you who have not already met to do so."

John held back and walked over to David who was standing beside Betty. They engaged in small talk about the food and how their team would outperform the Chinese. There was a long line when they entered the banquet hall. Since it was still light outside, John suggested that they go outside to get some air. John took out his phone appearing to try to access Google, seeming to temporarily forget it was disabled in China, and then left the phone on the table. He noticed a number of workers watching him as he walked toward the restrooms. No one, however, made any move toward him.

As he walked to the restroom, John turned to David and whispered in a very low voice, "No cell phones." Almost as inaudibly, David responded, "Don't worry, it's not a problem." John took his expert coder at his word.

John passed on the same warning to Betty who whispered back, "I never have one at meetings. My cell phone rang once during a meeting, and I was chewed out. Never again." John met them a few minutes later at the fountain in the courtyard.

As they approached the fountain, they noticed employees looking at them from one of the windows. John knew it wouldn't be long before someone would appear to monitor what was being said, since the noise of the fountain made it difficult to hear using traditional eavesdropping devices.

He quickly disclosed, "I have some very bad news. I was able to get into the research paddocks and saw what I'm sure was human testing of CRISPR technology. I am almost positive that they want to go even further with human testing using the algorithm and supercomputer to create human beings with incredible physical and intellectual capabilities, with total disregard of international norms and laws."

Betty thought, finally, it all made sense; the agreement to pay such a large sum of money upfront and the ease with which the transaction went through. She then said, "I don't think it would be against international law, but a number of international organizations would be appalled by and opposed to such testing. We also all signed nondisclosure agreements, so if any of us tell the story, then we all lose the money we received from the sale, and maybe more, even though much of it has been placed in accounts technically inaccessible to the Chinese."

David, unsurprised by these revelations said, "These guys are all the same. Whether they're Chinese, American, or otherwise, they always push the envelope to exploit my work. Like I told you, though, the joke's on them. The malware program I downloaded will meltdown their supercomputer in two days; then they won't have their grand algorithm. I know how to disarm the program, but I won't. The Silicon Valley jerk-offs tried to screw with me, and I got the last laugh, now I hate what these Chinese jerk-offs are up to, so let it meltdown."

John trying to keep the disgust from his face said, "I feel the same way and that we have to stop this. These people intend to abuse this power. Are we all agreed that we have to stop this?" Both shook their heads an emphatic yes, at the same time.

Betty liked John's new-found confidence but was upset as she thought what she'd been hoping would help her career, would instead turn into another setback. She reminded them both, "Be very careful about saying anything about this – that could cost you a fortune." At that moment, John saw three large Chinese men jogging over and John half-heartedly waved at them.

John, Betty, and David were escorted to the main building and into the room where the others were already eating. There was no longer a line and they picked through the remaining food, filled their plates, and then went to sit down at a table with three spots open.

John engaged in some shop talk with a few of the high-level scientists, discussing some of the new technologies, including the new Cas11. The other scientists were impressive, and all spoke English. It embarrassed him that he had almost no command of their language. Anyway, it turned out that their lab would be right beside his. There was even a large metal door connecting the two. He could not believe that these brilliant scientists would collaborate in human research, but they were likely handpicked and would be well-compensated if it all worked out. Maybe they were just as enamored as he was by the power of the technology.

As he was speaking with one of the scientists, he turned slightly and noticed Li Na was seated two tables away, talking with one of her colleagues. He excused himself and approached her table under the guise of introducing himself to the other scientists. He then greeted Li Na. Standing near her made him feel like taking her hand, racing out the front door, flying back to the states and never looking back. Unfortunately, at this point it was not possible.

98

John continued to work the room until most of the participants had left. Finally, he approached Li Na and asked, "Would you like to go for a walk?" Instead of speaking, she shook her head in agreement, stood up, picked up her handbag and they exited using the same door John had previously used. This time, the staff was not as attentive to them, probably because they thought she was one of their agents.

Once again, the fountain, with its loud gurgle, was the destination. When they got close to it, John leaned in and whispered, "I need your help. I'd like to switch the saline tubes from the American lab to the Chinese lab."

He looked for her reaction, to see if she'd had second thoughts, and it seemed she had not. Instead, she laughed as if he'd said something humorous to her, in case someone was watching. Then she quickly whispered, "The algorithm will be first used to figure out how to increase efficiency in human muscles so that a person will have the athletic ability of a gorilla. As you might expect, it's for military use. Testing on human subjects will begin in the next few weeks."

John whispered back, "I want to make the switch tonight. I'll be in my lab at 9:30 PM, and will open the shared door. Can you be in the Chinese lab then, so you can switch the vials?" She said, "Yes, but keep in mind your lab is constantly videoed and ours is not." John was looking deeply into her eyes during the entire exchange, and was 100% sure that she was on his side. He had to trust her, if he was to accomplish what he had planned.

At 9:05 PM, John went into his lab and pulled out all the saline containers. He placed the containers into two boxes, then positioned the boxes on the table adjacent to the door separating the two labs. Next, he sat down and flipped through the pages of a textbook for a few minutes.

After making it appear that he found what he was looking for, he turned off the lights and looked down the lab's hallway and saw his phone on the table near the shared door. He walked over without turning on the light, and as he picked up his phone, he stealthily reached over and gently clicked open the lock. He then retraced his steps out the door of his lab, turning off the remaining light in the hallway. It was 9:27 PM.

A few minutes later, promptly at 9:30 PM, Li Na opened the lock on her side, and slowly opened the door just enough so she could pass through. The light in her lab was off, so after acclimating her eyes to the darkness she could barely make out the outlines of the furniture from the exit light at the end of the hall. She had already moved the two boxes of saline vials that were in the Chinese lab to the table nearest the shared door.

She then warily entered the American lab, carefully picked up the boxes of vials of saline John had prepared and moved them into the Chinese lab. She quickly transferred the 2 boxes from the Chinese lab to the empty table in the American lab, then closed both shared doors, and locked the door on the Chinese side.

She carefully substituted John's boxes of vials for the original boxes in the Chinese lab, making certain that they were in the exact same position as when she began. She turned on an overhead light, began reading through some files and a textbook, then after another 20 minutes switched off the light as she left the lab.

99

Exactly 2 hours after the vials were switched, John and Betty were summoned to meet with Deng Ngo. It was late and John wondered what this was all about, but they had no choice in the matter.

John arrived at the conference room before Betty. Deng was already inside, with two other people who looked like aides or deputies. They both had electronic tablets as well as old-fashioned binders in front of them. Before John had time to formulate another thought, Betty arrived at the conference room.

What John and Betty were unaware of was that tapes from the more sensitive areas of the compound were systematically reviewed twice, after the video was viewed live. During the review of the tapes, John had been observed as he entered and made his way through the human testing paddocks. These areas were supposed to be off-limits to him and the American team.

The security officer who was monitoring it in real time had missed the breach somehow, by either walking away, falling asleep or looking at his phone. No matter why, this was a problem that had to be addressed instantly, and Deng Ngo and they were here for that reason.

Deng was smiling as he stood up to greet them, "I'm very happy to meet both of you in person, at last." Deng then shook hands with both of them before continuing, "I wanted to meet with you to go over the entire scope of our business. You are on the ground floor of something very big. Although the research is in its infancy, it is a rapidly advancing field of research. Our group, including both of you, consists of a very close-knit group of scientists and executives who are sworn to secrecy regarding the research performed."

Deng continued, "You might think that we Chinese are unique in our efforts to gain a competitive edge by spying on American companies. It is important that you know that the American government and others, also spy on us. We Chinese take the secrecy of our work very seriously.

We consider ourselves as the vanguard of our species. What we're doing can literally change the world – the way our species can think, defend itself, age, as well as to enhance every human ability. Can you imagine a world in which people select what they want to become, and are not limited by what they actually are? I think history will judge us very favorably."

He went on, "From looking at the algorithm, I believe our company is extremely close to being able to produce outstanding results. If you speak with the elite the world over, whether in the United States, Europe, South America, or Asia, they all support what we are doing and are interested in the fruits of our research. They are ready, willing and able to pay good money for positive results."

Betty, startled by what she was hearing, thought it was high time for the Chinese to put their cards on the table. John, for his part, wore his best poker face, revealing nothing as he listened to what this polished, Chinese suit had to say.

Deng, knowing he had their full attention, stated, "John, I'm just going to cut to the chase with you. We know you went into the human research paddocks, where you weren't supposed to go. It may have alarmed you, but I think it's important for you to also know that we have slowed our human testing down to a minimum, and you're the one who made it possible. The combination of your algorithm with one of the fastest computers on the planet, means our work will be infinitely safer."

Deng continued, "Our scientists already ran data through your program for one of our unsuccessful monkey experiments, and it accurately located the off-targeted mutations. We're optimistic that this may be successfully applied to human research subjects as well. So, if we put the entire genome into the computer for each human research participant, we're hoping to be able to avoid any of the off-target complications."

John was beginning to have difficulty controlling his anger. He strongly opposed the technology developed by him, his friends and colleagues being used in this misguided manner on unsuspecting people, who were treated as mere guinea pigs. He bit the inside of his cheek as he decided to take a page from his father's playbook, he'd pretend that everything was great, even when he knew it wasn't.

John began, "As you know, I'm a scientist first and foremost. This work fascinates me, and I believe in the technology that my, or rather, 'our' company, created. I'm all in – fully committed, as it were – to this research. I also have some hypotheses about turning genes on and off to cure old age through gene regulation, which may be of interest to you."

He continued, "Such cures have practical applications. For example, increasing testosterone or human growth hormone clearly makes men feel younger. In the US, a number of companies already sell testosterone to men in their fifties and sixties, imagine if the body's own DNA could do it naturally, we could make billions."

Deng was pleased by what he was hearing. He also knew a number of aging Politburo members, and members of the elite who would love having access to such a product and would pay handsomely if it worked. He knew that John was expendable, but his passion was something Deng could appreciate. It was also his responsibility to ensure that everything worked as planned, and any glitches were removed before Xian totally co-opted the technology, and this was accomplished more easily if he played nice with John.

Betty considered all that Deng had divulged, then asked, "Aren't there some repercussions if there is a death, or serious injury occurs? In the US, you'd be indicted for assault and battery, or even murder, if you conducted these types of experiments on people. Even when you do it on animals, the PETA people would be all over you. Do people have to sign consent forms? I get that we've signed your nondisclosure agreements, but we don't want to be part of a criminal conspiracy."

Deng actually grinned, thinking her very naïve for someone who worked for an important bank in the US. He wanted John to believe that it was safe and legal to proceed with the research, so that he and his tech guy would be willing to continue working with the Xian scientists.

Deng responded, "It's all taken care of, you do not have to worry about any of that. The people who matter, those who make the rules and can get things done very much want to see this go forward. They understand the implications, and believe the ends justify the means."

He went on, "Do not misunderstand. We still intend to be cautious and conduct simple research first, with the goal of curing diseases. The germline work to change traits will not commence until the algorithm amasses adequate amounts of data. And we have accessible information on hundreds of millions of people through genetic and social media data bases, which give us access to information on every conceivable human trait. We intend to access that for safety and reliability reasons. So, let's not get ahead of ourselves."

John, with a serious look on his face, said, "From what you've told us, it seems like a very well thought out plan, and a good way forward." He continued looking at Deng, without flinching, even though he was really thinking about the eyes of the human test subjects he'd witnessed in the paddock.

Betty offered, "That sounds like it's going to be extremely expensive. Do you mind telling us what type of financing you have in place?"

Deng, annoyed as he would be if a gnat continued to pester him, said, "There is no need to worry about the financing. Not only do we have tremendous assets in place, including access to funds from the Central Bank, but we also have access to the fortunes of potential clients, some heads of state, and still others who are captains of industry and finance."

Betty then asked, "If, as you say, the funds are unlimited, why did you not pay the full amount of the contract up front? Surely, you know the word on the street and the bad things said about the Chinese and their willingness to abide by contracts, particularly after they have the goods."

This warmed Deng's heart. It was clear that Betty was a banker, and a capitalist at heart, primarily interested in the dollars and cents. This, he understood well. He then said, "I think that both you, and David deserve an extra bonus. To show you how happy we are that you are on board, and how important you are to us, we can wire $3 million bonuses to each one of you, into your own personal accounts. We can even set it up in Switzerland if you like."

Betty, who still had no equity in this deal, felt as if she'd been hit by a bolt of lightning, and couldn't help but agree with Deng, after his demonstration of generosity.

Deng said, "Consider it a good faith gesture to all of you. Of course, we'd like some reciprocation of goodwill back. I will arrange for the transfer for tomorrow. Does that make you feel better about our solvency?"

Betty, overcome with her good fortune, could only shake her head. At the same time, John sat there, stone-faced. He felt that their lives were in danger, and he worried about how they could make a quick getaway once David's planned meltdown of the system commenced.

100

Larry Pan was at his desk at Langley when he got a call on a secure line from Chris Tuey, of the DC Field Office. Larry knew him from college, though he'd been a few years younger. Larry thought he was probably at the Agent III level by now.

Chris wanted to relay a story about a computer programmer, David Goldblum, who had worked for an American company, but was now supposedly working in China. One of Goldblum's friends, Jason Norton, had called Chris a few weeks ago, concerned for his friend's safety fearing that he might be being held against his will in China. Norton described Goldblum as an inspired programmer, a one in a billion talent, and not someone you'd want to fall into the wrong hands. Larry definitely wanted to hear more.

Norton told the agent that when he and Goldblum met, he had given his friend a malware program to be inserted into some special algorithm for a DNA cataloguing program Goldblum had developed. Larry quickly grasped the significance of what he was being told, and how it coincided with the case he was working.

Chris continued, Norton, a professional coder and malware expert, was concerned that Goldblum had gotten in over his head. According to what Goldblum told him, Norton thought that there was some business application that might've been, or was in the process of being, misappropriated by the Chinese. Thinking he was helping his friend avert this, Norton had given him the malware. Now he was having second thoughts, about whether this had been such a good idea.

Also, as far as Norton knew, Goldblum had not returned from China, and hadn't been happy about having to go there in the first place. This was the main reason Norton thought it possible that Goldblum was being held against his will.

Chris thought that Larry should look into it, and if the information was good, he could decide who else in the organization needed to know. He then provided Larry with the contact information for Jason Norton. Larry thanked Chris and asked him to keep him posted if there were further developments. They exchanged good-byes, then Chris returned to his more mundane responsibilities.

Larry Pan wanted to talk with Jason Norton immediately. He had instantly recognized Norton's name, and used the CIA databank to get more information and to confirm a working cell phone number. Larry then called Norton's cell phone. He picked up on the second ring.

Larry said, "Hello, this is Larry Pan. I'm a government coder. Is this Jason Norton?" Jason answered, "Yeah, you've got him."

Larry continued, "I'd like to talk to you a little bit about someone you know, David Goldblum. Is that alright?" Jason, happy to be talking with someone about his friend, said, "Sure. Whatever you need."

Larry opened by saying, "It has come to our attention that Mr. Goldblum may be working in China, which could have national security implications. That is why I decided to reach out to you, to get more information. Can you come to my office in Langley, so that we can discuss this further in a more secure setting?" Jason Norton said, "If you give me the address, I can be there in two hours."

Larry liked this fellow immediately, and gave him the address and the time that they could meet in his office. It was clear to Jason that this was a CIA inquiry, since he was going to Langley, and that gave him a good feeling about the chances of helping his friend.

At exactly 2 PM, Jason Norton arrived at the security gates of CIA headquarters in Langley, Virginia. He gave his name and was permitted entry to the visitor's parking area. When he entered the CIA building, he gave his name, was issued a visitor's badge and was directed to walk through a high-tech metal and explosive detection device. He was asked to wait for the person he was scheduled to meet with, who would accompany him to a meeting room.

Larry Pan arrived at the security area a few minutes later. He asked Jason to follow him to a small office located on the same floor. Its furnishings could best be described as spare, or even stark. The room contained a table, a half dozen chairs and a couple of traditional prints that hung on the walls. Once they were in the small conference room, Larry shook Jason's hand and introduced himself. Larry gestured toward one of the chairs, and Jason sat down as Larry sat down opposite of him.

Larry then said, "Thank you very much for coming here on such short notice." He continued, "The reason I've asked you here is we're conducting an investigation involving someone you know, David Goldblum. What did he tell you, and what can you tell us about his trip to China?"

Jason, a little reticent, began, "I don't want to get him into trouble or anything, but I'm glad someone is taking an interest in David. I can't imagine that he'd be involved in anything that would get him in trouble with the US government, or anything, but I can't say he might not be involved in something he can't handle with his new Chinese bosses."

Norton continued, "He was pretty spooked by some Chinese guys who were following him and approached him in some Mexican restaurant. This was when he worked for a company called, AlgoGene Corporation, before he even knew he'd be going to China. Actually, I think it was that night when he learned he'd have to go there."

Jason went on, "He mentioned something to me about creating an algorithm which apparently deals with genetic coding and creating new types of organisms. Anyway, he felt threatened enough to ask me for my most recent malware so he could take it with him, just in case."

Jason continued, "If he's in the kind of trouble I think he is, I'm almost certain that he used the malware and inserted it into his program. If he didn't change any of my coding, then his program will probably melt-down in two days. The malware is triggered from the day it's installed, and I think he left for China the day after we met, so he must've installed it the day I met him. That's how I calculated the number of days."

Concerned, Jason asked, "Is this just routine, or is he in big trouble, or what?"

Larry thought that this had been a very productive meeting, since he now knew that shortly, the algorithm would be destroyed. Also, if there was a need for an extraction or any kind of operation, it would have to happen quickly.

Larry then reassured Norton, "This is just a routine inquiry and I'm sure your friend will be fine. Thank you for calling this to our attention and we'll definitely look into it. Also, is the cell phone number where I reached you your best contact number? I may want to ask you some further questions about your malware code."

Finally Larry directed Jason, "Please treat this meeting as confidential and do not discuss it with anyone, as it may concern issues of national security. Again, thank you."

Jason thanked Larry, saying, "I appreciate your time, and if you could let me know what happens with David, that would be great."

Larry smiled, shook Jason's hand again, and walked him out of the room back to the security area, where they collected his visitor's badge before he left.

Larry returned to his desk, picked up his phone, and called an analyst at the NSA. He intended to find out exactly where Goldblum was, if he was in danger, and if so, what they could do about it.

101

John was racking his brain trying to figure out how to escape within the next forty-eight hours. He wished he had Dr. Duretts' brain, because he was not only brilliant but street smart. He figured the good doctor could have surely devised a plan to spirit the team out of China and back to the US before anyone was the wiser. Think, think, think. What would he do?

Then John pondered, what would his father do? How would he use his training to get out of this situation? John couldn't imagine. He didn't have special forces' training. He could certainly use one of them on his team right now.

His group was smart, but none were trained for this kind of situation. They spent most of their time in cyberspace, dealing with challenges posed in chemistry and mathematics. Their expertise was with chemical and mathematical equations, algorithms, or fixing software glitches, not life-and-death situations posed by a foreign government. Unless perhaps it was theoretical, on a gamer's screen, where real people didn't get hurt.

He wondered, could they just leave the compound? He didn't think so. What would they do to him, and his people, when the program crashed their system? Or when they found out that the CRISPR saline had been compromised? He'd made his decisions, but he hadn't prepared for the next step.

He hated thinking of what his father used to say, but he couldn't get it out of his head – in the heat of battle you make your choices and live, or die with the consequences. John had no choice but to do that now.

He'd try to figure something out with Betty, or David, or anyone else on his staff with whom he might be able to have a secret exchange. As a last resort, perhaps he'd approach a Chinese scientist. From his friend, Li Ming, now a victim in the paddock, he knew at least some of them opposed what was going on.

He sat on his couch, with his head in his hands, covering his eyes, trying to think, think, think. There had to be a way out of this, it just hadn't come to him yet. Still, he was fine with the decisions he'd made. It was better than being complicit in unethical science. Suddenly, there was a light tapping on his door.

John walked to the door, opened it and there stood Li Na. She wore her usual sweet smile on her face. She asked, "Is something wrong? You look worried." John replied, "No, I'm just tired."

Li Na then said, "I'm sorry to ask you to work some more, but I must insist that you come with me to our lab to show you some results and to get your input for further research." She winked at him and John shook his head in agreement. He followed her out of the apartment.

They walked beside each other down the hall to the elevators. They rode in silence, then exited and made their way to the Chinese lab. Li Na closed the door. After they made certain there was no one else in the lab, Li Na whispered, "I wanted to talk to you in private. First, I want you to know I have deep feelings for you. Also, I am good friends with Li Ming, and I and others are not happy with what has happened to him. We strongly believe it's wrong to do research on human subjects."

Li Na continued, "I have been asked to contact you by one of Li Ming's handlers, distraught by Li Ming's condition. A US military special operations team will attempt to get you and your team out of here at 6 AM the day after tomorrow. You need to get your entire team to a field a quarter of a mile north of here, where they will attempt extraction. They also want you to bring a copy of your software."

John, knowing the risk she had undertaken, could only say, "Thank you," as he embraced her.

Li Na, with a tear in her eye continued in a whisper, "The type of people they are experimenting on are the same as my father, mother and uncles, and this is not right." John felt a pang in his gut.

Although he usually had a difficult time expressing his feelings, this time they were flooding in like a tsunami.

He looked into her big brown eyes and said, "I can't leave without you. I want to be with you, too. You have to come to the extraction point and leave with us. I have more than enough money to take care of any problems you might have, and I promise you I won't abandon you when we're out of here. What I'd like to do right now is marry you, but under the circumstances, I think we have to wait," he smiled, to lighten the mood. Li Na's eyes told him everything he needed to know, without her saying a word.

He saw another small tear in the corner of Li Na's eye as she looked at the floor then said, "Yes, I will be there." John then gave her a gentle hug and a kiss as he thought he felt their hearts beat in rhythm with each other.

102

John had been sitting in his room for more than two hours debating how to tell his crew about what was going to happen tomorrow. He called Betty. When she picked up after four rings, he asked, "Hi, just wanted to check, did they transfer the bonus money into your and David's accounts?" She responded, "I already checked, the money appeared early in the morning in two accounts – one set up for each of us. This is on top of the initial payment that was made, which you already knew about." John said, "Thanks." He then hung up.

Satisfied, John went outside ambled down a path and finally reached the river, where he sat on a rock overlooking an area where there was some whitewater rushing by. As he sat there, he could hear frogs croaking in the background and saw a group of geese paddling in a calmer pool of the water. He smelled the earth and water and thought of all the life teeming in the habitat, from the single cell organisms to the flatworms, the marsh grass, fish and frogs. It all was interwoven in a tapestry of continuing cycles of life. What was supposed to happen, happens. Then, he thought of Li Na, how she made him feel, how he wanted to keep her safe, be with her and make her happy. But he didn't know what tomorrow would bring.

John knew that DNA was a peculiar molecule and the key to life in all its expressions. He was certain that it had to have been created by a higher being, and sitting here, it dawned on him again that all this, including the lake, was also part of a master plan. The larger question was, were people supposed to tinker with their own DNA? No? Maybe?

Yes, definitely yes, since, after all it was God-given talent that made it possible.

Isn't that the natural progression of life? Smarter and more clever animals sooner or later unlock the mysteries of their own DNA and then take evolution to the next level? He couldn't, however, forget the old adage he'd heard long ago that, 'With great power comes great responsibility.' He thought about the incredible power of CRISPR technology and the even greater potential for its misuse.

The scientists had done their part to unleash a technology that could have a great, if unknown, impact on the entire ecosystem. Now it was up to those in other disciplines to play their roles in determining how the technology should be used. The technical people should now be able to hand off what they developed to the ethicists and lawyers, those who were responsible for looking at the fine print, to make decisions on how the technology should be best managed.

If he got out of here, he promised himself he'd become involved in properly applying CRISPR. It was the right thing to do, even if it meant unending wrangling with politicians and others who controlled through their purse strings.

As John was walking back to the facility, he saw Betty walking toward him. He waved and when they met, asked, "So, where you heading to?" Betty replied, "Nowhere really, just out for a walk." John said, "There's an amazing waterfall that's not too far. Do you want to go?" Betty said, "Sure, why not?" and they began walking together.

John decided to continue the ruse that he was still a team player, since they could never be sure if they were under surveillance or not. Consequently, he said, "I'm really psyched about the research, which is right up my alley. If the computer system works like I think it will, we're on the precipice of changing everything. I think the Chinese are on the right track. Who knows, that Nobel prize I once joked about could become a reality."

Betty said, "Good luck with that, paisano, remember those little pieces of paper we signed, the nondisclosure agreements? I looked at them again the other day, and there's a million-dollar penalty for each disclosure. You don't just lose the money you already received, you also get stung by having to pay additional penalties. It would bankrupt you, probably all of us. Would it be worth it, just to satisfy your ego?"

John appeared flippant and with a smirk on his face said, "When you put it that way, I guess not. I've heard Nobel prizes are highly overrated, anyway."

They picked up their pace and walked in silence until they reached the waterfall. It was loud and you could feel the mist in the air. In a hushed tone, John asked, "Do you have your phone?" Betty replied, "No." John continued, "Neither do I. Just listen, so I can tell you what I have to say fast. Tomorrow at 6 AM, our military plans to pull our team out of here.

You'll need to help me make sure everyone's prepared to go, without raising suspicion. No one but me is supposed to be taking anything with us, so everyone should be in their rooms." Betty, standing close to John and looking up and down as if to appreciate the view, said, "Thanks for the heads up."

Betty said, "I actually think it's the right time to go home, anyway. Now that they have your intellectual property, they don't need us anymore, and I promise you, you'll see no more money from them."

She continued, "The experts I've talked to tell me that they expect the Chinese to close their economy to outsiders in the near future, when they implement their plan to be self-sufficient. The numbers don't lie. It's a result of the expansion of their own middle-class. Chinese companies increased their sales to their own people and now sell about 40% of their goods and services to Chinese companies and citizens. So, don't feel too bad, except that they just stole another piece of American intellectual property."

John said, "Maybe they did, and maybe they didn't." Betty looked surprised by the comment, but said nothing more.

They then just sat on a large rock, off to the side of the waterfall, and watched the water tumble to a large pool far below. Finally, about ten minutes later, they stood up to begin their return to the facility. Just in case they were being monitored, they engaged in fake gossip about the staff, and who they thought might stay in China to work on the project long-term, and who would want to return home at the end of their contract.

103

The USS Ronald Reagan, a Nimitz-class, nuclear-powered supercarrier, was deployed on routine maneuvers in the South China Sea when it was called up to be the launch point for a special mission. Col. Andrew Harrison and his SEAL Team were planning the operation, down to the last detail. The team knew it was a matter of national security – the Chinese had acquired certain CRISPR technology that could be used to create a force of supermen and biological weapons, and would be a game changer on the battlefield.

Whatever it could do, they had been ordered to repatriate the 13 Americans who had been involved in advancing the technology, who were now thought to be involuntary guest workers at a Chinese company, Xian Corporation. Col. Harrison and his lieutenants were in the situation room going over final details of the extraction plan, when the rest of the team was called in to join them. It was time for the final team briefing.

Col. Harrison began, "Our asset in the Xian Corporation compound told us that 13 Americans, employed by an American biotech company bought by Xian were originally guest workers. Among these are an organic chemist and a programmer who developed certain aspects of the technology that makes it ripe for military applications, which our government deems to be dangerous to national security. The group is now believed to be captives or prisoners who are not allowed to leave the compound. Like most things in China, there may be commercial ties between the Chinese government and Xian Corporation."

Col. Harrison cleared his throat, then continued, "We'll be using two Blackhawks for insertion and a Stealth Chinook for extraction. We'll fly in, pick up those who are at the extraction point, and then come directly back to the carrier. We don't believe there are any injured in the group, and don't anticipate any resistance from hostiles, since neither Xian Corporation nor the Chinese government has any reason to expect us. This operation should be a complete surprise to all but a few people, on our side, already on the ground."

We will fly low to avoid detection, land approximately a quarter of a click from the compound at 0600, secure the perimeter with one SEAL team, and use the other to shepherd the individuals awaiting our arrival to the extraction point into the waiting helicopters. All will then return to the Reagan.

Col. Harrison turned the briefing over to Lt. Rodriguez, who discussed specifics of the operation relating to security and schematics at the compound, with information received from their asset. Before dismissing the group for their final preparations, Col. Harrison asked, "Anybody have any idea what Xian means?" Lt. Rodriguez responded, "Funny that you ask. I Googled it, and it said it means 'the God of immortality.'"

Everyone around the table exchanged looks with each other, some with appreciation, others with disdain. However, it didn't matter because they all knew the same thing. The mission was a go. Let the masterminds in the Pentagon, at the State Department, and in the Commerce Department sort out all the political and commercial ramifications. Their role was simply to get the job done, and they planned so they could do just that.

104

Jo Chuang was overseeing the downloading of material into the 93 Peta Sunway computer. He loved this machine and took great pride in working on the greatest and fastest supercomputer in the world, even though the Americans recently developed one rumored to be slightly faster. He wasn't the best student at university, but he could certainly appreciate this fantastic piece of equipment.

He also had a rudimentary understanding of the material he was downloading, and understood its implications. He hoped to personally benefit from these technologies in his lifetime – maybe become a smarter person, a better athlete, a healthier specimen at the very least. He would like that.

Suddenly, he saw a glitch in the program. He tapped his monitor, thinking maybe a cable had come loose. He started seeing lists of numbers shooting down the screen which looked like machine language. He wondered, what the heck's wrong with the connection? It had to be a problem with the cables. It couldn't be a problem with the Internet or a firewall, since this computer wasn't connected to the Internet due to the sensitive nature of the material being downloaded and analyzed.

He looked at his watch and it was 5:45 am. He thought he'd give it five or ten minutes to let it settle down, and then call his boss, if it continued to have issues. As he watched the lines of numbers shoot by, fast then faster, he began thinking something was very, very wrong.

It had only been five minutes, when he decided to call his boss, just in case. He didn't want to be the person who sat by as some major development occurred without reporting to his superior. Such an error would be catastrophic for his career and his place in this cutting-edge facility. He liked it here, and he didn't want to screw it up.

Chuang picked up his cell phone and made the call. It seemed like an eternity, but four, five, six rings, and finally his supervisor answered with a groggy, gruff, "Hai". He said, "Hello, this is Chuang. I think there's a problem with the software. It's spewing out machine language. I've never seen anything like it before, and I think you should get a programmer down here to look at it immediately."

The supervisor didn't hold Chuang in high regard, and figured he was just worrying him for nothing, like usual. Chuang, a mere technician, with his basic vocational training was probably just misinterpreting what he was seeing. The supervisor said, "I'll get a programmer down there to look at the code. But you're sure that there was nothing unplugged or turned off, right? I was really expecting you to be able to do the simple download without needing more help."

Chuang embarrassed, said, "I checked, but I'll check again. I will wait for the programmer before calling you again." Chuang then hung up. A few seconds later the computer screen went completely blank. Chuang decided he couldn't wait for the programmer to arrive, and quickly redialed his supervisor.

When the supervisor answered, somewhat annoyed, Chuang said, "I think you need to get the programmer down here immediately. My computer screen just went completely blank. I'm almost certain it's not the hardware." The supervisor, on the other end of the line, shook his head in disgust as he thought about how much he hated incompetence, even though he, himself, knew little about computers.

The supervisor asked, "Are you sure you didn't do something to break it? That computer is the greatest computer ever built, and I bet it's doing its job. My question is, are you doing yours? I will have a programmer there in 15 minutes."

The supervisor totally aggravated, hung up then called the lead programmer and said, "Your idiot technician just woke me up, to say he thinks there is a problem with the computer. I need you to get someone down there, right now. The lead programmer said, "I'm up. I'll do it myself, I can be there in 10 minutes." It was 5:55 in the morning.

105

John emailed his entire team that tomorrow they would be meeting at 5:30 am in the cafeteria, so that they could come up with a plan for beating the Chinese team. He wrote that the meeting was mandatory – no exceptions.

He then went to talk with David Goldblum about the meeting. It was another one of those bathroom meetings, where he wrote a note which said, 'SEALS removing us 6 AM tomorrow. Bring software program.' David shook his head, yes, then took out a pen and wrote, 'Meltdown to begin 5:30-6:00 AM. Copy of program already in safe hands in US.'

Jesus, John thought, they couldn't have cut it any closer. They were getting out just in the nick of time, which hopefully wouldn't cause any problems, but he wasn't so sure. He then washed his hands, and soaked the paper towel he had written on until the ink was washed away and then he threw it out.

At 5:30 AM the next morning, he saw that everyone had assembled as requested, a few with smiles on their faces, others with looks of dismay at having been asked to begin their workdays so early.

John began, "I wanted this outing so that we could discuss what we'll be doing for Xian, how we can beef up our research to compete against the Chinese team, and to make my final pitch to make sure everyone stays on to help with this endeavor. And, after all, a little fresh air never hurt anyone." Hopefully that would be the case today.

John continued, "Why don't you all follow me, and we'll go north to a really cool waterfall that I found." They all ambled out the door, and after walking about a quarter of a mile, came to a large clearing.

John noticed a lone 'landscaper' had been following close behind. As John looked up at the sky, he commented on the beauty of the clouds overhead. It was exactly 6 am and they were in the middle of the clearing, as John stumbled and pretended to twist his ankle. He sat on the ground as he cried out, "Guys, I hurt my ankle. I need to stop to make sure I can keep going."

The 'landscaper' appeared to have stopped to tend to a plant about 100 yards south of John's team.

As John sat on the ground rubbing his ankle, the sound of helicopter rotors and engines broke the silence in the clearing. One helicopter landed abruptly on the south side of the clearing, and six armed men in fatigues jumped out and hit the ground running. They fanned out in a perimeter, except for one that ran into the wooded area where the 'landscaper' had last been seen.

The 'landscaper' drew his gun, then abruptly threw it to the ground in front of him. He then raised his hands over his head and without a sound, the SEAL was almost on top of him with his gun trained on his quarry's chest. The 'landscaper' looked down and saw the red target dot over his heart. Hoping to survive the day, he dropped to his knees and went face down on the forest floor.

Lt. Rodriguez, back at the carrier, was watching real-time footage. From one of the helicopter feeds he noticed a woman racing toward the extraction area. He also saw a few soldiers coalescing at the back entrance of the compound, and it looked like they were shouting at each other. It reminded him of how bees responded after an initial attack on their hive.

It didn't appear that the woman was armed, or that she was part of the compound's security detail. He radioed the teams on the ground and said, "One-Bravo-Charlie reporting, woman approaching from the southeast. She should be visible in approximately one minute. She appears to be unarmed. Intentions unclear, but she's running full bore."

He continued, "There's also a 10-man security force amassing due south. Don't take the woman out, but we may want to disable the security force if they make a move." The radioman said, "Affirmative." He went over and advised the lieutenant in command on the ground.

At the same time, the second helicopter landed, and six more SEALs hit the ground and fanned out. One ran over to John and sharply instructed, "Get your team into that bird," as he pointed to the Chinook. He continued, "Count them, make sure that they're all in there, and then get yourself in there, because we pull out in two minutes."

John was startled, as were all the members of his team who stood gawking at the helicopters, but had no choice but to act quickly. He stood up and directed everyone, "Quick, get into that helicopter. Now." He had no time to wonder about what happened with Li Na. When the last of the scientists was being helped into the helicopter, John heard what sounded like an explosion.

He turned his head and to the left, he saw Li Na. She appeared to be shouting at one of the SEALs. The SEAL immediately behind John shouted, "You, into that helo, now." John shook his head no, and then with little thought for his own safety, turned and bolted toward Li Na. He was in disbelief that she'd come, and as he got to the edge of the clearing, where Li Na stood, he shouted over the noise of the rotors, so the SEAL could hear, "This is Li Na, your informant. If you leave her here, she'll likely be killed."

Whether it was true or not, he was uncertain, but what he knew for sure was that he wanted her to come with them. The SEAL talked into his microphone, then said, "OK, both of you into that bird, now." They both ducked as they ran to board the helicopter.

John then heard another explosion to the south of the helicopter, but had no desire to figure out what it was. He was glad that they were on their way to safety, and more importantly that he was with Li Na.

106

Two days later, John felt like the entire episode had been a bad dream, except for Li Na. He was now at CIA headquarters in Langley, Virginia, where he was being debriefed. Agents Morse and Franklin were prepared to question him.

Agent Franklin did most of the talking. He asked John about what had occurred, what he had done, and to speculate about what the Chinese were up to. John was candid with them, and told them about the program, how it worked and what it could do. He suggested that they should talk with David Goldblum for specifics about the program, but it was clear that they would be debriefing Goldblum, too.

After John told them about the sale of his company to Xian Corporation, they advised him they were aware of Xian's purchase of his business and all the terms and conditions. Further, because the transaction was legitimate, he and his partners were allowed to keep the proceeds of the sale.

John then told them how he learned about Xian's human testing, and how once he'd realized it was going on, he decided to adulterate the saline, using a formula one of his scientists had come up with, to make test subjects sterile. He also told them about the software glitch that caused a meltdown, which had been David's idea. John was no longer interested in taking credit for the work of others.

What John really cared about was what was happening with Li Na. When he asked Agent Franklin about her, he was informed that it would take much longer for her debriefing because of the position she had held.

After that, she could seek asylum. Agent Franklin told John that Li Na had asked to see him, and that would be possible in a few days.

The agents advised John that everything he said to them was confidential, would not be disclosed to anyone, and that he should not discuss it with anyone else. John assured them that he would not. He knew it was always best to let sleeping dogs lie. After a daylong session of questions, John was finally told he could leave.

He wanted to talk with someone, so he drove to Betty's office at Kolb Kravath, LLP. It now seemed like ages ago that he'd first met her there. When he got there, he was greeted by the same receptionist. She called Betty and told her that John Ordell was there to see her. Betty waved at him as she walked down the hall toward him. He met her halfway and she turned and walked with him back to her office. When they got there, he could see she'd been packing up boxes and taking pictures and diplomas off the wall. He asked, "So what's going on with you, and why are you packing up, if you don't mind my asking?"

She said with a genuine smile, "My debriefing ended a few hours ago, and thanks to the $3 million that the Chinese gave to us the day before we left, 'I'm outta here,' as they say." She went on, "I'm able to do an early retirement, or possibly work as a consultant, if I choose."

She continued, "I'm glad you stopped by because I wanted to talk to you in person to give you the bank account numbers. I opened Swiss accounts for you, David, Lisa and me, to make it impossible for the Chinese to claw back the money. I think you have somewhere in the neighborhood of $250 million. Lisa also has a little bit less. If you want, I can reach out to everybody to give them their account numbers. Or, if you'd like to do it, even better."

John thanked her, and said, "You deserve every penny for all your hard work. I'd like to double that $3 million. If you give me the account number, I'll move the money into your account."

Betty then asked John, "So what will you do next?" John replied,

"The CIA guys floated me a possible job offer at NIH doing research on CRISPR, but I don't think it's for me. I'm definitely interested in continuing my CRISPR research, though, and I may even hold seminars."

He continued, "I'm considering setting up a foundation to hire ethicists and lawyers to figure out how to regulate CRISPR. That's an area above my pay grade, but we all know it must be done."

They both laughed and John continued, "I also was able to talk to Li Na and I think we'll be getting a place together when her debriefings are complete. She makes me feel so incredibly happy every time I see her. I'm looking forward to starting a new life with her and can't wait until she's released. I guess this must sound pretty sappy for a scientist."

Betty smiled and said, "I think it's sweet. I think we all deserve some happiness after the tumultuous couple of years we've had. She smiled at him turned her head slightly and then shook his hand and said, "John Ordell, I'm really glad I met you."

34758698R00211

Made in the USA
San Bernardino, CA
05 May 2019